DOCTOR WHO

INDEPENDENCE DAY
PETER DARVILL-EVANS

Published by BBC Worldwide Ltd,
Woodlands, 80 Wood Lane
London W12 0TT

First published 2000
Copyright © Peter Darvill-Evans
The moral right of the author has been asserted

Original series broadcast on the BBC

Doctor Who and TARDIS are trademarks of the BBC

ISBN 0 563 53804 X
Imaging by Black Sheep, copyright © BBC 2000

Printed and bound in Great Britain by Mackays of Chatham
Cover printed by Belmont Press Ltd, Northampton

Prologue

First of all...

A tiny circle of colour appeared from behind the distant forest of evergreens.

It was the signal. Madok watched the balloon, buffeted by the winds, as it rose into the pale violet sky.

He stamped his feet, holstered his revolver, and slapped his gloved hands against his arms. Kedin Ashar's summer workshops were to the north of the tropic, where the climate was never warm. The building Madok was guarding – the workshop without a name or number, whose location was known to no more than twenty people – was at the northernmost limit of habitation, concealed in the forests that covered the foothills of the ice mountains. He unlatched the outer door, stepped into the gloom, and struck the inner door until it reverberated in its frame. He hoped the banging could be heard inside the cavernous, noisy workshop.

'Yes, Madok?' It was the voice of Tevana Roslod, as calm and gently amused as ever, despite the distortion of the sound that brayed from the speaker of the address system.

'The signal, Tevana Roslod,' Madok said. He remembered not to shout, but he still felt ridiculous talking to the air. 'The Duke and his party are on their way to the house.'

'Come in, Madok.' This was Kedin Ashar's voice. 'Come and see. It's ready for its test flight.'

Madok smiled. Kedin Ashar took such enthusiastic pleasure in each new piece of machinery. This, Madok knew, was the most ambitious scheme yet. He felt a bubble of excitement expand within him as he fumbled his key into the lock of the inner door.

Madok stood in the doorway. He was motionless with wonder. Kedin, Tevana and their team of craftsmen were gathered at the winged base of the cylinder. It was thicker than the trunk of a beam-oak; it shimmered. Madok's gaze rose up the metal spire: its nose-cone almost touched the roughly-hewn planks that supported the roof.

'Well, come in, Madok,' Kedin Ashar shouted. 'Have you frozen solid out there, or have you been chewing on a spore-seed to alleviate the monotony of guard duty?'

'My lord,' Madok said as he approached the base of the rocket, 'it is exactly like the photographs you showed me. It's magnificent. But I didn't expect it to be so tall.'

Kedin Ashar grinned and shook his head, as if he could hardly believe it himself. 'Neither did I, Madok, to be quite honest. But the whole thing's packed solid with fuel, and even so Tevana assures me that there'll be only just enough thrust to take the damned thing beyond the atmosphere. And I can't argue with her calculations.'

'That's because they're correct, my love,' Tevana Roslod said. She appeared beside Kedin and twisted his ear. She was wearing craftsman's overalls, her blonde tresses were escaping from the rag with which she had tried to tie them back, and her face was smudged with dirt. Nonetheless it was still clear to Madok why his lord, for so many years a determined bachelor and rakehell, had become enthralled by her.

Kedin pulled away from Tevana's grip and retaliated by tickling her midriff. She squealed with laughter and began punching his chest.

'My lord,' Madok said. 'My lady. The Duke will be at the house within half an hour. If we leave now, and use the vehicle, we will be there when he arrives. However, there will be little time in which to prepare ourselves to welcome him. I should change out of this winter hunting gear and into a dress

2

uniform. And I can't imagine that Vethran would be much impressed with my lady's oily overalls.'

'Oh, Ked,' Tevana said, 'do I have to be there to greet him? You know how I hate these stuffy receptions.'

'Of course you have to be there, light of my life. I know I'm brilliant, but I'm prepared to let you take some of the credit.' Kedin grinned as he avoided a flurry of her punches. 'Vethran's got to meet you some time. I've told him that you and I are – well, you know.'

Madok shook his head. When Kedin Ashar and Tevina Roslod were together they seemed to forget that they were landholders and merchants. They acted and spoke with all the formality of farm children. And whatever the subject – the calibre of the air inlets of a carburettor, the burn rate of liquid petroleum fuel, the price per head of mountain-reared cattle or the selection of a tapestry – they could talk for hours.

It was time to abandon newfangled protocol. 'Kedin,' Madok said. 'Tevana. Put on your coats and come to the vehicle now. We must go to see Vethran. Forget about his bloody dukeship. Ignore the fact that he's the leader of our nation. Just remember that he's a potential customer. Let's go and clinch a sale.'

Outside, Madok announced that he would drive the vehicle. He was still more used to riding a camelope than trying to direct one of Kedin Ashar's roaring machines, but he knew that both Kedin and Tevana loved sitting in the driver's seat, and there wasn't time for a discussion about which of them should drive. In any case, Kedin and Tevana were engaged in an unspoken competition to discover which of them could coax the highest speed from one of their self-propelled vehicles, and Madok desired never again to be a passenger with either of them.

'It's ready to launch,' Kedin yelled over the noise of the exhaust. He clapped Madok on the shoulder. The vehicle bounced over the ruts of the track that wound downwards through the forest. 'Ready to launch, Madok. I can't wait.'

'You'll have to,' Tevana told him. 'I want to be sure that Vethran and everyone from the court is back in the capital before we send the rocket up.'

Madok gripped the steering wheel tightly and risked glancing back over his shoulder at his passengers. 'You don't intend to make the rocket available for sale?' he shouted.

'I shudder to think what uses Vethran would find for it,' Tevana said. Her flawless face was marred by a frown. 'I worry about letting him have the vehicles.'

'Anyway, Madok,' Kedin said, 'this rocket's merely for research. It's a toy compared with the one we have in mind. We still have to reinvent the technology for steering the damned things. And I don't want Vethran to know anything about it – at least until we're sure we can do it.'

Automatically, Madok looked upwards, searching in the cloudless expanse for the glint of reflected light.

'There,' Kedin yelled. His outstretched arm pointed towards the west horizon.

Madok slowed the vehicle, pulled the goggles from his face, and concentrated on the western sky. The tiny sliver of light was just above the tree tops, hardly visible against the bright lilac of the heavens.

It was known as the Moonstar. But Mendeb was a world without a moon, and the shining satellite did not circle the planet. Nor was it a star, being brighter and considerably less distant. Kedin Ashar had collected and studied the scraps of information about the arrival of people on Mendeb, and he knew the truth about the Moonstar. And about the Moonstar's dimmer sister, known only as Two, which was, apart from the sun by day and the eternal glittering backdrop of the fixed stars by night, the only other body to be seen in Mendeb's skies.

When he had been told the story Madok had at first refused to believe it. He still found that his mind reeled when he tried to imagine the distance from Mendeb to the Moonstar, and the further distance to the planet beyond it. He pictured a metallic pencil, hurtling skywards on a pillar of flame. His hands clenched on the rim of the steering wheel of the self-propelled vehicle. He restrained himself from shouting aloud with excitement. These were thrilling times indeed.

Less than an hour later Madok was in the thick of the crowd, chatting with Vethran's followers and summoning servants to bring mulled wine for the lords, cushions for the ladies, titbits for the fractious children. He listened to the comments of the sceptics: a self-propelled vehicle was intrinsically dangerous, would definitely explode, could not be faster than a thoroughbred camelope, and was an idea in very poor taste. Vethran, Madok noted, smiled at such comments but did not voice his own opinions; the Duke had known Kedin Ashar a long time, and knew that he was not to be underestimated.

The chattering of the courtiers was drowned, suddenly, by a roar that sounded like an avalanche. Some of the children started to cry; the adults looked about, struck dumb. Kedin Ashar strode from Vethran's side and stopped halfway towards the vast tent that had been erected on the lawn. He raised his arms. Servants severed ropes, and twenty balloons began to ascend, carrying with them the front panel of the tent.

Smoke billowed from within the tent. The roaring noise increased in volume. And from the swirling clouds of fog emerged five four-wheeled carriages, accelerating towards the crowd like carts careering down a hill. There was a universal gasp of surprise, and a few shrill screams. Madok tried not to smile as he saw several courtiers flinch, turn, and start to run away.

The vehicles slid to a halt in a diagonal line, and in each one the leather-coated, goggles-wearing crew stood and saluted. 'Hail Vethran, Duke of Gonfallon,' they shouted in unison. The five drivers sat, and turned their vehicles to face the eastern end of the lawn, where servants were pulling upright five wood-and-paper replicas of sword-wielding cavalrymen on charging camelopes. The uniforms were those of the elite guard of the Count of Dithra, whose territory lay adjacent to Gonfallon and with whom Vethran had for some time been provoking a quarrel.

The drivers set their machines in motion. The vehicles, spouting smoke and a fearsome amount of noise, gathered speed towards their targets. In the backs of the vehicles the gunners crouched behind their strangely shaped, unwieldy guns. Their fingers tightened on the triggers.

As one, they opened fire. The roar of the vehicles' engines was instantly drowned by a rattling cacophony that caused many in the crowd to cry out and cover their ears. Even Madok was stunned: he had had some part in the design of the rapid-repeating gun, but he had not previously heard five firing together. The racket was like a regiment of riflemen all shooting at once. Even the crackling boom of a field gun sounded less relentlessly offensive to the ears.

Spent cartridges flew in arcs in the wake of the speeding vehicles.

Madok, and those others in the crowd who had seen military service, managed to tear their gaze from the vehicles towards the targets.

The charging cavalrymen and their mounts were no longer recognizable. All that remained were stumps of wood and tatters of paper.

Madok shivered, and knew that his reaction had nothing to do with the icy wind blowing down from the mountains. As a cadet he had studied with men who were now officers in the

Dithran army. He knew that Dithran troops were generally a disciplined lot, well led and well equipped.

They wouldn't stand a chance.

The glorious Cathogh campaign had been concluded only the previous summer. Vethran had wanted the county's coal fields, and the Count Cathogh had rashly refused the Duchy of Gonfallon's offer of a treaty of permanent alliance. Madok had gone to the war in the entourage of Kedin Ashar, whose battlefield tactics were outshone only by his personal bravery. But Madok knew that it was the new guns, with their long, rifled barrels, that had won the war. Cathogh's men and women were valiant, but their muskets were accurate only within twenty metres. They died without sight of their opponents.

Kedin Ashar had devised the weapons almost as a by-product of the precise engineering he had had to develop for his secret projects, and had sold some to Vethran's army. After the war, Kedin Ashar had received his reward: he had become the largest landholder in County Cathogh. He had assigned most of his new possessions to Tevana Roslod. They had brought their new lands under the efficient administration Tevana had begun to apply to all of their estates, whose revenues funded their research.

It would be the same with Dithra. Vethran would buy as many self-propelled vehicles and rapid-repeating guns as he could afford. And he would be able to afford as many as he wanted, as Kedin Ashar could be paid in sequestered Dithran lands.

The demonstration was over. Kedin Ashar led his guests into the reception hall of his summer residence. In his father's day it had been a hunting lodge, and the stuffed heads of a dozen species stared glassily down at the procession of dignitaries and servants who processed through the ornately carved doors. Greatcoats and hats and scarves were discarded, and carried away in mounds by staggering servants. Pipes were lit. Glasses of sweet wine were selected from silver trays.

All the animated talk was of the self-propelled carriages. A sixth vehicle had been installed at the centre of the hall. Like the five that had been used in the demonstration it looked rugged, and was fitted with one of the rapid-repeating guns, an ominous metal structure with a cylindrical bullet-case and a wide barrel. This one, however, had coachwork that had been polished until it sparkled; two huge electrical lamps stared like unblinking eyes from its front; and the driver's position was protected with panels of armour.

Some sniffed and complained about the machine's vulgar appearance; others peered at the engine, exposed beneath panels of cowling lifted like a gull's wings, and tried to fathom the workings of the maze of rods, wires and cylinders.

Standing apart from the throng, Kedin Ashar and Duke Vethran were talking terms. Madok was at his lord's side, memorising the details of the discussion so that he could draw up the contract of sale.

'We can build twenty a week,' Kedin said. 'Complete with weapons and armour plating. You could have two divisions by mid-year,' he added shrewdly, 'which would leave enough time for a campaign before the rains.'

The Duke smiled and scratched his beard. 'But what about the drivers, eh?' he said. 'The sappers are only just getting used to the steam tractors you sold us two years ago, and anyway you can't send sappers into battle.'

Madok was ready with the answer. 'I'm an army man, as you know, my lord,' he said. 'And I'm sure there'll be no shortage of volunteers to drive these machines. We can train drivers and gunners, on the prototypes you've seen today, while we're building the rest of the vehicles. If your lordship is disposed to grant us an order, of course.'

The Duke grunted. 'Well, Kedin,' he said, 'if I take these machines off your hands – say, a hundred and twenty of them – what do you want?'

Kedin Ashar grinned. 'I could do with a deep-water port near my grain lands in Harran,' he said. 'I wondered whether your lordship would consider granting me the town and province of Bilton.'

Vethran's smile remained fixed on his face. Madok was sure that Kedin had gone too far this time.

'Bilton is one of the five Duchy ports,' Vethran rumbled, 'as you know very well. I had it from my mother. And it's worth eight hundred thousand marks a year.'

Kedin Ashar shook his head in pretend frustration. 'It's a small price to pay, Vethran,' he said. 'The Dithrans will pay that a hundredfold in taxes and reparations – once you've conquered them.'

'I can take Dithra without your machines, Kedin,' the Duke said.

Kedin shrugged. 'Yes, of course. But not this year, my lord. Not in a single campaign. And if you take Dithra this year, and grant us the stewardship and revenues of Bilton, I'm confident that by this time next year we'll be able to demonstrate something even more remarkable than these vehicles.'

The Duke was clearly on the point of agreeing. 'You sold rifles to Dithra,' he muttered.

'I'm a businessman, my lord,' Kedin said. 'But I'm also a patriot and an old friend. You can be sure I'll supply these vehicles to no one but you until next year at the earliest. Madok will insert the usual exclusivity clause in our agreement.'

'I'm not happy,' the Duke said. 'You're getting too wealthy, Kedin.'

'What nonsense!' It was Tevana Roslod's voice. She curtsied

in front of the Duke. 'I'm sorry, my lord,' she went on, 'but I cannot allow that it is possible for Kedin Ashar to be too wealthy. Why, he has to keep me in gowns like this.' She stood on her toes and twirled, so that the skirt of her dress fanned out into a spinning circle of jewelled silk.

Madok suppressed a smile. He had had to threaten to administer a spanking before Tevana had agreed to wear the dress: she hated dressing up and had never been presented at court. The green silk clung to her slender figure. She was vivacious, angelic, desirable. Vethran's eyes followed her every movement. She stood beside Kedin Ashar and tried to look demure.

'My lord,' Kedin said. 'May I introduce Tevana Roslod? She is my partner in – just about everything I do.'

'Tevana,' the Duke said, and lifted her hand to his lips. 'Delighted.' His gaze lingered on her pale shoulders before he turned again to Kedin. 'You haven't married, then?'

'No, my lord.' It was Tevana who replied. 'We're rather old-fashioned in that way. I hope you're not offended.'

'Not at all,' Vethran assured her. 'Quite the reverse. Kedin's told you, I'm sure, that he and I were at school together. Did he tell you that I was always ahead of him? Ah! I thought not. Well, Kedin has told me much about you, Tevana Roslod. Come into the drawing room with me awhile, and explain to me why Kedin thinks he needs to have Bilton. I'm sure we'll be able to come to an understanding.'

As the Duke led her away Tevana glanced over her shoulder. Madok saw her confused expression, her wide eyes. He made to follow, but felt Kedin's hand on his arm.

'We need Vethran to buy these vehicles,' Kedin whispered urgently. 'Tevana knows that. She'll be all right.'

Later, after dusk had fallen and all the guests had departed in their carriages, Madok tried to concentrate on the intricate wording of the contract. From the room above the study in which he was working he could hear Tevana, no longer sobbing but instead exclaiming angrily that Vethran was an animal, and that she would never see him again no matter what depended on it.

He heard Kedin assuring Tevana that she was safe, that Vethran would not try to carry out his vile suggestions, that Vethran depended on Kedin's advice and inventions.

But what will happen when Vethran has conquered the whole world, Madok wondered. He'll need no one then. Neither Tevana nor Kedin will be safe. The rocket: it must be made to work. We have helped to create Vethran; now we must be sure we can outrun him.

And then, some years later...

The only sound was made by insects buzzing angrily against the exterior of the translucent panels.

'It's awful hot here, Doctor,' Jamie said. He shook his kilt to create a draught around his legs. He could see the shapes of bugs the size of his hand clinging to the outside of the circular structure, and he hoped that the cloudy material was less flimsy than it looked.

'We're on the equator, Jamie,' the Doctor said, and continued his promenade around the curving desks.

'That's the wee line that runs round the middle of a planet,' Jamie said. One day, he thought, the Doctor would realize that he had acquired an education during their travels together.

It's as if he thinks that explaining the cause of the heat makes it more bearable, Jamie thought. And he can stare at those flickering lights and flashing numbers as long as he likes; I swear he's no more idea of what they mean than he has of how to read the console of the TARDIS. It's a miracle we ever get anywhere.

11

The TARDIS, incongruous as ever, stood like a weather-beaten hut that had been plucked from a hillside and set down in the centre of the circular room. The door was open, and Jamie knew that the interior was cool. And he'd never once found an insect anywhere in the ship's labyrinthine corridors. A bead of sweat trickled down his chest.

'Could we not go somewhere else?' he said. 'There's no one here. It's just a room full of electrical equipment,' he added, enjoying the ease with which the phrase slipped from his tongue.

The Doctor stopped, turned to face Jamie, frowned, fiddled with his bow tie, thrust his hands into the pockets of his vast, dusty frock coat, and then pulled them out to ruffle his already untidy mop of dark hair. 'I can't help thinking that the TARDIS must have brought us here for a reason,' he said. 'When we turn up somewhere unexpected, something usually happens.'

'Aye, and it's usually something bad.' And when do we ever turn up somewhere we've planned to, Jamie added in his thoughts. 'But whatever it is, it's not happening, Doctor. Not this time. We've been in this furnace a half-hour and we've seen no one and heard nothing. Perhaps we've arrived a wee bit early. We've a ship that can travel anywhere in time and space; let's go away and come back again after a while. I'm sure you can bring the TARDIS back to within an inch of its present position and in exactly six hours from now. By which time it might be cooler.'

'Now, now, Jamie,' the Doctor said. His face attempted to look simultaneously amused, hurt and severe. 'I'm pretty sure I know how to control the TARDIS, you know. The old girl simply needs a little sympathetic understanding.'

'Aye, Doctor,' Jamie said. 'So we'll go inside now, and you'll just move the ship forward by a few hours?' He stepped towards the TARDIS's welcoming doorway, and was delighted to see that the Doctor was doing the same.

'Well,' the Doctor began, and then stopped, stared into the distance, and started counting on his fingers and muttering to himself. 'I must admit, Jamie,' he announced at last, 'that I'm not confident of performing a manoeuvre of such delicacy.' His frown disappeared and was replaced by a toothy grin. 'But I'm sure I'll be able to do it one day. And, as you say, we can go anywhere in time and space. So it doesn't matter whether we decide to come back immediately, or in two weeks, or in twenty years. We can still arrive just here, and six hours from now.'

'That's if you can remember to come back, Doctor. You'll need a good memory if you're going to leave it for twenty years.' Jamie's opinion was that he'd rather trust a redcoat than the Doctor's memory.

The Doctor nodded enthusiastically. 'Of course, Jamie, of course. I'll need something to remind me. Something from here. Be a good chap and find something memorable, and bring it into the TARDIS.' He strode into the dark interior of the big blue box, leaving Jamie alone and perspiring in the circular room.

Something memorable, Jamie thought as he surveyed the rows of illuminated desks; there's nothing here that's different from anything else. When you've seen one range of flickering wee lights you've seen all of them. Ah! I'll take that.

It was the only unusual thing in the room: a tall column of brightly coloured wires, twisted together into a complex but organized shape. Better still, there was writing on the base of the column: Mendeb Two PCS. The Doctor couldn't fail to remember where it was from.

Shaking sweat from his hair, Jamie wrestled with the thing until he was able to pull it free from the desk into which it had been set. He staggered backwards: the object was heavier than it looked. As he turned towards the TARDIS the socket from which he had tugged the artefact seemed to gape at him like a mouth, open in outrage or warning.

'I've got something, Doctor,' he called. 'But I think it might be something important.'

'Oh, I doubt that, Jamie,' the Doctor's voice said from deep within the TARDIS. 'I thought you were keen to set off for somewhere with a pleasant climate. Come along.'

A vision of the Highlands swam into the young Scot's mind. Mist and drizzle; frost-rimed heather. He hefted the thing on to his shoulder and ran through the open doorway.

And then, later still...

'You've been redecorating.' The Doctor leant against the frame of the door of Ace's room. His piercing gaze darted from the walls, newly bare, to the shelving, now with weaponry and explosives stacked separately from recorded music, to the colourful new rugs. 'And tidying. I'm impressed.'

Ace laughed, for no reason other than that she hadn't seen the Doctor for a couple of days, and she was pleased to see him.

She couldn't even be bothered to find his lack of manners irritating, but for form's sake she scowled at him and said, 'Professor, I suppose you know you're supposed to knock, and wait to be invited in, before entering a lady's bedroom?'

He wasn't listening. He was staring at the metal and plastic structure which she had installed as an *objet d'art* on a table in the corner of the room.

'Where on earth did you find that?' he said.

She might have guessed. He was probably about to announce that it was a timed-fuse anti-matter bomb, or a crucial component of the TARDIS's hostile actions displacement mechanism. She'd had it sussed as part of a communications system. She resigned herself to losing it.

'Nowhere on Earth, that's for sure. Not from around my era, anyway. That's seriously futuristic technology. I found it lying at the back of one of the storage cupboards on the twelfth level. Can I keep it?'

The Doctor strode across the room and plucked the object up with his right hand.

And that's another irritating thing about him, Ace thought. I was sweating buckets by the time I'd hauled that object down here. Him and his Time Lord powers.

'It's part of a communications system,' he said. Ace smiled to herself. 'Have you noticed the lettering on the base?'

'Gibberish, I thought,' she said.

'Mendeb Two PCS,' the Doctor read. 'What do you make of that?'

Now that he'd said the words aloud, the meaning was obvious.

'Mendeb Two sounds like a planet,' she said. ' "PCS" could be planetary communications system, seeing as that what we think it is anyway.'

'Yes,' the Doctor said slowly. 'Do you know, Ace, I think you're right.'

'And you're surprised?' she protested, but he wasn't listening. He was already on his way out of her room, with the structure of twisted metal under his arm.

'This may be important,' the Doctor called over his shoulder.

I'll stay here, then, shall I? Ace asked silently. Nice to see you, Doctor, thanks for dropping in.

Then she smiled. Maybe the Doctor would land the TARDIS, once he'd worked out why her metal sculpture was important. She wandered over to the shelves that she hadn't yet dared tell the Doctor she called The Armoury. Maybe she'd have to blow something up again.

Chapter One

They would be there soon. That was all the Doctor had said. All there was for Ace to do was wait.

And that's just what I used to do, she thought, before the Doctor turned up in my life. I was waiting on tables in that grotty bar on Iceworld. And waiting for something interesting to happen.

Ace was lying, fully clothed, on her bed, a floor-level platform in the middle of her newly Spartan room. She looked at each of the four walls in turn.

She was feeling thoroughly fed up.

So this is it, then, she told herself. This is the lot of a Time Lord's assistant. The excitement and adventure of travelling in time and space. Was I worse off as a waitress? Not much.

It was the bare walls that annoyed her most, she decided. Because she had no idea what to decorate them with. Back on Earth, a lifetime ago, she'd known exactly what she wanted on the walls of her bedroom: pictures of sexy men.

At first she'd shared her bedroom with Adam Ant; then George Michael. Even when her musical tastes had moved on to Primal Scream and the Jesus And Mary Chain, she'd still secretly had a thing for George.

But who did she fancy now? She didn't even know how long she'd been away. Who was it cool to lust for these days?

The last film she'd been to see, just days before she was in the chem lab at school and carried out the experiment that had gone only slightly wrong but had swept her up in a time-storm anyway, had been an arty thing called *Withnail and I*. She'd thought it was really funny, even though her mates who were with her didn't get it. There had been a fanciable bloke in that;

now what was his name? He was definitely gorgeous. Who was he? That was it: Richard E Grant.

Why couldn't the Doctor be more like Richard E Grant? That, Ace was sure, would make life in the TARDIS much more interesting. Richard E Grant wouldn't treat her like an educationally sub-normal infant. He'd realise that Ace was grown up now, and had her own opinions; her own life to lead; her own feelings and desires.

Adam Ant; George Michael; who else? Who now?

Ace sat up suddenly. No use brooding. Might as well mix up some more high explosive.

Madok couldn't help looking up again and again at the dome. He recognised the geodesic steel polygons that contained the vast glass panes: Tevana's theoretical model, one of her last projects, transformed into grandiose, awe-inspiring reality thanks to Kedin's steel foundries and Vethran's boundless self-aggrandisement.

Every time he came to court there was something new. The last time he'd visited the Summer Palace he'd been amazed to find that the entire structure had been faced with pink marble. And now the great courtyard of Vethran's home Citadel had been roofed with this hemisphere of glass.

There was almost no trace of the compact fortress that Vethran had inherited with his dukedom: the sprawling, towering, expanding Citadel had smothered the older structure as completely as Vethran had obscured his relatively humble beginnings. Vethran's father had been considered an upstart when he declared Gonfallon a duchy: it was smaller than many mere counties. Madok had been a child at the time, but he remembered the scandal. It was little more than a decade since Vethran had come into the dukedom, and now every duchy, county and manor on the planet acknowledged Vethran as King.

'Remarkable, isn't it?' Balon Ferud said.

Madok lowered his gaze and forced himself once again to engage in courtly chat with the royal councillor. 'Quite remarkable, my lord,' he said, and couldn't resist adding: 'But of course, labour is – ah – cheap, these days.'

Balon's bluff, round face broke into a smile that deceived Madok for not a moment. The councillor swept out a chubby arm in a gesture that encompassed the filigree decoration on the girders of the dome as well as the army of gardeners at work in the newly planted borders and the omnipresent serving-women in their indecently transparent skirts. 'But surely you can't disapprove?' he asked mildly.

Madok's smile was as wide and as feigned. 'How could anyone?' he replied, as images of the aftermath of Vethran's latest conquest flashed through his mind. 'With all humility I can claim to have played some part in helping to bring all this about.'

With all humility, Madok thought. Oh yes. I'm Kedin Ashar's man, and Kedin made Vethran ruler of all. Great heavens, what have we done?

Balon raised a hand, and at once one of the women scurried to his side to refill his glass. Madok nodded and smiled at her: he didn't know whether he was more discomfited by the proximity of her nearly naked body or by her pathetic eagerness to please. She seemed perplexed to find that his glass was still full.

Madok drank and ate nothing during his visits to the royal palaces. He was aware of the expertise of the King's chemists. He was so hungry now that his stomach was cramping, but he dared not so much as sip the wine.

Balon leant forward. The gilt buttons and brocade on his uniform glittered; medals jingled ostentatiously on his broad chest. 'It's said that his majesty intends this entire courtyard to become his new throne room,' he whispered, as though

19

imparting exclusive news. 'And in due course the Council will award him imperial honours. In recognition of his valiant deeds.'

It was Madok's experience that Vethran always took whatever he wanted, and that if he wanted the title of Emperor he would have it. But he thought it undiplomatic to point that out to one of the King's councillors, so he merely adjusted his expression to indicate polite surprise.

'Did you see that?' Balon exclaimed, sweeping his arm up towards the apex of the dome and indicating the cloudy sky beyond the glass.

'What, my lord?' Madok said. This was, he was sure, another transparent attempt to lure him into revealing sensitive information.

'It's gone now,' Balon complained. 'Moved damned quickly. I think it might have been one of those flying darts that people have reported seeing.'

'Have they, my lord?' Madok said. 'I haven't heard these rumours.' So, Vethran and his councillors knew something about the scout ships. He suppressed the sudden pang of fear that his own ship might have been discovered: it was much more likely that his ship, or others, had merely been glimpsed in transit.

'I expect Kedin Ashar would know about such things,' Balon went on. 'But we never see him at court these days. Why is that?'

At last: a direct question.

'Kedin Ashar is kept busy, as you know, my lord,' Madok replied. 'Now that he has been awarded the title of Lord of the Skies he has to attend to the responsibilities that are entailed. And there is still a war on.' A direct answer, too, and truthful as far as it went.

'So he's –' Belon jerked his head up and lifted his eyes, indicating both an interrogative suggestion and a skyward direction.

'Exactly so, my lord,' Madok said. 'Kedin finds himself up there all the time. But he's keen to return.' And that was entirely true.

'So let me guess,' Ace said. 'We've arrived on Mendeb Two.' The Doctor hadn't summoned her to the control room, but she'd hurried there anyway: she knew how to interpret the changes in the hums and groans that coursed like the complaints of an antique central-heating system beneath the corridors of the TARDIS.

'Ah, well, yes,' the Doctor said, struggling into his jacket while simultaneously trying to make adjustments to the instruments on the scanner module. 'And no. Hello, Ace,' he added, as if he'd only just noticed her. He grinned. 'Good to see you again. All ready for the off?'

'So where are we, then?' Ace was in no mood to be diverted.

'We're approaching the Mendeb system,' the Doctor said. He had one finger raised: always a bad sign, it meant he was in lecture mode. 'It's really quite an interesting place. Three gas giants, in unusually close orbits.'

'But we're not going to the gas giants.' Ace wanted to cut to the chase. Once the Doctor got going there was no stopping him.

'Well, no, we're not. We're going to Mendeb Two. The smaller of the two inhabited planets.'

'Two inhabited planets?' This was more interesting. There could be scope here, Ace reckoned, for her to operate independently for a change. Meet some people. A thought struck her. 'Inhabited by humans, right?'

'Oh yes. Completely human, on both planets. Originally colonised by the TAM corporation.'

Ace grimaced. She'd frequently had reason to access the TARDIS's history abstracts relating to mankind's trek to the stars in the first half of the third millennium. 'We don't like the TAM corporation.'

The Doctor made one of his screwed-up faces. 'They were a particularly rapacious and unscrupulous bunch, even for the times,' he said. 'But they're long gone. Like so many of the corporations, they – ah – dramatically downsized during and after the wars. They pulled out of the Mendeb system four hundred years ago. And left the settlers to fend for themselves.'

Ace hoped that, if she waited, the Doctor would get round to telling her what they were doing in the Mendeb system. But she knew from previous experiences that she couldn't rely on it. So she had to ask.

'So,' she said, 'we've got a two-planet colony that's had four centuries to learn about self-government. What's the problem?'

The Doctor looked insufferably smug. 'Not a two-planet colony, Ace. That's the point. Two, entirely separate, single-planet colonies. Mendeb Two and Mendeb Three. During the wars the corporations had virtually all their interstellar ships requisitioned, and in any case TAM weren't in the business of being charitable to settlers – even those who farmed and mined the products that TAM traded in. When TAM left, they took everything they could take with them. They left a space station in orbit between the two planets, but they left no ships on the planets themselves. No manufacturing plant, no robots. No valuable high tech at all.'

'OK, so there are two separate planets, both with populations who have to pull themselves up by their own bootstraps. I get the picture. They're farmers, miners, hardy frontier types. Not good with computers or representative democracy. They've made a mess of it, and we're here to help out. A good guess? Am I warm?'

'We're here to stop a war, Ace.' The Doctor's eyes shone with excitement. 'An interplanetary war. Let me show you.'

He turned to the console again and began to fiddle with dials and switches. Ace had long since given up nagging him to update the systems with voice recognition. She reckoned he had an unhealthy obsession with obsolete technology.

The control room darkened until its corners were full of shadows. The time rotor at its centre rose and fell, its blinking lights casting beams of illumination like a mirror ball in a night club. In the air, between Ace and the Doctor, a hologram coruscated into being, and Ace saw simulations of the two planets, hanging like brilliant Christmas tree baubles in the surrounding darkness.

'This is Mendeb Two,' the Doctor said. It was a blue world of water, its surface covered by oceans and swirling white clouds.

'Pretty,' Ace commented. 'Where do the people live?'

'Two is the closer of the two planets to its sun.' The Doctor's voice came from the darkness beyond the hologram. 'Most of the surface is too hot for human habitation. The colonies were established at the poles, where the conditions are less extreme. If you look closely you can see archipelagos of islands.'

Ace stood on tip-toe and could see the islands scattered across the north polar region: like flakes of dandruff, she thought, on a bald, blue head.

She saw the indistinct shape of the Doctor move across the control room to the other pendant sphere.

'Three, on the other hand, is a cold planet. It's more Earth-like than Two, but due to its distance from the sun only the equatorial belt, between the tropics, is habitable. That's where the large land masses are, though, so the colonised area was substantial.'

The upper and lower thirds of the planet were so brilliantly white that to look at them hurt Ace's eyes. Between the ice caps, however, was a broad ribbon of green and brown and blue.

'And here,' the Doctor said, retracing his steps to stand between the two planets, 'is the space station. Abandoned centuries ago, but still in its orbit, equidistant between the two worlds.'

Ace studied the rotating, metallic cylinder. It looked like a standard space station. Big, though. Probably had its own half-normal gravity. 'And the situation now is – what, exactly?'

'That, Ace,' the Doctor said, 'is what we're here to find out.'

He was smiling just a little too broadly.

'You don't know, do you, Professor?' Ace said. 'This ought to be in the data store.' She stepped into the hologram, so that her black jeans and T-shirt came alive with colour, and she peered closely at Mendeb Three. 'I can't see any settlements,' she said. 'This hologram's based on the surveys TAM made from the station, before they brought any settlers in. It's ages old. I'm right, aren't I? Where's the up to date information? I thought the TARDIS could just download all this stuff from the Matrix.'

The Doctor looked miffed. Good, Ace thought.

'As I've said many times before,' the Doctor explained, 'time travel is not an exact science. In fact it's almost a form of art. The TARDIS is no mere machine, you know. And neither am I.'

'Yes, yes, yes,' Ace interrupted him. 'Don't go on. Just tell me what we don't know.'

'It's an area of uncertainty in the continuum,' the Doctor said with deliberation, as if that explained everything. 'An area of probabilities, rather than certainties.'

'What you're telling me,' Ace said, 'is that between your weird, alien, superhuman brain, and the TARDIS's vast computational power, and the entire resources of the Matrix of all Gallifreyan knowledge, you haven't got a clue what's happened to this system since the TAM corporation abandoned it. You're guessing, right? So what's your best guess?'

The hologram faded and then abruptly disappeared as the lights in the control room returned to normal.

The Doctor was leaning against the console. When he turned to Ace his face wore a look of anguish. 'It's a projection, Ace. Not a guess. That's all we ever have to go on. Please don't be so critical. We're doing our best.'

Oops. The Doctor really was upset. 'Sorry, Doctor,' Ace said. 'What do the projections tell us?'

He straightened. 'Mendeb Three had more settlers and had more natural resources. The settlers, left to themselves, would also have benefited from exploiting the large areas of arable land and forests. In time – in fact by now – they should have created a civilization with a level of technology similar to Earth's in the twentieth century.'

He walked to the hatstand and plucked his hat from it. 'The settlers on Mendeb Two would have had a comfortable life on the islands,' he went on, 'but it would have been difficult for them to organise, particularly as the inhabited parts are at either end of the planet. They would have developed technology more slowly than the people on Mendeb Two – but for one thing. The corporation left on Two a reasonably sophisticated radio system, with a communications centre on the equator to link the two communities.'

'Oh no,' Ace said.

She and the Doctor stared for a moment at the column of convoluted wires and metal that Ace had found in storage on the twelfth level and which was now standing incongruously next to the main doors.

'I just thought we should make sure they hadn't missed it,' the Doctor said. His voice was quiet. 'I feel responsible.'

Suddenly he was once again all smiles. He set his hat on his head at a rakish angle. 'But that's the beauty of being a Time Lord,' he announced. 'I can just turn up, whenever I choose, and make sure things don't go awry.'

Ace couldn't help smiling too. The Doctor's moods were infectious. Or was that just another of his uncanny, non-human abilities? Good grief, she was getting paranoid. Been around the Doctor too long. 'And what do you expect to go awry?' she asked.

'Well,' the Doctor said, 'by about now the peoples of both

planets should have reached roughly the same level of scientific knowledge. They're rediscovering existing texts, so progress will be fast once it gets going. The projections indicate that they will have recently met each other, and in fact the space station is now a busy trading post, with traffic going back and forth to both planets. So this is the time of danger. We have to make sure that they compete without recourse to warfare. That's probably why the TARDIS took me to Mendeb Two in the first place. But in those days I'm afraid I didn't always entirely understand the workings of the old girl.'

'And all we have to do is pop back to a few minutes after you took the communications core, and put it back.' Ace was disappointed. That didn't sound like any fun at all.

'Yes,' the Doctor said very slowly, and bent to examine the control console. 'Yes, that's the idea. Probably.' He straightened, and looked directly at Ace. 'The fact is, Ace, the records aren't as complete as they could be. The TARDIS has been through some damaging experiences since the early days of my travels.'

'Oh,' Ace said.

The Doctor tugged at his sleeves. 'I can't risk replacing the device before I took it, if you see what I mean. Terrible risk of temporal inversion. I've had to choose the latest possible moment before there's any likelihood of hostilities between the planets.'

'But you're still going to Mendeb Two?' Ace said. 'I come in peace, here's the vital piece of your communications network I borrowed, hope you didn't miss it, and by the way don't start a war with the other lot. That the idea?'

The Doctor scratched his head, nearly dislodging his hat as he did so. 'Well, yes. That's about it. Shall we go?'

'No,' Ace said, and waited until she was sure the Doctor had heard and understood. She grinned at the look of surprise on his face. 'You go and do that. It sounds fine, honest. I'm sure it'll go all right. But I like the sound of that space station. The trading post. It'll be buzzing with people, and things happening. I'll scout around, get talking to some of the traders, suss out what's going on.'

Got him! He obviously couldn't think of any reason not to let her visit the space station.

'We don't know exactly what the situation is,' he said at last. 'It could be dangerous.'

What wasn't, Ace thought. She brandished her backpack – the one in which she kept the explosive devices the Doctor forbade her from carrying. 'Danger is my middle name,' she said, 'or it would be if I had more than one. I can look after myself these days, you know. Besides, what can happen to me on a space station?'

There were four palace guards, mounted on camelopes. They remained about fifty metres behind Madok, making no attempt to keep out of sight or to overtake him.

They had been there while Madok's steed was picking its way down the forested slopes that surrounded the Citadel; they had accelerated to a trot, but no more so than Madok, when the road descended into the vineyards and orchards that had been the basis of Gonfallon's prosperity in earlier, simpler times.

Like Madok, the guards were armed with swords. He suspected that they also had firearms concealed within their uniforms, but he doubted whether they had guns that could fire as accurately or as rapidly as the machine pistol that he had in a holster slung round the pommel of his saddle. He hoped he wouldn't have to find out.

Hunger, the urgency of his mission, and an overwhelming desire to quit Vethran's domain all tempted Madok to spur his mount onwards and outrun his pursuers. He resisted the urge. He had been to the King's court on his lord's business; now he was returning to one of his lord's estates. It was perhaps surprising that he was alone, but it was not of itself unlawful. He had to do nothing that would arouse suspicion. The palace guards had not intercepted him while he was on the woodland tracks close to the Citadel, and they were hardly likely to now that he had joined a main highway.

He let the camelope use the broad sward at the side of the road: now that self-propelled vehicles were increasingly common, at least among the aristocracy, more and more roads were being surfaced with the mixture of gravel and tar that made them suitable for motorised vehicles but hard on animals' hooves.

The four guards were still behind him.

They were still there four hours later. The clouds had dispersed, and the rays of the midday sun seemed to have a physical weight, flattening the landscape and bearing down on Madok's shoulders. He was out of Vethran's fief at last: the fields on his left were still Gonfallon, but those on his right were in the manor of Horax.

The camelope plodded on. To Madok's left, the ground rose towards the hills that were owned by the Count of Orthalon. Later, as the shadows lengthened and a welcome breeze stirred the dust beside the road, Horax's neat fields gave way to ridges of scrub: the hinterland of County Harragon.

Still the palace guards were fifty metres behind him.

As dusk was falling he nudged the flank of his mount: the camelope turned off the road and trotted, home at last, through the open gates at the edge of Garthal Manor, one of Kedin Ashar's more modest estates.

Half a dozen of the household troops were waiting for him. Their camelopes were tethered under a stand of trees; the men and women were sitting in the long grass. Madok heard their voices before he saw them.

They sprang up when they heard the sound of his camelope's hooves. Madok reined in his mount and sat in the saddle, stretching his weary limbs, as the troopers brushed down their tunics and donned their helmets.

'Sire,' the captain shouted as he ran towards Madok, still adjusting his chinstrap, 'felicitations on your safe return. You had a fruitful journey, I trust?'

Madok slid from his saddle. 'I've had a bellyful of courtly manners, Gared,' he said. 'I'm as stiff as a board and as hungry as a marsh hog. So if I hear one more genteel phrase I'll give you a kicking. Understood?'

Gared laughed. 'Understood. We've food and wine with us, if you can't hold out until we reach the manor house. It's good to have you back, Madok. Everything went all right?'

Madok shrugged. He couldn't easily explain the remorse and revulsion he felt every time he visited the court. 'I've got the cargo,' he said, indicating his saddlebag. 'And the money.'

The troopers had lit lanterns: their burnished helmets and buttons glittered like fireflies. They were pulling flasks of wine and loaves of bread from their animals' packs. Madok would be able to relax soon, for a brief while.

'Gared,' he said, 'tell your troopers they're not on parade. They must be uncomfortable in full dress uniform. I don't need a guard of honour, you know. I've had an escort all the way from the Citadel.'

He pointed out to Gared the four stationary palace guards, as indistinct as shadows on the darkening highway. As he watched, they turned their mounts and began to retrace their many steps to the King's domain.

Madok breathed out a long sigh of relief. Another mission accomplished. There would not be many more. Perhaps none: events were reaching a critical point.

He would have a few hours' sleep in the safety of the manor

house, and Gared's troopers for protection and company on the short journey to the landing strip. He would have to be airborne before daybreak, even though it was perilous to launch a scout ship in the dark.

The evening air was rich with scents: the honey aroma of pollen, the clean tang of cut hay. Madok took in lungfuls of it, and wondered when he'd next have the chance to breathe air that wasn't filtered. He'd had enough of skulking and hiding and planning. It was time to act. Kedin must make his move soon. Things would be settled, one way or the other.

'I thought so,' Ace said. 'The gravity's not too bad.' She jumped into the air and experienced a momentary sensation of floating before her booted feet were pulled down to the floor.

The Doctor's head and shoulders tilted through the TARDIS's outer doorway. He looked to and fro, like a nervous bird.

Ace gestured with her hands. 'To my right, standard-issue space station corridor. Metal bulkheads, some sort of man-made material as cladding, heavy-duty rubberised flooring. Low-energy lighting. No people. To my left: exactly the same. The air's breathable, the place is obviously inhabited. You see? It's perfectly safe.'

The Doctor cocked his head, as if listening. Ace could hear nothing apart from the background hum of the life-support system and the echoing, distant clangs and squeaks that she'd heard every time she was in a space-going metal object.

'I'd rather you were with me, Ace,' the Doctor said.

Ace was aware of how small and crumpled he was. He always looked like that, of course: a short, slight man in dishevelled clothes. But usually he was being powerful and knowledgeable and mysterious, so you didn't notice his appearance.

She almost walked back into the TARDIS. 'All right,' she said, and then stopped when she glimpsed the satisfied smile that flitted across his face. Was he manipulating her again?

'I'll do my stuff here,' she said, 'and then you come and collect me. I'll know when the TARDIS gets back here.' She tapped the side of her head. 'I'm getting used to this time-travelling lark.'

'But, Ace –'

'Not another word, Doctor. You go and sort out the communications network on Mendeb Two. I'm OK here.'

She stood and watched as the big blue box shimmered and faded out of existence. The flashing blue light on the roof remained visible for a few moments, then with a rush of air it too was gone.

'At last,' Ace said to herself, 'I'm my own boss. So which way now?'

She looked both ways along the corridor. Either way it was gloomy and deserted. The metallic creaks and groans seemed louder now that she was alone. She thought that she could hear voices, too: distant, indistinct. It was impossible to tell from which direction the sounds came.

So this is the thriving hub of interplanetary trade, is it? Ace asked herself as she set off along the corridor. I hope the whole place isn't this lively and thrilling.

She spied a security camera set into the ceiling ahead of her. As she approached it she gave it a cheeky grin. She waved. Her smile faded as she realised that the camera wasn't moving to track her progress. It wasn't working.

Curiouser and curiouser, she thought.

Madok felt the cold sweat drying on his body. He relaxed at last into the contoured embrace of the padded seat. All around him banks of lights and dials flickered and hummed. Outside the craft the landing stage was filling with air. He kept his eyes on the tiny red bulb that would glow green when it was safe for him to disembark.

He had become almost confident about landing the ship on the planet. It wasn't so very different from piloting an aircraft. The controls worked by electricity, it seemed, rather than simple hydraulics, and he would have preferred to be able to feel the resistance of air against the rudder through a stick which he could wrestle with. But he could manage the lifeless, sliding control bars.

Landing in the space station was a different matter. He felt utterly helpless, surrounded by dials and switches whose functions he could only guess at. The ship didn't need him to pilot it, of course. Once he was beyond the planet's atmosphere he pressed the button marked automatic and the ship took itself to the station, and manoeuvred itself into one of the landing stages with a graceful competence that put to shame Madok's clumsy landings on the planet.

The light was green. With a hiss the doors slid open, and Madok unbuckled his seat belt and rose on shaking legs.

'Welcome back,' Horval said as Madok entered the control room that overlooked the landing stage. 'Everything go okay?'

Horval was at the side of the room, next to the levers that operated the doors of the landing stage. It never failed to disconcert Madok that the only way that the doors could be opened and closed was by means of a panel labelled *EMERGENCY – MANUAL OVERRIDE*. The space station had layers of secrets that Kedin and his technicians had failed to penetrate.

'Yes,' Madok said. He combed his fingers through his damp hair, and lifted into sight the saddlebags he was carrying in his other hand. 'The promissory notes from Vethran's exchequer, correct down to the last mark. Blood money. And another batch of hell-brew from the King's chemical works.' He was surprised at the vehemence of his own words. It didn't matter here: at last he was able to express his true feelings.

Horval shook his head slowly. 'It must be tough for you,' he said. 'Going back down there again and again. Dealing with those people. And you did a stint as a pilot during the invasion, too.'

Madok managed to smile. 'I'll survive,' he said. 'And at least we have justice on our side. Mainly.' He cast a significant glance at the saddlebags.

'The bad news,' Horval said, 'is that you'll have to go back again. That batch of SS10 will hardly be enough for the consignment we're holding. And Vethran wants another five thousand on top of that. We're using all the pods and transports. They're coming in as fast we can process them.'

Madok couldn't bear to think about it. 'Great heavens, Horval, they're people,' he yelled, clutching his head in his hands. 'Don't talk about them as if they're luggage.'

Horval blinked in surprise. 'I don't like it any more than you do,' he muttered. 'Kedin's got the chemists working all hours on the formula. You know that.'

Madok held out his hand. 'I'm sorry, Horval. It's not your fault. The last few days have been rather trying. Where is Kedin, anyway? I ought to report in.'

Horval took Madok's hand and shook it. 'It's all right,' he said. 'We're all tense and tired and frustrated. Even Kedin Ashar's feeling it. He's gone for a walk. By himself.'

'What?' Kedin could protect himself better than most, and the corridors were usually safe. All the same, it was an unnecessary risk.

'He insisted, apparently,' Horval said. 'That's what I heard.'

Madok sighed and cursed. 'I'd better go and find him. We need him. There are decisions that must be taken. Open up.'

The inner door slid open. Madok hefted the saddlebags on to his shoulder and set off into the space station.

* * *

'The hills are alive,' Ace sang, and stopped abruptly as she heard her voice echoing along the deserted corridors.

She had crossed a couple of junctions with corridors as featureless as the one she was in. She had tried to open a few doors: those that she succeeded in opening led only into empty rooms.

It's quiet, she said to herself. Too quiet.

The sounds, when they came, were sudden, loud and nearby. Voices raised in anger; running footsteps; a crash; a shout.

Ace ran towards the noises. There was another junction ahead. At the corner she stopped. She pressed her back against the wall and twisted her head round the corner, then ducked back.

There were people in the mouth of the adjoining corridor. It looked like a confrontation. No one had been looking in her direction. She took a step forward for a longer look.

There were half a dozen of them: mainly men, some women. An unkempt bunch, dressed in ragged clothes. The men were unshaven. They looked mean and nasty. They were in a half-circle around a single opponent: a man, tall and slim, dressed like a Ruritanian nobleman in a fancy military uniform, all buttons and epaulettes. He was holding the crowd at bay with a curved sword.

He didn't seem flustered. 'Look, I really don't want to hurt you,' Ace heard him say. 'Just back away. I should make yourselves scarce if I were you. My men will be here at any moment. They're right behind me.'

There was agitated murmuring in the small crowd. Then one of the men shouted, 'He's bluffing. Let's get him,' and lunged for the soldier's sword arm. The others gave an angry cry and all pressed forward at once.

This is more like it, Ace thought. A bit of action. And six against one just isn't fair.

She leapt into the fray.

Chapter Two

It wasn't difficult to find Kedin Ashar. Madok had scoured only one sector, and was entering another when he heard the sounds of battle. As he ran towards the source of the noise he recognised Kedin's voice.

He drew his sword as he approached the junction. He advanced more cautiously, keeping close to the side of the passageway. He wanted to find out what was happening before he became involved, and he knew better than to draw attention to himself. Information and surprise were often more important than strength of numbers.

The escapers from hold twelve had cornered Kedin. They looked desperate and half-starved, Madok thought, but there were enough of them to take Kedin down if they attacked together. Kedin was holding them off with his sword-point and a lecture on the futility of violence.

At Kedin's side, Madok noted, lashing out at the escapers with booted feet and a smooth wooden staff, was a young man dressed in black. Madok had never seen him before.

Not a young man. A young woman. Madok stared. She was giving a good account of herself, parrying and thrusting and kicking without much finesse, in Madok's opinion, but effectively and with enthusiasm. It was clear that together Kedin and his unknown ally hardly needed any assistance.

Madok shouted to Kedin; Kedin replied. With his sword raised before him Madok advanced towards the skirmish. The escapers fell back.

The young woman was grinning at the retreating attackers. She planted the tip of her staff on the floor and rested her fists on the end of the handle. She looked every inch a fighter.

Madok realised he was staring at her, and looked away. A woman fighter, he thought; that's a rare sight these days. And she'd been trained in martial disciplines that were unknown to him. Where could she be from? One of the barely civilized manors in the icy south, perhaps. And what was she doing here, on the space station? She was an enigma. Madok determined to find out everything he could about her.

The escapers were fleeing now. As Madok stepped up to greet Kedin both men sheathed their swords.

Madok saluted. 'Well, my lord. I've been to the planet, I've endured the hospitality of our enemy, and I've returned safely with the cargo. You, on the other hand, can't go for a short stroll in your own space station without getting into a fight.'

'Oh, it was nothing, Madok. A misunderstanding. I'm sure I would have been able to make them see sense.' As usual Kedin's tone was languid. Madok noticed that there was not one bead of perspiration, not even a hint of a flush of excitement, on Kedin's face.

'You had help, Kedin,' Madok said, turning towards the young woman. She was looking at them with keen, intelligent eyes. She didn't seem a bit daunted by the presence of two military officers, one of them the foremost of the nobility. Damn it, she was a handsome young thing, too. Heavens, but she was immodestly dressed: trousers, and tightly fitting, too. Her black jacket had the quality of reflecting shimmering light; it was embroidered with badges, sigils and meaningless groups of words.

'Ah, yes,' Kedin drawled. 'Madok, you haven't met my rescuer, have you? Well, neither have I.' He turned to the young woman. Madok saw her look up at him. Their eyes met. He saw her lips part and her pupils enlarge. Kedin never failed to have that effect on women. How did he do it? 'Madok, introduce me.'

Madok cleared his throat. 'Allow me to introduce Kedin

Ashar, Lord of the Skies, First Lord of the Vanguard, Councillor-in-chief to his majestic highness King Vethran.'

'Hello,' the young woman said, 'I'm Ace.' She held out her right hand towards Kedin.

Madok was struck dumb. Was the girl deaf? Or stupid? The honorific name alone was enough to indicate Kedin's rank. His titles demanded that she lower her head, at least. Most would consider it proper to kneel.

Kedin, also, was speechless. Then Madok saw the corners of his lips twitch, and his face lit up in a smile that became a gale of helpless laughter. Madok hadn't seen his lord as genuinely diverted as this for many months.

The woman called Ace frowned. Evidently she didn't like being laughed at. Her hand was still extended. 'What's so funny?' she said belligerently.

'Nothing whatsoever,' Kedin assured her. To Madok's amazement he took her hand and shook it, as if the two of them were equals. 'I apologise for my appalling manners. Thank you for coming to my aid.' He brought her hand to his lips and kissed her fingers. 'You have a fearless heart, young lady. And it's just "Ace"? You have no other names or titles? You make me feel very suddenly over-endowed.'

Madok saw Ace's eyebrows lift. She hadn't missed the innuendo. There were times when Madok despaired of Kedin. To be flirting at a time like this.

'Just Ace,' she replied. 'I like to travel light.'

'And if you wouldn't mind satisfying my curiosity,' Kedin said, 'where exactly have you travelled from?'

Ace grinned, and Madok knew that Kedin wouldn't get a straight answer. 'Everyone asks me that,' Ace said. 'It sounds like a simple question, but you wouldn't believe how difficult it is to come up with a plausible answer. Ask me something else.'

Kedin laughed. 'Would you like to join me and my officers for

37

a meal?' he asked. 'I warn you, I'll spend the whole time interrogating you.'

'OK,' Ace said with a shrug. 'I'm starved, as it happens. So lead me to the mess hall. Who's your friend, by the way?'

'How remiss of me,' Kedin cried. 'Ace, may I present Madok, my chief aide, my right hand, my stalwart companion-in-arms, my conscience and my friend.'

Madok's heart leapt in his chest as Ace's dark brown eyes met his gaze. He felt his face starting to blush. 'I'm delighted to meet you,' he said, trying to invest the trite words with particular sincerity. Her hand was cool and strong when he held it.

'Same here,' she said.

The touch of her fingers; the smile on her wide lips; the dark intensity of her look. All sweet; all fleeting. Once again she was attending to Kedin.

'You must have a title,' Kedin declared. He bent to inspect the smooth, tapering staff with which Ace had helped to defend him. 'Ace of clubs, perhaps?' His eyes were positively twinkling with mirth. He offered his elbow for Ace to rest her hand on. 'Or Ace of hearts?' he added, in a deeply significant tone that was immediately belied by the covert wink he directed to Madok.

Madok smiled and shook his head. Kedin expected women to be drawn to him. He hardly knew how not to flirt. And the signal to Madok was intended as an indication that Kedin was going to use his wiles to extract information from this mysterious young lady.

Nonetheless Madok's spirits slumped as he fell in behind Kedin and Ace. He saw her hand resting on Kedin's sleeve; he saw her face looking up at Kedin's as they bantered.

'It's Ace of here, there and everywhere, actually,' she said. 'Do you know,' she added, 'you look just like somebody famous.'

'Really?' Kedin replied. 'Even more famous than me?'

'Loads more. Have you ever seen a movie called *Withnail and I*?'

Kedin's face was a masterpiece of conspiratorial intrigue. 'Possibly,' he murmured. 'Tell me: what exactly is a movie?'

Ace laughed. 'Never mind.'

As the sun descended the room gradually filled with yellow incandescence. The long dusk was beginning. Soon, Bep-Wor told himself, he would have to venture outside. He would have to scavenge for food.

He watched bands of colour – orange, scarlet, ochre – stretch across the horizon. It was a spectacular sunset. He could see it clearly, as the back wall of the room had disappeared, had been smashed and scattered, and was now no more than a jagged hole and a pile of sand-coloured bricks.

On the patio, just beyond the wreckage, Bep-Wor used to like to watch the sun go down. After working in the fields he'd sit there, with a tankard of beer in his hand, listening to the chirruping of the insects. Listening to the sounds coming from the house. The sounds from the kitchen. Pots and plates rattling. Sizzling oil. Her voice.

Kia-Ga.

He shook his head violently. Everything reminded him of her. He gasped a silent, bitter laugh. There was, after all, nothing left: everything was broken, shattered, turned to ash and rubble. The bed they had shared was now charcoal. Her paintings were slashed and trampled. The flower garden had been crushed. There was nothing left, but still he couldn't forget. Even the beauty of the sunset reminded him of her.

He blinked. He must not cry. There was no use in crying. He'd wept enough.

But he would never forgive himself for being away from

home when the invaders came. He tortured himself by imagining her suffering. She didn't even know that he had survived. She would probably never know.

It was no use. Bep-Wor howled silently, his face contorted. How could he still have tears left in him? He felt the hot drops roll down his cheeks. Salty on his lips. Why did he bother to live any longer?

He heard a noise. Nothing natural. Like nothing he had heard before. A metallic groaning, the sound ebbing and flowing like waves on shingle. But getting louder. Getting closer.

It could only be the invaders. One of their infernal machines. Bep-Wor's hand closed around the handle of the pitchfork he carried with him when he went outside. It was useless against the machines and the weapons of the enemy, but it was all he had. He wiped his eyes and pulled himself from the floor. He picked his way silently across the fallen masonry.

Having risen to crescendo, until it sounded like a storm at sea, the strange sound had ceased. Bep-Wor could hear nothing: no sounds of soldiers marching; no voices; no machines. Holding the pitchfork before him, he stepped through the ruined side of his house.

Crouching, he scuttled to the low wall that surrounded his property. There were still no sounds. He lifted his head.

He knew what he would see. But he could not get used to it. At this time of day the village square would have been crowded with people, promenading in front of the neat, whitewashed houses and taking glasses of sweet tea in the two cafés. His neighbours. His friends.

All gone.

Some of the houses were still standing, their doors and windows gaping; others were no more than heaps of brick and timber. The slanting, golden sunlight was all that seemed familiar.

But this evening something had changed again. In the centre of the square, standing slightly askew on the rubble-strewn flagstones, there was a blue hut. At the apex of its sloping roof a lantern flashed. Its door stood open.

Bep-Wor struggled to understand what the structure was, and how it could have been placed in the square without him hearing the sounds of its construction. It looked nothing like the flying machines of the invaders, but Bep-Wor could imagine only that it had dropped from the sky.

He cursed. Soldiers from inside the hut must already be in the village, patrolling stealthily. Had he been seen when he last made a foray to find food? Had the blue hut been sent specifically to find him? He had to retreat into the house and lie low. He could go hungry for one more night.

He was about to scramble back to the house when he saw the man.

The stranger – not a soldier, Bep-Wor saw that at once – was sitting, motionless, in the long black shadow cast by the hut. He had his elbows resting on his knees, and his head cradled in his hands. He looked utterly miserable.

Ace hadn't expected to find the space station manned by sword-wielding chaps dressed like extras from *The Charge of the Light Brigade*, but she'd seen plenty of weird things in her time and she wasn't going to let her surprise show.

She was finding it more difficult to ignore the presence of Kedin Ashar: he was obviously the head honcho, what with his minions bowing and scraping all round him, and he was tall, skinny, resplendent in his uniform, very cool and very sexy. And he wouldn't stop chatting her up.

It was all very distracting. Ace had realised that whatever the space station was being used for, it wasn't a thriving trading post. So much for the Doctor's projections of probability. The only people she saw as Kedin showed her round were soldiers, all of them belonging to Kedin's battalion, or regiment, or whatever it was. And they were all men.

The only women she'd seen had been among the gang that had attacked Kedin. And that was another odd thing: Kedin hadn't explained why he'd been mugged, and managed to change the subject whenever Ace tried to ask.

'You men can return to your stations,' Kedin said over his shoulder to the troop of soldiers who had followed them throughout the tour. Ace had wondered all along why it was necessary to have a bodyguard.

'I must show you the observatory,' Kedin said, guiding her with his hand on her shoulder.

That kind of thing normally freaked her out, but she had to admit that she liked the touch of Kedin's hands. It made her feel shivery. Not nasty shivery: nice shivery. Very nice. 'Then you will have seen everything,' he concluded.

The exciting proximity of Kedin's slim body wasn't enough to make Ace fall for that line, however. She had a pretty good idea of the size of the station, and she knew she hadn't seen the half of it. The design of the place suggested that there must be large storage holds: Kedin hadn't shown her even one. Nor had he taken her to the docking bays or to the main control room. He had something to hide.

Well, Ace said to herself, if he fancies me I can use that to find out what's going on here. I'll just turn on my irresistible allure. He'll be eating out of my hand.

They were alone together now, standing in front of a closed door marked OBSERVATORY. Ace didn't move aside when Kedin reached past her to pull down the emergency door lever.

They haven't worked out how to use the electronic systems, Ace realised as she allowed herself to sway forward slightly, bringing the front of her T-shirt into soft contact with the back of Kedin's arm.

The door slid open. Ace didn't move, but remained standing in the doorway. She glanced over her shoulder at Kedin.

Now let's see him make his move, she thought. I suppose I ought to put up a bit of resistance when he does. I think I'm going to enjoy this Mata Hari stuff.

But Kedin didn't touch her. He stepped back, coughed discreetly, and made an elegant gesture indicating that Ace was welcome to precede him through the doorway.

Cursing inwardly, Ace smiled at him and walked ahead.

Ace couldn't understand it. The way he'd been acting, she'd thought he'd try to get physical as soon as he had her alone. Maybe it had all been an act, to impress his men. But he didn't seem the kind of bloke who needed to impress anyone.

'Prepare yourself for a shock,' Kedin said from behind her as she approached the end of the short corridor. 'I've known battle-hardened troopers to turn queasy when they first see the panorama of the stars.'

'Don't worry about me,' Ace said, and stepped from the mouth of the corridor into the transparent bubble beyond.

She didn't recognise the constellations, but she hadn't expected to. Every time she gazed up at an alien night sky she felt a pang of homesickness: it wasn't that she wanted to return to Earth, but she was assailed by a realization of how far away she was from her home world.

The sun of the Mendeb system, along with Mendeb Two, was out of sight, presumably on the opposite side of the space station. Mendeb Three was visible, however: a globe a little smaller than the Moon seen from Earth, brilliantly white in the full glare of the sun. Ace could see the corona of atmosphere around the planet, and within it swirls and lines of clouds.

Kedin exhaled a deep breath. 'That's my home,' he said.

Ace looked at him. He was staring at the planet. His face was set. His eyes were glittering. He looked sad and noble.

'One day,' he added, 'I'll be able to return.'

Kedin's an exile, Ace thought. That's really romantic.

He turned to Ace. His mouth was once again wearing its quirky smile. He gestured grandly at the heavens. 'And where is your home, Ace?'

Now that's a good question, Ace said to herself. I'm damned if I know the answer, these days. But I'd better tell him something. He's obviously worked out that I'm not from these parts. He probably wants to get his hands on the rocketship he assumes I used to get here. Better not say I'm from Earth, though – he's probably heard of it, and I don't know whether that's good or bad.

'I come from a world that's somewhere in that lot,' Ace said, pointing to the glittering swathe of stars that made up the Milky Way. 'Place called Perivale.'

'Ah,' Kedin said. 'I see.'

He looked completely mystified.

An hour later, the man was still sitting by his blue hut with his head in his hands.

Bep-Wor was still watching him, and still trying to decide whether he was one of the enemy. He wasn't in uniform: in fact his clothes looked almost as worn and untidy as Bep-Wor's. Perhaps he might prove to be an ally. At the very least he might have food in his hut. And he seemed to be alone.

Bep-Wor climbed over the wall. The man didn't notice him. Keeping within the long shadows, Bep-Wor crept round the sides of the square until he was at the closest point to the hut. Then he had no choice but to make a break into the open. He sprinted across the sun-streaked flagstones.

The man had heard his footsteps. As he reached the hut, the

man appeared round one of its corners. Bep-Wor lifted his pitchfork to keep the man at a distance.

The man raised his arms and showed his empty hands. 'Don't be alarmed,' he said. 'I'm not dangerous. I'm the Doctor. Who are you?'

Bep-Wor was confused. A doctor? But the man had said *the* Doctor. As if Bep-Wor should have heard of him. He was a short, slight man. His eyes were bright and unnervingly piercing, but he was smiling. For some reason Bep-Wor thought he could trust him. He lowered the pitchfork. 'My name is Bep-Wor. This is my village. Was my village.'

'What happened here?' the Doctor said, as if he was completely unaware of the invasion.

This wasn't the time to explain. 'We can't stay here,' Bep-Wor said. 'A patrol could come through at any time. We must take cover. But first, do you have food? I haven't eaten for two days.'

'Of course,' the Doctor said. 'Come into the TARDIS. No: wait.' The Doctor looked at Bep-Wor searchingly. 'Stay here,' the Doctor said. 'You've had enough shocks recently, I can see that. I'll be back in a trice.'

The Doctor disappeared through the doorway of his hut. It sounded to Bep-Wor as though the Doctor's footsteps were receding into the distance: as if the inside of the hut was a large, empty space. He shook his head. He decided he must have become delirious with hunger.

Suddenly the Doctor was emerging from the dark interior. He pulled the door closed behind him. Bep-Wor saw that he was carrying a small silver flask.

'Food,' Bep-Wor said. 'I need food, not drink.'

The Doctor grinned. He looked very pleased with himself. 'Just try a drop of this,' he said. 'It's really quite extraordinarily nutritious.' He proffered the flask.

Now Bep-Wor was very suspicious. There had been rumours

that the invaders pacified their captives with drugged drinks.

'It's perfectly safe,' the Doctor said. A note of impatience had entered his voice. 'Look, I'll have some myself.'

He unscrewed the stopper and lifted the flask to his lips. He drank.

'Don't drink it all,' Bep-Wor said urgently. The Doctor had surely drained the bottle. Perhaps the Doctor was mad.

'Don't worry,' the Doctor said with a crafty look. 'There's plenty left. It's on a permanent link to the food synthesiser.'

Bep-Wor had no idea what the Doctor was talking about. If he wasn't mad, he was certainly very strange. But the flask felt full in his hands, and when he brought it to his mouth he first smelt, and then tasted, a rich, warm aromatic broth that seemed to satisfy his aching gut even as the first mouthful entered his throat. He took gulps of the thick fluid, until he felt a hand pressing on his.

'That's enough for now,' the Doctor said. 'It is full of nutrients. Don't overdo it.'

'Thank you, Doctor,' Bep-Wor said. He handed back the flask, and as he did so he heard the distant droning of a machine. The doctor's head was cocked: he had heard it too.

'Run!' Bep-Wor said. 'It's a flying machine. This way.' He made for the side of the square, pausing only to make sure that the Doctor was following him. He realised that he felt stronger than he had for a week: the Doctor's flask contained a remarkably potent broth. The Doctor, too, could move surprisingly quickly, and both men were crouching behind the tumbled wall of Bep-Wor's house when the flying machine came into sight.

It was flying low, and the clatter of its engine was thunderous. Bep-Wor could see the flashing circle made by the whirling blades at the front of the machine. But for the noise it would have seemed as graceful as a bird as it swooped and circled over the square. The man sitting in the machine, his helmeted head visible above the metal flanks, had seen the Doctor's blue hut. Bep-Wor was certain that soldiers would be sent to investigate.

The Doctor was talking to himself. Bep-Wor heard him say, 'Surprisingly primitive construction.'

The engine roared louder as the machine curved upwards through the air and pulled away from the village.

'Primitive?' Bep-Wor said. 'Doctor, there are men in those machines. They can fly faster than any bird. They drop packages of explosives. Look around you. See what they can do.'

'Who are they, Bep-Wor? Who are the people who destroyed your village?' The Doctor's expression was intense, almost fearful.

When the invaders had attacked the village Bep-Wor had been at sea. There had been rumours of a war in the Links, the line of islands that trailed southwards beyond Big Hook Island; a trader, known for his liking for beer, had said he'd seen machines in the sky. But no one expected the invaders. There had been no reason at all why Bep-Wor should have refused his brother, who needed an extra hand on the fishing boat.

And while he was at sea – while he was enjoying the salty air and the easy comradeship of his brother's crew – the invaders had come.

Kia-Ga. Where was she now?

Bep-Wor shook his head and sniffed back his tears. 'I don't know,' he said.

The Doctor persisted. 'Are they from one of the other islands?'

'No. Of course not.' Bep-Wor was certain of that. His brother fished the waters from one side of the archipelago to the other. He would have known if any of the islands had started to build machines such as the invaders possessed. Everyone would have known.

'What about the people who live in the south polar region? Could it be them?'

Bep-Wor had considered the possibility many times. 'The southerners? Perhaps,' he said. 'But our leaders used to talk to their leaders. They live as we do, as far as we can tell. I never heard that they could fly in machines. We had a device, on Windsweep Island, that carried our voices to them and theirs to us. It stopped working a few years ago.'

'I know,' the Doctor said. He looked unhappy. 'That was my fault, I think. And so, maybe, is all of this.' His sad eyes scanned slowly across the ruined village.

Bep-Wor didn't understand. He still wasn't sure whether the Doctor was in his right mind. 'I've seen soldiers marching through here,' he said. 'I've met a few people from nearby villages, too. There's a rumour that the invaders don't come from this world at all; that they just dropped out of the sky.'

Bep-Wor expected the Doctor to ridicule his story. But the Doctor merely nodded with resignation, as if his worst fears had been confirmed. 'Well,' he said, 'I won't find out what's going on if I stay here. I'd better be on my way.'

'To where?' Bep-Wor said.

'To find the invaders, of course. I have to determine who they are. Then, somehow or other, I must put things right. And of course there's always Ace to worry about.' A look of anguish crossed his face. 'I seem to have made a spectacular hash of things this time.'

Bep-Wor wondered whether Ace was the Doctor's woman. And how the Doctor thought he could put things right. The strange thing was that Bep-Wor almost believed that the Doctor could do it. He was just one man, and not any sort of soldier, but Bep-Wor trusted him. The invaders had taken Kia-Ga. Perhaps the Doctor could find her.

He realised he was being pitifully hopeful. But the arrival of the Doctor seemed like a good omen.

'The invaders came from that direction,' Bep-Wor said, pointing south-east. 'They went north. I think some are still on the island. If we head northwards we'll find them. Or they'll find us.'

'We?' the Doctor said. 'Us?'

'I'm coming with you.' Bep-Wor looked around at his shattered home. 'I've nothing to stay for.'

Madok didn't like it. It was unseemly to hide in a young woman's quarters; it was worse to participate in playing a trick on her. He doubted whether Ace would be fooled, anyway: she was inquisitive, certainly, but it seemed unlikely that replacing the sign saying ESCAPE POD with one saying WEAPONS ROOM would be enough to entice her through the small door in the corner of her cabin.

'She won't be able to resist it,' Kedin had assured him. 'You'd be amazed at the things that girl's interested in. And she'll be quite safe: after all, you'll be there to switch the controls to automatic if she really can't handle it.'

And so Madok waited, crouching in the darkness, uncomfortably constricted in the narrow space behind the single seat.

He heard voices: Kedin and Ace.

'I'm afraid this is the best I can offer you,' Kedin said. His voice sounded thin and distant, even though the pod's door was slightly ajar. 'It's not the most luxurious of accommodation.'

'I've had worse,' Ace said.

Neither of them spoke for a while. As the silence extended Madok imagined Kedin pulling Ace into his arms. Touching her face. Kissing her. It was too much to bear.

'Yes, that's all pretty much as I expected,' Ace said. Her voice was louder than Kedin's. She had moved near to the door.

'Hello,' she said, her voice sharp with surprise. 'What's this? Weapons? That's not likely, is it? This is a pressure-sealed door.'

Light spilled into the pod as the outer door opened. Madok willed himself to keep still and silent as Ace crossed the threshold of the inner door.

'This is an escape pod,' she called over her shoulder to Kedin. 'You know, like a lifeboat on a ship.' As she finished the sentence Madok heard the outer door swing into its frame with a heavy thud.

'Oi!' Ace shouted.

At the same time Kedin's voice came weakly through the closed door. He was, Madok had to admit, making a good job of sounding close to panic.

'Great heavens,' he cried, 'the door's closed itself. I don't know what's going on. Don't worry, Ace. I'll get you out. I'll open the door. There must be a lever that will work it. Ah! I'll try this one.'

'Hold it!' Ace yelled, but communication with Kedin was cut off as the inner door slid shut. Madok peeked from behind the seat and saw Ace jump back to avoid being crushed.

'Bloody hell,' Ace said. She seemed more irritated than frightened.

'Emergency escape activated,' a woman's voice calmly intoned. Madok almost leapt from his hiding-place in surprise. 'Lift-off in ten seconds. Secure the seat straps.'

The voice belonged to the escape pod itself, Madok realised. Some of the troopers on the station had told him of hearing the ghostly voice of a woman: it was said to warn of danger. Madok knew that the explanation had to be technological, not supernatural. It was possible to send a voice across thousands of kilometres: every one of Kedin's military units had a radio set and a man trained to operate it. And it was possible to make a recording of a human voice. It wasn't far-fetched, therefore, to imagine a recorded message that turned itself on automatically. There was so much still to rediscover, despite the great strides that Kedin and Tevana had made.

'Bloody, bloody hell,' Ace said vehemently as she strapped herself into the seat. 'I just hope these controls are still working. I'll bet this thing hasn't been serviced for a good few hundred years.'

'Five,' said the voice of the escape pod, 'four.'

Madok peered over Ace's shoulder. She was scanning the boards, alight with flickering dials, that surrounded her.

'Life support's OK, that's the main thing,' she said to herself. 'Now, I must be able to pull up a graphic display. What about this?'

Madok almost gasped with surprise as a large blank area in the centre of the banks of controls burst into life. It looked like a swirling mist of colours.

'One,' said the voice of the escape pod, 'lift-off.'

Madok hunched into a ball. He felt the floor vibrate. A screaming roar filled his ears. His shaking body was pressed against the back of Ace's seat. He felt sick.

It went on for several minutes.

'Urgh,' he heard Ace say. Evidently the acceleration had been scarcely more comfortable for her.

He risked lifting his head again. Ace was still concentrating on the controls. The swirling slate of colours suddenly made sense to him: it was a picture. There was the vast, complex mass of the space station, exactly as he saw it from his scout ship; there, a tiny sliver of light drifting away from the station, was the escape pod.

'Thrusters,' Ace said, pensively. 'I wonder.' Tentatively she pressed a button. Madok saw the tiny representation of the pod begin to veer upwards.

'Brilliant!' Ace exclaimed. 'This is a doddle. Now if I can just identify a docking bay, I'll bring this thing in.'

Madok watched in admiration as Ace studied the moving picture, consulted the controls, and operated the thrusters to steer the pod towards the nearest docking bay.

'I wonder how I get the doors open,' Ace muttered as the pod floated ever closer to the metal shutters.

As Madok suspected, she didn't have to worry about it. 'Docking procedures initiated,' said the voice of the pod, and in the picture on the screen the shutters began to part.

A row of lights had flashed on in front of Ace. 'All systems to automatic,' the voice of the pod said.

Ace uttered a murmur of disappointment. 'Oh well,' she said, 'I can put my feet up.' And, to Madok's surprise, she did so.

'Now then,' Ace said to herself, 'what was all that about? That Kedin's a crafty old sod. Charming and very horny, but definitely crafty with it. I suppose he's trying to find out how much I know about all this futuristic technology. It's obvious he hasn't got the hang of all of it. I just wish I knew what he was up to on this godforsaken space station.'

My lady, Madok prayed fervently, I hope you never find out.

By the time the pod had landed and the docking bay had refilled itself with air, Madok had been crouched behind the seat for so long that his muscles were knotted and he had to grit his teeth to prevent himself crying out in pain. However, Ace remained unaware of his presence, and he allowed himself the luxury of movement only when the pod's door was open and he was sure she had disembarked.

Kedin was in the bay's control room. Madok could hear his voice as he greeted Ace.

'Ace, thank the heavens you're safe,' Kedin said. 'I've worried myself into an apoplexy. It's all my fault. How can you ever forgive me? And how the deuce did you bring yourself back?'

'I was very, very scared,' Ace said. Madok could imagine her big, dark eyes gazing up at Kedin's face. He couldn't prevent himself imagining Kedin's sympathetic arm resting on her shoulders. 'I didn't have a clue what to do. I think it all works automatically. I just sort of found myself back here. I'm so glad to be back – with you.'

Madok smiled. Ace was managing to invest her words with a quivering emotion that was almost convincing. She really was a splendid young woman.

But it wouldn't work, of course. If she succeeded in fooling Kedin, which was in any case unlikely, he wouldn't remain fooled for long. Madok had seen Ace piloting the escape pod, and it was clear that she knew more than Kedin did about the technology of the space station.

Kedin would consider her useful. He would encourage her to stay. And that was all that Madok wished for.

They walked, keeping close to the banks of hedge-ferns and hurrying between copses of broadleaves, until the sun was a vast golden ball melting across the horizon. Then they found shelter in an isolated barn, and Bep-Wor slept for the few hours of half-darkness.

When he woke he felt refreshed and full of hope. He found the Doctor sitting in the doorway of the barn, staring into the distance. Bep-Wor wondered whether the Doctor had slept at all. The Doctor looked up and said, 'Hello.' Bep-Wor nodded. They remained together in silence.

The world seemed to be at peace. The fields were freshly green, and full of the chirruping of insects. Stands of giant fern cast long, undulating shadows. In the distance, in the gaps between the tawny hills, the sea sparkled.

Bep-Wor could almost believe that it had all been a dream. That there had been no invaders, no damage. He knew he was deceiving himself, but the clear dawn light at least painted the world in optimistic colours. At last he had things to do, and the energy to do them: he would help the Doctor, and he would search for Kia-Ga. He had a purpose.

His good humour lasted until they reached Porgum. They had found a mule not far from the barn: it approached them, having no doubt seen no other people for many days. Once it had tasted the Doctor's broth it allowed itself to be ridden. The Doctor and Bep-Wor took it in turns to rest their feet, and they made good progress. Only once were they obliged to dive into a ditch to avoid being seen by one of the flying machines.

As they approached Porgum, however, Bep-Wor's new-found determination and cheer withered. As the mule jolted him from side to side he could see the signs of destruction: roofs torn open, columns of smoke rising into the air.

Porgum was the nearest settlement northwards from Bep-Wor's own village: a large, thriving place with a mercantile quarter, well-stocked shops, and a weekly grain and flour market that served the entire island. The annual music festival drew crowds from all over the archipelago.

There was nothing to say. The mule trudged onwards with the Doctor holding its halter, and with each step it became more and more obvious that Porgum had been devastated.

All too soon they were walking between the wrecked houses, picking their way round piles of tumbled masonry and smouldering fires.

The only sound was the clop of the mule's hooves. The town was deserted.

Bep-Wor scanned the skies. He told himself he was keeping a look-out for flying machines, but the truth was that he couldn't look at the scarred houses. The Doctor, he thought, was inquisitive enough for both of them: the strange little man, his face grim, peered along every choked alleyway and through every smashed wall.

'Bep-Wor,' the Doctor said at last, as they left behind the last ruined villa on the outskirts of the town, 'I saw no bodies. It looks like the aftermath of a battle, but there are no bodies.'

At first Bep-Wor failed to understand the meaning of the Doctor's words. When he understood, he was appalled. His stomach lurched and he felt nauseous. 'Bodies?' he said. 'You mean dead bodies? You think the invaders have killed people?' Could the invaders have killed Kia-Ga? It made no sense.

'I'm afraid it's not uncommon,' the Doctor said. 'It's the way invaders behave. And your people could have killed some of the invaders, as you defended yourselves.'

Bep-Wor barked a short laugh. 'Defend ourselves? Doctor, we have no defence against the invaders' machines. You've seen the flying machine. You've seen the damage caused by the explosives. The invaders come, and the people run before them. They herd us like cattle.'

The Doctor's keen gaze roved across the skyline of broken rooftops. 'So the invaders destroy the houses after all the inhabitants have fled?' he said.

'Yes, of course.' Bep-Wor had thought the Doctor understood that already. 'I watched them destroy my village.'

The Doctor nodded, but he looked perplexed. 'Let's continue on our way,' he said. 'I want to find these invaders and have a stern word with them.'

Bep-Wor insisted that the Doctor should take a turn riding the mule. Bep-Wor walked. They emerged from the northern outskirts of Porgum. Bep-Wor felt his spirits lift a little as they left behind the ruined town and found themselves trudging through small fields planted with sourwheat and squashes.

They were on higher ground, among thickets of tall ferns, when Bep-Wor noticed that the Doctor was listening to something. He had his hand cupped at his ear. They were approaching the edge of the plantation when Bep-Wor heard it: the sound of machines.

'Proceed cautiously,' the Doctor said. 'Don't go into the open.'

They stopped in the shade of the last spinney of ferns, and looked down into the flat valley below. Spike-grass and recumbent ferns covered most of the landscape in shades of green, rippling in the breeze. Here and there fields had been marked out and planted: winding tracks led from the fields to the road which descended from the tree-ferns and stretched away into the distance.

And in the middle of the valley, next to the road, the land was scarred and seared brown. A vast metal machine, the size and shape of a bow-roofed barn, stood in the middle of the burnt area. Nearby, and looking insubstantial alongside the big structure, were four flying machines. Still smaller machines, some of which Bep-Wor recognised as weapons which threw explosives, were drawn up in lines on a field between the burnt area and the hill on which Bep-Wor was standing. Other machines had wheels, and some of these were moving along the field-tracks and the main road. Bep-Wor realised that it was the movement of the wheeled machines that created the insistent racket.

'Internal combustion engines,' the Doctor said. 'Propellor aircraft, armoured cars. Field guns.' He turned to Bep-Wor. 'Your people have none of these?'

'No.' Bep-Wor felt defensive. Should he be ashamed? Of what? 'What would we want with machines that can only destroy?'

'Most humans I've encountered seem to want little else,' the Doctor said. 'Look: there's your enemy.'

Bep-Wor shielded his eyes and squinted. He saw one tiny

figure, emerging from one of the wheeled machines. Then three more, marching in a line along one of the tracks. The sunlight caught on the polished metal buttons of their uniforms. Now that he had seen a few he found it easy to see others: marching in columns, standing in rows, swarming around the machines.

'They're definitely human,' the Doctor said. He sounded disappointed. 'Why are they here? What do they want? Are they just taking a delight in wanton destruction? Or is this invasion a particularly brutal method of enforcing political hegemony?'

Bep-Wor could hardly believe his ears. The Doctor still hadn't understood. 'It's worse than that, Doctor,' he said. He could feel tears welling once again in his eyes. 'Look. Look: on the road, next to the biggest machine.'

The Doctor's gaze followed Bep-Wor's pointing finger. When he saw the line of people, stretching to the horizon, he said, 'Oh, no.'

'They're collecting us, Doctor,' Bep-Wor said. 'Like animals. They clear us from our towns and villages, and they destroy our homes so that we have nowhere to live. They herd us, round us up, and take us away.'

Having retired to her quarters with the excuse that she was upset – well, you would be, she thought, after being shot into space in an escape pod – Ace had spent some time trying to boot up the communications console.

It was no use: she couldn't get the thing to work. It was intensely frustrating. The system had power, and she could get up the introductory screen. But the console in her cabin seemed to be on a low security level, and she couldn't get into the system at a level high enough to kick it into life.

During her guided tour of the station Ace had noticed that

every screen she'd seen had been blank. It was obvious that Kedin and his men hadn't worked out how to use the station's communications system. Their knowledge of radio technology was rudimentary: she'd spotted one of the soldiers struggling to carry a wireless set the size of a suitcase.

The temptation to show off was almost irresistible. If turning on the station's communications couldn't impress Kedin, she was sure that a demonstration of the hologram projector would blow his mind. And she badly wanted to get Kedin's undivided attention.

The only thing that stopped her sharing her knowledge with Kedin was her nagging doubt about what he was doing on the station. Who were those low-lifes that had attacked him? Where had they come from? And why was Kedin being so cagey?

And she had to admit that she was rather enjoying her Mata Hari role. Kedin and Madok still had no idea where she was from, and she intended to keep them guessing – at least until she knew more about them.

When she'd finally given up on the communications console, she'd thrown herself on the bed and stared at the ceiling until she was thoroughly bored.

How long, she had asked herself, would it take for a defenceless young woman, alone in a strange environment and surrounded by grim-faced soldiers, to get over the shock of being ejected into space in a box not much bigger than a coffin?

No idea, she had answered herself. They probably expect me to have the screaming ab-dabs for days on end. But if I have to pretend to be having an attack of the vapours for much longer I'll go round the bend for real. I've had enough of this. Time to go out for a snoop about.

She'd tiptoed scarcely five metres from her room when Madok emerged from a side-corridor.

He's been waiting for me, she thought. Damn.

Madok had been polite, concerned, and anxious to reassure himself that she had recovered from her ordeal. However, no matter how often Ace told him that she felt fine, he didn't leave her alone. So much for snooping.

It was particularly difficult to shake Madok off while she was doing her vulnerable and feminine act. Madok lapped it up, and was pathetically eager to look after her.

Madok was all right, Ace decided as he followed her doggedly round the station. A regular bloke, once you got past the bluster and the stiff formality. She noticed that he was much more at ease talking to soldiers. He's a military man, she thought; a career officer. He probably hasn't spent much time in mixed company.

He was actually quite good-looking too. But too old for her. And too stocky.

Ace laughed aloud when she realised that she was comparing every man she met with Kedin. She had to pretend she was coughing, and endure Madok's anxious enquiries about the delicacy of her health.

The fact was that no one measured up to Kedin's score on the dreaminess gauge. Ace wanted to see him again: when she remembered his eyes the desire for him was physical, like a sudden pang in her stomach.

And she wasn't getting anything out of Madok, anyway. He seemed desperate to please her, but he managed always to evade difficult questions.

She'd found out that he and many others among Kedin's men could fly the ships that had been found in the station's docking bays. He admitted that he didn't understand most of the controls, and that he relied on the station's automatic systems to dock his ship. He was proud of the fact that he could bring a ship in to land on a planet, though, and Ace was genuinely impressed: it must have taken courage and skill.

'That's amazing, Madok,' she said. 'No, really, I mean it. You must be ever so brave.'

'It's nothing,' Madok said, but Ace noticed that his cheeks had turned pink. 'I'm sure you could do it, my lady.'

Yes, probably, Ace thought. How difficult can it be? But I'm not going to let you know it, mate. Even though it does mean I have to keep up this helpless girly act.

'I wouldn't have a clue,' Ace said, and managed to produce what she hoped was a fetching giggle. 'And now I'm sure I've taken up enough of your time. Didn't Kedin say that he wanted to see me again?'

'Yes, my lady, he did.' Madok looked uncomfortable and grumpy. 'But only if you're quite sure you're feeling better.'

'I'm sure I'll be fine,' Ace said, trying to look frail and wan. 'Where will I find him?'

Madok closed his eyes momentarily. 'I believe he is in his quarters, lady.'

Oh, good, Ace thought. I'll have him to myself at last. And in his bedroom.

Madok, blushing furiously, was struggling to express himself. 'But I would quite understand, lady,' he said, 'if you would prefer me to arrange an alternative rendezvous. I appreciate your sensibilities. This station isn't the most civilised of places, but there are certain standards of behaviour. What I mean is, my lord would not expect you to do anything unseemly.'

Ace had no idea what he was going on about. She was on the point of blurting out an entirely inappropriate question about Kedin's usual behaviour with women when she suddenly understood. Among these people it was considered scandalous for a respectable woman, alone, to visit a man's room. That was all.

Well, actually, Ace thought, I hope that's not all, in this case.

But I can't say that to Madok: he'd go purple in the face and explode.

She laid her hand on his sleeve. 'Kedin is an officer,' she said, 'and, apparently, the foremost aristo on the planet. This is a military post, and society's rules don't apply strictly here. So I'm sure my reputation will be safe.'

Madok seemed relieved. 'In that case,' he said, 'I will happily escort you.'

'I can find my own way, you know,' Ace said as she and Madok set off.

'I don't doubt it, my lady,' Madok said. 'But as you found out for yourself, these corridors are not entirely safe.'

'And that's another thing,' Ace said. 'You and Kedin still haven't told me who those creeps were.'

'Creeps?'

'The ones who attacked Kedin. You called them escapers.'

'Mutineers,' Madok said. 'We had them incarcerated. They'll be recaptured soon.'

'They weren't wearing uniforms.'

Madok appeared genuinely shocked. 'Of course not.'

It was almost plausible. Ace felt light-headed for a moment as the clouds of suspicion she'd been harbouring began to disperse. Maybe there was nothing untoward going on. Kedin's attackers were just criminals who'd escaped; large areas of the space station were locked simply because Kedin's men didn't need them, or hadn't worked out how to get into them; the distant, mournful voices were aural illusions of the kind you could experience in an almost disused warren of corridors.

Ace grinned. She'd spent too long with the Doctor. When he was around everything had a sinister explanation. She'd forgotten what normal life was like.

She turned to Madok and impulsively grabbed his arm. She

felt him flinch and then relax. 'If you want to know where your escaped mutineers are,' she whispered, 'why don't you use the cameras?'

Madok seemed at a loss for words. 'Cameras?' he stuttered at last.

Ace pointed to the ceiling. 'See that little box up there? With a glass eye? It can see what's in the corridor, and show you pictures of it. I'll demonstrate later, if you like.'

It was a relief not to have to pretend to be ignorant any more.

They had reached Kedin's quarters. The soldier on guard at the door turned to stare at Ace. His eyes lit up and he gave her a leering grin, which disappeared immediately when Madok glared at him.

Madok gestured impatiently at the door. The soldier rapped on it with the butt of his rifle.

A muffled voice called from beyond the sealed door. Madok shouted his name. The voice replied indistinctly. Madok tugged on the emergency door release handle.

They really need someone to tell them how to use this place properly, Ace thought.

'So this is the captain's cabin,' Ace said as she stepped through the doorway.

It was a suite of rooms. The main chamber was big, in Ace's opinion: accommodation was cramped on every other space station she'd visited. Despite not being able to use the colour and texture controls that Ace was sure were embedded in the grey walls, Kedin had succeeded in importing his personality and taste. The floor was covered in a carpet woven with a complex pattern; animal skins were laid here and there over the carpet. Tapestries covered most of the walls: a hunting scene, a troop of cavalry on animals that weren't horses, and a huddle of naked nymphs bathing near a waterfall. The furniture was large, heavy, generously upholstered, and well supplied with cushions. A vast, polished desk dominated the room.

Kedin wasn't in sight, but Ace could hear him moving in one of the other rooms.

Madok had followed Ace through the doorway. 'Kedin Ashar,' he called out. 'It's Madok. I've brought Ace to see you.'

'Excellent.' Kedin's voice came through one of the doors. 'Ace, please accept my apologies. I'm in the middle of a shave. I'll be able to give you my total attention in just a moment.'

Ace caught a glimpse of him through a doorway. The glint of a cut-throat razor; his naked torso. God, he had some muscles on him. Sinewy, she thought: that was the word.

Ace wandered about the room. She admired the jewelled scabbard and hilt of Kedin's sword. She heard Madok's indrawn breath as she picked up and inspected a delicate model of an old-fashioned rocket with swept-back fins and a bulbous nose.

Probably priceless, she thought.

Madok seemed ill at ease. He paced back and forth with his hands clasped behind his back. Several times Ace thought he was about to speak to her.

Kedin bounded into the room. He was dressed now, but not in full uniform: he had on soft suede boots, tight black trousers, and a brilliantly white shirt. Ace stole a glance at Madok. As she had expected, he was open-mouthed with shock. She supposed he considered Kedin almost indecently under-dressed. As for her, she was particularly happy with the tight trousers and the open shirt. Even the boots were sexy.

Kedin took her hands in his and stared into her eyes. 'Ace,' he said, 'can you find it in your heart to forgive me? I can't believe I was so incompetent. I endangered your life. I can't express my relief at finding you unharmed. I trust you've had sufficient time to rest and recuperate.'

He looked up, and seemed to notice Madok for the first time. 'Still here, Madok?' he said. He didn't release Ace's hands.

'At your service, my lord,' Madok said.

Kedin glanced at Ace. Their eyes met. His seemed to twinkle as he gave her a surreptitious smile.

'It's all right, Madok,' Ace said. 'I don't need a bodyguard any more. I'm sure I'll be safe with Kedin.' She couldn't stop her fingers trembling. She was sure Kedin would notice.

'My lord?' Madok said.

'I don't need protection either,' Kedin said. 'I'm sure Ace won't hurt me.' He tightened his grip on her hands. 'I can manage, Madok.'

Ace didn't hear Madok leave. Her heart was thumping, and she couldn't pull her eyes from Kedin's hawk-like face.

'Allow me to show you around my small domain,' Kedin said, retaining his hold on one of her hands. 'I've decorated the place as best I can. It reminds me of home. I hope you'll like it.'

'It's neat,' Ace said. She didn't trust herself to say much: she was afraid her voice might come out all wobbly. She couldn't pretend to be an expert on men: that was the trouble with growing up in the TARDIS and spending her time battling evil aliens. But she sensed that behind Kedin's casual elegance and carefree banter he was concealing a deep and tragic pain. It was all just too romantic.

'I insist that you tell me all about yourself,' Kedin said, 'now that we're alone together at last.' He stopped suddenly and turned to face her. He lifted his hand to her face and touched her cheek. 'I could make you talk, you know.' His expression was anxious – almost grim. 'I won't. I couldn't bear to do that to you.'

'It's OK,' Ace said. She put her hand over his. 'You won't have to get out the thumbscrews. I'm going to tell you.'

'Ace,' he murmured. And then his lips were touching hers, and she pressed herself against him and returned his kisses.

'Um - oh dear,' Kedin said after some time had passed. 'You've bewitched me, Ace. I don't intend - that is, I have no desire to compromise you, lady.'

Ace placed a finger on his lips. 'Hush. You were showing me round, remember. Which one of these doors leads to the bedroom, for instance?'

'Ah. It's this one. Would you like to -?'

He was even more kissable when he was looking confused. Hardly believing what she was doing, and with her legs feeling like jelly, Ace made for the doorway he had indicated.

She entered a bedroom that was sumptuous and dark with velvet and gold.

She glanced over her shoulder to make sure that Kedin was following her. She wanted to feel his hands touching her again.

He was standing in the doorway with his eyes closed. 'Tevana, forgive me,' she heard him say.

'Kedin,' she said, 'who's Tevana?'

Kedin's face broke into a grin. 'She's my personal goddess,' he said, and scooped Ace up in his arms. 'I think she'll forgive this transgression. I hope so.' He kissed her, and hugged her so tightly that she struggled for breath. 'I think you'd better say a prayer to your own deity, young lady. You're about to sin.'

Madok sat and stared at the endless rows of glowing lights and flickering numbers. He had thought that if he shut himself in the station's control room and concentrated on trying to understand more of the bewildering array he would be able to stop himself thinking about Ace. And Kedin. In Kedin's quarters.

He cursed himself for being a fool. The station's controls were almost entirely indecipherable: the winking lights mocked him and refused to give up their secrets. Kedin's campaign would just have to proceed with the technology he and Tevana had already researched, resurrected and refined. Unless, of course, it turned out that Kedin could coax some useful information out of Ace.

And there she was again, occupying the centre ground of Madok's thoughts. Her face seemed to be floating only inches in front of his. Her large, dark, laughing eyes. Her broad, sensuous mouth.

She was with Kedin.

The same thoughts marched round and round in his head. He shook his head. He had to pull himself together.

I'm not fit to be a soldier, Madok told himself. Still less an officer. I'm moping over a girl. I'm jealous of Kedin Ashar, a nobler man than I'll ever be, the lord to whom I've pledged my service. I'm ungrateful and disloyal. No one could have worked harder than Kedin, and still he strives and struggles, despite the terrible threat hanging over him.

I can't even help him to comprehend this station.

Madok could have wept with frustration and self-loathing. He closed his eyes and slammed his fist into the nearest bank of controls.

When he looked up one of the large, flat, blank areas was alive with lights. Madok thought it must be a picture, although he had no idea what was represented by the convoluted lines.

And I don't know how I created it, either, he said to himself.

He heard one of the doors slide open. He composed his face before he swivelled his chair, but he couldn't keep a note of surprise out of his voice.

'Kedin! Are you all right?'

Kedin Ashar was leaning against the door. He was holding his tunic slung over his shoulder, and his face was drawn.

'The things we have to do, Madok.' He covered his eyes with his hand. 'I stayed with her as long as I could. It was as though Tevana was in the room with us. I said I had duties to attend to. I hope I wasn't too abrupt.'

There was only one thing that Madok wanted to know. 'But Kedin, did you –?' he began, and then realised that he couldn't possibly ask the question. 'I'm sure you acted with your usual courtesy and charm,' he said.

Kedin grinned. 'Oh yes,' he said. 'I think our pretty visitor is satisfied with our hospitality. I'm no savage, Madok. I made her welcome.'

Madok's felt his heart sink into his stomach. Somehow he managed to smile. 'And did your pillow talk with Ace include any information that we can put to practical use?'

Kedin's eyes lit up. 'You wouldn't believe the science that's locked away behind the walls of this space station, Madok. It makes everything we've done up to now seem like – I don't know – crude building blocks piled up by children.'

As usual Madok found himself refusing to be swept along by his lord's enthusiasm. 'We can fly the ships we found here,' he pointed out. 'They are propelled by rockets much like the engines you and Tevana designed on the planet. The people who built this station were not so very far ahead of us.'

'You know that's not so,' Kedin said. 'You remember those old data cores we used to study? All those technical terms that were meaningless to us? Madok, there are whole universes of physics that we haven't dreamt of. There are particles, smaller than atoms, that obey different physical laws.' He strode to the banks of controls and stretched out his arms. 'And these lights and numbers and dials are speaking to us, Madok, if we could but understand them. They are the speech of the minds that control the station. Yes, Madok, my sceptical old friend: artificial minds, made of wires and as complex as a human brain.'

'The voices,' Madok said. 'The warning voices that the men say they hear. That I heard in the escape pod.'

'Ace says that the station will speak to us. And that we can speak to it. It will understand our instructions. She thinks she can communicate with it and make it obey my commands.'

This was too much for Madok to find credible. 'Can you be sure of this, Kedin? After all, we know nothing of Ace. How can she know the workings of devices that have defeated me, and you, and our best technicians?'

'I believe her,' Kedin said. 'Although I confess that I have been unable to discover any more about her origins, or her reasons for being here. But she is, ah, enamoured of me, Madok. I'm sure you've noticed it. She'll help us.' He stooped in front of Madok's chair and lowered his voice, as if there were a danger of being overheard. 'She knows about weapons, my friend. She says there must be weapons stored on the station. Weapons that make our guns and bombs look like toys.'

'That would certainly be useful,' Madok said. He always preferred to go into battle with every possible advantage. 'It's one thing to scare the wits out of those poor farmers on the other planet; quite another to invade our home world and overthrow its ruler.'

'Indeed.' Kedin's face once again showed the strain he was under. 'But we must do it, and soon. It's the only way to stop this vile trade and to rescue Tevana. And Ace will help us.'

Madok put his hand on his lord's shoulder. 'Then we had better be sure that she has no opportunity to find out what we're doing here,' he said.

The mule was grazing on the hillside, not far from the ferny hollow in which the Doctor and Bep-Wor were lying on their stomachs. They had crept and slithered down the slope, and were now close enough to the invaders to be able to see clearly what they were doing.

It came as no surprise to Bep-Wor that the prisoners were being herded into the cavernous belly of the domed machine. The Doctor, however, seemed outraged.

'That's a cargo pod,' he spluttered. 'It's not meant for passengers. Perhaps,' he added pensively, 'they're just using it as a prison. A holding pen. A refuge, even.'

'I don't know, Doctor,' Bep-Wor said. 'The invaders just take us away. All of us, except the very old and infirm.'

'But where, Bep-Wor? Where are the prisoners taken?'

Bep-Wor didn't know. And the rumours he'd heard were not believable. 'I spoke to an old woman a few days ago,' he said. 'One who was rejected and turned away. I don't know if her words can be relied on. She was confused and frightened.'

'That's not surprising,' the Doctor said. 'What did she say?'

'She heard two of the soldiers speaking. They speak our language, apparently, but strangely. She thought she could understand them. They were joking about taking prisoners away in the big machines – like that one, the one you call a cargo pod. And she said they spoke of taking the prisoners up into the sky.'

'But did she find out the destination, Bep-Wor? Where are the cargo pods taking your people?'

Bep-Wor hesitated. It seemed such a stupid thing to suggest. He extended his arm. 'You see that point of light, just above the horizon? Far away in the skies. It glints like a jewel. A daytime star.'

The Doctor simply accepted the notion. In fact, it seemed to confirm his worst fears. 'The space station,' he said. 'And that's where I left Ace. I shudder to think what danger I've placed her in.'

The Doctor turned on to his back and stared up into the skies. 'Bep-Wor,' he said, 'I am an incompetent, bungling Time Lord. So far I have done nothing right. I must try to make amends. And I must rescue Ace.'

He sat up, placed his hat on his head, and scanned the hillside for the mule. He put two fingers into his mouth and emitted a piercing whistle. The mule's ears twitched, and it began to pick its way toward the hollow.

'Doctor,' Bep-Wor hissed urgently. 'The invaders will hear you. Keep down, out of sight.'

'No, no,' the Doctor said. He stood up, and waited for the mule to reach him. 'I'm going to turn myself in. If I hurry, I'll be able to join that batch of prisoners and get a ride to the space station.'

He hoisted himself on to the mule's back and nudged the animal's flanks with his knees. Bep-Wor watched him as he began an ungainly descent into the valley. He looked absurd. He shifted from side to side with each step that the mule took. He kept one hand on his head, to stop his hat blowing off. He was small and defenceless, and he was heading towards certain imprisonment. The invaders had no mercy.

As the Doctor rode away, Bep-Wor's sense of purpose evaporated. His home and his village were in ruins. Kia-Ga had been taken. He had nothing to live for. But perhaps, if he could reach the little jewel in the sky, he would be able to find Kia-Ga. It was a tiny, futile hope, but it was the only hope he had.

'Doctor,' he called out. 'Wait. I'm coming with you.'

Ace was feeling very, very pleased with herself. She suspected that if she looked in a mirror she would find her face wearing a stupid, smug smile.

She hugged herself. I've definitely been too long in the TARDIS, she thought. Too long with that grumpy old

Gallifreyan. I'd forgotten how much fun you can have with an ordinary human male.

Suddenly restless, she began to wander through the suite of rooms. Already she was missing Kedin: she found herself wondering when he'd return.

She pulled aside a brocade curtain, stepped through the doorway which it had been covering, and was in a small room whose walls consisted of blank monitor screens. There was just room to walk between the well-padded seat and the control panels that surrounded it.

Now that's more like it, Ace said to herself. This must be an auxiliary control room. Not surprising, really. Kedin would have the best quarters on the station, and I suppose the guy who was in charge of the place when it was being run by TAM would have had these rooms.

She settled herself in the chair and began studying the banks of switches. There was a drawer below the console in front of her. She pulled it out and found a QWERTY keyboard and a mouse.

Blimey, she thought, that's primitive. Emergency use only, I should think, in case the interactive systems fail. She touched the dusty plastic, and was assailed by a wave of nostalgia for Earth.

She shook herself, and experimentally pressed a few keys. The monitor in front of her crackled and hummed, and displayed the same holding screen as she had been able to call up on the comms console in her cabin.

Now then, she thought, let's kick some life into these communications. I must be able to get into the system from here.

It was disappointingly simple. Ace had only to press a red button, conveniently labelled Reset, for the station's soothing female voice to ask her, 'Do you wish to reset the control configuration?'

71

It took a little longer for Ace to persuade the computer that she was the acting director of the space station, but once she'd pointed out that several hundred years had passed since the death of the previous director, the computer realised the futility of requiring the previous director's authorization of Ace's appointment as his successor. After several minutes of conversation, the computer reluctantly agreed to recognise Ace's voice pattern as a sufficient password to gain access to all security levels.

Ace grinned and punched the air in triumph. Wait till Kedin sees this, she thought. This'll knock his socks off. Now: what shall I get on-line first? I know: let's get those cameras working.

'Check the visual monitors,' Ace told the computer. 'Internal and external. Report any faults.'

She sat back in the chair as the station began to test all of its cameras. On the screen in front of her a succession of images blinked on and off, almost faster than she could watch them. An empty corridor; a corridor with two soldiers in it; a view of the dining hall; a small room containing a stack of boxes.

And then something that made Ace sit bolt upright. For a moment she was too shocked to think.

'Stop,' she said. 'Go back to the previous camera. That's not it. Back again.'

Ace stared at the screen, which was showing her a view of a large, poorly lit space. The floor was entirely taken up with lumpy, cloth-covered shapes, some of which occasionally shifted. One stood up, stretched its arms, and subsided again. Each shape was a person.

'What part of the station is that?' Ace asked.

'The current view is of cargo hold twelve,' the station replied.

'Zoom in,' Ace said. 'And give me sound, too.'

They were human. Men and women, crowded together in the darkness of the hold so that each had barely enough room to lie down. As far as Ace could make out in the dim light, they were wearing ragged clothing and looked as though they hadn't washed for days. The men were unshaven.

Most were lying or sitting still; a few were rocking from side to side. When the sound came on Ace heard no raised voices: just a susurration of breathing and snoring, some muttering, and occasional sobs and moans.

'Close down,' Ace said. The screen went blank.

Ace sat very still and tried to work exactly how many things she was angry about.

One: there were people on the station who were being held prisoner in terrible conditions.

Two: Kedin and Madok had lied to her, or at least had failed to be completely honest.

Three: perhaps they'd been trying all along just to use her.

Perhaps he doesn't even like me, Ace thought.

She shivered. She felt suddenly cold, as if her guts had turned to ice.

She couldn't think about Kedin. Not yet. What should she do? That was the important question.

Play it cool, she advised herself. I know more about them now than they know about me. And I'm in control of the station. Keep a low profile, play along, find out more about what's going on. That's what I should do.

Sod that, she decided, and stood up. The heat of her anger dried the tears in her eyes. That long streak of aristocratic effluent has some explaining to do, she said to herself. Where's my baseball bat?

For the fifth time in as many days, Kedin was poring over maps of Gonfallon. Every flat surface in the station's control room was covered with unrolled charts and lists of military units.

This, Madok realised, was the closest activity to relaxation that Kedin allowed himself. When the burden of conscience and anxiety became insupportable, Kedin resorted to planning, yet again, the campaign to dethrone Vethran.

Kedin looked up. 'What was that?'

Madok had heard it too: a stifled cry, followed by a thump, outside the door. He drew his sword and leapt towards the doorway. He could hear nothing now. He caught Kedin's eye, put his finger to his lips, and slipped behind the tapestry that hung next to the door.

The door slid open. Ace strode in. She was holding the long, smooth club with which she had been armed when he had first seen her. She was smiling, but Madok perceived the belligerence in her stance.

She didn't notice Madok. She was interested only in Kedin, who sprawled comfortably in his chair.

'Kedin,' she said conversationally, 'you're a lying toerag. I think it's time you told me the truth about what's going on.'

Kedin sighed. 'Oh dear,' he said. 'There are things that I didn't want to have to tell you. What would you like to know?'

Ace kept her distance from him. 'Everything,' she said. 'But, for starters, who are the prisoners in cargo hold twelve? And why are they there?'

Kedin spread his hands to indicate the maps all around him. 'My entire planet has fallen under the control of one man. He used to be my friend. I regret to say that I helped him. I'm still helping him. But the more territory he acquired, the greedier he grew. And less stable. Now I'm planning to oppose him. That's what I'm doing here.'

'Yeah, sure,' Ace said. 'Very noble. But what about the people in the hold? What are you doing with them?'

Kedin drew his hand across his face. 'I'm buying time, Ace. I'm buying Vethran's confidence. And I'm buying weaponry.'

Without seeing Ace's face Madok could tell that she wasn't impressed with Kedin's explanation. 'So you're still doing this guy Vethran's dirty work, whatever it is, and you're hiding out up here, off the planet, making lots of plans to save your planet. One day, when you can be bothered.'

He can't tell her, Madok realised. She thinks he's a coward, but he can't explain why he has to be so careful. After the love they have so recently shared, how can he tell her about Tevana Roslod?

Kedin uttered a short, bitter laugh. 'Not much of a freedom fighter, am I, Ace?' he said. 'I imagine that you'd adopt a more direct approach. Quite right, too.'

Ace hefted her long club. Kedin made no move to draw his sword. 'Don't try to get round me, Kedin,' she said. Her voice was unsteady. 'What about those people in the hold?'

Kedin took a deep breath. 'Vethran has an inexhaustible appetite not just for power, but also for land. Once he had made himself king of our world, he began to turn against his own subjects. I thought to divert him by directing his attention to worlds beyond our own. I built a rocket which, more by luck than engineering, enabled me to reach this space station. Here there were other, better ships. Craft with which we could take a small army to our sister planet.'

'You helped him invade Mendeb Two?' Ace's voice shook with disgust.

'I had no choice,' Kedin said quietly, but Ace was speaking again, quietly, to herself.

'Oh my god,' she said. Madok could make no sense of her next words. 'The Doctor's landed in a war zone.'

Kedin shook his head. 'There's no war,' he said. 'The people there don't even try to defend themselves. They run away, and

75

we collect them. We bring them here, and we ship them to our own planet. Vethran has the monopoly in the trade, of course. His agents pay me ten marks for each person I land. They're slaves, Ace.'

'Oh, right,' Ace said. To Madok's ears she sounded strangely calm. 'I get it. You're funding your war of liberation with the money you make from being a slave trader. That's good business sense, I suppose.'

'I don't like it, Ace,' Kedin said. His eyes were bright with hope. Perhaps, Madok thought, he really believes he can make her understand. 'As I said, at the moment I have no choice.'

'And I expect you'd like me to tell you how to operate the weapons on the station? Because, of course, I'm so grateful that you've lowered yourself to take an interest in me.'

Madok stepped cautiously from behind the tapestry. Something in the tone of Ace's voice worried him. He couldn't stand her to be upset. He thought she might be about to swoon or to burst into tears.

'Yes,' Kedin said. He was smiling now. He clearly thought that Ace could be won round. 'Yes, I'd like you to help us, Ace.'

'I'll bet you would,' Ace said. 'And do you know what? There's not a chance, mate. As far as I can see you're a nasty piece of work, and I'm going to put a stop to your filthy slave business. Starting now.'

She brought her club down on the map-strewn console in front of Kedin, and then lifted it so that the rounded end was pressed against his chest.

'Now then,' she began.

Forgive me, Ace, Madok prayed, and brought the hilt of his sword down on the back of her head.

She said, 'Ow,' half turned, and then fell to the floor.

'Thank you, Madok,' Kedin said.

The two men looked down at Ace's prone body. Madok

realised for the first time that she was younger than her confident manner had suggested.

She's not much more than a girl, Madok thought; she looks about as dangerous as a puppy.

Kedin's feelings were clearly similar. 'Madok, I hate this,' he said, his voice choked with emotion. He barked an abrupt laugh. 'Add this to the list of crimes that Vethran will be made to pay for.'

'What are you going to do with her?' Madok said. He knew that Kedin could be ruthless when he deemed it necessary.

But Kedin was unusually indecisive. 'I have no idea, old friend. I've already treated this poor girl more cruelly than she deserves. And now that she hates me and has pledged herself to oppose my plans, I fear that instead of making amends I'll have to aggravate the wrongs I've already done to her.'

'We could lock her away,' Madok suggested. 'In her cabin.'

He knew that it was an insufficient solution.

'She'll escape, Madok.' Kedin ran his hands through his hair in exasperation. 'You know she has the determination and the ability. I can't keep her here. She has the knowledge to turn the station against us.'

'Don't kill her, my lord. I beg you.'

'Do you have an alternative suggestion, Madok?'

Madok grimaced. 'Yes, Kedin. I have. The consignment in hold twelve will soon be ready for despatch. Let's process Ace and send her down to the planet.'

Kedin was aghast. 'Madok!'

'At least she'll be alive.' A sudden idea bloomed in his mind. He was so excited he could hardly speak. 'Kedin! Didn't you tell me –? Neroda – the new formula!'

Kedin nodded, and a wide smile spread slowly across his face. 'Yes, of course. Neroda has synthesised a substitute for SS10. It mimics the effects exactly. But the tests aren't finished.

She doesn't know how long it lasts. That's why we haven't started using it.'

'What would one dose matter, Kedin? Vethran won't get to hear about one slave acting strangely. At least it's better than giving her SS10.'

'It's ironic,' Kedin said. 'Neroda and her team have worked like slaves themselves to create and test the new formula. And now we'll have virtually no time to use it.'

Madok stared at Kedin. 'My lord?'

'It's almost time, Madok. I won't skulk up here in this tin box any longer. Ace was right.'

They looked down in silence at the girl.

'Goodbye, Ace,' Kedin said at last. 'I hope one day you'll think better of me. But I suppose that's not likely. Not after what's going to happen to you.'

Chapter Three

While the Doctor argued with the soldiers, Bep-Wor stayed silent at his side. The Doctor seemed to be digging himself ever more deeply into trouble, but there was nothing Bep-Wor could do to help.

He kept his head lowered at first, and saw little apart from the soldiers' boots. Under the dust and dried mud they still shone like polished jet. He could see the muzzles of the soldiers' long guns.

When it became clear that the Doctor wasn't going to stop talking or be shot dead, which were the only two alternatives the soldiers had offered him, Bep-Wor dared to lift his eyes. No one was paying any attention to him.

This was the first time he had been close to the invaders: close enough to talk to them, or to strike them with his fists. He wanted to do both. He wanted to know why they had come; he wanted to express his anger and despair. He stood silently and watched.

They were just men, after all. Their uniforms were dashing and gilded when seen from a distance; Bep-Wor saw now that their trousers were splashed with mud, tunics had lost buttons and were stained with sweat, caps were torn. The men had sunken eyes and stubbly jaws.

Behind and between the raised voices of the Doctor and the officer with whom he was arguing, Bep-Wor heard the listless conversation and grim jokes that the soldiers exchanged. There was an altercation at the head of the line of prisoners.

'Oi, kid. How old are you?'

The boy, clutching a blanket around himself despite the heat, looked to Bep-Wor's eyes to be no more than ten.

'Fourteen,' the boy muttered. He didn't look up at the soldier.

'Yeah, and I'm the king of the ice apes. Get out of line. Clear off. We don't want you.'

The boy looked angry rather than relieved. 'You've taken my mum and my dad,' he said. 'I want to go too.'

The soldier turned away, cursed and spat. 'You don't, kid,' he said. His voice was urgent and, Bep-Wor realised, almost breaking with emotion. 'You really don't want to come. Look, I'm giving you a chance. Take it, for heavens' sake. Go. Get out of the line. Before an officer sees what's going on. That's it. Run. If anyone stops you, say you're only nine. Run!'

The soldier thrust out his gun, and at that the boy raced away. The soldier stood cursing and shaking his head. 'I hate this job,' he yelled at the line of captives. 'And I hate you lot. Keep moving along. Come on, don't hang about.'

The Doctor was having the same problem as the boy. The officer was becoming irate.

'I keep telling you, you irritating little man, that we won't take you. You're too old and frail. We're going to take your friend here,' the officer said, indicating Bep-Wor with a casual wave. 'He looks fit and sturdy. But you're staying here.'

'You must take me,' the Doctor said. He struggled in the grip of the two soldiers who were restraining him. He suddenly went limp, and exhaled a great sigh of exasperation. 'Appearances can be deceptive, lieutenant. Allow me to demonstrate.'

The Doctor suddenly jerked and wriggled and, moving faster that Bep-Wor's eyes could follow, he was suddenly free – and holding the long, metal gun that had been slung across the back of one of the soldiers.

All around Bep-Wor and the Doctor, soldiers shouted in surprise and swung their own guns to point at the Doctor. The Doctor looked annoyed rather than fearful. He turned slowly in a circle, like a conjuror about to perform a trick, making a show of the fact that he was holding the gun by its barrel. The surrounding soldiers relaxed slightly. Then the Doctor's hands moved very quickly, in a complex pattern. He held up the gun, as if expecting applause. Its barrel now had two right-angled bends.

There was a stunned silence. The line of prisoners had stopped moving forwards; the guards and their captives were staring at the Doctor.

Only the officer seemed unimpressed. 'Very clever,' he said. 'All right. There's obviously something unusual about you. And there's always a demand for novelties. Get in the line.'

The soldiers behind the Doctor pushed him forward. Bep-Wor extended his arm to stop the Doctor falling. He glared at the soldiers, daring them to touch the Doctor again.

The officer had turned on his booted heel and had begun to stride away. 'Just a minute, lieutenant,' the Doctor said. 'I haven't finished with you yet.'

A murmur ran along the line of prisoners. Even some of the guards were grinning broadly.

The officer stopped. Very slowly he turned again. His face was set in an expression of barely restrained rage, but Bep-Wor noticed that his body was not at all tense. Perhaps, he thought, even the officer finds it diverting to bandy words with the Doctor. He's pretending to be angry because he knows it's part of the role he's expected to play.

'What?' the officer demanded. 'Do you have more tricks with which to entertain us?'

'Of course not,' the Doctor spluttered. 'This is a serious matter. Are you intending to transport these people in that vessel?' The Doctor pointed at the line of prisoners and then at the metal container with the vast curved roof.

The officer nodded, as if dealing with a simpleton.

'It's a cargo pod,' the Doctor shouted. 'It's not meant for ferrying people. It's unheated and, most importantly, it isn't pressurised. You'll kill everyone.' Another murmur, this time of fear, rose from the line of prisoners.

The officer scowled irritatedly. 'Keep them quiet!' he called to the guards. He looked at the Doctor as if seeing him for the first time. 'You're beginning to interest me,' he said. 'I've not heard a single one of these Twos refer to our ships by their correct designations. Still less know anything about the need for pressurization. I don't believe you're a native. You're not from Mendeb Two.'

'You're quite right,' the Doctor said. 'I'm from Gallifrey. But that's neither here nor there at the moment. I assume you're taking us to the space station? Then we'll need air.'

The officer beckoned to the Doctor and then set off towards the front of the line, where the prisoners were trudging, single file, into the cavernous interior of the metal container. The Doctor hurried to follow him, and Bep-Wor trailed after the Doctor. Two soldiers marched behind Bep-Wor.

'I suppose I should be surprised that you know about the space station,' the lieutenant said, as if chatting with a fellow officer. 'But it seems you know about everything. This is how you'll be transported.'

He stood at one side of the gaping doorway and gestured into the interior. He kept his other hand fastidiously across his nose.

There was indeed a stench. As Bep-Wor peered over the Doctor's shoulder into the container he almost choked as a particularly strong odour wafted past him. The smell was that of human beings: sweat and excrement.

It was coming from the hundreds of bodies already packed inside what the Doctor called the cargo pod. People were sitting and lying on the floor, their attempts to preserve their own personal spaces continually being undermined by the inexorable arrival of more prisoners.

'It's a short trip to the station,' the officer said. 'We don't like using these ships, but the more civilised transports are needed for the other half of the journey. We do the best we can. By crowding in as many of these Twos as possible, we keep the temperature up. As for air: we release oxygen into the pod at intervals. We're not barbarians.'

The Doctor's face was taut with anger. 'How many deaths?' he said through gritted teeth.

The officer took a deep breath, and then coughed and swore. 'Mostly they survive. We don't attempt the trip until the planet and the station are at their closest alignment. It's the best we can do.'

'Oh, well done, lieutenant,' the Doctor said with heavy sarcasm. 'You're a credit to your nation. I hope you're very proud of yourself.'

The officer seemed suddenly very tired. 'Just get in,' he said. The soldiers pushed Bep-Wor and the Doctor through the doorway, into the stinking darkness. 'And don't waste your breath complaining.'

The pilot's tuneless whistling echoed along the corridor. He turned the corner, saw Madok, and stopped at attention. 'Sir!'

'Easy, Parek,' Madok said. 'This isn't a formal inspection.' They were standing outside the door to one of the docking bays. 'All ready to go?'

'Yes, sir,' the pilot said. 'Another full load.'

There was a moment of uncomfortable silence as Madok and the pilot considered the implications of those three innocuous words.

'Take care, Parek,' Madok said. 'The girl's in this shipment. She's been given the new formula. Tell the guards to keep an eye on her. If she behaves in any way differently from the rest, don't offload her. Bring her back. Understood?'

'Of course, sir. May I ask – the new formula?'

Madok sighed. 'It's been slow progress. We don't have the facilities here. Or Tevana and her chemists. But we think we've succeeded. Keep it quiet for now.'

'That's good news, sir,' the pilot said. His restrained words were belied by the huge grin that appeared on his face.

Madok couldn't help his own expression reflecting the pilot's relief. 'So keep the ship well pressurised,' he said. 'There's one young girl in this consignment who might not be better off dead. Who might be able to thank us one day.'

'Or who might turn round and blame us, of course,' the pilot said.

Madok grunted in agreement. 'And she'd have every right to. Parek, will you do one more thing for me?'

'What is it, sir?'

'When you've offloaded, try to stay long enough to find out which agent gets the girl. You've seen her, while she's been on the station? You'll recognise her?'

'She's not one you'd forget in a hurry, is she, sir? I'll find out for you.'

'Thank you, Parek. Both Kedin Ashar and I will be very grateful. We're concerned for her. But don't endanger the ship: we know Vethran wants to get his hands on one of these vessels. I doubt if he'd risk jeopardising our trade with him, but be careful. If any of his troops get too close, take off immediately. You know the drill.'

'Yes, sir.'

The door next to them started to slide open.

'Parek!' a voice bawled through the widening gap. 'Where the hell are you?'

A soldier appeared in the doorway. He took a deep breath, in readiness for an even louder shout, and then saw Madok and the pilot.

'Sorry, sir,' he said to Madok. 'Sir, I must ask you to excuse Parek. The transport's ready to go, and we need the bay for an incoming cargo pod. We can't keep them waiting.'

'I know,' Madok said. He pictured the wretched mass of Twos fighting for breath in the freezing pod. 'Go, Parek. My best wishes go with you.'

And my heart's desire, he thought. Ace, will you ever forgive us?

Nothing could be more comfortable than to lie in bed with Kia-Ga. Her body was soft and warm. The bedclothes were soft and warm. Everything was soft and warm.

A distant voice was telling him to wake up. But it wasn't morning: there was no light. In the long nights of winter it was better to stay in bed. Soft and warm.

'Wake up, Bep-Wor! Wake up.'

Someone was rocking the bed. Was he at sea, sleeping in a hammock? No. Kia-Ga – where was she? Gone. He couldn't feel his limbs. The smell. The terrible smell. His head hurt. His body ached.

Stop shaking me. Leave me alone. Leave me in the soft and warm.

'That's it, Bep-Wor. Think. Feel. Breathe.'

The same voice, louder now: 'All of you. Don't let anyone fall asleep. Try to keep moving. Everyone must stay awake.'

The Doctor. That was the voice. Funny little man. Why was he shouting?

Then Bep-Wor remembered everything, in a sickening slide of recollections. He flailed his arms and tried to sit up. He wanted to scream.

'Bep-Wor,' the Doctor said. Bep-Wor felt a warm hand on his chest. 'Try to keep still. The air's very thin.'

Then the Doctor raised his voice again. It echoed eerily in the vast dark space. 'Everyone must try to hold on. Don't let go. Feel the cold. Feel the pain in your lungs. Hang on to those feelings. Just a few more minutes. We've arrived. We just have to hold on for a few more minutes, until the doors are open.'

A feeble chorus of muted moans and cries answered the Doctor's exhortations. Bep-Wor sat with his head in his hands, trying to control the shivering of his limbs.

There was a resounding, metallic bang. The floor shook. Suddenly there was light, and a rushing wind. Bep-Wor took gasping breaths of the warm air. All around him men and women were choking, gulping, retching and crying out as they filled their lungs.

The wide doors were sliding open, and soldiers stood silhouetted against the yellow light.

'Everybody out,' yelled a voice. 'Come on, get moving.'

'Where are we?' Bep-Wor asked the Doctor.

The Doctor helped Bep-Wor to his feet. 'We're on the space station,' the Doctor said. Under his breath he added, 'I just hope I can find Ace quickly.'

Bep-Wor and the Doctor joined the stampede towards the doors. As the ragged crowd pressed round them and carried them along, the Doctor did his best to help those who were still dazed, sitting or lying on the floor, in danger of being trampled in the confusion. Bep-Wor followed the Doctor's example.

'Slow down,' the Doctor called out. His words echoed. Bep-Wor wondered how such a little man could have such a powerful, commanding voice. Bep-Wor's throat was raw and he could still hardly draw enough breath to speak. 'Go carefully,' the Doctor shouted. 'Stop and help those who can't walk. We must all help each other.'

The shuffling throng emerged through the doors, between

two lines of grim-faced guards with guns, and into a square hall even larger than the hold of the cargo pod. The Doctor, holding Bep-Wor by the arm, fought his way to the edge of the crowd. 'We have to stay near the pod,' he said, but offered no explanation.

Bep-Wor and the Doctor were standing just beyond the guards. Bep-Wor's eyes were drawn upwards: the ceiling was so high that he could hardly discern it, and the cargo pod which had seemed so unnaturally large when squatting amid the fields was now dwarfed by the chamber it was resting in. He could see, behind the pod, a pair of metal doors each the height and width of a cliff. The prisoners dispersed across the floor of the chamber: they were no bigger than insects milling about in the village square.

'Who built this?' Bep-Wor whispered.

The Doctor was trying to look over the shoulders of the soldiers, but he turned briefly to answer the question. 'The TAM corporation,' he said. 'But I expect your ancestors did a lot of the manual work.'

The stream of prisoners pouring through the pod's doors became a trickle. Those worst affected by the cold and the thin air emerged staggering, or crawling, or supported by others.

Some of the soldiers wrapped cloths around their faces and went into the pod.

Across the expanse of the great chamber the prisoners were becoming more animated. Some wandered, still dazed and exhausted; others paced urgently from group to group, searching for friends or members of their families. Bep-Wor was torn between staying with the Doctor and entering the throng. There was a chance that he might find Kia-Ga. But, he had to admit to himself, he could see no one from his village. He recognised many people from Porgum, and some from other, more northern, towns and villages. As the volume of the babel of voices increased, Bep-Wor's heart sank. He remained at the Doctor's side. The flame of hope that he nurtured was flickering and dying.

The soldiers who had gone into the pod began to return from inside. As they strode out they tore the cloths from their faces and took deep breaths of the clean air. For some reason they were smiling broadly.

'That's the best yet,' one of them shouted towards the line of guards standing in front of the Doctor. 'Only lost one.'

The last two of the soldiers emerged from the pod. Between them they were carrying the lifeless body of a young man.

Bep-Wor recognised the figure. 'That's Hap-Lor,' he told the Doctor. 'He's a boat-builder from Kragen. Is he dead?'

The Doctor tapped on the shoulder of one of the guards. The soldier turned. The Doctor doffed his hat.

'Let me through,' the Doctor said. 'I'm a doctor.'

The soldier shrugged, and the Doctor pushed past him. The soldiers carrying Hap-Lor lowered him to the floor as the Doctor and Bep-Wor approached.

Hap-Lor's face was pale. His eyes were closed and his lips were blue. His chest wasn't moving. Bep-Wor could tell that he was dead. He wondered whether Hap-Lor's wife, Noa-La, was in the crowd. And where were their children?

'Your cape,' the Doctor said. 'Bep-Wor, give me your cape.'

Without thinking Bep-Wor unlaced his cape and gave it to the Doctor. It didn't matter. Nothing mattered any more.

'More!' the Doctor shouted. 'Bring me more clothes. I have to get him warm.'

'He's dead, Doctor,' Bep-Wor murmured. He noticed that all the prisoners had started to converge on the entrance to the pod. A dense circle of inquisitive faces surrounded the patch of floor where the Doctor was kneeling beside Hap-Lor's body. The soldiers struggled to hold back the crowd. Some of the prisoners tore off their grimy clothes and threw them over the heads of the soldiers, towards the Doctor. Bep-Wor collected the garments and helped the Doctor to pack them around Hap-Lor's cold corpse.

'He's not dead yet,' the Doctor said. 'Not until I say so. There must be something I can do right.'

The Doctor put his ear to Hap-Lor's chest. He massaged Hap-Lor's torso and throat. Then he tipped back Hap-Lor's head, opened the blue lips, and kissed the dead man.

It was a long, intense kiss. The Doctor pulled his head away, took a deep breath, and kissed Hap-Lor again. Bep-Wor realised that the Doctor was blowing his own breath into Hap-Lor, as if he believed the vital exhalation of a living man could restore life to the dead.

The crowd was silent now, but for the constant murmured questions of those too far back to see. The soldiers, too, had all turned to face the centre of the circle.

The Doctor lifted his head again, and brought his fist down hard on Hap-Lor's ribs. Again. And again. Another long kiss. Another pounding on the chest.

Once again the Doctor listened for a heartbeat. Bep-Wor thought that he detected the ghost of a smile on the Doctor's lips. 'Bep-Wor,' the Doctor said, 'help me.'

Bep-Wor knelt beside Hap-Lor, facing the Doctor.

'Lift him up a little,' the Doctor said, and when Bep-Wor had hauled the dead weight of Hap-Lor's torso into a sitting position, he noticed the flask in the Doctor's hand, concealed under his jacket.

'Come closer,' the Doctor whispered, and as Bep-Wor leant forwards the Doctor did likewise, so that no one could see him bring the neck of the flask to Hap-Lor's lips. Thick liquid trickled into Hap-Lor's slack mouth.

'Hold him steady,' the Doctor said, and stood up, as he did so returning the flask discreetly to a pocket inside his jacket.

The Doctor stroked his chin as he looked down at Hap-Lor. The crowd was silent. The guards stared intently.

Bep-Wor was the first to know that Hap-Lor had come back to life. He felt the man's body shake, as if with an ague. Bep-Wor let out a cry, and almost allowed Hap-Lor to drop from his hands.

Hap-Lor's eyes blinked open, and shut again. He coughed, and then drew a raucous, rattling breath. His lips were no longer blue.

And then a wave of shouting swept through the crowd, and Bep-Wor cowered on the floor as the noise grew and overwhelmed him. He held Hap-Lor in a warm embrace, and felt the man's fitful movements and increasingly confident breathing.

The soldiers waved their guns and drew their swords, and gradually the shouting died away. There was still a buzz of conversation, however. Bep-Wor could hear one question, repeated over and over again by hundred of different voices: 'Who is he?'

Bep-Wor rose, and helped Hap-Lor to stand. He put his hand to his face, and realised that he was crying.

'He is the Doctor!' Bep-Wor shouted. 'Trust him. He can save us all.'

Tragar knew that he would be summoned. He was waiting for the call.

He had returned to Underton by self-propelled vehicle, leaving Jellod in charge of the carts and camelopes that would bring the bulk of the purchases home to Balon Ferud's city residence. As soon as he had arrived he had conscientiously submitted his purse and his receipts to Bared, the keeper of Balon's accounts.

Then he had retired to his lodgings in the old castle. He had bathed, he had changed into the heavy, formal costume that Poa-Nan had prepared for him, he had packed a pipe with smoke-leaf and a sprinkling of dried spore-seed, and he had settled down in the window seat of his study to enjoy the view of Underton's rooftops.

He had smoked only half the pipe, and his senses were beginning to relax into a gently narcotic cloud, when he heard footsteps hurrying up the stairs. There was a knock on the door.

'Enter,' Tragar called out.

Poa-Nan stood in the doorway. In his hand was a stiff envelope bearing a large seal.

'I know,' Tragar said. 'Balon wants me.'

Poa-Nan looked troubled. 'No, sir,' he said, holding out the envelope. 'A message.'

Tragar smiled. These Twos could be so literal in their thinking. 'Yes, Poa-Nan,' he said, taking the envelope and knocking it against the man's head. 'And the message will say that Balon wants to see me.'

Poa-Nan's face resumed its usual expression of vacant bliss. 'Yes, sir,' he said.

Tragar tore open the envelope and read its contents. 'Balon is on his way here,' he said. He felt pleased with himself. His extravagance had clearly piqued his lord's curiosity. 'Come, Poa-Nan. Let's go and greet him.'

Tragar took one last pull on his pipe, sucked the sweet smoke deeply into his lungs, and sighed with regret as he laid the pipe on the windowsill. 'Help me,' he said, and went to stand in front of the long mirror while Poa-Nan brushed the shoulders of his brocade coat and adjusted the lace ruffles at his neck and wrists.

It wouldn't do to appear as expensively dressed as his lordship. Tragar wondered whether he should quickly change into one of his plain, black silk coats. No time for that. And in any case these days Balon's uniform was so festooned with medals that the King himself looked hardly less gilded.

'Follow me,' he said, and strode from the room.

As Tragar entered the reception hall of the east wing, Balon Ferud and two uniformed attendants were being ushered through the doors that opened on to the courtyard. Balon's medals and ornate sword-belt jingled as he marched across the flagstones. He could move surprisingly quickly, Tragar knew, considering he was a head shorter than Tragar, was running to fat, and was carrying enough gold and silver on his clothing to buy a dozen Twos.

'Three hundred and fifty marks,' Balon shouted at Tragar as soon as he saw him. 'Three hundred and fifty marks, Chamberlain Tragar. Have you lost your senses?'

Tragar stopped in front of Balon and bowed. 'Good day, my lord,' he said. 'I'm honoured to receive you. How can I be of service?'

Balon Ferud's face was red with indignation. 'You can be of service, Tragar, by not wasting my money. Do you have any explanation for this expense?'

Tragar put on an expression of mortified hurt. 'Your lordship's finances are my prime concern,' he said. 'I take a modest pride in the economy with which I run your lordship's household. I venture to suggest that I take no less care than Bared himself.'

'Then what's your explanation for this, Chamberlain?' Balon pressed a chubby finger into Tragar's chest. 'Three hundred and fifty marks for a poxy Two? You could have bought seven or eight of the smelly beggars for that amount. Prices are coming down, if anything.'

Tragar glanced at Poa-Nan. The slave was, of course, unaffected by Balon's insulting words and was smiling vacantly. Tragar wondered whether he would ever get used to owning Twos.

'There was considerable competition for this particular Two,' Tragar said. 'If you'll allow me to demonstrate her to you, I believe you'll see why. I am sure that she will prove a sound investment. If your lordship would follow me?'

'This had better be worthwhile,' Balon grumbled as he followed Tragar towards the door to an anteroom of the reception hall.

Tragar had left to his domestic staff the tasks of making the new slave presentable and of coaching her in the basic rules of behaviour. As he ushered Balon into the anteroom he saw that his domestics had done a good job: the slave was wearing her own unusual clothes, washed and pressed, and was standing quietly with a distant smile on her lips.

Tragar noted that he had no reluctance to think of this one as a slave. The Twos were bought and sold, but people didn't usually refer to them as slaves: perhaps, Tragar thought, there was beneath all the imperial pride a sense of unease at exploiting prisoners of war. But there was something different about this one: she wasn't like a Two. She was unique. It pleased Tragar to think of her as a slave. As his slave, even though she was Balon's property.

'Great heavens, Tragar,' Balon cried, 'what have you dressed her in? She's positively indecent.'

'These are her own clothes, my lord,' Tragar said. 'I confess I was confounded myself, at first. That she wears trousers is shocking enough, and they are a disgracefully tight fit. And the bare arms! But consider, my lord, that it's said the womenfolk of our forefathers used to dress like the men. And she is decently covered, after all.'

Balon grunted and paced around the slave. 'I've never seen one like this before,' he said. 'Is she from the northern islands?'

Tragar shrugged. 'She was in the latest consignment. It consisted entirely of Twos from the northern islands. I don't believe our armies have yet started to conquer the south. But ask her yourself, my lord.'

Balon looked suspiciously at his chamberlain, as if he suspected a trick. And Tragar could hardly conceal his mirth, because he knew that Balon was in for a surprise.

'Hmm,' Balon said. 'Very well. Girl, what's your name?'

'Ace, sir,' the slave replied, and favoured Balon Ferud with a dazzling grin.

'What's that? Ace? Just Ace?'

'Yes, sir. Just Ace. No other names at all.'

Balon turned and looked at Tragar. His face showed his amazement. Tragar lifted his hands and his eyebrows.

'She's got a peculiar accent,' Balon said. 'And a very strange name. Are you sure she's a Two?'

'Ask her, my lord. Ask her.'

'Well then, Ace,' Balon said cautiously. 'Where are you from, eh?'

'Perivale, sir,' Ace replied. Tragar stifled an urge to laugh. The girl was remarkable.

'And where, pray, is Perivale?' Balon persisted.

'It's a suburb of Deadsville, sir,' Ace said earnestly. 'The back end of nowhere.'

'I see,' Balon said. He and Tragar had another wordless exchange. He turned again to Ace. 'And what was your occupation, before you were brought here?'

Ace screwed up her face as she considered her answer. 'I was a time traveller, I suppose, sir. A righter of wrongs, a fighter of monsters. I used to be the assistant to this meddlesome old Professor.'

Balon was about to ask another question, but abruptly he turned on his heel and moved close to Tragar. 'Is this some sort of prank, Tragar?' he said in a low voice. 'If so I shall not be amused.'

Tragar held up his hands again. 'I assure you, my lord, everything is as it seems. I bought her yesterday, fresh from Kedin Ashar's transport ship.'

'But has she been correctly processed, Tragar? Her answers are nonsensical.'

'I saw her leaving the ship with my own eyes, my lord,' Tragar said. 'She must have been processed along with all the others. She learns. She obeys. Allow me to demonstrate.'

Tragar tried to think quickly. He hadn't expected Balon to be this sceptical. How could he demonstrate the slave's obedience? Disfigurement would damage the slave's value. And he didn't want bloodstains on his carpets.

'Poa-Nan,' he said, 'go and stand beside Ace. Keep still and don't make a noise. Ace, eat Poa-Nan's right ear.'

'Yes, sir,' the two slaves said in unison. Tragar and Belon watched as Ace grasped Poa-Nan's head, bit into the tough cartilage of his ear, and began to rend and chew with her strong, white teeth.

Poa-Nan gritted his teeth, clenched his fists, and began to gasp with pain. But he didn't cry out or try to move away. Once again Tragar marvelled at the technical skill of the King's chemists.

'Enough, Tragar,' Balon said. 'I'm convinced she's been dosed with the potion.'

Tragar breathed a sigh of relief: blood from Poa-Nan's ear was dripping on to the Two's tunic. He hated wasting money on new clothes for the servants. 'Stop, Ace,' he said. He gave her a handkerchief. 'Wipe clean your mouth.'

'Yes, sir,' Ace said. She looked very pleased with herself. 'Thank you, sir.'

Balon looked once again into her smiling face. Tragar

95

noticed that Balon and Ace were the same height. 'One more thing, Ace,' Balon said. 'What are your particular skills?'

Tragar saw that once again Ace considered her answer before replying. A thoughtful slave: that was unusual in itself.

'Shove ha'penny football, sir,' Ace said. 'I was always dead good at that. Computers, these days. Explosives – for use in demolition, as weapons, and just for the fun of it, really. And I once had a job as a waitress, sir.'

'Remarkable.' Balon was chuckling. 'Quite remarkable.' He turned to Tragar. 'Well, chamberlain, I think you might be right. She is unique. And she claims a bizarre range of talents. Young and pretty, too. I'm not convinced she's worth 350, but I'm willing to give you the benefit of the doubt for the time being. I'll leave her in your hands. Train her up, and keep me informed of your progress.'

Bep-Wor wondered whether the Doctor ever slept. There was little else to do in the dimly lit chamber into which the prisoners had been herded. There was enough room for each person to lie down, and there was air and warmth. In all other respects conditions were little better than during the journey in the cargo pod.

Bep-Wor dozed, drifting in and out of sleep.

Sometimes when he woke the Doctor was sitting beside him, conversing in whispers with one of the succession of wretched men and women who made their way through the maze of prone bodies to ask his advice. Some were ill; others were simply overwhelmed by the disasters that had befallen them – the destruction of their homes, separation from their families, fear of what was still to come. And some were simply curious about the little man with the strange clothes who had brought Hap-Lor back from the dead.

The Doctor listened patiently to each one, and did his best

to offer comfort and reassurance. Bep-Wor was amazed at the Doctor's stamina. For himself he could hardly bear to overhear the recurrent accounts of pain and loss, and he would cover his ears and try to sleep again. The Doctor simply absorbed the distress of everyone who came to him: he soaked up the anguish, and the petitioners went away with brighter eyes and a surer step.

At other times when Bep-Wor awoke the Doctor was absent. His voice could be heard from near the single door of the chamber. He would be in animated conversation with one of the guards who were posted outside. He asked for medicines, fresh dressings for wounds, water and, more and more urgently, food. His requests, except for the last item, were usually granted.

Hunger was making it more and more difficult for Bep-Wor to sleep. His stomach was hollow, and ached.

'Why won't they give us food, Doctor?' he asked when there was a brief respite from dealing with the tribulations of the prisoners.

The Doctor tipped back his hat and scratched his head. 'I don't know, Bep-Wor. But I can't believe that they've brought us all this way just to starve us to death.'

Bep-Wor hardly dared to ask, but hunger drove him to it. 'Could we not take some sustenance from your silver flask, Doctor?'

'Emergency use only,' the Doctor said. 'There must be a reason why they're refusing us food. I want to know what it is.'

'What will happen to us, Doctor?' It was the question that the Doctor had been asked a hundred times already, and Bep-Wor was reluctant to irritate the Doctor by asking it again. But he was afraid, and he wanted to know. 'What are they going to do with us?'

'I wish I knew,' the Doctor said. 'I'll tell you everything I've been able to deduce. You know, don't you, that your world travels in a circle around the sun?'

'Yes, of course.' Bep-Wor wondered how this basic truth could be relevant to their predicament. 'That's how we have the cycle of the seasons: the long winter nights, the long summer days, and the two festivals each year when the day and the night are equal.'

'Good. And what do you call your world?'

Bep-Wor thought long and hard, but could come up with no clever answer. 'It's just the world.'

In the near-darkness Bep-Wor could see the Doctor's toothy smile. 'Your ancestors were brought to your world by people who travelled between the stars.'

Bep-Wor was not surprised. 'There are old stories that say so.'

'Those travellers,' the Doctor went on, 'called your sun Mendeb. And your world was named Mendeb Two, because it is the second planet from the sun.'

A thought appeared in Bep-Wor's mind, like a coin glinting in freshly-turned soil. 'The soldiers,' he said. 'They call us Twos.'

'Well spotted,' the Doctor said. 'That's right. And therefore I believe they're not from your planet, but are from another world. And they have discovered records about the history of this planetary system.'

It was almost too much for Bep-Wor to comprehend. 'Another world, Doctor? What other world?'

The Doctor sighed, as if facing up to an unpalatable truth. 'I think they're from Mendeb Three,' he said. 'Your neighbour planet. Their ancestors were brought there at the same time as your ancestors were settled on Mendeb Two. Unfortunately they seem to have rediscovered some advanced technology rather more quickly than you have.'

Bep-Wor gazed up at the titanic bulkheads that supported the prison chamber roof. 'Did they build this place?' he asked.

'No, no,' the Doctor said impatiently, as if the question was absurd. 'This is a space station. It's been here for centuries. It's fifty kilometres in diameter, for goodness' sake. It's remarkable that the people of Mendeb Three have reached it. But now that they have, they have access to some even more sophisticated machinery. Such as the cargo pod in which we were brought here.'

'And what do they want with us, Doctor?' This was the crucial question. 'Why have they brought us here?'

The Doctor pursed his lips. 'I can think of only five reasons why an entire population is rounded up and taken away. The first stems from racial intolerance: the idea is to exterminate a people that is regarded as inferior or unclean. I don't believe that can apply in this case. The Threes don't know you, and have had no opportunity to develop a fear or hatred of you. And the soldiers seem sympathetic, if anything.'

'That's good,' Bep-Wor said cautiously. He didn't like the sound of extermination.

'Second is a desire for living space. If Mendeb Three were threatened with climate change, or ecological catastrophe, or overcrowding, they might try to clear your planet so that they could move to it.'

The idea horrified Bep-Wor. It seemed so horribly plausible. 'But wait,' he said. 'Why then do they bother to bring us here? Why not just kill us in our homes?'

'Precisely,' the Doctor said. 'Good thinking. So we can rule out that explanation, probably.'

'The third possibility?' Bep-Wor asked.

'It's not likely,' the Doctor said, 'but it's possible that for some reason the people of Mendeb Three have become infertile, and they need you for breeding stock.'

Bep-Wor winced as an image of Kia-Ga flashed into his mind.

'But there seem to be plenty of Threes,' the Doctor said, 'and they're taking men as well as women. So we come to the fourth possibility.'

The Doctor paused before resuming.'I hope it's not this one,' he said, 'because it's particularly unpleasant. Sometimes a society in the grip of religious or political fervour finds itself in a spiral of ever-increasing violence. The gods demand ever more propitiation; the ideologues see traitors everywhere. In the end everyone has to be sacrificed: the citizens of the society itself, and everyone with whom it comes into contact. So we may be on our way to ritual execution.'

'Oh,' Bep-Wor said. He couldn't conceive of killing an entire population for so little reason.

'But it's probably not that,' the Doctor said. 'I've seen no evidence of religious zeal or dogmatic ideology among the guards or their officers. So that leaves only the fifth reason for taking an entire people into captivity.'

'Yes?' Bep-Wor said. 'What's the reason?'

'Forced labour,' the Doctor said. 'They need workers.'

While Bep-Wor was turning over this conclusion in his mind, the door slid open.

'Form a line,' shouted the soldier who appeared in the doorway. 'There's plenty for everyone.'

Two more soldiers wheeled into the chamber a trolley on which was a large metal cylinder. This was followed by a second trolley piled with beakers.

Hundreds of pairs of eyes watched the soldiers and then, as the air from the doorway percolated throughout the chamber, carrying the aroma of cooked vegetables, hundreds of pairs of nostrils began to twitch, and hundreds of stomachs rumbled. The soldiers had brought food at last.

Everyone stood. Everyone moved towards the door.

The soldiers drew their swords and stood in a line in front of the trolleys.

'Keep back,' one of them shouted. 'If you can't form an orderly line, there'll be none for any of you.'

The prisoners shuffled and shoved. Arguments flared, and died quickly because the opponents were too hungry to fight. Eventually the hundreds of captives had organised themselves into a queue that snaked back and forth and filled the chamber.

'That's better,' the soldier said. 'Now step forward one at a time. You'll get a beaker of soup. It's good stuff, so don't waste any.'

The soldiers positioned the trolleys across the doorway and stood behind them. Bep-Wor and the Doctor were near the head of the queue, and they shuffled forward each time another prisoner reached the front and stepped forward to receive a ration of soup.

Soon there were only three people between the Doctor and the front of the queue. Bep-Wor, standing behind the Doctor, noticed that the guards seemed nervous and uneasy. Another prisoner was served, and sipped the hot soup from his beaker as he wandered back into the depths of the chamber; then another. Bep-Wor was fascinated by the expressions on the faces of the guards. They might have been expected to enjoy providing food for hungry prisoners, but instead they looked tired and tense. They didn't speak to the prisoners, or even to each other.

The Doctor stepped forward to collect his ration. He took a beaker from the first trolley and stood in front of the second while one of the soldiers took the beaker from him, ladled soup from the metal cylinder, and passed the full beaker back to the Doctor.

The Doctor began to carry his soup back into the chamber. He lifted the beaker to his face and inhaled the rich aroma of vegetables and spices. And then, as Bep-Wor watched, the

Doctor's appreciative smile turned into a grimace of disgust.

'Come on,' the soldier with the ladle shouted. 'Keep moving. Let's have the next one.'

Bep-Wor started. He was holding up the queue. Before he could step forward, the Doctor clutched his arm.

'Don't touch a drop,' the Doctor whispered. 'It's poisoned. Don't make a fuss. As soon as you've got your soup, go and tell the others. Try to stop them eating it.'

'Come on!' the soldier yelled, and the woman behind Bep-Wor pushed him in the back.

As the soldier ladled soup into Bep-Wor's beaker, Bep-Wor looked over his shoulder. The Doctor was moving along the queue, whispering his urgent message.

'You there,' one of the soldiers shouted. 'You with the hat. Stop talking and go and eat your soup. Stay clear of the line. No second helpings.'

The Doctor lifted an arm to acknowledge the instruction, and disappeared into the gloom of the chamber. Bep-Wor did the same, looking for the prisoners who had been in the queue ahead of the Doctor.

'Don't eat it,' he whispered, as loudly as he dared, as he approached a group of prisoners holding beakers. 'The Doctor says it's poisoned.'

The warning was too late. Some of the prisoners had already drained every drop: they seemed sleepy, their speech was slurred, and their only concern was to lie down and rest. Others, who had eaten less, insisted that the soup was good, and would not listen to Bep-Wor. A few looked worried and confused, and stopped eating.

The Doctor appeared out of the darkness. 'I've tried to warn everyone still in the line,' he said. 'Now I've got to be out of sight. I'll be in the corner near the privy, where there's least light. Bep-Wor, send everyone to me. Tell them I have food for

102

them. But they mustn't eat the soup.' He pulled open his jacket, and Bep-Wor saw the metallic gleam of the flask in the Doctor's pocket.

'Yes, Doctor,' Bep-Wor said. He had no idea what the Doctor intended to do, and it was easier to follow the Doctor's instructions than to try to work out what was going on. 'Follow the Doctor,' he told the prisoners who hadn't eaten all of their soup. 'He will feed you. Don't eat the soup.'

He went as close to the door as he could without attracting the attention of the guards. He wandered back and forth. He pretended to sip from his beaker. 'Don't eat it,' he told all the prisoners he managed to intercept as they made their way from the doorway. 'The Doctor has better food. This is poisoned. He's in the corner near the privy. Go and see him.'

He tried not to wonder how the Doctor would feed so many people with the contents of one small flask.

He stayed at his post until the last of the prisoners had collected a beaker of soup. It was Nam-Gar, a metal worker from Porgum whom Bep-Wor knew slightly. Nam-Gar had been last in the queue because he was lame in his left leg. Bep-Wor supported him and half-carried him into the darkness towards the Doctor.

Wherever he peered into the gloom Bep-Wor saw prisoners drinking from beakers. As he approached the darkest corner, where the Doctor had found a drainage hole and had decreed that it should be reserved for the prisoners' waste, he put his hand over his face in an attempt to lessen the stench.

He saw the Doctor, standing next to the drain and apparently unaffected by the noxious smell. The last few prisoners were with him. He took the beaker from each of them, and poured its contents into the drain. Then he turned his back, and when he turned again he presented the prisoner with a full beaker. To the prisoners this seemed like magic, and although Bep-

Wor knew that the sustenance came from the Doctor's flask he was as perplexed as they were about the original never-ending source of the Doctor's bounty.

The Doctor urged the prisoners to move away, and to act as if they were eating the soup that the soldiers had provided.

When Nam-Gar's soup, and Bep-Wor's, had been disposed of and replaced with the Doctor's delicious broth, the Doctor led Bep-Wor towards the centre of the chamber. The prisoners they passed, still amazed that the Doctor had poured away all the soup and had replenished all the beakers as if by magic, stared at him as he passed. 'The Doctor,' they muttered under their breath. 'Praise the Doctor.'

'But why did they give us poison, Doctor?' Bep-Wor asked. 'Do they want to kill us?'

The Doctor sniffed his beaker, which was still full of the soup that the guards had provided. 'I don't think so,' he said. 'It's a narcotic of some kind. Did we manage to stop everyone from eating it?'

Bep-Wor shook his head. 'No, Doctor. There were a few who had eaten before I found them, and a few others who wouldn't listen to our warnings.'

'They were very hungry, Bep-Wor,' the Doctor said. 'We can't blame them. And,' he added, with a grim smile, 'they'll be useful. The guards will be watching us, to make sure we behave as they expect. We'll have to copy the actions of those who ate the soup.'

'It makes them sleepy,' Bep-Wor said. 'They just want to lie down.'

The Doctor's look of disappointment was almost comical. 'Well, that's not very interesting,' he said. 'However, everyone must do the same. Spread the word: copy the behaviour of those who ate the soup.'

'Yes, Doctor,' Bep-Wor said. 'What are you going to do?'

'I'm going to perform a crude analysis of the drug in this soup,' the Doctor announced, 'and without the facilities of the TARDIS I'll have to do it the basic way.' Before Bep-Wor could stop him, the Doctor had put the beaker to his lips and drained its contents.

'Very good,' the Doctor said, wiping his lips with a large patterned handkerchief. 'But a little heavy on the black pepper.'

He collapsed to the floor and lay with his eyes closed.

Bep-Wor knelt beside the Doctor and shook him. 'Doctor! Doctor! Wake up!'

The Doctor opened one eye. 'Do you mind?' he said. 'I'm pretending to be asleep. Now go and tell everyone else to do the same.'

Later, as he lay on his back, listening to the breathing of the hundreds of prisoners lying all around him across the floor of the chamber, Bep-Wor heard booted feet approaching. The soldiers were walking among the prisoners. He reckoned there were at least six of them.

If we rise up and attack them now, Bep-Wor thought, we will overcome them easily. He dismissed the idea. There were more soldiers – many more – and they had guns and swords.

'Is that the lot?' one of the soldiers shouted.

'Every beaker accounted for,' another shouted back. 'And they're all empty. No troublemakers in this consignment.'

A soldier standing close to Bep-Wor spoke under his breath. 'The poor bastards,' he murmured. 'No one deserves what we're doing to them.'

The gleaming white circle grew larger with each minute. Now Madok could see the corona of atmosphere, and the swirls of cloud within it; he could make out the shapes of the continents around the planet's central belt. Once again he was on his way home.

He had plenty of time to think during these trips to and from the space station. He was becoming used to the feeling of weightlessness: it seemed to free his mind. Unlike most of Kedin's pilots Madok preferred to fly the scout ships, rather than the cumbersome cargo pods and transports. He didn't mind flying solo. In the black, spangled gulf between worlds a scout's metal shell seemed negligible, and Madok could fancy himself alone with the stars; once within a planet's atmosphere the small ship was almost reminiscent of the fragile aircraft, prototypes made of wooden panels held together with wire, in which Madok had learnt to fly on Kedin's summer estates.

It all seemed so long ago.

Everything had been simpler then.

Madok was not a native of one of Kedin's estates. He was from County Vandorn, a small, insignificant domain, three-fifths desert and scrub. As the family's second son he had had no expectation of owning land, and had entered the military academy because he had few options. But he had found that a soldier's life suited him, and as the academy's most promising cadet he had been offered, and had enthusiastically accepted, opportunities to travel and to train with cadets from other lands.

He had graduated, with the rank of lieutenant, while he was seconded to the army of the Duke of Brann. He had seen active service, at the head of a cavalry troop, during the border conflict between Brann and Gonfallon, and he had seen for himself the proficiency of Vethran's disciplined, well-equipped army. His troop had done well to withstand the whirlwind charge of the Gonfallon cavalry, led by the youthful and charismatic Kedin Ashar. The rest of the wing had been swept away and had fled from the field. The Duke of Brann had surrendered, had been assured of his rights and privileges, and had nonetheless seen his duchy sequestered by Vethran and parcelled out to Vethran's minions.

Madok had returned to Vandorn when the County's army was mustered to defend the land: frontier conflicts were erupting across every continent. But Vandorn was surrendered without a battle being fought. The Count died without an heir, and due to Vethran's influence the County was gifted to Vethran's military genius, the newly created Duke of Jerrissar, the dashing Kedin Ashar.

Madok had expected to dislike his new lord. Kedin Ashar was from a family of no particular note; he had a reputation as a womaniser and a rakehell; he seemed reckless in battle, and his unbroken succession of military successes was ascribed to luck, or to reliance on new and frankly ungentlemanly gadgets and tricks.

They had met on the battlements of Castle Vandorn. Madok had gone outside, hoping to avoid being presented to the new Count. Kedin had come looking for him.

Madok had heard his name being called, and had turned from the view of dusty Vandorn town to see a tall, slim figure striding towards him along the walkway. He had recognised Kedin Ashar immediately, and knelt on one knee with his head bowed.

'Get up, Madok,' Kedin had said. 'On your feet, man. Let me shake your hand. If the Duke of Brann had had three more cavalry officers with just half your spirit, the battle would have gone the other way.'

Shocked in equal measure by Kedin's friendliness and informality, Madok had been able only to mutter a few words of thanks. He had been struck by Kedin's youth: he was no older than Madok himself.

'I want you on my staff, Madok,' Kedin had declared. 'I've seen your record as a cadet and an officer. Come with me to what I suppose I will have to get used to calling Jerrissar – pompous name for a duchy, don't you think? Vethran's idea, of course. I've got people working on a new design for a musket. Yet another idea inspired by reading the old books. You load in the breech, not the muzzle. It'll change the way we wage war.'

They had walked together then around the circumference of Vandorn's walls. By the time they had returned to the main hall, where the county's notables were waiting to introduce themselves to their new lord, Madok had decided to throw in his lot with Kedin. The Duke of Jerrissar was excitable, talkative, indiscreet – and made it clear that promoting Vethran's ambitions was merely incidental to transforming the world.

Kedin Ashar had been an idealist even then. Once he had met Tevana Roslod, he had become a crusader and an inspiration.

And he still was, Madok thought.

A burst of light against the browns and greens of the world's central belt caught Madok's attention. It was the transport ship that had left the station the day before Madok had set out: his scout had almost caught up with it. It was firing its engines in preparation for entering the atmosphere.

Another consignment of wretched prisoners from Mendeb Two. They represented funds for Kedin's war chest. They represented cheap, disposable labour for the more ruthless owners of mines and farms and factories; entertainment for the jaded appetites at Vethran's court; cannon fodder for Vethran's armies.

Ace had been in the previous consignment. She had been on the planet for several days already. Madok tried not to think about what might be happening to her.

Madok was close enough to the planet now to discern the

dark green heartland of the largest landmass: the equatorial forest, within which lay Gonfallon, Vethran's home domain, the source of the canker that had contaminated the entire world.

To begin with the pace of change had been exhilarating. Then they had all been young: Vethran, whose ambition and drive had seemed admirable; Kedin and Tevana, so brilliant and so in love; Madok himself, volunteering to experiment with each new weapon and vehicle that Kedin's technicians created.

Looking back, it seemed that not a day passed without some new discovery or adventure: the serendipitous understanding of an arcane diagram in one of the old books; the testing of a prototype engine; dousing the fires that were the inevitable result of most of Tevana's experiments with new fuels.

Now, in the serene silence of space, Madok could see that Kedin had become swept up in the hurricane of innovation that he had himself created. And he, and Tevana, and everyone around them, had underestimated Vethran.

Kedin had had the ideas, and the workshops, and the new machines. Vethran had had the money and the soldiers and the guns, and an appetite for power that increased as it was fed.

It was not until Kedin had taken the space station that he finally became aware that Vethran's desires were insatiable. Newly crowned King, Vethran had sent a new strategic plan to each of his generals and advisers, including Kedin. Madok had brought the document by scout ship to the space station, and had been present when Kedin broke the seal and read aloud Vethran's intentions. Madok would never forget the silence that had settled on everyone in the control room when Kedin finished reading.

They had thought that once Vethran controlled the world, his ambitions would cease; instead, his orders to Kedin were to transport an invasion army to Mendeb Two. They had thought that Kedin and Tevana had recruited all the most brilliant technicians and mechanics; now they discovered that Vethran had his own teams of specialists, including chemists who had distilled essences of terrifying potency which Kedin was instructed to use.

From that moment Kedin Ashar resolved to resist Vethran's plans. Kedin had the space station; he had some technological advances that he had not yet supplied to the Gonfallon army; he had all the pilots who knew how to fly between the worlds.

But Vethran had Tevana.

It was a stalemate. Kedin continued to manifest an allegiance to Vethran, to transport Vethran's troops, and to supply the vile trade from the conquered planet to the home world – but he didn't take the risk of going to the royal court. The King continued to pay Kedin, to use Kedin's space ships and pilots, and to load Kedin with honours – but he didn't allow Tevana to leave her residence.

The deadlock would break soon. The end game was about to begin. Madok smiled grimly. He hated to be inactive.

On the space station Neroda, Jerol and Tered, Kedin's ablest physicians, had succeeded in analysing SS10, the dreadful potion supplied by Vethran's chemists. They knew how to alter its composition. Soon, when the physicians knew how long the effects of the new formula lasted, it would be given to every man and woman captured on Mendeb Three instead of SS10.

And some time later Vethran would realise that Kedin had crossed him. Then, at the latest, Kedin would have to move against Vethran – before Vethran could harm Tevana.

There was still much to organise. From the space station Kedin kept in contact with his scattered domains by radio but, no matter how often the frequency and the code were changed, there was the possibility that one of the few other receivers on the planet would pick up a transmission.

So Madok travelled back and forth in person, holding in his memory the latest plans and codes.

Mendeb Three filled the forward window. Madok leant forward and pushed the button marked MANUAL. Soon he would be in Jerrissar.

The floor vibrated, and the humming that had been so consistent that Bep-Wor had ceased to notice it suddenly increased in volume.

'What's happening?' Bep-Wor whispered to the Doctor.

'We'll be landing soon,' the Doctor said quietly. 'On Mendeb Three, I imagine. Have the sleepers woken yet?'

Bep-Wor lifted his head and looked across the sea of recumbent prisoners. 'If they have, they're not moving,' he said.

The Doctor pondered for a while. 'How many do you think we saved from taking the narcotic?' he asked.

'Perhaps only half,' Bep-Wor replied. 'Some ate the soup knowing it was poisoned. They were very hungry.'

'We did what we could,' the Doctor said gently. 'And we don't know what's in store for us. Perhaps they'll be better off than us.' He sighed in the darkness. 'We have to try to be ready for anything,' he whispered. 'Spread the word to everyone. When the ship lands, we must try to ensure that the ones who took the drug are taken off first. Then we can see how they behave, and copy them. I don't want the guards to know that we're not affected.'

'I understand, Doctor,' Bep-Wor said. 'Everyone will do as you say. They know you will care for us.'

Bep-Wor gave the Doctor's instructions to those around him who were merely pretending to be asleep, and urged them to

111

pass on the message. As he lay on his back, staring at the monstrous girders and panels that disappeared into the blackness above him, he was surprised to find that he felt no fear. He was a captive on an unknown world, but he was intrigued rather than terrified.

It was the Doctor's presence that made the difference. The Doctor was a man of power. He revived the dead; he sniffed out poison; he fed the hungry; he was immune to sleeping draughts. The Doctor would keep everyone safe.

The vibration stopped after a while, although the noise remained loud. The sleepers continued to sleep. Then the floor began to shudder, and the noise became a shriek. Bep-Wor covered his ears and tried to prevent his body bouncing up and down. He heard several loud bangs, felt a couple of violent shocks, and then the noise and the shuddering gradually quietened. 'We've landed,' the Doctor whispered.

In the eerie silence that ensued Bep-Wor received whispered communications from across the floor of the chamber. 'Some of the sleepers have woken,' he told the Doctor, 'but they're not stirring. Our people have moved away from the door. The soldiers will find the sleepers first.'

The door slid open. Fresh air flooded through it. Bep-Wor thought that he could see slanting rays of sunlight in the corridor beyond, and had to fight an urge to jump up and shout with relief.

Soldiers stood in the doorway. Bep-Wor squinted at them. 'Different uniforms,' he told the Doctor.

'Come on, sleepy-heads,' one of the soldiers shouted. 'Wake up. Stand up. Don't speak. You Twos are slaves. You will do as I say. Walk slowly to the door. Walk through the door. Follow the Two in front of you.'

Bep-Wor gave the Doctor a mystified glance. Why was the soldier addressing the prisoners in such a strange manner?

'The chemical in the soup was a complex organic molecule,' the Doctor whispered. 'I believe it acts on the hypothalamus. Watch.'

Near the door men and women were beginning to stand up. They were among those who had eaten the soup and had fallen asleep afterwards. Bep-Wor noticed that there was something strange about their behaviour. They didn't talk to each other as they rose; they didn't even glance at each other. They didn't stretch, or scratch, or yawn. They walked towards the door; one of the soldiers pulled the nearest prisoner through the doorway and the others followed, one at a time, exactly as they had been instructed. They looked straight ahead.

'They've become suggestible,' the Doctor said. 'It's as if they have no will of their own.' He shook his head sadly. 'Well, we know what we've got to do. Stand up, Bep-Wor.'

The Doctor stood up, as if unrolling himself from the floor, and began to walk slowly towards the door. Bep-Wor copied him, and stole a glance backwards to make sure that all the others were beginning to follow the Doctor's lead. They were. Bep-Wor concentrated on keeping his steps regular and his face expressionless.

The prisoners threaded along a corridor, down a ramp and out of the vast metal container. Bep-Wor felt sunlight and a fresh breeze on his face. Plodding forwards, keeping two paces behind the Doctor, he peered from the corners of his eyes to inspect the world of his captors.

The line of prisoners snaked back and forth, slowly filling a flat square of packed earth. Around the edges of the square were carriages and carts, some drawn by strange beasts and the others, Bep-Wor supposed, propelled by machines. Men sat in the vehicles and stood between them, watching the prisoners. Some wore military uniforms similar to those worn

113

by the soldiers who had invaded Bep-Wor's world; the remainder were in a bewildering variety of costumes. Beyond the vehicles there were tents and pavilions, with pennants fluttering above them. And beyond the tents there was countryside: meadows, and then woodland, and then hills.

Bep-Wor felt a sudden yearning loss that almost made him stumble. He could not see the sea. At home, on the archipelago, the ocean was hardly ever out of sight. The sheer extent of the land on this world was oppressive.

He heard a shout. 'Is that the lot, captain?' The words were so strangely accented that Bep-Wor could hardly understand them.

Another voice, from the direction of the transport ship: 'They're all out, commissioner.'

The first voice again: 'Twos. Turn towards me.'

With a sideways glance to make sure that he was moving in the same way as the drugged prisoners, Bep-Wor shuffled to face the direction from which the voice had come.

Standing on a platform at the edge of the square was a big, bearded man in a resplendent suit of dark brocade. His eyes swept back and forth along the rows of prisoners; his keen expression hardly altered, but his lips moved soundlessly.

He's counting us, Bep-Wor realised.

The commissioner turned to one side and spoke to another, younger man, much less richly clothed. The young man listened, and wrote a note on the paper he was holding.

The commissioner peered again at the prisoners. He seemed to be looking for a particular one. He raised his arm and pointed. Bep-Wor was grateful that the pointing finger was not directed at him.

'You,' the commissioner said. 'The slave with the blue rag around your neck. Step forward. Stand before me.'

Bep-Wor recognised the figure who walked slowly from the

ranks of the prisoners and stopped in front of the platform, looking up at the commissioner. It was Mor-Pia, the wife of one of the krake-fishers Bep-Wor had sometimes sailed with. Bep-Wor had been unable to convince her that the soup was poisoned: she had eaten it, and had slept.

The voice of the transport's captain came again from behind the prisoners' heads. 'Don't worry, commissioner,' he shouted, 'they've all had a dose of the potion. Every one of them.'

'No harm in checking,' the commissioner called back. 'Just a random sample. This one won't fetch much anyway. She's too old and too scrawny.'

Bep-Wor knew that something terrible was about to happen. Mor-Pia stood, unmoving, in front of the platform. Bep-Wor willed her to run, or at least to take some interest in her surroundings.

The commissioner leant forward and spoke to her. His voice carried on the breeze. 'What's your name?' he asked her.

Mor-Pia's reply was inaudible.

'Mor-Pia,' the commissioner said, 'place your left hand on the platform. Here, in front of my feet.'

Mor-Pia bent forwards and obeyed.

'The rest of you Twos,' the commissioner shouted, 'keep still and keep quiet. Sarid,' he added, to the young man at his side, 'bring me an axe from the cart.'

A silence fell on the square as the young man hurried away. Mor-Pia remained motionless, her left arm extended on the planks between the commissioner's feet. The pennants snapped and rustled in the wind.

Bep-Wor stole a sideways glance at the Doctor. The little man's face was drawn, and his glittering eyes were fixed on Mor-Pia.

'Thank you, Sarid,' the commissioner said as the young man, out of breath from running, handed him a small axe. The blade glinted in the sunlight.

The commissioner bent to place the axe on the platform, then straightened. 'Mor-Pia,' he said, 'pick up the axe with your right hand and use it to chop off your left hand.'

Bep-Wor saw Mor-Pia's fingers grip the haft of the axe. He saw her lift it above her head. She was going to do it.

'Mor-Pia!' shouted a voice. For a moment Bep-Wor believed he had called out himself. He had wanted to. But the voice was not his own. It was the Doctor's. 'Mor-Pia! Stop! Put down the axe.'

Bep-Wor turned towards the Doctor. 'Keep still, you fool,' the Doctor hissed as he strode forward, pushing between prisoners as he made his way towards the platform.

Mor-Pia had placed the axe on the platform. She had turned round, to face the direction from which the Doctor's voice had come, but her face showed no expression.

As the Doctor emerged from the ranks of the prisoners half a dozen soldiers with drawn swords converged on him. He held up his hands. 'Mor-Pia,' he called out, 'return to your place in the line.'

Without hesitation Mor-Pia walked back into the rows of prisoners, her face as blank as theirs.

'Come here, you Two,' the commissioner shouted to the Doctor. 'Captain!' he called out even more loudly, 'I thought you said every one of these Twos had been dosed.'

'So they were,' was the answering cry.

'It's true,' the Doctor shouted, struggling to be seen above the heads of the soldiers surrounding him. 'Everyone took the drug. It affected all the others.'

'Bring another dose,' the commissioner shouted, and then he looked down at the Doctor. 'Stand clear of him, you clods,' he told the soldiers. 'He's no threat to us.' When the soldiers had withdrawn a little the commissioner peered down at the Doctor.

The Doctor lifted his hat. 'Hello,' he said. 'I'm the Doctor. Whom do I have the pleasure of being ordered around by?'

'Commissioner Dallid,' the commissioner said absently. 'His Majesty's commissioner for the importation of Twos and the regulation of their sale. You don't look like any Two I've ever seen.'

'I apologise for my appearance,' the Doctor said. 'I suppose I have always thought of myself as a unique personality.'

'Shut up,' the commissioner said. 'Are you are a Two? The same as the rest of these slaves?'

The Doctor drew himself up to his full height. His eyes were level with Dallid's knees. 'I arrived on the same transport ship, didn't I?'

The commissioner turned away in exasperation. The captain of the transport was approaching, carrying one of the ship's beakers.

'Who is this fellow, captain?' the commissioner said. 'Are you Jerrissarians playing some trick on us?'

'I haven't noticed him during the voyage, commissioner,' the captain said. 'But we don't inspect the Twos closely. They all took the potion, though. I'd swear to it.'

'This one didn't,' the commissioner growled.

'Oh yes I did,' the Doctor said. 'It doesn't affect me. I'm immune.'

'We'll see about that,' the commissioner said. 'Take this bowl of soup. Eat it.'

The Doctor took the beaker from the captain's hands and brought it reluctantly to his face. 'It's cold,' he said. 'Have you no moral scruples at all?'

The commissioner gestured to the guards, who moved closer to the Doctor and held their sword-points at his body. 'You heartless sadist,' the Doctor said. He pinched his nose with one hand and with the other tipped the contents of the beaker into his mouth.

He handed the empty beaker to one of the guards. 'That

117

wasn't too bad,' he said. 'Rather refreshing. Now then,' he began, but instead of continuing his speech he began to sway, and then to crumple slowly to the ground.

Bep-Wor couldn't believe his eyes. The Doctor was vulnerable after all. Perhaps, while one dose of the poison was not enough to harm him, two would make him as mindlessly obedient as Mor-Pia.

'Wake up, slave,' the commissioner said. 'Stand up and face me.'

The Doctor rose and stood motionless in front of the platform.

'Step back.'

The Doctor moved backwards.

'Stop. Come here again.'

The Doctor walked up to the platform.

'Pick up the axe and sever your left hand.'

The Doctor picked up the glinting axe. He hefted it in his hand. 'Oh, bother,' he said. 'All right, you've rumbled me. Still not turned into a mindless zombie. Sorry.'

Bep-Wor wanted to shout and cheer. Instead he released as a sigh the breath he had been holding in his chest. Most of the undrugged prisoners reacted in the same way to the Doctor's miraculous recovery, and the multiple exhalation sounded like a sudden gust of wind across the square.

The commissioner looked up with a puzzled frown, and then returned his attention to the Doctor, who had pulled his handkerchief from the pocket of his trousers and was wiping it across his brow.

'It's warm work,' the Doctor said, 'processing all those toxins and complex organic compounds.'

'Oh, shut up,' the commissioner said, 'you irritating little man. You're going to the capital. The King's interrogators will want to see you. Then you'll be only too pleased to talk. Captain, I'm not paying you for this one.'

The captain protested that it was not his fault that the Doctor was immune to the potion, and an argument ensued. Bep-Wor, meanwhile, was racking his brains to think of a way to remain with the Doctor.

Even if he could organise the prisoners to act together, to run away or to attack the soldiers, he realised that they would be cut down by the soldiers' swords and guns. The only thing he could think of was to convince the commissioner that all of the prisoners were in some way unusual.

He kept his head lowered. He took a deep breath. In a low, resonating voice he intoned the single word, 'Doctor.'

He didn't dare to look up to find out whether the commissioner had heard him. 'Doctor,' he said again in a deep voice.

The commissioner and the captain had stopped arguing. There was a long silence. Then, from the row behind Bep-Wor, another voice boomed. 'Doctor.'

Bep-Wor briefly lifted his eyes. The commissioner wasn't looking in his direction. 'Doctor,' he called again.

A third voice rang out. Then a fourth, and then a fifth. Soon the sepulchral word 'Doctor' was echoing around the square as prisoner after prisoner joined in the ragged chorus.

Bep-Wor looked from side to side. He was amazed to see that even some of the prisoners who had taken the drug were intoning the word.

'Quiet!' the commissioner yelled. 'Twos, be silent.'

The swelling chorus receded and died away. Once again the only noise in the square was the fluttering of the flags.

Into the hiatus Bep-Wor spoke again. 'Doctor.'

And the word was repeated by another voice, and another, and then from prisoners' mouths across the square.

'Silence!' the commissioner roared. His face was red above his beard. The prisoners took no heed, and the word 'Doctor' continued to ebb and flow like a tide washing through the ranks of motionless, expressionless slaves.

The Doctor jumped on to the platform and stood between the commissioner and the captain. He raised his arms, and lowered them slowly. The prisoners' voices faded.

'Crowd control,' the Doctor said to the commissioner. 'It's a matter of charisma. You've either got it or you haven't.'

The commissioner ignored him. 'I'm withholding payment for the entire consignment,' he told the captain. 'You can argue about it later. I've got twenty traders who have come here to buy and I'll have to tell them they've had a wasted journey. That's my priority. They won't be happy. I suggest that you and your men wait on your ship. I'll see you later.'

He stood with his hand on his hips and his beard jutting belligerently above the Doctor's head towards the captain.

'We did everything correctly,' the captain said mildly. 'Perhaps this batch of the potion was sub-standard. In which case I'll be requiring compensation from you. As you say, we'll meet later.' He turned on his heel and stepped from the platform.

The commissioner watched him leave. 'Sarid!' he shouted. 'Muster all of our men. And any of the King's guards you can find. I want them here now. And I want these Twos – every one of them – in chains. Hire manacles from the traders if we don't have enough. They're all coming back to the capital with us.' He turned to the Doctor. 'This one,' he said, 'I want particularly well secured.'

Tragar had resisted as long as he could. Each day the overseer brought him a report on the new slave's progress, and each day he had conquered the urge to see for himself. But it had been almost a week since Ace had arrived in the house, and he was burning with curiosity to see her again.

Therefore he had rescheduled his regular meeting with Bared about the household budget, he had brought forward his discussion with Balon's chef about the menu for the evening's banquet, and he had the afternoon to himself.

He had smoked a pipe to relax his nerves: talking to the chef, particularly when a large dinner was in prospect, was always trying. He had dressed in one of his more colourful coats. As he stood before the mirror, inspecting his face and failing to find any pimples or protruding nostril hairs, he suddenly laughed aloud.

I'm preening myself, he thought, as if I'm about to have an assignation with the wife of one of Balon's guards. All this for a mere slave.

He heard a knock at the door.

'Come in, Poa-Nan,' he called. He had recognised the Two's hesitant raps.

Poa-Nan came into the room. Tragar didn't turn, but by looking in the mirror he was able to study his manservant. Poa-Nan stood with his hands folded together on his slightly rotund stomach. He had a gentle smile on his lips. He was gazing at the floor.

There was something unnerving about Twos, Tragar thought. He wondered how they behaved on their home world, without the benefit of the potion that made them so obedient. The traders said that Twos, in their natural habitat, were savages. Looking at Poa-Nan, Tragar found that hard to believe.

Still, they were cheap. That was the main thing. Always willing to serve, and never requiring to be paid. Tragar had invested wisely, and had been able to replace several of his servants with Twos. He had already saved in servants' wages more than he had paid for the Twos.

He wondered, not the first time, how long Poa-Nan would

stand and wait if he ignored him. For ever, he supposed, or at least until he collapsed from hunger or exhaustion. The first instruction that Twos were given, long before they were sold to their owners, was to speak only when spoken to.

He sighed. Twos were cheap, but real servants were better conversationalists. 'Yes, Poa-Nan?' he said.

Poa-Nan lifted his head. 'The overseer says that she is at your disposal, sir.'

'Thank you, Poa-Nan,' Tragar said. Why did he bother to be polite? It was wasted on Twos. Force of habit, that was all. 'Go and tell her I'll be there shortly. Then proceed with your chores.'

'Yes, sir.' Poa-Nan plodded from the room.

Tragar spent another few minutes in front of the mirror, impatiently plucking from his coat almost imperceptible loose threads. Having told Poa-Nan to announce his visit, he now had to wait for the Two to carry out the mission.

He couldn't wait any longer. He had to know how his new slave was shaping up. He corrected himself: Ace belonged to Balon Ferud, and Balon would be unhappy if she proved to be worth less than the exorbitant price his chamberlain had paid for her.

Anxiety clenched Tragar's innards. He strode to the door.

Such was Tragar's preoccupation that for once he forgot to count as he hurried along the length of the corridor that connected the rooms that made up his suite of apartments. It was ninety-seven paces from the door of his study to the top of the main staircase of the east wing. The corridor in Bared's apartments in the west wing was only eighty-three paces long. The differential never failed to provide Tragar with a warm glow of satisfaction. Whenever Tragar found himself having to listen politely while Bared censured him for overspending by a few marks on anything from fine wines to household repairs, Tragar would repeat to himself: you are merely the keeper of the accounts, while I am the chamberlain – and my corridor is longer than yours.

Tragar clattered down the back stairs. He descended from the realm of airy rooms with tinted window glass, hanging tapestries and thick carpets into the lower depths of Balon's residence. Here the flagstones and walls were bare, and daylight streamed in through small, high windows.

He slowed his pace. As he looked from left to right he saw Twos at work: rolling out pastry in the kitchen, stacking logs next to the ovens, scrubbing the floor of the meat store. These were Tragar's own Twos: in the lower floors of the central block of the mansion, an army of Balon's Twos were no doubt performing the same tasks on a much grander scale.

It irked Tragar that Bared owned more Twos than he did. But Tragar had to admit, although only to himself, that he found the presence of even his own few Twos slightly unsettling. Apart from Poa-Nan he didn't know their names, and he rarely visited the lower floors of his apartments. His reliable overseer, Rigora, managed the Twos: she was his chamberlain, just as he was Balon Ferud's.

He strode into the cubicle – a square room between the kitchen and the dry store – that Rigora used as her office.

Rigora was seated behind her desk. Her meaty arms were resting on piles of ledgers and provisioners' bills. Her cheeks were flushed. Tragar wondered whether she had been at the wine already, and if so whether he should upbraid her. He decided to ignore the problem: he didn't want to aggravate her, she was entitled to her perks, and in any case he had other business on his mind.

The other business was standing beside the desk. As he had instructed, Ace was wearing a new tunic and new trousers modelled on those she had been wearing when he had bought her. Like any other Two waiting for orders she was gazing at the floor with a vacant smile on her face.

'Chamberlain,' Rigora said with a nod.

'Good afternoon, Rigora,' Tragar said. His eyes scanned the room. It was a long time since he'd visited Rigora in her den: normally he summoned her to his study. How could she work in such clutter and gloom, he wondered?

'Any difficulties today, overseer, down here in your subterranean workshops?'

Rigora shifted her weight from one ham to the other. 'None worth bothering you with, chamberlain.'

'Ah, good.' With the formalities over Tragar could devote his attention to the intriguing new slave. He turned to Ace and inspected her.

Rigora had been keeping her clean and well fed, he noted with satisfaction. The overseer's standards were usually high, but he'd known the overseer to ignore his instructions on occasion. He looked behind Ace's ears and pulled back the neck of her shirt: thoroughly scrubbed. He sniffed. The girl smelt clean, too: in fact he detected a hint of cheap scent, which to his surprise made him tremble with a sudden physical desire.

He stepped back. Rigora had been tending this slave particularly conscientiously. The new outfit had been competently tailored, presumably by another of the Twos, and Rigora hadn't skimped on the quality of the cloth. Tragar was not surprised that the overseer hadn't been able to find a match for the heavy material of Ace's original trousers, but the black linen was a suitable substitute, and the new garment clung to the girl's legs even more tightly than the old. The new black shirt was an improvement, too: as before Ace's arms were left scandalously bare, but now she had buttons and a collar, so that the costume was more than ever a parody of respectable attire.

'You like what you see, chamberlain?' Rigora said. She was leaning forward, and her vast bosom was flattened against the piles of paperwork on her desk. Tragar thought that she might be preparing to lift herself out of her chair.

'You've done well, overseer,' he said. 'At least in the matter of appearances. Has she taken instruction well?'

'Well enough.' There was a pause while Rigora pushed herself from her chair. 'I've reported every day, as you know. Ask her, if you want. She'll tell you.'

'I will, overseer.' Tragar turned again to Ace. 'Tell me, Ace, what have you been taught here? Can you remember what you learnt on your first day?'

'Yes, sir,' Ace said. Her face was more animated now: she was looking and smiling at Tragar. 'That's easy. I did basic duties, eating and washing, forms of address, and the rules of the household.'

'Very good, Ace. And on the second day?'

'The routine chores of the kitchen, sir. I'm a wizard with a mop and bucket now.'

Tragar couldn't help laughing, and when he did so Ace's smile widened. She really was a remarkable discovery. Despite the effects of the potion the embers of her personality still glowed within her.

Rigora misunderstood Tragar's fascination with Ace. 'Don't you worry, chamberlain,' she said, 'she's been properly processed, even though she sometimes answers back a mite too freely. But I've trained her in kitchen, deportment, table service, even a bit of cooking, and she always does as she's told. Ask her about the hot plates. Go on.'

'Very well.' Mystified, Tragar addressed Ace. 'Tell me about the hot plates, Ace.'

'Yes, sir,' Ace said brightly. 'Madam Rigora told me to take six clean white plates from the kitchen to the bakery. I saw clean white plates on the range, so I picked up six of them and took them to the bakery. They were the wrong plates. They were hot.' Ace held up her hands. They were bandaged.

Tragar spun round. 'She's damaged,' he cried. 'Have you any idea how much of Balon's cash I spent buying her? What have you done?'

'Don't fuss,' the overseer said. 'It was just a mistake. Every Two gets the odd knock during training. She's young. She'll heal. The point is, she didn't make a scene or drop the plates. She's properly processed, like I said.'

'And how do you feel, Ace?' Tragar asked. It was a question he'd never previously thought to ask a Two, and he wondered how Ace would reply.

Ace pursed her lips as she thought about her answer. 'I feel all right, thank you, sir,' she said. 'No worries.'

Behind him, Rigora snorted. 'Stupid question,' she huffed. 'Twos feel whatever we tell them to feel. Rest of the time, they don't feel anything much. Not such a bad life, if you ask me. It beats worrying about these bloody butchers' bills.'

She shuffled towards the door. 'Come along, chamberlain,' she said, 'I've got something to show you. Ace, follow me.'

The overseer led Tragar out into the passageway, and stopped at a pair of wooden doors that were black with age.

'Where are we going?' Tragar asked, while Rigora struggled with the latch. He couldn't remember ever seeing these doors open, and he didn't want to admit that he had no idea what lay beyond them.

'You'll see,' Rigora said, panting from her exertions. 'She's full of surprises, that one. Ah! That's it.'

The latch gave way, and the overseer pulled open the doors. Daylight illuminated the stone corridor, revealing stains and mildew that had passed unnoticed for years. The doors gave on to a small courtyard: its floor was flat stones, its four sides were the grimy walls of the east wing's kitchens and outhouses, and it was open to the sky. There were no other doors.

Standing in one corner was a Two: Tragar recognised him as the one who usually worked in the meat store. He was a big, ugly fellow, and he looked no better on this occasion for being stripped to the waist. Tragar noticed with alarm that the Two was carrying a cleaver, and his hand went automatically to the hilt of his sword.

'Rigora,' Tragar said from the corner of his mouth, as if he didn't want the Two to hear him, 'what's that brute doing here?'

'Don't fret, chamberlain,' the overseer said. 'I put him in here earlier. Like I said, I've got something to show you. Now let me have a word with young Ace.'

Rigora beckoned to Ace. 'You remember, Ace,' she said, 'what you did here yesterday afternoon? With the lad from the kitchen? Well, when I say the word, you just do the same again. Understand?'

'Yes, madam,' Ace replied. Then, to Tragar's surprise, she looked at her empty, bandaged hands, and a confused expression appeared on her face.

'Don't worry, dear,' Rigora said. 'There's your stick, in the corner. Make yourself ready, then pick it up.'

Tragar looked into the corner of the yard, but was immediately distracted. Ace was removing her clothes.

'Overseer!' he said. 'What licentiousness are you proposing?' He was appalled and, he realised with a pang of self-disgust, excited in equal measure at the thought of Ace performing with the Two from the meat store. He couldn't take his eyes from her.

Rigora laughed: an unpleasant, gurgling sound. 'None whatsoever,' she replied. 'She's just getting ready. Stand in the doorway with me, chamberlain. And prepare to be amazed.'

There was barely enough room in the doorway for both the chamberlain and the overseer. Tragar was slender, but Rigora more than made up for his narrow girth. Ace, without a thought for her own modesty, had removed her shirt and her trousers. She was wearing only a cloth tied around her bosom, a pair of brief shorts, and heavy boots. In her hands was the stick she had collected from the corner of the yard: it was in fact no mere stick, Tragar saw, but a staff of seasoned wood.

Ace and the male Two stood impassively in the courtyard.

'Good-looking, for a Two, isn't she?' Rigora said.

Tragar shrugged.

The overseer chuckled. 'Ready to be amazed, then?' she asked. Without waiting for an answer she called out, 'Ace! Har-Gur! Fight each other.'

'What?' Tragar struggled to turn in the doorway to face his overseer. 'Are you mad? He's twice her size. And he's got a meat-axe.'

Rigora merely laughed. 'Just you watch,' she said.

Ace and Har-Gur circled each other for a while. Both were eerily silent, and the only sound was the padding of their feet on the stones. Ace began to lunge with the staff, forcing Har-Gur to parry. Tragar was no warrior, but he had seen Balon's household troops in training, and he knew that Ace's technique was poor. Her movements were awkward when they should have been fluid; her opponent was able to predict the swing of her staff. Nonetheless, Tragar couldn't deny that guiltily he was enjoying watching her move.

Ace stepped back, opened her mouth, and emitted a howl that echoed around the towering walls. Then she attacked.

The fight was over within seconds. The staff in Ace's hands

became a blur; her arms worked like the pistons of a steam engine. She pressed forward, driving Har-Gur into a corner. Tragar closed his eyes as he heard the sound of the staff striking Har-Gur's flesh. The Two sank to his knees, and still Ace harried him with the end of the staff.

'Stop!' Rigora shouted.

Ace immediately became still. Her bosom heaved as she drew in deep breaths. Her legs shone with the sweat of her exertions.

'Well, chamberlain,' Rigora said, jolting Tragar from his reverie. 'What do you think? I reckon she could be one for the arena. That's big money, if she's good enough.'

'Indeed, overseer,' Tragar said. 'It's unusual to find a Two who retains so much spirit.'

'You're not wrong there,' Rigora said. 'I'm glad I didn't meet this one before she had the potion.'

Tragar grunted in agreement. His eyes were once again fixed on Ace. She was a Two with many possibilities. He'd considered her as an amusing domestic, but she might be more valuable fighting in the arenas. Then again, she would earn back Balon's investment many times over, Tragar now realised, if she were trained for pleasure.

Tragar had no doubt. He had secured for Balon Ferud a most valuable asset.

Some of the traders had insisted on buying Twos: they had arrived with specific commissions from aristocratic patrons, and they refused to leave the landing-site with nothing to show for their journeys. Commissioner Dallid had been unable to resist the cash offers, and had set up an informal, hurried auction at which he disposed of a few score of the most obviously docile Twos.

The remainder – one hundred and fifty-three men and

women – were put in chains as they stood in the square. There were still some among them who had eaten the drugged soup, and who were as a result without any will of their own; the majority, Bep-Wor reckoned, were, like him, merely pretending.

Bep-Wor had a manacle bolted around each of his wrists. A length of chain connected the manacles. Surreptitiously he tested the strength of the metal: it was heavy, well-made iron, and he knew that he would not be able to remove the shackles without a hammer and a pick.

The Doctor's bonds were much more substantial: his ankles, as well as his wrists, were shackled, and a long chain was wrapped around his torso. He was carried away, struggling, and placed in a cart.

Bep-Wor could think of nothing better to do than to endure the chains, continue the pretence of being affected by the drug, and wait. Bep-Wor was the Doctor's mouthpiece, and the other prisoners were becoming accustomed to following his lead. Therefore they also waited.

Bep-Wor, tanned from years of working in the fields and on board ship, was used to the heat of the sun. But he had never before known it to shine directly above his head. He marvelled at his own shadow: a black patch around his feet. On his home world the sun was always low in the sky, and shadows were always long. As he stood staring for hour after hour at the dusty ground, Bep-Wor fought back the waves of homesickness and despair that threatened to overwhelm him.

He told himself he had to be strong. He was the Doctor's chief follower, and all the others were depending on him. While he was alive and still had his wits, there was a chance he might find Kia-Ga. The Doctor would not let his followers remain chained for long. There was hope.

The sun had passed its zenith, and the midday heat had

begun to dissipate, before the prisoners were moved. The auction had ended: some of the traders had disappeared into their tents, and others had trundled away in their vehicles with their purchases stumbling behind. The soldiers from the transport ship had long since retired inside their vessel. Commissioner Dallid and his staff were in their pavilion, and apart from half a dozen guards the lines of prisoners were the only people to be seen across the wide panorama of the valley.

Now, at last there was movement. Bep-Wor lifted his head a little, and saw the commissioner's assistant, Sarid, emerge from the pavilion. He was clutching a bulging purse. He called to two of the guards, and strode to the enclosure where several large, four-legged beasts were standing lazily in the sun.

The animals were taller than any Bep-Wor had seen on his own world, but it was clear that the men were going to ride them. Bep-Wor could see that with their long legs the animals would make good speed. As the commissioner's assistant and the two guards mounted their steeds and galloped away in a cloud of dust, Bep-Wor concluded that the threesome was an advance party: the commissioner had sent them ahead, with a purse of money, to procure food and lodging for the unexpectedly large host which the commissioner was bringing with him.

Sure enough, shortly afterwards the commissioner and four more of his underlings emerged from the pavilion. The commissioner stood and watched while his staff carried bags and bundles from the pavilion to the three nearby carts. After a while a thought struck him, and he strolled to one of the carts, knocked on the side, called out, and waited for a reply. Bep-Wor realised that he was checking that the Doctor was still in the cart.

The guards abandoned their posts near the prisoners and went to fetch animals from the enclosure. As some of the animals were saddled, and others were manoeuvred between the thills of the carts, Bep-Wor realised that no one was guarding the prisoners. He dismissed the idea of escape as soon as it arose in his mind: they wouldn't get far burdened with heavy chains, and Bep-Wor had no way of knowing in which direction to lead them. In any case, he wouldn't leave the Doctor.

A thunderous clattering interrupted Bep-Wor's thoughts. He squinted towards the pavilion, and saw smoke issuing from the back of a vehicle parked next to the carts. It was the type of vehicle that moved by itself, without the need for draught animals: Bep-Wor had seen many of these machines on his own world. There the noise and appearance of the machines had scared him: they were alien, and the invaders used them for destruction. Now, he realised, he was no longer afraid. He had seen the worst that the invaders could do, and he had survived; he had been transported from his world to theirs, and he had survived; they had tried to poison him and destroy his will, and he had survived. They might yet enslave him, or even kill him. But at least he'd never again hide from the sound of their raucous machines.

It seemed to him that he had the Doctor to thank for that.

The motorised vehicle, with the commissioner inside it, started to move. The cart containing the Doctor followed it. The guards, mounted on their steeds, rode towards the prisoners.

'March!' they shouted. 'Come on, you lazy Twos, get moving. Follow the cart. Don't stop until you're told to.'

The rows of prisoners unravelled into a single line, plodding in step behind the cart. The long column wound away from the square, and on to a road that ran along the valley, between fields full of crops and types of trees that Bep-Wor had never seen before.

The line of prisoners marched up hills, through a narrow pass overhung by rocks, down a corniche road perched half-way up the side of a gorge, into a wide valley, and across a sluggish stream. Bep-Wor, who had lived all his life on islands dotted across the ocean, could hardly comprehend the vast majesty of the landscape.

There were no stops for rest or refreshment. Having been dosed with the drug, the prisoners were expected to obey instructions: they would walk until they were told to stop walking. Bep-Wor's feet were blistered and his legs ached: he wondered how Hap-Lor was managing to keep up the pace.

The sun had descended into a bank of clouds beyond the distant peaks of a range of mountains, and had stained the horizon a vivid crimson. Bep-Wor, his feet moving automatically beneath him, didn't realise that both the day and the journey were coming to an end until he walked between two stone pillars and found himself on a track illuminated by flaming torches.

The place was a farm. Bep-Wor recognised the smells, the wooden fencing, the barns and outhouses. Despite the weariness of his limbs he smiled: he was pleased that farms were the same, even when worlds apart.

The mounted guards rode alongside the line of prisoners. 'Turn left at the end of the path,' they shouted. 'Into the stockade. Then stop walking. Find somewhere to lie down. You can rest. Don't leave the stockade.'

Bep-Wor stumbled along the prescribed route, and into a fenced area of dry earth already milling with the prisoners who had preceded him. His legs felt as heavy as anchors, and the manacles were chafing his wrists. He was so tired that he was no longer hungry or thirsty. He wanted only to find a space in which to stretch his aching body on the ground.

The daylight was failing fast, but Bep-Wor saw that the

fenced area included an open-fronted barn with a thatched roof, as well as a farmhouse. The barn contained hay: it looked to Bep-Wor as welcoming as a feather bed. Also in the barn was a cart – the cart that contained the Doctor.

In an instant Bep-Wor forgot his weariness: like many of the prisoners, he began to amble towards, and then into, the barn. He risked looking over his shoulders, and found that no guards were watching over the stockade. They thought they could be sure that the obedient prisoners would make no attempt to escape.

Bep-Wor straightened his shoulders and made straight for the cart. A crowd of prisoners was already pressed around it, and more were converging all the time.

As he approached, Bep-Wor heard the prisoners' whispered conversation.

'Is the Doctor in there?'

'Somebody should look.'

'Here comes Bep-Wor. Let him through.'

Bep-Wor found the throng of prisoners parting before him. 'It's all right,' he said, 'we can speak freely. The guards have gone to the farmhouse. We'd be free if it weren't for these chains. Has anyone spoken with the Doctor?'

'No, Bep-Wor,' said a tall man standing at the tailgate of the cart. 'We were waiting for you.' Bep-Wor recognised the man as Lep-Tar: he had been a merchant and investor, based in Porgum, and had once refused to loan Bep-Wor the funds to purchase seed-corn. Now, wearing rags and chains, he deferred to Bep-Wor.

'Help me up,' Bep-Wor said. 'Lep-Tar, make a step with your hands.'

Lep-Tar locked his fingers together to form a stirrup, into which Bep-Wor placed his left foot. He reached up and gripped the top of the tailgate. Lep-Tar straightened, lifting

Bep-Wor up, and Bep-Wor was able to pull himself over the tailgate and into the cart. He landed with a jangle of chains.

'Bep-Wor,' the Doctor said. 'How nice of you to drop in.'

'Doctor,' Bep-Wor said, crawling on his hands and knees and feeling his way. 'Where are you?' The interior of the cart was dark, and crammed with oddly shaped bundles any one of which could have been the Doctor's chained body.

'Up here,' the Doctor said.

Bep-Wor raised his eyes and saw the unmistakable silhouette of the Doctor, with his hat perched on his head. He was sitting on a bulging sack, his knees drawn up to his chin.

Bep-Wor reined in his exclamation of amazement. He wondered whether he was beginning to get used to being amazed by the Doctor. He sat on his haunches.

'Doctor,' he said. 'I can see you're no longer in chains. How did you break free?'

'Ah,' the Doctor said. 'Have I mentioned that I once knew Harry Houdini? The name wouldn't mean anything to you, of course. He was an escapologist. Taught me every trick he knew.'

'And which trick did you use to escape today?'

The Doctor's teeth gleamed in the darkness. 'None of them, as a matter of fact. I was getting very uncomfortable in the back of this cart. Appalling suspension. I was being jolted about like a die in a shaker. So I just wriggled, and the chain around me fell off. I think they forgot to fasten it. Then I pulled my hands through the manacles – it's one of the advantages of having slim, artistic hands – and then, once I'd taken my shoes off, I did the same with the rings round my ankles. I think the chains were made for someone much larger than me.'

The Doctor rubbed his wrists and ankles. 'It's all very tiresome,' he said. 'Being held prisoner restricts one's freedom of movement, I find. I haven't got time for imprisonment. I really must get on with looking for Ace.'

Bep-Wor shook his head. He thought that he'd never understand the Doctor. There was a knocking on the side of the cart. The prisoners were impatient to know whether their saviour was safe. Bep-Wor had an idea.

'Doctor,' he said, 'stand up. On those barrels. I'll come up with you. Spread your arms.'

Bep-Wor could imagine how the Doctor looked from among the crowd gathered around the cart. The Doctor, with Bep-Wor beside him, suddenly appeared above the crowd with his arms outspread, wordlessly demonstrating that he had freed himself from the chains that had bound him.

The prisoners gasped in unison. 'Doctor!' one of them cried out, and others took up the shout, which became a repetitive chant. 'Doctor! Doctor! Doctor!'

As the Doctor and Bep-Wor tried to silence the chanting, prisoners from all over the compound were drawn to the noise. Soon the rest of the stockade was deserted: all of the prisoners were in the barn, standing round the cart, looking up at the little man who could not be enslaved by poison or held by chains.

'Someone's coming,' the Doctor said, and jumped down into the cart, out of sight.

Bep-Wor peered into the empty stockade, illuminated now only by the last glimmerings of the pale sky above the mountains and the dancing light from the torches. There were soldiers standing at the gates. Bep-Wor saw them looking about, puzzled by the absence of prisoners. They drew their swords, opened the gates, and proceeded cautiously across the packed earth. Beyond them there were more people, walking in a line, carrying burdens from the direction of the farmhouse.

'It's all right,' one of the soldiers shouted to the others. 'I can see them. They're all in the barn.' Bep-Wor could hear the relief in his voice. 'I was beginning to think we'd lost the whole lot.'

Bep-Wor gestured with his hands, telling the prisoners to move away from the cart. By the time the first soldier arrived in the barn the prisoners were milling about, silent and apparently purposeless. Bep-Wor could hear the Doctor moving: it sounded as if he was wrestling with the chains he had discarded.

'Right then, you Twos,' the soldier shouted. 'Form a line. One behind the other. There's food on the way. Step forward one at a time. Take your food. Move away. Eat the food. Don't come back for more.'

'Help me get out,' the Doctor said to Bep-Wor. 'I have to taste the food.'

The Doctor had struggled back into his shackles. Bep-Wor pulled him up to the top of the cart's side, and winced as he heard him fall to the ground. Bep-Wor followed. With their heads lowered, and walking somnolently, Bep-Wor and the Doctor emerged from behind the cart and attempted to look aimless as they made their way to the front of the winding line of prisoners.

The soldiers were paying little attention. They were slapping their hands against their arms, trying to warm themselves. A chill wind was gusting across the stockade.

The jangling of chains died away: the prisoners were standing in a line which snaked across the floor of the barn. The Doctor was at the head of the queue, and Bep-Wor was behind him. Bep-Wor saw that the five women carrying food from the farmhouse were more of his people: Twos, unthinkingly obeying the instructions of the soldiers.

'Set the cauldron down here,' one of the soldiers said to the women, indicating a space just inside the barn. 'Bread here. You know how to serve this up? Half a loaf and a ladle of stew for each person.'

'Yes, sir,' the women said in unison.

'Right then,' the soldier said. He called to his companions.

'We'll leave them to it. They've all got their orders. Should be no trouble. Let's get out of this wind and into that back parlour.'

'Let's get into that bottle of brandy,' another soldier shouted back. They sheathed their swords and loped towards the farmhouse.

Wordlessly the five women began to prepare the food. One removed the lid from the cauldron; another stirred the contents with a ladle; the remainder started to unpack loaves of bread from baskets, and tear them in half. The loaves were hollow, and the woman with the ladle poured a helping of stew into the half-loaf proffered by her companion. The first meal was ready. The Doctor stepped forward.

Bep-Wor could hardly bear the suspense. The smell of the stew had made him suddenly ravenous, and he was sure that all the other prisoners shared his hunger. If the stew proved to be dosed with the potion, he wasn't sure that he would be able to prevent himself, let alone anyone else, from eating it. The brew from the Doctor's flask was delicious and invigorating, but it wasn't substantial. His stomach was keening for solid sustenance.

The Doctor bit into the bread and slurped at the stew contained within it. He chewed contemplatively. He craned his neck to check that the soldiers were out of sight and out of earshot.

'It's delicious,' he said. 'And quite safe. The bread has been made with a yeast that could prove dangerous to the Sontaran physiognomy, but I'm fairly sure it's harmless for humans.'

There were times when Bep-Wor found the Doctor's gnomic utterances particularly trying. His stomach rumbled. 'So we can eat it, Doctor?'

'Oh, yes,' the Doctor said. 'Of course. Here, take mine.' He handed his dripping half-loaf to Bep-Wor. 'Shall we converse with the canteen staff while our comrades are taking their dinner?'

The Doctor and Bep-Wor stood by the cauldron while the women served stew to the prisoners one at a time. From their position they could reassure everyone that the stew was safe to eat, they could keep watch in the direction of the farmhouse – and the Doctor could chat with the women who were serving the food.

Bep-Wor took no part in the conversation at first, as he was completely preoccupied with filling his stomach. The stew was hot and tasty, and the bread was freshly baked. Never had a meal been so welcome.

'Hello,' the Doctor said, doffing his hat to the women. They didn't look at him. 'I expect you've been told not to talk to the Twos. But it's all right. I'm not a Two. So you can talk to me.'

The five women paused in their work. They frowned.

'I'm the Doctor,' the Doctor said. 'And I say that you are permitted to talk to me.'

'The Doctor is our leader,' Bep-Wor added, hastily swallowing a mouthful of bread. 'He is the leader of the Twos. You must do as he says.'

The women looked at the Doctor. 'Yes, sir,' they said together.

The Doctor recoiled slightly from their ardent gaze. 'You,' he said, beckoning to the woman who had least to do. 'Come here and talk with us. This is Bep-Wor, my friend and companion. What's your name?'

The woman stepped from her place behind the bread baskets and stood between the Doctor and Bep-Wor. Her expressionless eyes were directed at the Doctor's face. 'My name is Sab-Ma, sir.'

'Where are you from, Sab-Ma?' the Doctor asked.

'Tilk,' the woman replied.

The Doctor looked at Bep-Wor, who bolted down another mouthful in order to speak.

'It's a village on the island of Yollund,' he said. 'To the south-east of my island. Very warm climate. Good fishing.'

'I see,' the Doctor said. 'And how long have you been working on this farm, Sab-Ma of Tilk?'

Sab-Ma frowned again. Bep-Wor assumed that she was out of the habit of thinking for herself. 'Two hundred days, sir,' she said, although she sounded uncertain and Bep-Wor thought it unlikely that she had counted the days. It was unlikely, after all, that her owners had instructed her to keep track of time, and Bep-Wor now realised that anyone who had taken the potion would do only those things that he or she was told to do. Sab-Ma did nothing of her own accord.

'Are you happy?' Bep-Wor blurted out. He needed to know what Sab-Ma felt about her new life as a slave on a strange world.

Sab-Ma looked confused.

'Are you content?' the Doctor put in.

At this, Sab-Ma smiled. She suddenly looked alive and attractive. 'Yes, thank you, sir,' she said. 'I am very content with my work and my accommodation.'

The Doctor smiled sadly and shook his head. 'And have you been told that you should be content?' he asked.

Sab-Ma continued to smile. 'Yes, sir,' she said. 'The master and the mistress have told me that I must always be content, and I am.'

Bep-Wor closed his eyes. He had eaten his meal too quickly: he felt queasy. He considered how close he had been to drinking the soup containing the drug, and he felt even sicker. It was the most evil potion imaginable: its victims were left with no will, no personality, no feelings of their own.

The Doctor's thoughts had apparently been running along

the same path. 'If this has been done to Ace,' he muttered to himself, 'I will never forgive myself. I must find her.'

Bep-Wor was determined to seek out whatever spark of individuality remained within Sab-Ma. 'You are permitted to tell us your own feelings,' he urged her. 'You must have feelings of your own.' The woman looked at him: her face was blank. 'Has anything made you sad?' he asked, his voice rising in desperation. 'Tell me about something that has happened recently that you didn't like.'

Sab-Ma's face contorted as she tried to obey Bep-Wor's instruction. 'A new Two,' she said at last. 'A new one came, a few days ago. But the master sold her again, very soon. She's gone now. It was good to have another Two at the farm. I was sad when she went. Her name was Kia-Ga.'

The Duchy of Jerrissar was not a single, contiguous tract of land. It was a name that Vethran had invented, when he had granted Kedin a dukedom, to encompass Kedin's various landholdings. Kedin's ancestral lands were small: a county in the north of the central continent, mountainous even in its most fertile parts and extending into the high, frozen wastes above the tropic. Kedin had added to this through chance inheritance, by purchasing small tracts of land, and through the generosity of Vethran, who gifted conquered territories to Kedin in return for Kedin's military achievements and technological innovations.

To complicate matters further, Kedin's influence extended over domains that were not included in the Duchy of Jerrissar: Tevana held lands in her own right, as to a lesser extent did a handful of aristocrats who were Kedin's allies.

This patchwork of estates, from the largest, which contained an inland sea, to the smallest, which was no more than a town and the hill it stood on, constituted the bastions from which the onslaught on Gonfallon would be launched. Most of the territories were, like Gonfallon itself, in the planet's central continent. Some of Kedin's holdings were, in fact, within the Duchy of Gonfallon, and were held by him as fiefs from Vethran; the remainder were dotted around and threaded between the sprawling lands which Vethran had accumulated for himself.

In theory, since Vethran had proclaimed himself King, all lands in all three continents belonged to him and were held by others entirely at his pleasure; in practice Vethran still relied on the ancient families to administer those lands which he did not directly rule.

The estates of Kedin Ashar – even the province of Harran, whose highly productive prairies stretched like a golden carpet into the heart of Gonfallon – were particularly safe from Vethran's acquisitive nature. Kedin and Vethran, Jerrissar and Gonfallon, were dependent on each other. Each was the other's most valuable trading partner. And Kedin's troops were a match for Vethran's.

Therefore, although the overthrow of Vethran would be carried out by shock troops arriving directly from the space station, the attack would begin on land: a multiplicity of pincer movements, emerging from Kedin's domains and striking into Gonfallon.

Madok was bringing the order of battle to the commander of Kedin's household troops.

Jerrissar – the province, rather than the entire duchy on which its name had been conferred – was one of Kedin's earliest territorial acquisitions. He had bought it, cheaply, from the old Count of Larriman, who had considered Jerrissar the least valuable of his lands, and who had then lived long enough to see Kedin and Tevana transform the province's lower slopes into fertile terraces growing profitable crops of silk, tea and spore-seed.

Kedin's motives in buying Jerrissar had not been entirely economic, however: the province straddled the equator, and provided Kedin with a domain that lay adjacent to Gonfallon and midway between his northern and southern estates. And while Jerrissar's lower slopes could be made productive, the mountainous hinterland had the advantage of being impregnable.

On his infrequent visits to his least favourite domain, the Count of Larriman used to stay in the palace in Jerris, the province's only large town. Kedin had other plans. He used explosives to blast a new road from Jerris into the mountains, and he appointed masons and engineers to rebuild and modernise the ruined fortress known as the Bridge.

Jerrissar was a province with its back to the sea. At its front, the mountains – often snow-capped despite their latitude – sloped relatively gently, down to Jerris and the fertile terraces, and then down again to the Tavent, the river that separated the province from Gonfallon. On the other side of the province, the mountains dropped precipitously, in vertical curtains of stone, to a narrow coastal strip. Here the inhabitants of a dozen villages, strung along the shore, made their living from fishing and remained almost unaware that they were part of Jerrissar. Only one track wound back and forth from this coast, up the steep cliffs, into the mountains and through a narrow defile between the highest peaks in the range.

From this pass the track continued, down slopes that were gentle only by comparison to those on the seaward side, to Jerris.

And at the highest point, on the levelled peaks of the twin spires of rock that formed the pass, in centuries past a lord of Jerrissar had built two fortresses. His successor, anxious to outdo his father's monumental work of building, had had a wide stone bridge constructed to link the two forts. Hundreds of labourers, it was said, fell to their deaths on the road below during the building of the bridge. The newly-unified fortification took its name from its most notable feature. It proved costly to maintain and was abandoned within five years of being completed.

The Bridge was now Kedin's communications centre. The new road, guarded by five strategically-placed forts between the Bridge and Jerris, provided rapid access by land to the main commercial route alongside the Tavent, and to Gonfallon. A funicular railway transported goods, vehicles and passengers in fifteen minutes from the Bridge to the coast, where one of the fishing villages had been developed into a deep-water port.

Madok had first visited the Bridge while the improvements were being made, and he had been back several times since. The first sight of the fortification never failed to leave him speechless, however.

The vehicle – a six-wheeled, self-propelled vehicle with a goods container behind the cabin – had grumbled and roared up the new road. It was all uphill work, twisting back and forth up the breast of the mountains. The sun had sunk behind the summits, and the road was in deep shadow. At each of the steepest points the vehicle would struggle up to a peak, and there Madok would find himself staring into the mouths of the big guns squatting in one of the defensive forts. The higher the self-propelled vehicle crept, the taller and more vertiginous the surrounding mountains became. From time to time, as the driver hauled the vehicle round another hairpin bend, Madok was granted a view back down the mountainside: the green terraces, gilded by the slanting rays of the setting sun, seemed impossibly small and far away.

And yet, as Madok knew, none of these sights, spectacular

though they were, would diminish the effect of his first view of the Bridge. Madok found himself leaning forward and peering upwards expectantly.

'Round the next bend, sir,' the driver said.

'Thanks.' Madok laughed. 'I suppose you get used to seeing it.'

'Not really, sir,' the driver said. 'It always looks unnatural. I've heard,' he added, 'that we'll be going into action soon.'

'You know I can't talk about operational plans,' Madok said. 'I think we're all tired of waiting. And – great heavens, there it is.'

The self-propelled vehicle had turned a sharp corner, and the road ran straight ahead between sheer cliffs. Ruddy light poured through the gap, even though the sun itself had dropped out of sight. At the point where the road disappeared over the brow of the slope, the cliffs were tallest – thirty metres or more above the road – and it was there that the Bridge connected the two peaks. Its straight edges and rectangular shape looked incongruous against the wild, jagged imprecision of the rocks. It was as if a giant had rested a book across the two mountains.

The arches on which the Bridge rested appeared too delicate to support such a solid structure, yet Madok knew that it was built of many stone blocks, each the height of a man. It was wide enough for an army to march across, and two stories high. Lurking in its strongpoints were the heaviest guns ever cast. Never had a road been so well guarded.

The self-propelled vehicle laboured up the slope and under the Bridge. Madok shivered: he hoped he would never find himself attempting to attack this fortress. From the road, little could be seen of the two mountaintop castles which were joined by the Bridge; only apparently natural fissures in the cliffs hinted at the tunnels, reservoirs, store rooms, gun emplacements and secret passages which honeycombed the mountains on which the fortress squatted.

Having passed under the glowering gaze of the Bridge, the self-propelled vehicle began to descend. Madok saw the ocean: far below, and stretching to the horizon, where the red ball of the sun was melting into the fiery water. The road became no more than a bumpy track, and as ever Madok was alarmed to be reminded of the angle at which it sloped down the face of the mountain range. The self-propelled vehicle didn't follow the road, however: the driver pulled the vehicle to the left, on to an even rougher path, and began the final, winding, uphill section of the journey to the almost inaccessible heart of Kedin's domains.

The Castlain was waiting in the outer bailey. Credig was as Madok remembered him: a little more grizzled now, perhaps, and a little more leathery, but as tall and upright as ever.

'Madok,' he said as Madok jumped from the cabin of the self-propelled vehicle. 'Saw your vehicle from the bridge. Knew it had to be you. Good trip?'

Madok took Credig's hand. The old soldier's voice was more welcoming than his face, which remained grimly unsmiling. 'I had no trouble, Castlain,' Madok said. He looked around at the massive walls, and up to the concentric rings of towers. Only the whistling wind and the circling lizardwings gave any hint that the vast courtyard was perched on the flattened peak of the highest mountain in Jerrissar. 'It's been a while since I've been here.'

'What have you brought for us?' Credig asked. Madok remembered that Credig was a man of little conversation.

Madok gestured towards the back of the self-propelled vehicle. 'New radio equipment,' he said. 'A more powerful transmitter, and more receivers.'

Credig grunted interrogatively.

'We've learnt how to use the space station to relay signals,' Madok explained. 'Don't ask me how it works – it's not my area of expertise. But with this transmitter you'll be able to bounce signals off the station and then down to any of our receivers – anywhere on the planet. It will give us ten times the reach you've had from up here. The King has nothing like this.'

Credig nodded, and raised an eyebrow. For Credig, this was an unrestrained expression of amazement. 'I imagine we'll soon be needing every advantage we can muster,' he said.

Madok led him a little further from the self-propelled vehicle, out of the driver's hearing. 'All forces are to be made ready,' he said quietly. 'We have to get the transmitter set up as soon as possible. The order to begin the operation could come within days. I have the precise plans here.' He tapped the side of his head. 'As well as the codes and frequencies to be used for communications, and the schedule for changing them.'

'Good.' The barest hint of a smile touched Credig's lips. 'I'll be glad to see some action at last. We need to cleanse Vethran's filth from the world.'

Madok could only agree. 'I was at court a week ago,' he said. 'In the capital. He's going to have himself declared Emperor. There are Twos everywhere. It's all got to be stopped.' Once again Ace's face appeared in his thoughts, and as ever he fought against imagining the life she could be living now.

He took Credig to the back of the self-propelled vehicle and pointed out four of the boxes. 'Are the rockets ready?' he asked. The mountains around the Bridge concealed deep pits from which six rockets, not unlike the one which had first reached the space station, could be launched at targets anywhere on the continent.

'Of course,' Credig said.

'The boxes contain new components for the warheads,'

Madok said. 'There is still much we don't understand about the space station, but we're sure we can use our own radio signals from the station to control the flight of rockets launched from here. At last we should be able to target the warheads accurately.'

Credig nodded. He was clearly impressed. 'Never did see the point of rockets,' he said. 'Send them up. No idea where'll they come down. This is much better.' He grunted. 'Getting old,' he said. 'These days soldiering's all about rockets and electricity. Used to be hot blood and cold steel.'

'If things go badly,' Madok said, 'there'll be plenty of old-fashioned slaughter.'

Credig's eyes brightened. The thought of battle must have reminded him of food, as he next asked Madok if he had eaten dinner. 'Come in,' he said. 'Freshen up. Come to the mess. I'll send out a team to unload your vehicle.'

Madok shook his head. 'Thank you, Castlain. But I can't rest until the transmitter's set up and tested. It's already getting dark. I'll pass the plans on to you, and then I'll have to be on my way again.'

'Tevana Roslod?' Credig asked.

Madok nodded. 'And then we can make our move.'

Credig turned towards the self-propelled vehicle. 'Driver,' he shouted, 'go to the lower barracks and get some help to unload. Then have this vehicle refuelled and made ready to leave.'

The driver saluted. 'Yes, sir,' he said, and ran across the courtyard to the inner gateway.

'You have a –' Credig lifted a hand into the air, 'a flying machine of some kind?' he said.

'A scout from the station,' Madok said. 'I landed at the northern strip. I have room for five,' he added. 'I think it would be wise to take some men with me. Can you spare me four of your best? They must be utterly trustworthy.'

'Of course, Madok,' the Castlain said. 'Now let's get this transmitter set up. You're going to set off in the dark?'

Madok looked about him. Only the highest towers of the castle were still golden in sunlight. The courtyard was in deep shade. He knew that lights could be fitted to the self-propelled vehicle, but the drive down the road to Jerris would nonetheless be perilous. And there were no lights at the landing strip: he'd have to take the scout ship up in complete darkness. And land again before dawn.

'Damnation,' he said. 'No, Credig, I'll have to stay overnight. No doubt the rest will do me good. I'll leave at daybreak.'

Bep-Wor had never thought that he would find himself arguing with the Doctor. They spoke in urgent whispers as the line of prisoners shuffled forwards to receive their meals.

'Please try to understand,' the Doctor said. 'It's imperative that I reach the capital. That must be the centre of government on this world. There I will be able to negotiate with people in authority. I might find a way to put a stop to all this.' He waved his arm in the direction of the prisoners. 'The commissioner is going to the capital. I must let him take me there.'

'And I must find Kia-Ga,' Bep-Wor replied. 'The farmer sold her only a few days ago. Perhaps only yesterday. She can't be far away. There are tools in this barn. We can break our chains. We can make the farmer tell us where she is.'

'In order to do that, Bep-Wor, we will have to reveal that most of these people are free of the effects of the drug. Do you think that the commissioner will just shrug his shoulders and forget about you? Of course not. He'll bring more soldiers. He'll hunt you down.'

Bep-Wor could not believe the words he was hearing. The Doctor seemed to want to remain a captive, and to keep all the

149

prisoners captive with him. 'I'll take that chance,' he said. 'I'd rather be free and hunted than taken in chains to the capital. Who knows what will happen to us in a big town? We might be separated, or shut up in prisons. We may never get another chance to free ourselves. If we escape now, we can all remain together. We will take the soldiers' swords and guns. We will have you to lead us. We will have some hope.'

'If I don't go to the capital,' the Doctor said, 'I may never find out where Ace is.'

'And if I don't free myself now,' Bep-Wor replied, 'I will never find out where Kia-Ga is.'

The two men had run out of words. They glared at each other. Bep-Wor realised he was shaking with emotion. He felt sick. He and the Doctor had travelled together across the gulf between two worlds. He had thought that they had a common purpose – a shared destiny. Suddenly he was aware that the Doctor's motives were utterly different from his own. He felt foolish and betrayed.

The women were handing out half-loaves to the last few prisoners. All over the barn men and women who had devoured their meals were holding whispered conversations, or trying to loosen their shackles. They were dressed in rags; they were dirty; they were tired. And yet Bep-Wor knew that they were no longer the confused, beaten, hopeless rabble they had been when crammed into the deathly cold of the cargo pod. He heard it in their voices, and saw it in their faces: a pride in having survived, and a determination to continue surviving. Where the commissioner and his soldiers saw mindless slaves, Bep-Wor saw a small army. An army that would rather fight to be free than live as slaves.

The Doctor had made the difference. He had given Bep-Wor's people hope. How could he think of abandoning them now?

Bep-Wor held his head in his hands. I'm a farmer, he said to himself. I help out on the fishing boats. I know about soil and seeds, wind and waves. And here I am on another world, where even the plants look different, responsible for 150 of my fellow countrymen, on a hopeless quest to find Kia-Ga. It's too much. I can't be expected to do this.

He looked down at the chain hanging between his wrists.

There really was no point in giving up. He had to keep fighting, or end his life as a slave.

Think, Bep-Wor, he told himself. Think clearly.

He marshalled his thoughts. The starting point was that he would no longer remain a prisoner. He and all of the captives must be freed. He might have been prepared to continue the pretence of being drugged, but the knowledge that Kia-Ga was nearby changed everything.

He wanted the Doctor to go with him. The Doctor inspired the group; he had wondrous powers and knowledge; above all – although Bep-Wor had never before dared to speculate about this – he might be able to reverse the effects of the drug, and restore Kia-Ga. He had, after all, brought Hap-Lor back from the dead.

Freedom and Kia-Ga were Bep-Wor's objectives. Freedom and Kia-Ga might prove unattainable, or only partially attainable, without the Doctor's help. But to follow the Doctor, away from Kia-Ga and into certain slavery, would gain nothing that Bep-Wor wanted. Nor would it help the 150 men and women who also had wives and husbands to find.

The way forward was clear. Bep-Wor had his hand on the tiller, and he knew the heading he had to steer.

'Doctor,' he said. 'Listen to me. If we proceed, as slaves, to the capital, we may lose our only chance to be free. And I will lose my only chance to find Kia-Ga. If we free ourselves now, you will still be able to go to the capital and look for your friend Ace.'

The Doctor began to speak, but Bep-Wor hushed him.

'I'm going to break free,' Bep-Wor said. 'I'll ask the others: any who wish to can come with me. If you decide to stay, I think many will choose to stay with you.'

The Doctor rubbed a hand over his face. 'You're serious, aren't you?' he said.

I don't know, Bep-Wor thought. But this is the only way I can think of to persuade you to come with me.

He nodded. 'Deadly serious.'

'You'll split the group, and go without me?'

Bep-Wor nodded again.

The Doctor sighed. 'I can't let that happen, Bep-Wor. All right, I'll come with you. As long as everyone agrees. I won't leave anyone behind. And as long as you agree that once we've found Kia-Ga we'll head towards the capital.'

Bep-Wor could have shouted for joy. 'Thank you, Doctor. I'm sure this will be for the best. And once they know that you are leading us, all the people will follow you.'

The Doctor was about to speak again, but Bep-Wor pointed over his shoulder.

'The women from the farmhouse,' he said. 'Look: they're getting ready to leave. We must keep them here.'

The Doctor looked puzzled.

'They've heard us talking,' Bep-Wor explained. 'If they're asked, they'll tell what they've heard. Tell them to stay here.'

The Doctor turned. 'Sab-Ma,' he called out. 'And you others. Come here, please.'

The five women abandoned the empty cauldron and baskets and, with blank faces, walked the few paces to the Doctor. Bep-Wor stepped outside the barn for an instant. 'All clear,' he said. 'I'll tell our comrades to start breaking out of their chains.'

He set off into the depths of the barn to find heavy tools and the strongest of the prisoners. Two of them, he knew, had been metal-workers in Porgum. Behind him he heard the Doctor telling the women that they must not return to the farmhouse, and five voices saying, 'Yes, sir,' in reply.

When Bep-Wor returned to the front of the barn the Doctor was still talking to the women.

'It's very strange,' he was saying. His hat was tilted on his head and he was scratching his scalp. Bep-Wor realised that he was talking to himself more than to the women, who were standing in a row and gazing at him. 'It's as if an entire level of consciousness has been eroded from the hypothalamus. They think, but are they aware of their awareness of their thinking? Are they even aware that they think?'

The Doctor turned as Bep-Wor approached. Bep-Wor held up his arms to show that the manacles had gone from his wrists.

The Doctor grinned. 'I suppose I'd better slip out of these again,' he said, performing a little dance to jangle the chains at his wrists and ankles. 'You're right, Bep-Wor. Life's better without chains.'

He indicated the row of women. 'I thought,' he said, 'that perhaps I could counteract the effects of the drug by making use of the absolute obedience that it seems to instil in its victims. I've been trying to find a way to instruct these poor women to think for themselves.'

'What do you mean?' Bep-Wor asked.

'I'll demonstrate,' the Doctor said, 'but I don't think I'm getting anywhere.' He addressed the women. 'I order you to do whatever you like,' he said.

The women's faces showed that they were struggling to understand. One of them, having reached a decision, began to comb her hair with her fingers. Another began to eat the piece of bread she was holding in her hand. A third started to rummage under her clothing.

'Stop!' Bep-Wor said quickly. 'Doctor,' he explained, 'they are doing things that they like doing, not things that they have chosen to do.'

'Yes, I see,' the Doctor said. 'Pity. I thought I'd cracked it. It's volition that is still missing. Let's try something else.' He turned again to the women. 'You are free,' he said. 'You no longer have to obey any orders.'

The women did nothing. They stood, slack-jawed and slump-shouldered, before the Doctor.

Bep-Wor stepped in. 'The Doctor is your master,' he told the women. 'You must do as he says. Follow the Doctor, and be glad. He will lead us all to freedom.'

At these words some animation returned to the faces of the women. They smiled at the Doctor, and looked at him expectantly.

'I'm not –' he began, and then tutted with irritation. 'Oh, go and help the others remove their chains,' he said, waving into the depths of the barn.

'Yes, sir,' the women chorused, and with smiles on their faces they scampered away.

'They're not free,' the Doctor said to Bep-Wor.

'No,' Bep-Wor replied, 'but they're happy enough. Sometimes it isn't easy to tell the ones who are free from the ones who have had the drug, when they're busy with something.' He looked back into the barn. 'The two smiths are getting on well with breaking the chains. We'll be ready to leave soon.'

The Doctor peered out of the barn. 'It's very dark,' he said. 'We'll let everyone get some sleep, and leave at dawn.' His face was illuminated by a sudden thought. 'How will you know where to go?'

Bep-Wor held up the hammer he was holding. 'I'll take a few of the men and we'll ask the farmer where Kia-Ga is.'

'No violence, Bep-Wor,' the Doctor said. 'There's no

justification for revenge.' Another thought struck him. 'The farmer, the commissioner and the guards are all in the farmhouse,' he said. 'They'll know we've escaped, and they'll raise the alarm. You'll have to restrain them.'

'Don't worry, Doctor,' Bep-Wor said. 'We've plenty of spare chains. I'll take a few men and we'll tackle the farmer, the commissioner and the guards at daybreak.' There was no hurry: better to give the soldiers time to get helplessly drunk on the farmer's brandy.

The atmosphere inside the scout ship was bearable, given that there were five men crammed in the cabin and that one of them had been sick. Madok presumed that among the many automatic systems that Kedin's technicians had yet to understand there was one that filtered the air.

Madok was flying high, above the clouds. He didn't want the ship to be seen. The four troopers with him had never flown before: whenever he looked over his shoulder they were still staring, open-mouthed and pale-faced, at the sunlit banks of cloud below them and at the miniature landscapes visible through the gaps.

'Sir,' one of them said, in a hesitant voice, 'may I ask a question?'

Madok smiled. He had wondered whether any of the troopers would have both the intelligence to calculate the direction of the flight and the nerve to question an officer. 'Go on, soldier,' he said.

'Well, sir,' the trooper said, 'from the position of the sun I think we've been travelling to the south of due west. Shouldn't we be flying to the north?'

'Well spotted,' Madok said. 'I'm taking a detour. I'm going to call at the main landing site – the one the transports use. The one we let the King know about.'

The silence from the back of the cabin was as eloquent as any criticism. The troopers knew the purpose of Madok's mission; they knew the need for speed and secrecy.

Madok couldn't deny that their unspoken disapproval was justified. The detour to the landing site would not take long, but any delay was unwarranted. And unlike the troopers Madok knew that there were usually a few soldiers, either from one of the King's regiments or hired by the King's commissioner, policing the landing site: landing the scout ship there could hardly fail to be noticed, and might entail some risk.

Nonetheless, Madok clung to his course. Kedin had not instructed Madok to make the detour, but he had given Madok considerable discretion to act on his initiative. And Madok was sure that Kedin would understand.

'Don't worry, men,' Madok said over his shoulder. He directed the ship down, into and through the clouds. 'This won't take long.'

Just long enough, Madok thought, for me to find a trader who remembers Ace, and who can tell me who bought her.

Breathing heavily, Bep-Wor rested his back against the wall of the barn. Gathered in a circle around him, their faces ghostly in the pale light of dawn, were the men he'd taken with him to the farmhouse and the Twos – three men – they had found there and freed.

When he leant his head against the wall, he heard from the other side of it the voice of the Doctor, organizing the men and women into groups in preparation for leaving.

Bep-Wor straightened his body. This was no time to show weakness. He hoped his face did not reveal the shock and doubt he saw in those around him. When the soldiers from this world invaded his, he reasoned, they had shown no mercy.

156

They were the enemy, and sometimes it would be necessary to fight them with their own weapons.

'Clean those swords,' he said, pointing to the blades hanging from the trembling hands of four of the men. He tore a strip from his clothing and used it to wipe the blood off the hammer he was carrying.

'We did what we had to,' he said. 'There is no reason to feel guilty.' Somehow, he managed to smile. 'You did well,' he said. 'I'm proud of you.'

He saw the men around him nod their heads. They visibly relaxed, and smiled grimly at each other. Even the Twos from the farm, who were under the influence of the drug, had animated expressions.

Bep-Wor forced himself to remember all the details of the brief struggle in the farmhouse. The surprise and outrage on the faces, fixed there by sudden death. The soldiers, barely sober enough to comprehend what was happening to them. Making the farmer tell him where Kia-Ga had been sold, and where the money was kept.

It had been easy. And now, as he went over it again, Bep-Wor felt surprisingly little remorse. He had never previously killed anything larger than a fish.

He beckoned the group to come closer to him. 'You all know that the Doctor will lead us to freedom,' he whispered. 'But he is a man of ideas, not actions. We have to act for him. And sometimes, like tonight, we have to do things that he would not like to hear about. So don't let him know what we've done. He will be happier if he thinks we left the farmer and the soldiers bound in chains. Do you all understand?'

Everyone around him nodded.

'Good,' Bep-Wor said. 'Keep the guns hidden until we have to use them.' He pushed himself away from the wall, shouldered his hammer, and strode round the corner of the barn.

'Doctor!' he called out. 'Is everyone ready to leave? We've loaded a cart with food.'

The Doctor emerged out of the gloomy interior of the barn. For a moment Bep-Wor was unnerved by the searching light in the Doctor's eyes. 'Well done,' the Doctor said.

Bep-Wor refused to answer the Doctor's unspoken question. 'I've found some money, too,' he said. 'And we took the soldiers' uniforms. We can make ourselves look like a group of prisoners being led by guards, and with the money we can buy provisions if we need to.'

'Theft,' the Doctor said, making a face as though the word tasted in his mouth like a sour fruit.

'Survival,' Bep-Wor countered. 'And,' he continued, changing the subject, 'the farmer told me that Kia-Ga is close: he sold her to the next farm to the north. Lead your army northward, Doctor.'

'Army?'

'Your followers, Doctor. Your host of freed Twos. We will go where you lead us.'

The scout ship howled and shuddered as Madok cut the thrusters and raised the air-baffles. He had hurled the small craft through the sky from the landing site, and in his anger and impatience he had almost overshot his destination.

Balon Ferud had bought Ace. His chamberlain had won the auction with the highest price ever paid for a Two. The only satisfaction to be had was that Ace's value had been recognised, and that Balon had had to pay dearly for her.

Everything else Madok had been able to learn was worrying. He had been hoping that Ace would have been bought by a farmer, or the owner of a mine or a plantation: then it would have been a simple operation, a quick and clean attack with a few of Kedin's men, and Ace would have been free. But Balon had a number of residences, and none of the traders had known which of them Balon's chamberlain had taken Ace to. Balon had only a small retinue of household troops, but they were well trained and well armed: even if Madok had known where to strike, he couldn't have risked doing so. Not now, at this critical moment.

As he pushed the scout ship to its limits Madok had to admit that it would be impossible to rescue Ace before Kedin began to move against Vethran. He would have to leave Ace in the hands of the odious Balon Ferud. The situation could hardly be worse: only the Citadel itself would be more difficult to extract Ace from.

'What's happening?' one of the troopers said. He sounded as though his teeth were chattering.

'This is more exciting than guard duty on the Bridge!' Madok shouted above the roar of the wind. 'We've arrived over County Cathogh. The castle's below us. We've made up some time,' he added, although the troopers could hardly have failed to notice that the scout ship had been screaming through the air since Madok took off from the landing site. 'It's still early morning here.'

On his previous visits Madok had brought his ship down in the neighbouring manor, which belonged to an ally of Kedin, and had made his way to Cathogh by camelope. He had keys to the postern gates of the castle: the guards knew he was there only if he wanted them to.

Now there was no time for subtlety and subterfuge. He would bring the scout ship down in the castle park. On his previous visits there had been no more than six guards in the castle: most of the squadron was garrisoned in the town, below the castle walls. He and his four men would be in and out before the main body of Vethran's guards could react.

'Weapons ready?' Madok said, as he banked the ship around

the topmost turrets of Castle Cathogh. 'Remember: shoot anyone who tries to stop us. I want a volunteer to stay with the ship, and –'

'Sir!' Madok's instructions were cut off by the excited shout of the trooper sitting behind him. 'Down there, sir. Look. Camelopes and carriages.'

Madok swore. The inner courtyard of the castle was swarming with cavalry steeds. The entire squadron, he realised, was inside the castle walls. As the scout ship swooped over the battlements, Madok saw cavalrymen in the King's livery emerge from doorways and point skywards as they tried to calm their mounts. He cursed again. He would be unable to take the castle in a direct attack, no matter that the guards wouldn't be expecting a flying machine to land in the gardens: his force was five men, and the defenders were twenty times as numerous. And now that he had flown over the heads of the cavalrymen there would be no point in landing at a distance, as he was wont to do, and proceeding by stealth and on foot: the King's men knew that only Kedin had such machines, and they would be ready for any attempted infiltration of the castle.

'Stow your guns,' Madok told the troopers. 'We can't fight our way in against that lot. Swords only, and keep them sheathed unless I give the word. I'm going to land in the park, as planned. The story is that I'm simply on a visit from Kedin Ashar. You're my personal guards. We'll improvise once we're inside. But be aware that we'll probably have to abort the mission. And don't eat or drink anything.'

By the time the scout ship rolled to a halt on the flat sward at the rear of the castle, two dozen of the King's men were in position on the terrace above. They were armed only with muskets, but at such short range, Madok knew, the old-fashioned guns would be deadly.

He slid open the outer door and emerged with his hands empty and raised. The troopers followed him.

Madok didn't expect to be gunned down as he ascended the wide stone stairs that led up to the terrace, but it was nevertheless unnerving to know that he was in the sights of twenty muskets. He was relieved when he saw an officer step through the wide doorway from the castle.

'Is that Madok?' the officer called.

'The same,' Madok replied. He reached the top step and held out his hand. 'How are you, Kaped?' He couldn't remember having met the officer, but he knew the name of the commander of the squadron on duty at Cathogh Castle.

'Well enough,' the officer said. He peered at Madok's uniform. 'No badges of rank, eh? What are you these days, Madok? Captain? Major?'

Madok ignored the subtle insult. 'I'm here as the special emissary of the Duke of Jerrissar,' he said. 'A civilian mission. It's a private matter between Kedin Ashar and Tevana Roslod. And it's urgent. I apologise for my haste, but may I see her?'

Kaped smiled, in a way that Madok found unsettling. 'Of course,' he said. He looked over Madok's shoulder. 'Your men will have to remain in our barracks, however.'

Madok raised a hand. 'I'm happy to carry out my commission alone,' he said, 'but if my men can't be with me I'd prefer them to stay with my flying machine. It's a prototype. Very fragile.'

Madok watched Kaped's face as the officer considered his reply. He would want to have Madok's troopers mixing with his own men: he wouldn't dare use SS10, but a milder formula, or even a few glasses of wine, might be enough to loosen the troopers' tongues. And while the scout ship was untended Kaped could search it, or boobytrap it.

On the other hand, Kedin Ashar was the King's premier subject: still the most important person on the planet, after

161

Vethran himself, despite his long absence from court. It wouldn't do to antagonise Kedin's special emissary.

'Of course, Madok,' Kaped said. 'As you wish. I'll have refreshments brought out to them.'

'Thank you, commander,' Madok said, as he waved his troopers back down the stairs, 'but we have provisions on board. Please tell your men to stay well clear of the flying machine. Now, may I see Tevana?'

Kaped's smile remained fixed on his face. 'Follow me,' he said.

When seen from a distance, Cathogh Castle appeared unchanged since the days of spears and crossbows. Its walls of reddish stone were pierced by arrow-slits and surmounted by battlements; its towers were tall and cylindrical, not having been lowered and reshaped as defence against artillery.

A closer view revealed that the curtain walls had long been demolished, so that the castle's park and gardens stretched in uninterrupted vistas right up to the moat, which served now as a decorative lake. Terraces and conservatories had been built against the lower floors of the once-forbidding walls, and new windows now allowed light into the ancient halls within.

Inside the castle any lingering thoughts of the structure's martial origins were finally dispelled. It had been used as the principal residence of the Counts of Cathogh for three generations, and therefore its internal architecture was entirely domestic. When Tevana Roslod had acquired Cathogh she had set about modernizing the castle, so that as Madok followed Kaped across brightly tiled hallways and up whitewood stairs he found, as usual when he came to Cathogh, that the palace within made him forget the castle outside.

Madok noted that the ceramic floors, the glass canopies and the brass lamps were not smirched by so much as a mote of dust. Servants were busy everywhere, and each one greeted Madok with a quick bow and a friendly smile. Madok was reassured: Tevana clearly still had income enough to maintain her household; her servants were still the loyal Cathogh staff she had inherited with the castle; and she had not been obliged, for reasons of economy or because of pressure from Vethran, to keep any Twos.

The billeting of the King's cavalry in Cathogh town had not prevented Tevana from managing her estates: although she was not permitted to leave the castle, she was able to receive her stewards and send out messengers. And, although Kaped attended each of Tevana's audiences and read all of her letters, he knew nothing of the secret communications carried by Madok on his covert visits to Cathogh. Despite being confined to her residence Tevana had been able to keep herself informed of the political and military situation; she had even been able to offer suggestions about analysing the formula of SS10.

Things had not changed, apparently, since the last time Madok had been at Cathogh: the restraints on Tevana had not been made any stricter. Still, he wondered why the entire cavalry squadron had come up to the castle. Was it possible that the King's councillors had had warning of Madok's mission? If so, there was a spy in Kedin's staff.

He had to see Tevana.

Kaped stopped in front of the doors to Tevana's apartments. It irritated Madok to see that two cavalrymen were standing on guard, as if Tevana were a common prisoner. Kaped knocked, and spoke briefly to the woman who opened the door.

Then the doors were thrown back, and Kaped and Madok walked in. Madok looked towards the top of the curving stairway, where he expected to see Tevana emerge from her bedroom. Instead her voice came from the drawing room on Madok's left.

'Madok. What a lovely surprise.'

Madok turned. Although the sun was barely over the horizon Tevana was dressed in working clothes: a linen dress and an apron. Curls of blond hair were escaping from the scarf wrapped round her head. Madok formed the impression that she had been up for some time, and had been busy at some task.

He bowed. 'My lady,' he said.

Neither time nor tribulation had altered her. Her face was still unlined; her smile was still as warm and uplifting as sunlight. Nonetheless, Madok thought that she looked concerned.

He indicated her apron. 'You are up early, Tevana,' he said. It would do no harm to let Kaped know that he and the Countess were on familiar terms.

Tevana averted her face. Madok was sure he had seen tears in her eyes. 'And you are late, Madok,' she said. 'Too late.'

Suddenly she was vivacious again. 'I'm leaving Cathogh,' she said with a laugh. 'I'm off to Gonfallon. Come into the drawing room, Madok, and I'll tell you all about it. We'll have one of our interesting tripartite conversations.'

For a moment Madok couldn't move. He became aware that his hand was clenched on the pommel of his sword, and that his guts had gone as cold as ice. For a moment he considered striking down Kaped and attempting to take Tevana to the scout ship. But he'd be unlikely to get past the guards at the doors, he realised, let alone the hundred other men between him and the ship.

He shook himself and followed Kaped and Tevana.

'Gonfallon, my lady,' he said, as if making conversation. 'Which province, may I ask?'

Tevana seated herself on a couch. Madok sat opposite her in a straight-backed chair. Kaped stood, like an over-attentive servant, between them.

'I'm going to the capital, Madok. To the Citadel itself, perhaps. I've been summoned by Vethran.'

Madok leant forward. Her eyes were bright. He could see fear in their depths.

'His Majesty has invited the Countess to reside in Gonfallon,' Kaped said, 'in view of the unsettling nature of the recent news. His only concern is her ladyship's safety.'

Madok looked searchingly at Tevana. He could see that she was as perplexed as he was by Kaped's reference to unsettling news.

'May I see the order?' Madok said. He hoped Kaped would have to have it fetched, and that he and Tevana could thereby snatch a moment of private conversation.

'I have it here,' Kaped said, producing a scroll from within his tunic. 'The Countess has perused it several times, as you can imagine, but by all means study it again.'

Madok took the document impatiently, checked its royal seal, and unrolled it. 'There can be no legal basis for this,' he said, scanning the dense text. 'What's this? "Under the provisions of the law relating to the disposition of lordless estates . . ." This is preposterous, Kaped. That law was approved by the council only after Vethran arrested and replaced two councillors. It's highly dubious. And it was intended to deal with lands left in the hands of children or idiots. In which category do you place Tevana Roslod?'

'The order is signed not only by the King himself,' Kaped pointed out, 'but also by the Ducal Attorney. It may be that a legal counter-argument could be made, but my instructions are clear. County Cathogh, and all of Tevana Roslod's lands, are now administered by the Council on behalf of the King. His Majesty has generously permitted the Countess to retain her title in respect of Cathogh and, now that she is landless, has furthermore offered her secure accommodation within his ducal domain. It's all in the order.'

'I can see that,' Madok said. He resisted the temptation to tear the document into fragments. 'You can fight this, Tevana,' he said.

Tevana shook her head. She looked sad rather than defeated. 'Possibly,' she said. 'But Vethran is very insistent that I leave Cathogh immediately. And once I'm in "secure accommodation" I doubt I'll have many opportunities for discussions with lawyers. Times are changing, Madok. Vethran's code of laws extends beyond Gonfallon now: every landowner must adhere to it. And Gonfallon law now denies property rights to unmarried women.' She laughed, briefly and with an edge of bitterness. 'Kedin and I agreed not to marry. After all, our parents would never have considered doing so. We thought it was a passing fashion, and that it would constrain us. It's ironic. If I had a husband now, my lands wouldn't be forfeit to the King.'

'Don't blame yourself,' Madok said. Blame me, he raged at himself; if I had arrived only an hour earlier I could have taken you away. 'If you had been married, Vethran would have found another pretext.' He noticed that the order carried a third signature. He pretended to study the text again, and concentrated on deciphering the spidery handwriting. The scrawled name was Pelod, he was sure of it: the castlain of Grake castle.

He brought his hand to his face to conceal his smile from Kaped. This was the first piece of good news he had had today. He now knew where Tevana would be incarcerated. And he knew that Grake, while notoriously difficult to escape from, was far from impregnable to an attack from outside. There was still hope.

He thrust the scroll towards Kaped. 'The document's in order,' he said, 'inasmuch as injustice is ever in order.' He glanced towards Tevana. She nodded: she had seen his smile, and she had understood.

166

'Commander,' Madok said to Kaped, 'I have come here in haste on a private mission from Kedin Ashar. The subject is a delicate one, and I am under instructions to speak to no one but Tevana Roslod. Would you leave us alone for a few minutes?'

Madok had no expectation that a direct request for privacy would prove effective, but there was no harm in asking.

Kaped shook his head. 'My instructions are also clear, sir. I and my men are here to protect her ladyship. His Majesty has the utmost concern for her safety, and I am to leave no one alone with her, other than the ladies of her chamber.'

Madok shrugged. 'Well, then, Tevana, we must talk of other matters.'

'Tell me, Madok,' Tevana said in a rush of words, 'how is Kedin?'

'He's well,' Madok said. 'He misses you, it's obvious, but he manages to remain cheerful. And resolute.' It occurred to him that he could tell Tevana about Ace, the strange girl who had appeared from nowhere and who understood the space station better than Kedin himself. But then, on reflection, he decided not to.

'Tell him I'm counting the days until I see him again,' Tevana said.

'I'm sure you won't have to count many,' Madok said, with a significant look. He was sure that once Kedin learnt that Tevana was imprisoned in Gonfallon, nothing would restrain him from launching the assault. 'Has his Majesty graced you with a visit recently?' he asked.

Tevana pulled a face. 'Not for a few weeks,' she said. 'I'm running out of ways to say no. He won't believe that I won't marry him. I'm sure he thinks I'm just haggling for a better offer. Apparently if I accept him now I'll be an empress.'

'He's still sending gifts?'

Tevana sighed with impatience. 'The cellar room I allocated is full now,' she said. 'The latest evidence of his devotion is piled up at the foot of the cellar stairs. He doesn't seem to notice, when he comes here, that I never wear the dresses and jewellery he's sent.'

Madok lowered his voice. 'He's obsessed with you, Tevana. Be careful.'

'I know. Sometimes I almost pity him.'

Kaped cleared his throat. 'Countess, we should be leaving soon. And I feel obliged to warn both of you to be cautious in your speech. The King disapproves of treasonous conversations.'

Madok looked up at Kaped. Madok's adult life had been spent as a soldier, and he found it hard to hold any fellow-officer in contempt. Hard, but not impossible. 'Tell me, Kaped,' he said, 'what is the unsettling news you spoke of earlier?'

'There are reports,' he said, 'that there was something wrong with the last consignment of Twos.'

'In what way?' This was worrying: if Vethran suspected that Kedin was double-crossing him, it was not surprising that he wanted Tevana closer to his seat of power.

Kaped shrugged. 'They were just a bit different, that's all I heard,' he said. 'The commissioner's bringing them all to the capital. So there's been a considerable loss of trade.'

Madok turned slowly to look at Tevana. She would be as troubled by this news as he was, and she would jump to the conclusion that the Twos had been given the new formula instead of SS10. Sure enough, she was frowning at him intensely. He mouthed the word 'No,' and turned his head slightly from side to side.

She understood, and like him she was even more perplexed. He widened his eyes and shrugged.

Things were moving fast: out of control. The Twos that had

168

been landed the previous day would be among the last to receive SS10. There was now sufficient of the new formula on the space station to dose all prisoners with it, and it would be used as soon as Kedin knew how long its effects would last. The slave trade was as good as over – although it would be some time before anyone realised it.

But it had been Twos dosed with SS10 who had behaved strangely, and had prompted Vethran to bring Tevana, his hostage for Kedin's good behaviour, closer to him.

Madok didn't understand. But he knew that Tevana's move from house arrest to prison would prompt Kedin to launch his assault.

Someone had lit the fuse, and in a way it didn't matter who had done it: within days the powder would explode.

'We will meet again, my lady,' Madok said. He stood up and saluted. 'Soon.'

169

Chapter Four

The trees here were so unlike those of his home world. Bep-Wor held a thin branch in his hand and studied it: a maze of brown, woody stems, from which green leaves sprouted. Nothing like the giant cycads he was used to, which blocked the sun's rays and made slabs of black shadow on the soil. These small leaves scattered the sunlight.

He used his hand to shield his eyes as he peered between the trunks of the trees. The men he had posted as sentries at the edge of the spinney were still in position. The rest of the group was sitting and lying under the trees. The Doctor – where was the Doctor?

Bep-Wor found the Doctor pacing back and forth at the edge of the woods.

'Come further in, Doctor,' he called. 'You can be seen out there.'

The Doctor scrambled across a barrier of thorns. 'We should move on, Bep-Wor,' he said, tugging his trouser legs free. 'We found a stream for everyone to wash in. We found a place to stop and eat. Now we've found the farm. Let's proceed.'

Bep-Wor led the Doctor to a gap between the trees, through which they had a view of the farmhouse, nestling in the valley below them, surrounded by barns and other outbuildings. 'I can tell you're not a farmer,' Bep-Wor said. 'Look, Doctor: the farm itself is deserted. There may be a few workers in the kitchen or the livestock sheds, but on a fine day such as this almost everyone will be out in the fields. You can see them: there, and there. And earlier I saw a party going over the brow of that hill.'

This was the largest farm Bep-Wor had ever seen. As far as he could tell, all the land between the hills on the horizon and the wooded hill on which he stood was part of one estate. All around the farm buildings the countryside had been divided into a patchwork of fields: some contained grazing animals, some were rippling with growing crops, and others were recently ploughed.

'The sun is descending,' Bep-Wor pointed out. 'Summer days are short on this world. We'll see the workers return from the fields. Then we'll go down to the farm.'

'Very well,' the Doctor agreed. 'I suppose there's not much point in making a social call while no one's at home. Are you going to wear that uniform? You're not exactly up to parade-ground standard, you know.'

Bep-Wor stroked his chin as he looked down at the uniform he was wearing. He hadn't shaved for almost a week, and his stubble was becoming a beard. The tunic was too big for him, and the trousers were too short: the soldier he'd stripped had been stocky.

'No one would take me for a native anyway,' he said. 'As soon as I speak I'll betray myself as a Two. You'll have to do the talking, Doctor. You're good at that.'

Later, as the last long shadows merged into a chill dusk, the Doctor and Bep-Wor led the escaped prisoners out of the wood, down the hillside and towards the farm buildings, where windows were yellow with lamplight.

The farm buildings were arranged in a square around a courtyard, the entrance to which was between two high, wooden barns. The main house stood on the opposite side of the square: light and the noise of conversations spilled from the windows.

Bep-Wor stopped at the entrance. He looked over his shoulder and saw nothing but rows of anxious, eager faces. He held up one hand. His army was stationary and silent.

'Go on, then, Doctor,' Bep-Wor said. 'Try to get Kia-Ga out of there. If you can buy food as well, so much the better. And if you need help, we'll come running.'

The Doctor smiled. 'Don't worry, Bep-Wor,' he said. 'I think you'll find I can conduct a simple negotiation without any difficulty.'

He had taken only three steps into the courtyard when a shout went up from the upper floor of the barn on the left of the entrance.

'Farmer! Farmer Bretod!' It was a young man's voice. 'There's a crowd of Twos here. Standing outside the gate.'

The conversations in the farmhouse were suddenly hushed. The central door was flung open. The silhouette of a large man filled the doorway. He hitched up his trousers.

'What's that?' he shouted. 'Namtol, was that you calling? Twos, you say? At the gate? Are they ours? Ah, I see them.'

The Doctor stepped forward. 'Good evening,' he said. 'Farmer Bretod, is it? Pleased to meet you. I'm sorry to trouble you, but I was wondering –'

The farmer gave the Doctor one puzzled glance and then ignored him.

'You Twos,' he shouted. 'Get away from here. Go back to your shed. Brainless idiots.'

Bep-Wor clenched his fists. He heard a hiss, a collective indrawing of breath, from the men and women behind him. He raised his hand to quieten them, but they pressed forward, so that Bep-Wor and others were pushed into the square.

The farmer looked puzzled. He stepped backwards. 'Holred! Conbal! Come out here. And bring me my shotgun. Something's amiss with these Twos.'

'They're not ours, Bretod,' shouted Namtol from the barn. Other voices were calling from inside the house. Behind Bep-Wor the escaped prisoners were continuing to press forward

173

into the courtyard, and were shouting to each other. The enclosed square was filling with people and noise.

Farmer Bretod was once again in the doorway of his house. 'Only one thing these Twos understand,' he said, and turned to face the crowd. Now he held a long-barrelled gun in his right hand. He stepped forward and began to lift it.

The Doctor stood in front of him. 'There's no need for that,' he said. 'We don't want to trouble you. We're looking for a woman named Kia-Ga.'

'Doctor! Doctor! Doctor!' the escaped prisoners chanted softly.

The farmer's face was a mask of confusion and anger. 'Out of my way,' he said, and knocked the Doctor aside with the barrel of his gun. 'Quiet!' he yelled, and retreated into the doorway, where he was joined from inside the house by two more men uncertainly holding curved swords. The courtyard was full of Bep-Wor's people, chanting more loudly now and advancing towards the farmer.

'Be quiet!' he shouted again. He grabbed the Doctor's jacket. 'Get back, or I'll shoot this fellow. Understand?'

The chanting ceased. In the sudden silence a woman's voice rang out: 'He touched the Doctor!'

There followed another brief silence, and then from the back of the crowd came a wordless cry that grew in volume. Bep-Wor was pushed in the back as those behind him surged forward.

The farmer, still clutching the Doctor, turned as if to pull his captive through the doorway. He tripped as he turned, and fired his gun. The explosion rang around the enclosing walls.

Before the echo died the crowd engulfed him.

Bep-Wor, elbowed aside, found himself on his hands and knees next to the Doctor. Their followers flooded like a tide

174

above and around them, entering the house through every door and window.

'Doctor,' Bep-Wor said, 'are you hurt?'

'Of course not,' the Doctor snapped. 'Now stop those people before they do something violent.'

Bep-Wor stared at the Doctor. He shrugged his shoulders. The tide had passed over them: from inside the house came shouts, bangs and crashes. 'It's too late for that,' he said.

They had ascended the 248 steps to the top of the highest turret on the Bridge. The pretext was to inspect the newly-installed radio mast; the true purpose was to discuss the situation freely without fear of being overheard.

The tower was half its original height: it had been lowered and widened to protect it from artillery and to accommodate large cannon. It could have been described as short and stubby, were it not for the fact that even now it soared above the surrounding towers. Its summit was the highest point in the province of Jerrissar. Through the gun ports that pierced the reinforced walls, Madok could look north along the mountain ridge, and see its peaks and the monumental block of the Bridge itself far below him; east across endless rocky crags, into the evening darkness where lay the fertile terraces of Jerrissar; south, where the mountain ridge curved away to the horizon; and west, down the vertiginous slope to the purple ocean into which the sun had recently slipped.

But Madok was in no mood to admire the views. He had seen them before. He was only a little more interested in the spire of metal that was rising from a circular opening in the centre of the roof of the tower. The sound of chains and pulleys came from the depths of the building.

'It's a precaution,' Credig said. 'I don't think we can be attacked from the air. As far as I know Kedin hasn't supplied

Vethran with any craft that have sufficient range. But it's reassuring to know that the aerial can be lowered and is always safe.'

The frail-looking structure was already taller than Madok, and still rising against a backdrop of brightening stars. 'Leave it up, Castlain,' he said gloomily. 'We're going to need it tonight.'

'I see no alternative,' Credig said.

Madok hugged himself to keep out the cold wind. 'If only I'd arrived earlier,' he said. 'I'll never forgive myself. Tevana would be here now. Safe, among friends. With Kedin within a few days.'

The Castlain pointed a gloved finger at Madok. 'Stop chastising yourself,' he said. 'That would be an order, if I had the authority. You'll be no good to Kedin Ashar if you're drowning in self-pity. At least we know that Tevana has been taken to Gonfallon. In the end, the result is the same.'

'Is it?' Madok said. He didn't understand.

'Yes,' Credig said. 'If you had stolen Tevana from under the noses of Vethran's household cavalry, we would have had to launch the operation immediately. I can't believe that Kedin would wait for Vethran to strike first. Now that we know that Tevana has been taken to Vethran, we will have to launch the operation immediately. The result is the same.'

'Except that thanks to my tardiness our priority is still to make Tevana secure. We will lose momentum. We will have to divide our forces.'

Credig uttered an exasperated curse. 'A diversionary attack was always part of the plan, Madok. You know that. You devised the damned thing. The attack on Grake Castle will act as our diversion. Vethran will assume our mission is to rescue Tevana. While he's concentrating on Grake we'll take the Citadel. Now stop punishing yourself. Let's decide on the actions we have to take tonight.'

'You're right, Credig. Let's get on with it.' Madok looked up again at the radio mast. 'The first thing is to contact Kedin.'

I have failed to protect my lord's beloved, Madok thought to himself. And I've failed to protect Ace. I must not fail again.

Bep-Wor found the Doctor in the upper floor of the farmhouse. He was in a bedroom, lit by a single lamp, staring down at the bed.

'Was this necessary?' the Doctor said, before Bep-Wor could speak. The Doctor turned, and Bep-Wor recoiled from the lambent fire in his shadowed eyes. He looked instead at the bloody body lying on the bed. He sighed.

'This is a time for celebration, Doctor,' he said gently. 'Not for regret. We have freed thirty of our people tonight.'

The Doctor raised a pointing finger. 'Bep-Wor,' he began.

Bep-Wor was in no mood to receive a lecture. He was too full of joy. 'Doctor,' he said, 'I must show you something. Come here.' He extended a hand towards the Doctor.

When he was sure the Doctor was following him Bep-Wor left the room. There, on the landing, where he had left her, Kia-Ga was waiting for him. He took her hand in his.

'Look,' he said as the Doctor emerged from the room. 'This is Kia-Ga.'

The Doctor knotted his brows and merely glanced at Kia-Ga. He was clearly going to be truculent. The Doctor's problem, Bep-Wor knew, was that he was too sensitive and thoughtful. No doubt thought and sensitivity were necessary if a person hoped to achieve knowledge and wisdom such as the Doctor's. But emotion and practicality were sometimes more important. He had to try to make the Doctor understand the importance of the evening's triumph.

'Doctor,' he said, caressing Kia-Ga's arm, 'please listen to me. On my world, on the islands of the archipelago, people mate for love, and a couple love, together, for life. Kia-Ga and I have grown together: we are the two halves of a single fruit. When she was taken from me I no longer wanted to live. Only my cowardice prevented me from killing myself. Now I have found her, and entirely thanks to you. If I had not met you, I would be dead by now, or enslaved. You have saved me, and you have brought me to Kia-Ga.'

The Doctor's face showed only pain and sorrow. 'Bep-Wor,' he said, 'she has taken the drug.'

The icy weight that Bep-Wor thought had disappeared for ever from his heart was there again. 'I know, Doctor,' he said. He turned to Kia-Ga and stroked her cheek. 'But you know who I am, don't you, Kia-Ga?'

'Bep-Wor,' Kia-Ga said, and smiled.

'And you remember our life together, before the invaders captured you?'

'Yes,' she said. Her voice became excited. 'Blue walls in the kitchen. Cooking fish. Sunlight on the bedroom wall. Kissing you. Warm bread in the morning. Wine in the evening.'

'You see?' Bep-Wor said to the Doctor. 'It's all there. She remembers everything.'

'But she has no volition,' the Doctor said. 'She does only what you tell her to do. You are simply her new master.'

'No, sir,' Kia-Ga stated. She bowed her head to the Doctor. 'I am free now. Bep-Wor has told me. All of our people will be free, as long as we follow our new master. You are our lord.'

The Doctor grasped the sleeve of Bep-Wor's uniform and with surprising strength pulled him across the landing.

'This nonsense must stop,' the Doctor whispered urgently. 'I'm a scientist, not a miracle-worker. I don't want your people to think of me as their master.'

'I understand, Doctor,' Bep-Wor said. He wondered whether the Doctor was merely being modest, or whether he truly doubted his own powers. Whichever was the case, it was important to placate him now. 'This is a matter of being practical. Those who have taken the drug act more normally when they are told that you are our leader. They copy the behaviour of those of us you saved on the journey from our world to this. We are all your followers.' He decided to change the subject. 'I have asked all the freed men and women if they have heard of the woman named Ace. I'm afraid none has.'

Bep-Wor was relieved to see that his ruse had worked. The Doctor was once again preoccupied with finding his oddly-named friend.

'I must find the centre of government on this planet,' the Doctor muttered. 'I may be able to do some good there.' He looked up at Bep-Wor. 'I'm going to the capital,' he stated.

'I promised to follow you,' Bep-Wor said, 'once I had regained Kia-Ga. I won't let you down. We will all follow you.'

There was a barely-audible hiss. That was all. No crackles; no whooping noises like the calls of demented birds. When Madok had tested Kedin's first radio set, only five years previously, he and Kedin had been in adjoining rooms, and the reception had been so poor that the sound in the headphones had resembled a forest full of wailing beasts. Now Kedin and he were thousands of miles apart, separated by the vacuum of space, and he could hear Kedin as clearly as if he were in an adjoining room.

Madok was trying to apologise. 'But I was too late, my lord. If I had arrived only an hour earlier –'

'Don't blame yourself, Madok,' Kedin's voice cut in. 'Of course I would be happier if I knew Tevana was safe. But at least we know that she is well, we know where she will be kept, and we know that we can rescue her. And if you had succeeded in taking her from Cathogh, Vethran would have known that we were about to move against him. He would have been prepared. Now he believes that he has Tevana even more securely imprisoned, and he will expect us to continue to fly his armies back and forth and to ship him ever more of these wretched Twos. He will be confident that he can control me. He is in for a surprise.'

'You agree, then,' Madok asked, 'that we should strike now?' He wanted to be sure that there was no doubt. Once the operation had begun there could be no turning back.

'Yes, Madok. There's no time like the present. The operation starts now. Within four days we'll take tea in whatever remains of Vethran's new throne room.'

Holding the mouthpiece in front of his face and the earphones on his head, Madok turned from the desk to look at the Castlain. 'Understood, Kedin. We start immediately.'

Credig nodded. A grim smile spread across his face. Madok recognised the expression: action at last.

'First,' Kedin said, although both he and Madok had rehearsed the order of events a hundred times, 'I'll pull all our ships off Mendeb Two. Vethran's invasion army will be stranded there, and they have no way of contacting the Council.'

'Are you ready to send decoy messages?' Madok reminded him. 'A sudden silence from the invasion army will alert the Council as surely as a warning would.'

'They rely on us to transmit their signals,' Kedin said. 'We know their codes and their protocols.'

'The new transmitter is working here,' Madok went on. 'I'm sure you've noticed the improved quality of the signal. The Castlain will co-ordinate the sending of orders to our forces down here. The covert teams will move into Gonfallon and converge on the palace. The motorised and airborne units will move by night to the camouflaged bunkers and landing strips.'

'The strike force will set off from the space station precisely one day from now,' Kedin said. 'We'll pretend to be one transport ship: remind Credig to monitor our signals and listen for the code words.'

'And I'll make for Grake castle,' Madok said.

'Maintain radio silence unless we have to deviate from the plan,' Kedin said. 'And: good luck, Madok. Your part of this operation is the closest to my heart. Bring Tevana to me, and we'll drink a toast to the overthrowing of tyrants. In four days, Madok. Just four days.'

It was now three days since the chains had been struck from Bep-Wor's wrists. He had been a slave; now he was leading a crusade. He had been filthy, unshaven, and dressed in rags; now his skin smelt of perfume and the buttons of his uniform glittered.

He was riding one of the tall beasts, which he had learnt were called camelopes. The Doctor insisted on walking.

As the Doctor's confidant and mouthpiece, Bep-Wor found that almost as many offerings were made to him as to the Doctor himself. A second plate of food would appear in front him at meal times; men would bring him the best trinkets and weapons that they had found in the farms and cottages they had liberated; women would come to him at night. Like the Doctor, Bep-Wor refused all such offerings. Unlike the Doctor, Bep-Wor allowed himself a few privileges: a camelope to ride, a daily shave, clean clothes, and a separate room each night, in whatever house they had sequestered, for himself and Kia-Ga.

No one had ever seen the Doctor wash, or shave his face, or change his clothes, or sleep. And yet he remained clean, grew no beard, and remained alert. When questioned about it, Bep-Wor would smile inscrutably: it did no harm to let the people believe that he was privy to the Doctor's secrets.

Protected by the uniform, a gun, a sword, and the speed of his steed, Bep-Wor had cantered ahead of the Doctor and the long column of marchers. He had swung south, to check that the column was still proceeding parallel to the main-road that led to the capital, and that there were no soldiers on the road. He had pressed on, into the increasingly dense woodlands, to blaze a trail and to search for settlements, whether so large that they were to be avoided or sufficiently small that they could be overrun.

He had found not so much as a cottage, but there were tracks running through the woods that indicated that the forest had some populated areas. Through the trees he had seen that in the distance the woodlands merged into a dense forest that covered the flanks of the jagged peaks ahead.

At every farm and cottage the prisoners had passed since their escape, Bep-Wor had sought information as well as opportunities to free other slaves. Sometimes he bought intelligence; sometimes, when the Doctor wasn't nearby, he used threats. He therefore knew that somewhere in the woodlands, before the ground rose towards the distant peaks, he and his people would come to a wide river. They would have to cut south to the road, where they would be able to cross the river on a bridge. There was a farm there, and a trading post and a store: more slaves to liberate, plenty of food, roofs to sleep under for the night.

Once over the river, they would be in Gonfallon: the lands owned by the leader of all the people of this world. He called himself by the title of King. His name, Bep-Wor had learnt, was Vethran.

Bep-Wor knew, but would not admit to knowing, that the woman with whom he had been lying for the past two nights was not the same Kia-Ga he had loved on his own world. In the same way he knew that the Doctor's rag-tag army of escaped prisoners and freed slaves could not prevail against the soldiers of this world, with their guns and their loud vehicles and their flying machines. And he knew that the lands of the King would be heavily guarded.

But the Doctor wanted to go to the capital, and Bep-Wor and all the others would follow him.

I will view the capital, Bep-Wor vowed. I will see the city at the heart of this world. And then I'll let the Doctor go on without me. I'll lead whoever will follow me into the forests, and we'll survive as best we can.

He urged his camelope to a trot, and set off to return to the marching column.

It irked Tragar that no matter how many extra-stipendiary purses and occasional gratuities he obtained from Balon Ferud; no matter how many times he overstated prices and skimmed off the excess coins for himself, without that fool Bared even noticing; no matter how much gossip about his lord's household he was able to sell to the chamberlains of Underton's other great houses; no matter how hard he tried to accumulate wealth, he never had quite enough to afford his own pleasure Two.

He had, of course, found plentiful opportunities to taste such sweetmeats. Pleasure Twos – the most attractive, voluptuous, dextrous and pliable of the ever-willing migrants from Mendeb Two – were bartered and sold between the greater nobility with a frequency that was unsurprising, given that aristocrats have preternaturally-jaded tastes. And as chamberlain of Balon Ferud's household, it was Tragar's responsibility to oversee the despatch and receipt of such merchandise. Security was paramount, as pleasure Twos were valuable. Almost as important was secrecy: the very existence of pleasure Twos was merely a scandalous rumour as far as the wives, servants, soldiers and tenants of the noblemen were concerned.

Tragar unfailingly used his position to sample the goods in transit.

I wouldn't do it, he told himself, if the Twos objected. But they're always so happy to oblige.

Nonetheless, he resented the fact that he couldn't afford one of his own. Particularly as Balon Ferud, who was more interested in hunting and politicking than the erotic arts, kept two or three pleasure Twos at a time locked in an attic room above the south wing.

And so it was that Tragar found himself facing a dilemma. Rigora had completed her training of Ace. The girl was ready to enter Balon's service, in almost any capacity from kitchen drudge to arena warrior. It was Tragar's duty to inform Balon that Ace was ready, and to have her taken from Tragar's apartments in the east wing to whatever part of the house Balon deemed appropriate, or to another of Balon's residences. Balon might even have Tragar send her to a trader for re-sale.

Tragar couldn't bring himself to send the news to Balon. In any case, Tragar reasoned, Balon would have no opportunity to put Ace to any use in the immediate future: the King had summoned all the members of the Council to the capital. Balon was due to leave that very afternoon, and would be away for at least a week.

It was Tragar who had seen the potential in Ace, and who had won the bidding for her. It seemed to him only fair that he should have the girl to himself for a few days, until Balon returned.

He realised that, deep in thought, he was walking in circles around his study. He paced deliberately to the window, and took several deep breaths as he looked out across the town.

The view usually calmed him, even after he had been locked in disputation with Bared about the household finances. It reassured him to know that while Balon was above him, and while that upstart Bared was prepared to challenge him, he, Tragar, was superior to even the wealthiest of the tradesmen and merchants in the squalid houses whose roofs he looked down on.

Today, however, his hands wouldn't stop trembling. Heavens, he wanted Ace so badly he'd defy his lord to have her.

I should smoke a pipe, he told himself. I should let the spore-seed calm me, and then, once Balon has departed for the capital, I will venture down the stairs, and fetch Ace.

No. I can't wait. I'll have her now.

He strode to the door, pulled it open, and called down the length of his hallway. 'Poa-Nan! Go downstairs, go to Rigora, and tell her that I want the Two named Ace in my apartments immediately.'

He closed the door and leant against it. What if Balon should want to see me before he leaves? he thought. It would be typical of him to make a fuss about the house, just as he's leaving it for a week. What if he summons me while I'm in the middle of...? His thoughts became incoherent as he imagined, for the hundredth time, some of the activities that he might perform with Ace.

He smiled. So much the better, he decided. It would be amusing to leave Ace in order to discuss the stocking up of the pantry, or some such trivia: to bow, and murmur reassurances to Balon, while half-way through using Balon's most expensive Two.

Poa-Nan knocked at the door.

'Enter,' Tragar called. The door opened, and Ace walked into the room, followed by Poa-Nan.

She looked to left and right as she approached him. Once

185

again he marvelled at her. Twos didn't do that: they were universally uninterested in their surroundings, unless told to look at something. What had Ace been like, he wondered, before she was processed for use as a Two? She must have been a tempestuous girl; uncontrollable.

It gave him a thrill of pleasure to think that this once-wild girl would now happily obey the most humiliating instructions.

'Leave,' he ordered Poa-Nan. 'Shut the door behind you. And don't disturb me until I call for you.'

'Yes, sir,' Poa-Nan said. The Two left the room.

At last Tragar was alone with the most costly Two on the planet. He resisted the urge to touch her immediately. There was no need to rush. Every delay simply sweetened the tasting.

Ace stood still, smiling slightly, as he walked around her. When should he order her to undress? Not yet: she was so perversely appealing in her tightly-fitting, masculine, black costume.

'Walk to the window, Ace,' he said. 'Lean on the sill and look out across the town.'

'Yes, sir,' Ace said, and did as she had been instructed.

Tragar folded his arms and watched her. How unselfconsciously she moved; how unaware she was of the provocative pose she had adopted as she gazed through the window.

Which should he try first: the Plough and the Furrow, perhaps? Or Covering the Bitch? How many of the Hundred Forbidden Acts would he be able to teach her before Balon returned from court?

Poa-Nan's knock sounded on the door.

'Enter,' Tragar said, automatically, a second before he remembered that he had told Poa-Nan not to disturb him.

He turned towards the door, gathering the breath with which to shout his anger at the Two. But he let the breath go with a sigh. Poa-Nan was a Two, and a Two never disobeyed. Therefore Tragar's instruction had been overruled by someone in whom Poa-Nan recognised an authority even higher than Tragar's. And there was only one such person.

'Balon Ferud wishes to see me,' he said.

Poa-Nan was momentarily confused. 'His lordship is in the reception hall, sir,' the Two said. 'He told me to tell you that he wants to see the Two named Ace.'

Tragar closed his eyes. His desires had been so close to fruition.

'Tragar!' Balon's voice echoed along the hallway, as did the sound of his heavy footsteps on the stairs. 'Where is she, Tragar? Where are you hiding that girl?'

'Come here, Ace,' Tragar said. He could have wept with anger and frustration. 'Stand in the centre of the room.' He raised his voice. 'In here, my lord. In my study.'

The portly figure of Balon Ferud filled the width of the doorway. He was dressed for the royal court in military regalia: his broad chest had hardly sufficient room for its array of medals and badges. 'Stand aside!' he barked at Poa-Nan, and strode into the room.

'I'm delighted to report,' Tragar said, 'that Ace's training is now complete. I anticipated that you might wish to see her, my lord, so I had her brought here. I was just about to bring her to you.'

'Were you, indeed?' Balon said, with a sceptical glance. His attention was taken by Ace. As Tragar had done, he walked around her. He admired her costume. He stopped in front of her.

Ace lowered her head. 'My lord,' she said. 'How may I serve you?'

'I'm told you're a fighter,' Balon said. 'Is that so?'

Ace grinned. 'I can look after myself, my lord,' she said. 'I don't mind a bit of aggro. You want to start?'

Balon looked at Tragar. He chuckled. 'She still has the most remarkable character of speech,' he said. 'I'll take her with me. I think his Majesty will be amused. He might even want to buy her, Tragar. I'll make sure I make a profit on her, too.'

'I was sure she would prove to be a worthwhile investment, my lord,' Tragar said. His only consolation was that his dangerously profligate expenditure of Balon's money was beginning to look like an inspired gamble.

'The carriages are ready to leave,' Balon said as he strode towards the door. 'Bring her down immediately.'

Tragar, Poa-Nan and Ace stood in silence as Balon's footsteps receded. Tragar extended his hand. He could at least touch her before she went. A kiss, perhaps; some fleeting, intimate caresses. No – what was the point?

'Poa-Nan,' he said, 'take Ace to the outer courtyard. Ace, go with Poa-Nan and then follow the instructions of the guards.'

He watched them leave, and then he went to the window and filled his pipe.

The settlement, Bep-Wor discovered after the battle, was called Felling Bridge. It had not, in truth, been much of a battle: the traders and travellers had stared open-mouthed from the windows of their cabins and of the inn while Bep-Wor, astride his camelope, had led his ragged army along the rutted street towards the bridge. Half a dozen soldiers had lined up hurriedly to defend the river crossing: they fired their guns into the air and, when they saw that the crowd running towards them was not going to stop, they ran across the bridge into Gonfallon.

Bep-Wor had posted his own guards on the bridge, to make

sure the soldiers didn't return to recapture it. He had had no difficulty in persuading the merchants and the innkeeper to surrender their properties: the very idea of free Twos was enough to terrify them into submission.

In the dining room of the inn, after a meal from the innkeeper's pantry washed down with wine from the innkeeper's cellar, the army had cheered Bep-Wor and the Doctor, and had joined in the chorus of the hastily-composed ballad, 'The Battle of Felling Bridge'.

The next morning, the army crossed the bridge and entered Gonfallon.

The land was forested, but criss-crossed with paths and scattered with clearings. As on the other side of the river, Bep-Wor led the column away from the road, but followed its direction. The terrain undulated, but tended to go uphill rather than down.

At midday Bep-Wor brought the column to a halt in a clearing. He set sentries. The army's numbers had been swollen again, by the addition of Twos set free at Felling Bridge, and those under the influence of the potion now outnumbered those whom the Doctor had saved from taking it. Bep-Wor found it increasingly difficult to remember which men and women were drugged. They all behaved the same: afloat on a wave of success, and with the Doctor as their steersman, they were all happy to obey Bep-Wor's directions.

'We'll rest here a while,' he said to the nearest group of men. 'Break open the rations, and eat sparingly. Drink, but nothing intoxicating. And keep the noise down. Pass the word to everyone else.'

He watched as the men threaded their way through the throng in the clearing, disseminating his orders. Bep-Wor was sure that the group he'd spoken to had been on the transport ship with him; but had they taken the drug, or not? He couldn't be sure. And it didn't matter.

The next task was to see to the Doctor. Arduous cross-country marches didn't seem to tire the Doctor, who usually strode ahead of the main column and who fidgeted impatiently at any delay. Bep-Wor knew that the Doctor would become bad-tempered if given nothing to do; and reluctant as Bep-Wor was to forego his midday meal, he knew that it would bolster his authority if he were to spend time alone with the Doctor.

He found the Doctor at the edge of the clearing, peering into the forest. 'Let's scout ahead,' he suggested, 'while the others take a rest.'

The Doctor pulled a dial from his pocket and studied the numbers on its face. 'It's been almost a week,' he said. 'And I still don't even know where she is.'

'We're going as fast as we can, Doctor,' Bep-Wor said. 'It would be dangerous for you to go alone, even if we could persuade the army not to follow you.'

The Doctor smiled. To Bep-Wor's relief the Doctor had been less irritable since the bloodless battle at the river crossing. 'I know,' the Doctor said. 'The guards who ran from the bridge must have retreated along the road we're following. I'm surprised we haven't already come across more soldiers out looking for us.'

'All the more reason for us to look at the way ahead,' Bep-Wor said. 'I'll rest my animal. Let's go on foot.'

He looked round as he and the Doctor passed from the light of the clearing into the shadow of the trees. He waved. He wanted to be sure that his departure was noticed: the army would think that he was going to discuss arcane mysteries with the Doctor.

Some time later he and the Doctor were crouching on the treeless summit of a small hill.

'We should return,' Bep-Wor said. 'They'll start to get restless if we're away too long.'

He thought that the Doctor hadn't heard him, and was about to repeat his words, when the Doctor glanced round and lowered his outstretched arm: he wanted Bep-Wor to keep down.

Bep-Wor lay on his front beside the Doctor. 'Look,' the Doctor said, 'the road goes in a wide curve around those two peaks.'

Bep-Wor squinted. He had been renowned for his keen eyesight, but he suspected that the Doctor could see more and further than he. Now he could make out the snaking thread of the distant road.

'We should keep to the south of those hills,' he said. 'We'll save ourselves an hour's marching.'

'That's true,' the Doctor said. 'More to the point, however, is the fact that we'll also avoid being shot. Look there.'

Bep-Wor rubbed his eyes and stared. Beyond the two hills there was movement on the road. It was a column of soldiers: he saw the glint of weapons. There were hundreds of them.

He felt ridiculously proud. The King of this world had sent out a vast force of his crisply uniformed soldiers to deal with Bep-Wor's little band. 'They're not taking any chances with us,' he said.

'That's not all,' the Doctor said. 'There are just as many off the road. I can see them moving through the forest on both sides. They mean to catch us.'

'Well, they won't,' Bep-Wor said, stepping backwards from the summit, 'thanks to your sharp eyes. We'll keep south, and they'll miss us.'

The Doctor joined him. 'There will be others,' the Doctor said. 'We're only a day's march from the capital, according to the innkeeper. We can expect the King's forces to be more numerous the closer we get.'

'Then we'll continue to scout ahead,' Bep-Wor said. 'It's just a matter of –'

He stopped. Watching him and the Doctor was a man, standing still and almost invisible among the trees that ringed the summit of the hill.

Bep-Wor's hand went to his gun. But the man wasn't a soldier: he had a long beard, he was wearing clothes sewn from animal skins and, although he had at his belt a long knife in a decorated scabbard, he wasn't threatening. He was just watching them.

Still, Bep-Wor thought, it didn't do for anyone to see them. How much had this man overheard? He would have ensured the man's silence – if the Doctor hadn't been with him. With a silent curse he let his hand fall from the gun.

The man remained where he was while the Doctor and Bep-Wor regained the cover of the trees, but he didn't address them.

'Who are you?' Bep-Wor asked him. 'What are you doing here, dressed in such strange clothing?'

The man didn't answer, but slowly ran his gaze over Bep-Wor's purloined uniform and the Doctor's crumpled jacket and trousers. 'Strange clothing,' he repeated, slowly.

He turned and strode away into the trees. 'Forester,' he called over his shoulder. 'Come. Eat in my house.'

Bep-Wor and the Doctor looked at each other.

'I suppose that's his function,' the Doctor said, 'rather than his name.'

'We should follow him,' Bep-Wor said. 'We need to be sure he won't send the soldiers after us. And I am hungry.'

The forester lived a short way down the side of the hill, in a wooden cabin that was no more than a hut. It had a covered porch with a spectacular view across the surrounding wooded hills.

'See the city,' the forester said, pointing towards the horizon.

It was true. Bep-Wor could see the towers and spires of a town, shimmering in the gap between two of the hills.

'Forester,' Bep-Wor said. 'This is the Doctor, and I'm –' He hesitated, unwilling to reveal his name. He was dressed as soldier; he would invent a rank for himself. 'I'm the General,' he concluded.

The forester nodded thoughtfully. He opened the door of the hut and called inside. 'Dab! Here.'

A man emerged from inside the hut. He was tall, slim, and younger than Bep-Wor. He was dressed in a cotton robe and his hair was as long as a woman's, but Bep-Wor recognised him as a fellow-countryman – a Two.

'Dab,' said the forester, indicating the young man. He pointed to his guests. 'Doctor. General. Dab, talk to them.' He plunged into the dark interior of the hut.

'Yes, forester,' Dab replied. He turned towards the Doctor and Bep-Wor. 'Good day to both of you, and welcome to the forester's house. We live simply here, and we have few visitors. We were about to eat. Would you like to share our meal?'

Bep-Wor and the Doctor exchanged a glance, and then both nodded. The forester emerged from the hut carrying a rickety table, which he placed on the deck of the porch. 'Talk,' he said. 'Good.'

Dab smiled, and made a graceful gesture with one arm. 'The forester has a monosyllabic habit of speech,' he said. 'He's become unaccustomed to intercourse, other than with me.'

'Are you –?' Bep-Wor began. 'Are you from the other planet? From Two?'

'Why, yes,' Dab replied, 'of course. My full name is Dab-Tar. I grew up on Starpoint Island.' He frowned, as if the memories of his childhood were unpleasant.

Bep-Wor knew the island. It was obvious to him that Dab-Tar

193

was one of his people, but he couldn't decide whether the Two was under the influence of the drug. The forester, who said nothing as he arranged chairs around the table and carried trays of food and crockery from the hut, seemed more servile than Dab.

'The forester, as his title suggests,' Dab said, 'cares for the forest. He is one of twenty-four such, appointed by the King's First Huntsman to inhabit the depths of the King's sylvan wilderness, there to protect the fauna and flora.'

Bep-Wor had never heard a Two, drugged or otherwise, speak in such convoluted sentences. 'Is the pay good?' he asked.

Dab fluttered his hands. 'Financial remuneration there is almost none,' he said. 'But the forester's needs are few and simple.'

Bep-Wor realised that there was no alternative: he would simply have to ask, and apologise afterwards if necessary. 'The forester had enough money to afford you, though.'

'I was inexpensive,' Dab said. He was silent for a moment, frowning again, and then he smiled. 'None of the traders wanted me. I am too delicate for manual labour, and I had barely survived the journey to this world. I was expected to die.'

The incongruity of Dab's cheerful expression as he spoke convinced Bep-Wor that Dab was under the influence of the drug.

The forester struck a plate with a wooden spoon to attract attention. 'Dab: a bargain,' he said, a grin gleaming in the depths of his beard. 'Eat now.'

The four men sat round the table. Dab opened the lid of a casserole, and stirred the contents with a spoon. 'The forester is also the hunter and the chef,' he said. 'I'm afraid I don't recognise the birds and beasts that he brings home. But this is a stew of fowl and roots, I know that much, and here we have a salad of cresses, and unleavened bread, and potted meat.'

Bep-Wor's stomach was groaning for food. While Dab spooned stew on to his plate he managed to comment that the meal looked tasty, but as soon as the plate was set in front of him he forgot all about conversation. He grabbed a piece of bread and began shovelling the stew into his mouth. It was hot and good.

The Doctor, of course, merely toyed with his food, and therefore had time to think about the strange behaviour and speech of the Two named Dab.

The forester was as silent as Bep-Wor, but for much slurping of soup and sucking of beard. Like Bep-Wor, he seemed content to listen to the animated conversation of Dab and the Doctor.

'You have a very extensive vocabulary,' the Doctor said. 'Do you read a lot?'

Dab laughed. Bep-Wor, his spoon halfway to his mouth, stared at him: he had never before heard a drugged Two laugh. Not even Kia-Ga, not even when he gave her pleasure.

'My purpose is to read,' Dab said. 'I sometimes think the forester's books are more dear to him than I am. He has a small library of ancient texts, but lacks the learning to comprehend the printed words. Every evening I read to him, by lamplight, before we retire to bed. He says he likes to hear my voice.'

'Ah, yes,' the Doctor said. 'I understand now. And the forester has instructed you to talk, and to use your voice.'

'Yes, Doctor. The forester wishes me to be at all times loquacious, if not positively verbose.'

'What a remarkable and convenient arrangement,' the Doctor cried. 'Don't you think so, ah, General? Dab is the forester's voice – his interpreter of books, his spokesman with strangers. Are you happy here, Dab?'

'Very happy, Doctor. I am happy for the first time in my life. The forester and I care for each other.'

Bep-Wor put his hand on the Doctor's sleeve. 'He has to say that, Doctor,' he whispered. 'He's taken the drug. He's obeying the forester's instructions.'

The Doctor pursed his lips. 'That's true. But still –' he said, and might have said more, had the forester not slowly risen to his feet with his hand on his scabbard. The silence of the forest was broken by a shout.

'There they are,' the voice called. 'Doctor! Doctor!'

The forester pulled Dab from the table and stood in front of the young man.

The Doctor and Bep-Wor also stood. Bep-Wor could see a few figures now, running between the trees.

'Your army has come to find us,' the Doctor said. 'You'd better go and keep them quiet, or we'll have all the King's men here before you can say Humpty Dumpty.'

Bep-Wor set off down the steps from the porch, but before he had reached the ground his people emerged from the surrounding trees. The entire army had decamped. 'Doctor! Doctor!' they chanted, as they converged on the forester's hut.

Bep-Wor held up his hands, trying to silence the crowd. But they seemed excited at having found Bep-Wor and the Doctor, and he found it impossible to keep them quiet.

'It's all right,' he said, trying to make himself heard. 'There's nothing to make a noise about. I'm safe. The Doctor's safe. This is the hut of the forester. He lives here with one of our people.'

The men and women, jostling with each other on the thin circle of clear ground between the forest and the hut, gradually fell silent. Then one voice – Bep-Wor recognised it as belonging to one of the men who had been with him and the Doctor on the transport ship – shouted, 'One of our people? Free him!'

196

The cry was taken up by others around the circle. As he tried to calm the crowd Bep-Wor reflected that his general instructions to the freed Twos – that they should copy the behaviour of those who hadn't taken the drug – did not always produce the desired results.

Suddenly the crowd roared, and surged forward. Bep-Wor turned to see that the Doctor had appeared at the head of the short stairway from the porch of the hut. He gestured for the Doctor to move back, out of sight, but instead the forester appeared behind the Doctor.

There was nothing Bep-Wor could do to control his army. As the men and women ran up the steps, pushing him aside, he could only watch as events unfolded with a tragic inevitability.

The forester, no doubt concerned to protect Dab, drew his long knife from its scabbard. Bep-Wor's followers howled: they saw only a bearded stranger threatening the Doctor with a blade.

It was all over by the time Bep-Wor pushed through the crowd and reached the topmost stair. The forester was dead; Dab, his face showing only confusion, was being carried in triumph on the shoulders of his liberators.

The Doctor was kneeling by the forester's body. He looked up as Bep-Wor approached.

'Doctor,' Bep-Wor began, 'I tried –'

'I know,' the Doctor said. He shut his eyes for a moment and sighed. 'There was nothing you could do. Let's get on.' He pointed towards the turrets of the distant capital. 'Let's get this finished.'

The men had been marching all through the night, and now they were resting: each one sitting with his back to the tall trunk of one of the evergreen needletrees that covered the slopes around Grake Castle. Some were dozing; some were

197

cleaning their weapons. They wore no uniform, no badges of rank: they were dressed as farm workers. Each had a vial of deadly poison hanging from a chain around his neck: better to die than to be captured and interrogated, particularly as the King's interrogators made free use of SS10. If the attack were to fail, the King would have no prisoners, and no proof of the identities of the attackers.

Hidden in a convoy of hay wains they had come into Gonfallon two days previously from the neighbouring domain of Harran. When dusk fell the convoy had stopped, but the soldiers had kept moving: on foot now, in the darkness, into the hills around the capital, following the phosphorescent trail that Madok had sprayed from the craft he'd flown from Jerrissar.

The men from Harran marched by night and concealed themselves during the days. Madok, meanwhile, made two more flights, dropping at the rendezvous point crates containing rations, a radio set, ammunition, and heavier weapons than those being carried by the men.

There was no landing strip in the needletree forest that surrounded Grake. On his final flight, just as dawn was breaking, Madok had jumped from his machine and parachuted on to the rendezvous site. He'd rigged the controls so that the craft continued to fly: over the castle, and into the rocky slope beyond it. As he pulled himself to his feet Madok saw the orange burst of flame as the machine struck the hillside, and then heard the dull noise of the explosion. A spiral of black smoke ascended into the lightening sky.

He had smiled with satisfaction. If the guards at Grake stir themselves to investigate anything today, he had thought, they'll head towards that beacon of fire and smoke. And we'll come from precisely the opposite direction.

Shortly afterwards six rough-looking countrymen had

wandered into the clearing where Madok, rifle in hand, was guarding the crates of supplies. The men were the advance guard of the Harran detachment, and they had arrived a little earlier than expected. Madok was impressed. Everything, so far, had gone according to the plan. Madok didn't believe in omens, good or bad, but the successful rendezvous was encouraging: he would be able to proceed with a full complement of fully-armed troops, against defenders who had had no warning of the attack. None of the contingencies would be required.

Soon Tevana Roslod would be free.

Now Madok was lying on his stomach among the trees, inspecting the walls of Grake through his telescope. As a castle, Madok reckoned, Grake was a passable hunting lodge. Although it occupied the peak of a hill, it was overlooked by higher peaks, such as the one on which Madok's force was encamped. Not for the first time Madok regretted that he had been unable to equip himself with artillery. Still, it would be easy enough to storm the defences. The curtain wall lay in ruins, and trees had been allowed to grow up to the central square of buildings. Madok had provided himself with explosive charges powerful enough to bring down entire walls; the trees would allow his men to place the charges undetected.

It would be almost too easy. Then Madok's eye caught a movement on the far side of the castle. He focused the telescope, and saw a troop of the castle guards marching down the hill, away from the castle and towards the burning wreckage of his flying machine. Now, he thought, it will be even easier.

'Sir!' The Harran commander was crouching behind Madok, keeping out of sight of the castle's watchtowers. 'I thought you might be interested to listen in.'

Madok stood up. 'Don't worry too much about being spotted,' he said. 'The sentry points face inwards: they're more concerned with keeping their prisoners in than keeping anyone out.' He looked into the clearing, where a group of soldiers had gathered around the radio set. 'You're not transmitting?' he said.

'Of course not, sir,' the commander replied. 'But we've picked up incoming signals from Kedin Ashar.'

Madok ran towards the radio set. 'Let me share a set of phones,' he said, and pressed his ear against the other side of one of the thick discs.

'I can only repeat my apologies,' Kedin was saying, his voice thin and overlaid with crackles. 'Tell commissioner Dallid that the consignment will be delayed by one-and-a-half days at most.'

A second voice, so distorted and obscured by hisses that Madok could not make out the words, replied to Kedin.

'Really?' Kedin said. 'How unfortunate. Well, tell the new commissioner, then. Tell his Majesty himself. Our ships have to be serviced from time to time. The next consignment will be delayed by one and a half days.'

Madok lifted his head away from the earphone. He had heard enough. Kedin's transmission purported to be from the space station. The one-and-a-half days' delay was the coded signal to the Bridge: it meant that Kedin was not transmitting from the station, but from one of the fleet of ships that was now half-way to Mendeb Three.

The main assault force was on its way.

Bep-Wor knew for a fact that the largest town on his world – or at least the northern half of it – was Norport. He had been there: he had sailed into its harbour, he had walked along its main avenue, he had haggled in its market, he had become lost in its back alleys.

200

Norport was a mere village compared to Gonfallon city, the capital of this new world's King.

Even the Doctor, Bep-Wor thought, had been taken aback by the size of the city. Its streets and walls coated the floor and sides of a wide valley, around which were the forested hills that had become familiar during the previous days of marching. A wide river ran through the valley and bisected the city. Bep-Wor had counted the bridges that spanned the sluggish flow: there were eight, all of them built of stone. The river was alive with barges and other boats; the bridges swarmed with people and vehicles. On either side of the river the city was a maze of streets and alleys, mansions and hovels, fields and yards and towers and mills. Smoke rose from the tall stacks above workshops, from domestic chimneys, and from bonfires.

Near the centre of the city was the oldest quarter: a warren of small streets, zigzagging about the sides of a low hill, enclosed within an ancient rampart. The top of the hill consisted of just one agglomeration of buildings, covering an area larger than the rest of the old city. Its highest towers were so tall that they seemed to rise into the clouds; its monumental walls contained entire parks; the glass dome at its centre shimmered in the sunlight. This was the King's palace.

All this Bep-Wor could see from the wooded hillside across which he and his army were making slow progress. They had stopped again, following his example, to gaze down at the city from behind the screen of trees.

The Doctor, who had gone ahead, came bustling through the forest. 'What's holding you up, Bep-Wor?' he said. 'You must get your people off the hillside. We know there are patrols of soldiers out on these hills.'

It was true. Bep-Wor had almost walked into a heavily-armed troop of the King's soldiers only that morning. His army's march of liberation had become a scurrying between trees, a hiding from patrols. They were too near the city: too near the seat of the King's power.

But Bep-Wor couldn't bring himself to leave. He and the Doctor should have parted company by now: they could have done it last night, under cover of darkness, giving the army no opportunity to follow the Doctor down into the valley.

'What's wrong with you, Bep-Wor?' the Doctor said. 'We've spent the whole day dodging soldiers. I'm no nearer the capital, and your people are in constant danger of capture. You must lead them away from here.'

'I know, Doctor.' Bep-Wor sighed. 'But it will feel like a retreat – like an admission of defeat. Part of me wants to lead our little army down into those wide streets, just as an act of defiance. And I suppose,' he added, feeling his face redden as he spoke, 'that I don't want to be parted from you. Our lives have been intertwined since you appeared outside the ruins of my house.'

The Doctor grimaced with embarrassment and exasperation. 'I'm very grateful to you, Bep-Wor,' he said, 'for providing me with an escort on this journey. But I have to travel alone on the final part of the road, and you and your people must move to somewhere safer.' He looked up at the sky. 'It's getting dark. I've scouted round this hill, and I think it's clear of soldiers. Let's make camp on the far side.'

'Agreed,' Bep-Wor said. He waved his arms in the air, indicating to his people that they should hurry around the hillside and then stop for the night. 'And during the night?'

The Doctor shrugged. 'I'll slip away quietly. Tell your people the truth: that I've gone alone to seek an audience with the King.'

Bep-Wor thought that even now he might be able to dissuade the Doctor from such a foolhardy mission. 'It will be dangerous, Doctor. You will certainly be captured.'

'Don't worry, Bep-Wor. They won't know who I am. It's only when I'm with your army that I can be identified as an escaped prisoner. Alone, I'll simply be a visitor. Don't worry about me. I'm used to doing this sort of thing. It's almost a hobby of mine. The ruler of the planet Chloris, for instance, tried to have me killed by throwing me into a pit. It didn't work, of course, and it didn't do her much good, either. As you know, I have a few tricks up my sleeve.'

Bep-Wor studied the sleeves of the Doctor's jacket. He couldn't think of anything to say. He knew the Doctor was right. He became aware that the Doctor was no longer looking at him, but had instead turned his face towards the sky. Then he realised that the evening wasn't silent: a noise like a continuous rumble of thunder was getting louder – getting closer.

'Look!' the Doctor said. 'Over there. Coming down beyond the next hill.'

Six dark shapes were descending on pillars of fire.

'Friend or foe, I wonder?' said the Doctor.

Throughout the day Madok had remained close to the radio set. There had been plenty to do: breaking out the supplies, distributing the ammunition and rations, going over the attack plan, drilling the men. Nonetheless it had felt like a day spent waiting.

The signal came at dusk.

'Sir!' the radio operator called. Madok was at his side in an instant. 'Coded message, sir.'

Madok put the spare set of earphones to his head.

'All ships are now berthed at the station,' he heard. It was Kedin's voice. 'I repeat, all ships are now berthed at the station. The recovery operation can begin at once. Please acknowledge.'

This was it. Kedin's message told Madok that the main assault force had landed. In the unlikely event that anyone else had picked up the signal, it would convey only misleading information.

Madok was impressed: he had been listening for the sound of the landing, and had been watching the skies for any sight of the ships. The capital was only five kilometres away. Kedin and the pilots had brought the ships down surreptitiously.

'Acknowledge,' he said. 'And then pack up the kit. We're going in.'

Madok took up his telescope and made a final scan of Grake Castle. Lights were burning in a few of the windows, but not in any that overlooked the wall where the first charges were to be placed. Only one of the watchtowers was occupied by a sentry. The party that had left that morning to investigate the crash of Madok's flying machine had still not returned. The weather was clear, and as night fell his men would have the cover of darkness as well as of the forest. Conditions for the attack could not have been better.

The men from Harran were gathering in the clearing, organising themselves into the three attack groups. In their rough clothing, and with their faces blackened, they looked more like bandits than soldiers. Their teeth gleamed in the darkness as they joked with each other and jostled into line.

Madok held up his hands to stop the whispered conversations, and then addressed the men.

'We will proceed immediately,' he said. 'We have the advantage of surprise, we outnumber the defenders, and we have superior weaponry. And, of course, you are of Harran, and they are merely of Gonfallon.'

The soldiers cheered. Madok smiled: no problems with troop morale on this mission.

'If the Castlain has any sense,' Madok continued, 'he'll

surrender quickly. However, his men are defending a prisoner whose importance to the King cannot be overestimated. We may find ourselves fighting through every doorway in the castle. We know that we are taking the first step to overthrow a tyrant. If we fail, however, we will be no more than traitors. Therefore we succeed or we die in the attempt.'

The men cheered again.

'Group One will make and hold the breach. Group Two will guard the exits: it is vital that no messenger leaves the castle. I will lead Group Three: we'll go in and we'll take and hold the prison tower. Then Groups One and Two will post sentries and will move into the castle. Commanders, use your loudhailers: we want the defenders to surrender rather than fight. Speed is essential. It is possible that the Castlain is under orders to harm Tevana Roslod if an attempt is made to free her. And our sole aim is to bring Tevana out, unharmed. Are you ready?'

The men were oddly quiet. Then one of their Group commanders began to sing, and the entire troop joined in. Their voices filled the clearing with words of defiance and glory. Slavery would be ended, injustice would be ended, and the men of Harran were going to do the work.

Still singing, more quietly now, and carrying explosive charges in their backpacks, the men of Group One jogged into the dark forest, making towards Grake Castle.

Night had fallen. Bep-Wor tripped over tree roots and pushed through undergrowth as he tried to keep up with the Doctor, who seemed uncannily able to see in the dark.

They left their army of followers on the side of the hill that faced away from the lights of the capital city. The Doctor was in a hurry, and was not prepared to wait for the entire column to stumble through the forest in his wake.

'Tell them to set up camp here,' he told Bep-Wor. 'It's too dark now to march through these woods. You can assure them that we'll return soon. Now we must try to find the place where those ships landed.' He paced back and forth, twiddling his thumbs, while Bep-Wor gave hurried instructions. And then he plunged into the black shadows under the trees, and Bep-Wor followed him.

Although he had to concentrate on keeping up with the Doctor and on avoiding the thorns and branches of the woodland, Bep-Wor had time to think about the massive machines he and the Doctor had seen descending from the sky. He was sure they were transport ships, similar to the one that had brought him and the Doctor to this world. That meant they were from the space station, the artificial world built in ancient times and set between his own world and this one. The Doctor said that he had to find out what the ships were doing here, but Bep-Wor suspected that the Doctor had another reason for his desperation to reach the ships: the people from the space station might have information about his friend Ace.

The ships had landed further away than Bep-Wor had first thought. He followed the Doctor down from the hill on which they had left their followers, up the side of another hill, and down again towards a wide valley. He was scratched, footsore and exhausted. The capital city could no longer be seen. There were no lights; the only sound was of the Doctor's footsteps, leading him onwards.

He didn't realise they had reached the ships' landing site until he caught up with the Doctor. He bent double to relieve the ache in his side and to breathe deeply. It was only as he straightened that he saw that he and the Doctor were surrounded by uniformed soldiers. The soldiers' guns were pointing at his chest.

'It's all right,' the Doctor said, holding up his hands. 'I'm not armed. Do you think you could take me to your leader? That seems to be the appropriate phrase. He will want to see me.'

The soldiers' uniforms were not exactly like Bep-Wor's own. He recognised them as the same as those worn by the guards on the cargo pod and the transport ship.

The soldiers studied the Doctor and Bep-Wor. The Doctor tapped his foot impatiently while the soldiers held a short debate about whether the two of them should be shot immediately as spies.

'Take them to the Duke,' one of them decided. 'Keep them covered, and wing them if they try to run. Send back a couple of men to maintain the cordon.'

Followed by two of the soldiers, the Doctor and Bep-Wor continued to push through the forest. The trees soon thinned, and they found themselves descending into the valley, a flat-bottomed bowl of open land surrounded by hills.

The transport ships, sinister black shapes, squatted in a rough circle that spanned the valley. The ships were showing no lights, and the valley might have been deserted but for the muted sounds of men and machines issuing from within the circle.

As he was led beside the vast metal hull of one of the ships, Bep-Wor realised that large numbers of soldiers and vehicles were on the move – and that they didn't want to be noticed.

In the centre of the circle, like an island in the sea of swarming troops and manoeuvring vehicles, stood a craft that was small, at least in comparison to the other transports. Bep-Wor supposed that it must be a flying machine, such as those used by the invaders of his world, although it had only stubby wings and no circular fan at its nose. The two soldiers brought Bep-Wor and the Doctor to the side of this craft, where they were met by two more soldiers in more ornate uniforms.

'Sir,' one of their escorts said, 'we picked up these two at the perimeter. This one says he wants to speak to the Duke.'

The officers exchanged a look. 'We've no time for that,' one of them said. 'The transports have to lift off again in a few minutes.'

A door slid open in the side of the craft, and a slim figure stood silhouetted against the yellow light inside. 'It's all right, Lafed,' he said. 'There is always time for visitors. Come in, please. I'm afraid the accommodation is rather cramped.'

The soldiers shrugged, and then made way for the Doctor and Bep-Wor to climb the few steps to the doorway.

Bep-Wor stood blinking in the light. He had thought that he was becoming accustomed to seeing mechanical marvels, but he could only stand and stare at the array of winking lights and glowing screens. He knew, instinctively, that like the transport ships this craft was as far above the invaders' vehicles and flying machines as those machines were above the fishing boats he used to crew. It had been made by the ancient ones: the people who had brought his ancestors from the stars.

And it was, indeed, very cramped. The tall, slim man folded himself into the single seat at the front of the cabin, and swivelled it to face the Doctor and Bep-Wor, who squeezed into the two seats at the back.

The man perused his two visitors for a long moment. 'Well,' he said at last, 'I'm Kedin Ashar, Duke of Jerrissar, Lord of the Skies, and so forth. And you,' he said, looking at Bep-Wor's uniform, 'appear to be a corporal in one of the King's regiments.'

'And you thought you were a general,' the Doctor murmured.

'I am Bep-Wor,' Bep-Wor said, stifling the urge to address the man as 'sir'. 'I am from the world you call Mendeb Two.'

Kedin Ashar sat back in his seat. 'Great heavens,' he said, 'I believe you are. So he belongs to you,' he went on, turning to the Doctor.

'Of course not,' the Doctor snapped. 'He's a free man. And there are a couple of hundred more like him camped two hills away.'

Kedin nodded. 'Of course,' he said. 'The consignment of Twos that proved to be sub-standard. Obviously you've managed to escape. Do you mind me asking how you avoided falling under the influence of that dreadful potion?'

'That's easy,' the Doctor said. 'They didn't take it. I stopped them. Bep-Wor helped me.'

'And you, I take it,' Kedin said, leaning forwards to peer at the Doctor, 'are not from Mendeb Two?'

The Doctor lifted his hat. 'I'm the Doctor,' he said. 'I expect you've heard of me.'

Kedin frowned. 'Do you know,' he said, 'I believe you're right. Now where could I have heard of you? Ah!' he said, as though he had suddenly remembered. A look of anguish contorted his aquiline features for a moment. 'I should have guessed, I suppose.'

It was the Doctor's turn to lean forwards. 'And where is Ace?' he said.

Kedin looked up at the cabin's ceiling. 'I don't know,' he admitted. He stared at the Doctor, his eyes seeming to plead for understanding. 'I have been remiss. I should have taken better care of her.' He curled his lip and tossed his head, disgusted with the inadequacy of his excuse. 'I've been very busy lately.'

'Where is she?' the Doctor said. Bep-Wor saw icy fires burning in the Doctor's eyes.

'She's on this planet, Doctor,' Kedin said, spreading his arms. 'That's all I know. My aide, Madok, may have more information by now, but he isn't here. He's engaged on another mission.'

Kedin raised a finger to forestall the Doctor's next question. The Doctor scowled.

'I am engaged in an act of treason,' Kedin said. 'Reluctant as I am to stoop to melodrama, it is no exaggeration to say that the fate of this planet, as well as that of Mendeb Two, depends on the actions we take within the next few hours.'

The Doctor appeared sceptical. 'You would claim to be fighting for freedom and justice, I imagine,' he said. 'But for all I know you're simply mounting a *coup d'état*. One military leader replacing another.'

Kedin smiled wryly. 'You have every reason to doubt my motives, Doctor,' he said. 'And I can't claim that I have a grand new vision for my planet, nor that I'm acting from long-held principles. I'm a soldier and a scientist, not a politician. In the days when I helped Vethran to power I was complacent; as soon as I realised the extent of my errors I found myself coerced. I have some idea of the concern you feel for your companion, Doctor. I, too, care for someone: someone whom Vethran has kept within reach of his power, in order to ensure my compliance.'

'I understand,' Bep-Wor exclaimed. Kedin's words had conjured the image of Kia-Ga into his mind. He saw that Kedin would destroy the world to save the one he loved. And to Bep-Wor that seemed entirely reasonable.

There was a knocking on the outside of the craft. A soldier put his head through the doorway. 'Sorry to interrupt, sir. The road is secured, both directions, and we've started to move the vehicles out. Lift-off in five minutes, if you're ready.'

'Thank you,' Kedin said. 'I'll be with you shortly.' The soldier withdrew. 'My apologies, Doctor, Bep-Wor. This is a time for deeds, not words. Oh yes! I remember: I was trying to dissuade you from the notion that I'm no better than the King I intend to dethrone. What can I say that will convince you? Vethran is mad for power; he has a lust for conquest so insatiable that an entire planet has not satisfied him, and he has forced me to assist him in invading Bep-Wor's home world; he rules a society in which the wealthy own slaves; the formula which destroys the will of his captives and makes them slaves was created under his personal direction. No matter what shortcomings I may have, Doctor, don't you think I have every justification for removing him from his throne?'

'That all sounds very plausible,' the Doctor replied. 'And do you hope to fight your way across the King's capital city with the troops and vehicles you've assembled here?'

Kedin's eyes shone with excitement. 'By no means, Doctor. I have as many men again already in the city. They have been gathering for days, disguised as farmers, merchants, travelling showmen. The King has summoned the court to the Citadel, so the city is thronging with visitors. And then I have a third force, which I will lead myself, in an aerial attack.'

'And now that we know your plans,' the Doctor said, 'I suppose you'll have to kill us.'

Kedin threw back his head and laughed. 'Great heavens, no, Doctor,' he said. 'On the contrary. I want you to join me. Lead your army of free slaves into the city.'

He turned towards Bep-Wor. 'If Vethran remains in power, your people have no hope of freedom. This is your chance to make a difference.'

He turned back to the Doctor. 'And you, Doctor, are too wise to shirk your duty. You know I have right on my side. I would value your advice.'

Once again there was a knocking on the side of the craft. 'Ready for lift-off, sir,' a voice called.

Kedin shrugged. 'We have run out of time for talking,' he said. 'It will be bullets and sword-strokes from now on.' He stood up. 'I must ask you to leave now. Please consider my words. If you wish to join us, bring your people here. I'll tell Lafed to expect you.'

Deep in thought, the Doctor and Bep-Wor stepped down from the craft. Beyond the black shapes of the transport ships soldiers waved their arms, beckoning to them. 'Clear the area,' voices shouted. 'Hurry up! Get clear!'

Bep-Wor took the Doctor's arm and pulled him onwards. They ran between two of the vast vessels, and continued to run up the slope and into the forest as the roar of the engines of the transport ships became an unbearable scream.

'This will do,' the Doctor panted, and he stopped on a hillock. Bep-Wor stood beside him as they watched the six huge shapes begin to rise, imperceptibly at first and then with shocking speed, into the night sky. Kedin's much smaller craft spiralled upwards after them.

The valley was silent. The soldiers and vehicles had withdrawn.

'Well, Bep-Wor,' the Doctor said, 'what do you think?'

'I think we should return to the camp quickly, Doctor. We know there are soldiers from the city out in these hills.'

'You're right,' the Doctor said. 'Can you remember the way back?'

Bep-Wor turned. He could see only the darkness of the sky and under it the deeper darkness of the mounded hills. The view in every direction was similar. 'No, Doctor.'

'In that case it's a good job one of us has a sense of direction,' the Doctor said. 'Follow me. And tell me what you think we should do.'

As they fought their way up and down the forested slopes, the Doctor and Bep-Wor discussed whether either or both of them should support Kedin's attack on the city.

Bep-Wor was certain of what he had to do. Kedin had been right: regardless of the vices or virtues of the protagonists in the struggle, and regardless of the legality of the actions of either side, and regardless of the chances of Kedin's attack being successful, it remained true that unless the present King was overthrown Bep-Wor's people would continue to be enslaved. Bep-Wor saw no choice: he would have to bring his small army to join Kedin's forces.

After some debate the Doctor accepted the inevitability of Bep-Wor's decision. 'You've right, Bep-Wor,' he said, stopping for a moment to disengage his jacket from a thorn bush, so that Bep-Wor almost collided with him in the darkness. 'And I'll come with you.'

Bep-Wor was relieved. He had not been sure that he would have been able to persuade his army to go anywhere without the Doctor.

'As I said previously,' the Doctor went on, 'my main concern is to find the seat of power on this planet and to rectify the appalling mess that both worlds have got into. I can't do that by turning my back on this imminent conflict. And, of course, I have plenty of experience of this sort of thing. I expect I'll be able to sort things out.'

'Hush!' Bep-Wor said. He had heard a noise among the trees. 'Are we near to the camp?' he whispered.

'Yes,' the Doctor said. 'It's just –'

He was suddenly silent. Bep-Wor turned to look at him. For a moment his mind refused to understand what his eyes were seeing. There was a man standing behind the Doctor. A man in uniform. A soldier, with his gun pointed at the Doctor's body. Then something was thrust into his own ribs: something hard.

The barrel of a gun.

'Looks like we've found two more runaways,' the soldier behind the Doctor said.

'Drop your weapons,' the other ordered. 'Don't even think of making a run for it. We've a regiment on this hill, and all your sorry crew are already in chains. That's it: the carbine and the sword, on the floor.'

'We've got two more!' the first soldier shouted into the darkness.

'Bring them,' another voice replied. 'Let's get the whole lot down to the city and into the dungeons.'

Madok leant back in the Castlain's chair and rested the heels of his boots on the Castlain's desk. He gazed at the figurine that had pride of place on the polished surface, and then nudged it with his toe until it fell to the floor. The Castlain's taste in ornaments left much to be desired and little to the imagination. He ran his fingers through his hair and yawned. 'Four hours, lieutenant,' he said.

'Fast work, sir,' said the commander of Group Two. He had his arm in a bloodstained sling and a smoking pipe clenched between his teeth.

'It would have been faster if they hadn't defended the kitchens,' Madok complained. 'Did they think we'd broken in to get our breakfast loaves?'

The sound of marching feet echoed along the corridor outside the Castlain's quarters.

'That will be the Castlain,' the lieutenant said, strolling towards the door.

'Send him in immediately,' Madok said. 'We have unfinished business here.'

Escorted by two of the lieutenant's men, Castlain Pelod strode into the room and stopped abruptly when he saw the man sitting behind his desk. His grey-bearded jaw dropped open, and for a moment he was unable to speak.

'Madok!' he spluttered. 'Madok, by all the heavens what are you doing here? Are you responsible for this bloody violence? You've taken leave of your senses, man. You'll hang for this.'

'Or worse, I shouldn't wonder,' Madok said. 'Calm yourself, Pelod. Take a seat. It's been a tiring night for all of us.'

Pelod broke away from his guards and advanced towards Madok. 'You killed six of my men,' he said.

'And your men killed three of mine,' Madok said. 'There will be time to mourn our losses later. The important matter now is this: do you surrender Grake Castle to me?'

Pelod shrugged. 'Yes,' he said. 'I have no choice.'

'Thank you,' Madok said. He pulled his feet from the desk and turned to the lieutenant. 'Announce the surrender. Disarm any of the garrison we haven't yet captured. And then set up the radio and send the message that we've accomplished our mission.'

'Yes, sir,' the lieutenant said, and marched from the room.

'Now then, Pelod,' Madok said. 'Please be seated. We have searched the cells in the prison tower. I trust you'll save us the chore of searching every cell in the main block and below ground. Just tell me where she is.'

Pelod sat opposite Madok. He perched on the edge of the seat, leaning forward, his face still red with indignation. 'Where who is, Madok?'

Madok banged his fist on the desk. 'Don't play games, Pelod. You have only one significant prisoner here. I'm looking for Tevana Roslod.'

Pelod leant back. A slight smile appeared on his lips. For the first time since he launched the attack on Grake, Madok felt a shiver of doubt.

'So this is the work of Kedin Ashar,' Pelod said. 'I might have guessed. I always thought Kedin would prove unworthy of his Majesty's trust, in the end. You've allowed yourself to be seduced into treason, Madok.'

'Where is Tevana Roslod?' Madok persisted. 'If she's come to any harm you will pay for it.'

Pelod folded his arms. 'I am a loyal subject of King Vethran,' he said. 'I have defended his Majesty's castle to the best of my ability, and I have surrendered it according to the requirements of military law. I am not required to answer your questions.'

Madok stared at the Castlain. 'Vethran's reign is about to end,' he said. 'You will gain nothing by hindering me now.' Madok did his best to invest his words with conviction, but he knew that were he in Pelod's position he too would refuse to co-operate with his captors.

Pelod said nothing. He sat stolidly in his chair with his arms crossed over his chest.

'Take him away,' Madok told the soldiers. 'Put him in a cell. We'll have to search this castle from the cellars to the battlements.'

Bep-Wor, with Kia-Ga at his side, had led his army in chanting 'Doctor! Doctor!' throughout the long march through the dark streets of the city. The blows and curses of the King's soldiers had done nothing to dampen the spirits of the captives, and Bep-Wor had felt a sense of victory as his people entered within the high walls of the palace.

Now, however, he was finding it difficult to keep his spirits up. His army was silent; the only noises were the dripping of water from the damp walls of the dungeon, and the Doctor's footsteps as he paced back and forth. There was no light: even in the middle of the long winters on his home world Bep-Wor had never known such impenetrable darkness. It lay like a black blanket, smothering thought and hope alike. He had no way of knowing how long he and his people had been kept underground. Was it still night above them, or had a new day dawned? Would he ever see another day? The pressure of Kia-Ga's body against his provided no comfort: perhaps he would never see her face again.

He lifted his head: he had heard the sound of marching feet. The sound became louder; nearer. A shaft of light fell across the huddled bodies: a door had opened, high up. There were torches, soldiers, shouts.

Bep-Wor's eyes adjusted to the illumination. A row of soldiers, with their guns aimed at the prisoners below, were standing on a stone gallery halfway up one of the ancient walls. Wide stone steps – the steps down which Bep-Wor had stumbled when he had been thrust into the darkness – led down from the gallery to the unwholesome floor of the dungeon.

A voice rang out, and echoed from the vast vaults: 'Make way for his Majesty the King!'

The soldiers stood to attention. In the ensuing silence Bep-Wor heard the Doctor's voice saying, 'About time, too.'

A tall figure appeared in the doorway. The medals on his chest, the buttons of his uniform, the jewels sewn into his robe, all glittered in the torchlight. The soldiers saluted. This was Vethran, the King of this world. Bep-Wor had expected – he didn't know what he had expected. Someone more remarkable, perhaps: a man whose face betrayed an inner evil. Vethran was tall, imposing, with keen, intelligent eyes and a full beard. And that was all.

The King gazed down at the prisoners as his entourage followed him through the doorway and filled the gallery. Most of them were dressed in finery almost as rich as their monarch's. Some held lace-trimmed cloths to their faces.

'This place stinks,' the King said at last. He paused to listen to his words rebounding from the slick stones. 'It's fit only for vermin,' he went on. 'And that's what it contains. Councillor Traban!'

One of the glittering figures stepped forward. 'Your Majesty?'

'Am I to take it, Traban,' the King said, ' that this pathetic, unwashed rabble of Twos is the mighty army that has eluded your men for almost a week?'

The Councillor hesitated before replying. It was clear to Bep-Wor that Vethran's courtiers were in fear of him. 'I believe so, your Majesty. We have succeeded in capturing all of them, with no losses to our forces.' Traban had obviously decided that it was better to stress the positive aspects of the situation.

The King grunted, and Traban visibly sighed with relief. 'So be it,' the King said. 'Although I'm sure it wasn't necessary to mobilise half the household guard merely to round up a gang of escaped Twos.'

'Your Majesty's security is always my prime consideration.'

'That's as it should be,' the King said. 'It's true there have been curious rumours about shadowy forces moving through the night. However, the problem has been resolved. Stand down the guard, Councillor, and bring the patrols back to their barracks.'

'Of course, your Majesty.'

Bep-Wor found that he could still smile: a grim twist of his lips. Vethran had decided that with the escaped Twos recaptured, there was no further danger. Kedin's preparations for his attacks could now proceed with less danger of discovery.

'I should execute the lot of you,' the King announced, addressing the prisoners. 'But I'm in a merciful mood. And in any case, to kill you all would be a waste of valuable Twos. You will all become obedient servants, and that will be the end of this short-lived rebellion. I will, however, make one exception. Which is the one known as the Doctor?'

A young man pushed through the courtiers to stand at the King's side. Bep-Wor recognised him: Sarid, the commissioner's assistant, whom Bep-Wor had last seen riding away from the landing site on the day the transport ship had landed.

'That's him, your Majesty,' Sarid said, pointing down to the dungeon floor. 'At the front, in the strange clothes and hat.'

The Doctor began climbing the steps. 'Yes, I'm the Doctor,' he said, 'and I have a number of things to discuss with you.'

The King appeared amused. 'Is that so?' he said. He turned to Sarid. 'I understand this fellow is unaffected by SS10?'

'Yes, your Majesty. He claims he took the potion while in transit, and he certainly took a second dose on the orders of commissioner Dallid. As you can see, he retains his own will.'

'Doctor,' the King called out. 'Stop there!'

The Doctor continued to walk up the steps.

A look of mild surprise appeared on the King's face. 'It's true, then,' he said. 'Seize him, some of you.'

Four soldiers ran down the steps to intercept the Doctor, and soon he was struggling in their grasp next to the King.

'We must talk,' the Doctor was trying to say. 'This is important.'

'He's a noisy little fellow,' the King announced. The courtiers laughed politely. The King addressed the Doctor. 'Be silent,' he said, 'or I'll have the guards damage you.'

The Doctor's struggles subsided.

'If you don't fall under the thrall of SS10,' the King said to the Doctor, 'you are worse than valueless. I would turn you over to my chemists, so that they can analyse you, but frankly I can't be bothered to take the trouble. You have already caused enough inconvenience.' He spoke to the guards around the Doctor. 'Hold his head.'

The King produced from a pocket in his robe a slender glass tube. 'This is distilled from the venom of bile worms,' he said. 'I made it myself. It corrupts the internal organs. Death is inevitable and very rapid. Let's see you remain unaffected by this.'

The Doctor was fighting again to be free, but there were

soldiers all around him. Bep-Wor saw hands clamped on to the Doctor's head, twisting it and forcing his mouth open. He saw the King smiling as he tipped the contents of the tube into the Doctor's throat.

'Stand aside,' the King said. The soldiers cautiously stepped back from the Doctor.

The Doctor stood alone at the top of the steps. His eyes were wide with shock. His limbs began to convulse. He gave a weak cry, and his knees gave way. He fell forward, and tumbled down the steps.

Bep-Wor watched the Doctor's body. It lay motionless at the foot of the steps. The Doctor's hat was floating on a stinking puddle next to his head.

Now, Doctor, Bep-Wor silently urged. Now is the time to rise up. Come on, Doctor. Amaze them. Be alive. Be alive, Doctor.

The Doctor didn't move.

'Collect the body,' the King said. 'I'll have it put on display. Have these Twos interrogated, and then dose them with SS10 as necessary. This little crisis is as dead as the Doctor.'

There was nowhere left to search. The men from Harran had torn up floorboards and had even knocked holes in the walls where they had sounded hollow. Men had climbed into the roof spaces and down into the drains.

Madok had to face the truth. The men needed to rest. And if Tevana Roslod had ever been held in Grake Castle, she was there no longer.

Madok sat at the Castlain's desk with his head in his hands. He consulted his pocket-watch. By now Kedin would be committed to the final assault. And Tevana was still in Vethran's hands.

Chapter Five

Above and beyond the vast glass dome that roofed the new throne room, night had fallen. Inside it was still as bright as day: glowing bulbs containing electric filaments were strung along the polygonal frames of the dome's structure, creating a filigree tessellation in the heavens, while far below gas lamps in ornate shapes burnt alongside every avenue and at the centre of every table.

It was a room as spacious as a park. It contained an ornamental garden, a dining area, arcades and fountains and, on a terrace constructed of old stone blocks and decorated with friezes that depicted Vethran's conquests, the throne itself.

Architecturally, Ace thought, it was a right old dog's dinner.

She thought it odd that she hadn't noticed before how grandiose and muddled the whole room was.

'Ace!' the King called to her. 'Traban Yonfar needs more wine. He has reason to celebrate this evening.'

Dinner was in full swing. Every table was occupied by stuffy-looking lords and ladies wearing costumes that must have weighed a ton. The medals and jewellery were dazzling, and the noise of conversation and clattering cutlery was deafening.

'Yes, your Majesty,' Ace said, and carried her pitcher of wine towards the military-looking type with waxed moustaches.

From waitress to waitress, via a spot of time-travel and saving a few civilisations, she thought. As she squeezed between tables she was aware of all the nearby men looking at her. She was the only woman in the throne room wearing trousers, and she knew by now that everyone thought she was indecently dressed. Occasionally she felt a hand grope at her legs as she passed.

It's a good job I've been told that I'm happy doing this, she said to herself, because otherwise I think I'd be quite pissed off.

She poured wine into Traban's glass. 'May I serve you further, sir?' she asked him.

'I'll say, you pretty thing,' the old buffer exclaimed. 'Come here and sit on my knees, eh?'

Not bloody likely, she thought. I'll pretend I didn't hear that.

'Thank you, sir,' she said. She turned and walked away, ignoring the expostulations behind her.

I can't believe I just did that, she thought. I should have obeyed his instructions. I should have sat on his bony old knees. I would have been happy to do it. I've been told I'll be happy to obey every instruction I'm given.

What's happening to me?

'Ace!' It was the King calling her again. 'Ace, come here. I want to show you to the Count of Martolin. I might lend you to him, I think, for an hour or so.'

You're joking, aren't you? Ace said to herself. She'd already identified the Count of Martolin as a grade-A slime-ball.

Smiling, and with a determined stride, Ace made for one of the stairwells that led down into the service areas. Her wine pitcher was almost empty: if challenged she would say that she had been told to refill it.

As she walked steadfastly towards the wine cellars she blocked out the noise around her and tried to work out what was happening.

She had been told to do as she was told. She had been told that she was happy to do as she was told. It was stupid, circular illogicality. What if she wasn't happy?

And she wasn't happy. In fact, how had she ever put up with

them? That greasy fop Tragar, that vicious old witch Rigora, that wily politician Balon, and that fruitcake of a King. She remembered some of the things that they had made her do, and she felt her cheeks burning as she blushed.

She wasn't happy. She was angry.

There were Twos and other servants carrying pitchers and bottles in and out of the entrance to the cellars, but inside the low, gloomy, bottle-lined corridors Ace was able to find a place where she could be alone.

In the cool quiet she sat on a barrel, inhaling the musty aroma of old brandy, and she realised that for the first time in weeks she was enjoying an experience without having been told to enjoy it.

The curious thing was that she remembered everything. She had been herself – wanting things, knowing her own opinions, doing as she chose – in the TARDIS, and after the Doctor had left her on the space station. And then she had ceased to be herself. She had had no thoughts of her own: no wants or wishes, no emotions other than those she was told to have. She had done exactly as she had been told, always, because there had been no alternative.

And now, just as suddenly, she was herself again.

What I should concentrate on, she said to herself, is getting out of here. And doing as much damage as I can in the process. This whole set-up stinks. Mister high-and-mighty Vethran is in charge of a society that uses people from another world as slaves. This is exactly the sort of nonsense the Doctor and I should be putting a stop to.

But I can't help wondering how it was done. How did I become like that? A mindless slave?

Oh, god. It had to be. There was no other possibility.

That's the last time I fall for someone because he looks like a film star, Ace told herself. It was Kedin. All those people in cargo hold twelve; the ones I travelled with on that gruesome transport ship. It must be a drug, or something. And Kedin's doing it.

As Ace remembered the things she'd said and done on the space station, she clenched her fists so tightly that her nails cut into her palms.

'That bastard,' she whispered. 'I'll kill him.'

Kia-Ga, along with all of Bep-Wor's people who had taken the drug on the transport ship, had been taken away. The Doctor was dead.

Bep-Wor had been left with nothing. Soon he would be given the potion, and he would live out the rest of his life as a slave on this alien world.

The dungeon darkness enveloped him like a shroud. All around him, he knew, were his comrades – the army he and the Doctor had led from victory to victory, freeing slaves as they marched from the landing site to the King's capital. And yet he felt utterly alone. The damp cold had penetrated into his heart and soul, and rendered him numb. Even if he had had a weapon, he knew he lacked the spirit to kill himself.

Nothing. The end. Blackness.

He wondered how long the noises had been going on. Down here every sound, except for the dripping of water from the walls, was muffled. He lifted his head. He heard murmurings from around him: others had begun to notice the occasional, distant, dull thumps that echoed, more vibration than sound, in the dark void above them.

He had heard similar noises before. On his home world, when the invaders had come. Before anyone knew the coming danger, soft booms like these had been heard from over the horizon. These were the sounds of explosives.

The attack had begun, then. In the streets above the dank

stillness of the dungeon, men were fighting, firing weapons, thrusting swords.

Perhaps there was a little hope. But Kia-Ga was gone, and the Doctor was dead. And with the Doctor had died Bep-Wor's gossamer dream that Kia-Ga could be returned to her former state.

Bep-Wor smiled bitterly. Just enough hope, then, to make him realise the hopelessness of his situation.

They had found only six camelopes in the stables of Grake Castle. Having transmitted to Kedin the grim news that Tevana had not been found, Madok had asked for five volunteers to accompany him.

He knew that every one of the Harran men was as battle-weary as he was.

He had told them that to accompany him would be more taxing than taking the castle had been: they would have to ride fast, in the dark, on unfamiliar terrain, into a well-defended city. The mission was suicidal. Every man had volunteered. Madok had been so moved that he had felt tears stinging his eyes.

The heavens seemed to Madok to be dispensing good fortune arbitrarily. After the disappointment of failing to find Tevana, things were once again going well. The camelopes were strong, and seemed accustomed to night travel. The riders made good speed across the wooded hillsides: none of the steeds tripped or was made lame. They encountered none of the King's forces.

Madok called his little troop to a halt as they reached the final hilltop. From it they looked down on Gonfallon city.

'It looks peaceful,' one of the men said.

Madok extended his arm. 'Look,' he said. 'There are fires burning in the outer quarters. Our covert teams have begun their work. They will draw the King's guards out across the city, dispersing Vethran's strength.'

A vivid burst of light flashed among the distant streets. It receded, and then flared again as a column of flame and smoke. A rumble, like thunder, rolled across the panorama.

'Explosive charge,' grunted one of the riders.

Madok's lowered his arm slightly. 'One of our motorised units has reached the West Gate of the inner city,' he said. 'They're equipped with a weapon that we discovered on the space station. It fires a beam which seems to disrupt matter in its path. They should be able to take the gate. We'll try to enter the city there.'

'All's quiet at the Citadel,' another of the riders said.

Madok nudged his heels into the flanks of his camelope, and began to pick his way down the side of the hill. He kept his eyes on the vast, ornate structure that dominated the city: at its centre the dome of the new throne room glowed with light. 'There's a feast in progress,' he said. 'The entire court's in residence. It looks quiet, but that new dome of Vethran's will be shaking, what with the music and the talking. I doubt if they've even heard the explosions. It will be some time before the city's garrison commanders can get word to Vethran that there are attacks in progress.'

'No sign yet of Kedin Ashar's ships,' the rider behind Madok said.

'He'll be there soon. Vethran's in for a surprise.'

I've heard of hiding in plain sight, Ace thought, but this takes the biscuit.

Balon Ferud had presented Ace to the King only that morning but, thanks to her infamously indecent costume she was already recognisable to just about everyone in the palace. Now she found that because she was so well known her presence was taken for granted. Carrying her wine pitcher, and with an expression of docile contentment fixed on her face, she was able to walk the corridors unchallenged.

Most of the people marching or scurrying along the passages were Twos or soldiers: they had their own orders to follow, and barely looked at her at they passed. Otherwise she saw only a few of the palace servants, or retainers of the courtiers, or sometimes the courtiers themselves: these would look at her, certainly, as she was something of a celebrity. But she was known to be a Two, and the King's property, and it was assumed that she was fulfilling an instruction given by his Majesty. What other explanation could there be?

Once she realised that no one would molest her, Ace decided to explore the whole palace. Something was up: the soldiers who passed her in the corridors were running now, rather than marching, and they were clutching rifles rather than the ceremonial swords they usually carried in the palace. The atmosphere had changed. It crackled almost audibly with an electric, exciting buzz. In the same way that one knows one is approaching the coast, even though there is no sign of the sea, because of the salt and seaweed smells in the air, Ace knew she was approaching something exciting. She could smell it. Conflict. Danger. Thrills and spills.

Adrenaline in her veins.

She found a terrace: a stone-built walkway with glassed arches, like one side of a cloister. The windows, she assumed, provided views of something worth seeing, when there was daylight to see by. The terrace was, as far as she could judge, near the perimeter of the palace buildings, and it was here that she heard the explosion.

She recognised the sound immediately, and grinned.

That's more like it, she thought.

She took the risk of dropping her pretence of mindlessness

for a moment, and peered out into the darkness. There were fires burning in the distance; flashes of light, followed by deep rumblings; the crackle of gunfire.

It's an attack, she told herself. Someone's attacking the palace. Well, now: any enemy of King Vethran is a friend of mine, I'd say. I really ought to lend a hand.

A baseball bat worked against Daleks, and gold coins did for Cybermen. Neither, Ace thought, would be of much help in the storming of a fortified palace. Ace considered what she knew about besieging castles, and decided she didn't know much. She concluded that, when in doubt, she should arm herself with some explosives.

And, she thought, casting her mind back to black-and-white films about Ruritania and men in iron masks, there are probably dangerous, swashbuckling prisoners who'd be handy in a punch-up, if released and armed.

Dungeons and ammo stores. Both downstairs, probably.

Bep-Wor woke with a start. He had been dozing, curled on the floor, dreaming. He had been sitting on the verandah, watching the crimson sea, with the aroma of frying herbs and fish floating by him on the warm breeze. From the kitchen came a voice, calling him. Kia-Ga.

He sobbed with anguish when he remembered where he was.

He could see the walls. There was light. The door, high up, at the top of the stairway, was open. Not much light: just the glimmer of a torch in the corridor beyond the door.

A lone figure stood in the doorway. A boy – no, a young woman.

'Blimey, what a stench,' the woman said. Then she raised her voice. 'Anyone down there?'

Whoever she was, she wasn't one of the King's guards.

'Here,' Bep-Wor called out.

His voice emerged from his throat as a whispered croak. He hadn't spoken for hours. He tried again. 'Over here! There are about a hundred of us.'

'Who are you?' the woman shouted.

'We're from the other world,' Bep-Wor shouted back. 'The world called Mendeb Two. We used to be free.'

'You'll not be chums of the King, then,' the woman said. 'Good. Well, you're free again. Something's going on: an attack on the palace, I think. War, rebellion, that kind of thing. Join in, if you want. I'm off to find some dynamite.'

'I know something of this attack,' Bep-Wor started to say, but the young woman had gone from the doorway.

But the door remained open.

Bep-Wor stood on trembling legs. 'Up!' he exhorted the prisoners. 'Come! Let us leave this pit.'

By the dim light he could see the shapes of his comrades moving sluggishly as they tried to rouse themselves.

'Would the Doctor want us to remain here as slaves?' he cried. 'No! The Doctor would lead us up, and into the light. For his sake, let us march once more. We may yet die. But we will die free.'

'Doctor! Doctor!' The chant began, quietly at first, and then with increasing force as the men and women dragged themselves up from the foetid floor.

Still chanting, they followed Bep-Wor up the steps.

When Madok reached Carracton Square he rode his camelope straight into the patch of green lawn at its centre. Here, at least, there was comparative peace. On all sides of the square, citizens of the city were leaning from their upper windows, hurling questions and rubbish on to the brawling soldiers below. As far as Madok could tell none of the soldiers were

Kedin's men: the fight seemed to be between a troop of the King's guards and a contingent of the citizens' militia.

His five men followed him into the tree-ringed haven.

'Dismount,' Madok said, 'and tether your steeds. We'll go on foot from here. We're too visible riding.' He tied the reins of his camelope to the outstretched hand of the statue of Count Carracton.

'It's slow progress either way,' one of the Harran men said. 'Half the city's locked itself indoors. The other half's out on the streets and fighting mad.'

'And not much sign of the covert units,' Madok said. 'Although that's as it should be. Plenty of evidence of where they've set fires and charges.'

'It's keeping the guards busy just fighting the flames.'

'Keep your guns hidden, if you can,' Madok said. 'Now we're on foot we may once again pass as farmers.' He stuffed his handgun into the front of his jerkin. He didn't feel comfortable out of uniform, but it would have been folly to ride into the King's capital as an identifiable follower of Kedin Ashar.

'We've seen enough of the skirmishing in the suburbs,' he told his men. 'The indications are that the main forces have advanced into the inner city. Everything's going to plan. We'll make for the Citadel gates.'

He pushed his hands into the pockets of his rough woollen trousers, lowered his head, affected a slouch, and set off into the burning, brawling streets.

He and his men walked as two groups of three, so as to look less threatening. They were uniformly tall and strong for farm workers, and they walked with a sense of purpose that was strange to see in out-of-towners on a late-night spree, but the citizens and soldiery of Gonfallon city had too many other concerns to inspect too closely two groups of slightly-drunken country folk.

They passed a warehouse with flames leaping from its roof. Furtive figures were running from its broken doors, carrying away bundles of loot.

They entered a wide avenue, only to find it blocked with a barricade of merchants' carts. The soldiers behind the barricade, militia commanded by officers from the King's guard, had their weapons aimed and ready to rake the avenue with bullets. But there was no sign of an enemy for them to shoot at.

They heard, nearby, the sounds of an intense gun-battle. They heard, distantly, occasional explosions. The sky was orange with reflected fire; the air smelt of smoke.

Three guards emerged from an alley to challenge Madok and the two men beside him. Madok prevaricated, acting drunk, until the other three came up behind the guards. It was six against three: the guards fell before they could summon aid.

They passed the sites of earlier battles: blood running between the cobbles, the smell of gunpowder, ungainly bodies in stained uniforms. Madok was relieved to see that few of the dead were Kedin's men.

They came upon a crowd in a wide street: the people, quiet and curious, were surrounding an abandoned machine. Madok held up his hand to indicate that his men should remain in the shadows; he staggered across the street and pushed his way into the crowd.

'Never seen anything like it,' a woman said. 'It's unnatural.'

'The self-propelled vehicle is modern, that's a fact,' a man said, 'but as for the device on top of it . . .'

'Could it be a bomb?' someone else said, and the crowd drew back as one.

Madok recognised the machine at once. It was one of the weapons taken from the space station, mounted on one of the latest self-propelled vehicles. It was the disrupter that had shattered the gate of the inner city and allowed in Kedin's main force, led by Lafed. It was destroyed: its funnel-shaped barrel was broken, its casing pierced with bullet-holes.

'That's bad,' Madok muttered to his men when he rejoined them. 'Lafed will find it hard going at the Citadel gates without the disrupter.'

'We're almost there,' one of the men pointed out. 'I can hear the fighting.'

They rounded two more corners, and it became obvious that a fierce battle was in progress nearby. Two cargo vehicles, parked sideways, blocked the street ahead of them. The rattle of guns and the whine of bullets were continuous. Any slight hiatus was filled with the shouting of orders and the cries of wounded men. Shadows danced against the lurid colours of the flames that coated the tall buildings.

'Stop!' a voice shouted from behind the vehicles. 'No further or we'll shoot.'

These were Lafed's men: the rearguard, defending his position against attack from behind. And to judge from the few troops guarding the rear, Madok concluded that Lafed had found it necessary to commit virtually all his forces forward.

Madok held up his hands. 'I'm Madok,' he said. 'Aide to Kedin Ashar.'

There was a silence. Madok imagined the whispered discussion between the sentries. 'Advance,' a voice said.

Gesturing to his men to stay back, Madok walked towards the vehicles. He hoped that the sentries – no doubt the least experienced of Lafed's troops – had steady trigger fingers.

'It is Madok,' a voice rang out. 'I saw him once. It's him.'

Madok ran forward and squeezed through the gap between the vehicles. He was appalled to find only three men, and youngsters at that, on duty.

'Those are my men,' he said, jerking his thumb over his shoulder. 'Let them pass. We've ridden here from Grake – we took the castle earlier this evening. My men are exhausted. I'll leave them here with you. It looks as though you could do with reinforcements. Where's Lafed?'

'At the front, sir.' The lad pointed up the street, although it was obvious where the battle was taking place. The twin towers of the Citadel gateway loomed above the tall mansions that lined the street; in front of the wedge-shaped bases of the towers, each as large as the prow of an ocean-going ship, a ribbon of men and machines sheltered behind a makeshift barrier of vehicles, fallen statues, and the bodies of the dead. Bullets and grenades rained down from the towers; intermittently, rockets and bullets were fired from the ground towards the battlements.

Madok didn't like the look of it at all. Lafed's force had been pinned down in front of the gates, and without the disrupter there seemed no prospect of breaking through.

Crouching, and keeping under the eaves of the houses, Madok ran towards the cacophony of the battle. He found Lafed directing his troops' fire from behind the low garden wall of the last house.

'Madok! What in heaven's name are you doing here?' Lafed's face was black with smoke. His eyes were bloodshot.

'Couldn't bear to miss the fun,' he said, attempting to be lighthearted. 'This doesn't look too good.'

'It isn't.' Lafed shook his head. 'We can't get through here. I've sent a radio message to Kedin's assault group. I'm waiting for the signal to withdraw and regroup.'

A bullet struck the parapet of the wall, and splinters of stone exploded. Madok and Lafed ducked their heads. Madok's ears were ringing; he felt a trickle of blood down his cheek.

'You won't get it,' he said. 'Tevana Roslod wasn't being held at Grake. She must be in the palace.'

Madok watched Lafed's face as he absorbed the news and

233

understood its meaning. 'Yes,' Madok said. 'Kedin will have to go in. He won't leave Tevana here.'

Lafed's eyes were wide. 'His group will be cut to pieces if they go in without support.'

'And so we have to keep trying,' Madok said. 'If we can't get into the palace, at least we'll keep some of the guards busy.'

'Until we're all dead,' Lafed said. Suddenly he grinned. 'Right then. Let's see how long we can keep fighting.'

Ace studied the base of her pitcher. It wasn't so much as cracked. She looked down at the unconscious guard whose head she had just struck. Crockery that was harder than a soldier's head – she was impressed.

She dragged the guard away from the door he had been standing beside, round a corner and into the shadows below a flight of stairs. She frisked the still body. The guard had a sword, but no gun: that was no good, a sword was too noticeable. No keys, either.

Ace poked her head round the corner. The corridor was still empty. She hadn't yet found a weapons store, and despite the reassuring solidity of the wine pitcher she was getting desperate for something with some real firepower. She was about to set off along the corridor, when the door whose sentry she had just knocked out seemed to draw her attention.

She tiptoed towards it, pressed her ear to the solid wood, and listened. She could hear nothing. She knocked.

'Yes?' said a female voice. 'Enter, by all means, if you have a key.'

A woman prisoner. And with a dedicated guard, too. Ace's curiosity was piqued. 'Who's in there?' she said, as loudly as she dared.

There was a long silence. When the woman spoke again, it was clear to Ace that she had moved close to the door. 'I am

Tevana Roslod,' the woman said. Her voice sounded calm and amused. 'I'm surprised you didn't know. And who are you?'

Tevana. Ace thought she recognised the name, but she couldn't remember from where or when.

'My name's Ace.'

'Is that all?'

'Yes.'

There was another pause. 'You have me at a disadvantage, Ace,' Tevana said. 'I regret that I've not heard of you. You should go. I'm not supposed to receive visitors, other than Vethran and my guards.'

'The palace is being attacked,' Ace said.

'I know,' Tevana said. 'I've heard the explosions.' She seemed not at all surprised.

Ace was becoming exasperated. 'Well, do you want me to try to get you out of there?'

Tevana laughed. 'I'll be quite safe,' she said. 'I'm very valuable to the King. But you sound young, my dear. You should look to your own safety, and go.'

Ace stared at the door. Evidently the woman locked behind it was important. She didn't know what she should do.

The sound of marching feet echoed along the corridor.

'Someone's coming,' Ace said. 'Sounds like guards.'

'Don't worry yourself,' the gentle voice said. 'I'm in no danger. Now go.'

Ace struck her forehead with her hands. The sound of marching feet was becoming louder. Ace realised that she would have to conceal herself. 'Goodbye,' she said, and ran to the corner.

She pressed her back against the wall. Just in time: the footsteps were in the corridor now. At least two guards. If only she'd been able to find some weapons. The wine pitcher wouldn't be much use in a frontal assault on two or more armed soldiers.

'Where's the sentry?' one of the guards said.

'Don't know, sir,' another replied.

'Called away, perhaps. No matter. Unlock the door.'

Ace heard the rattle of keys. She turned, and risked a glance along the corridor.

There were four of them, armed to the teeth. No hope of jumping them. One of them was carrying a tray, on which Ace could see a plate of food and a goblet.

It was just a mealtime visit. Nothing to worry about. The woman named Tevana would be safe for a while, at least.

Ace determined to continue her search for weapons. Maybe she'd be able to come back and release the woman later.

Bep-Wor had quickly given up his attempts to persuade his people to move stealthily. Their cry of 'Doctor! Doctor!' echoed along the corridors, preceding the miasma of dungeon odour that wafted around them. They streamed and surged into rooms and up stairways. With unkempt hair, wild eyes, and damp, flapping rags as clothes, they seemed to strike fear into whoever they met. Servants and courtiers ran; any soldiers who tried to hold back the human flood were overwhelmed, their weapons plucked from their hands.

As they poured through the innards of the palace their numbers grew: every Two they found they instructed to join them. Bep-Wor's army was reconstituted, and was once again on the march.

He found Kia-Ga in the kitchens. As his people swarmed alongside him, he stood still in the waves of heat emanating from the long iron ovens. He held Kia-Ga's face in his hands, and stared into her eyes. He could not be sure that she even recognised him.

236

He realised that there had been no point in finding her. He could hold her in his hands: she was warm, alive. But she had gone forever.

'Follow me,' he told her. 'Obey no more orders from anyone other than me.'

'Yes, sir,' she replied.

He sobbed, and wiped tears from his eyes.

'Don't call me sir,' he said. 'Call me Bep-Wor.'

'Yes, Bep-Wor.'

The kitchen had emptied as suddenly as it had become crowded. His army had sped on and he, its leader, risked being left behind.

Onwards. Upwards, into the light. There was nothing left but vengeance.

'Come on, Kia-Ga,' he said. 'We must hurry. Run!'

'Yes, Bep-Wor.'

The pitcher was now very heavy. It contained ten cylinders that, in Ace's opinion, were sticks of explosive. They had red warning signs stuck on them, and fuses made of something that looked inflammable.

There was, Ace thought, only one way to find out just how much of a bang they'd make, and she had therefore lifted from the weapons room, along with the cylinders, two books of matches.

She also now had a gun in the inside pocket of her jacket.

She had emerged from the subterranean passages below the palace: she was making for where the noise of battle was loudest.

As she walked through a low doorway, she found herself in the open air. She was in a narrow, curved courtyard, with high walls on both sides. In the crescent of night sky above her there were stars, obscured by drifting smoke. The noise –

gunfire and shouting – was much louder, and came from the far end of the courtyard.

She hefted the pitcher on to her shoulder and set off across the flagstones. She could see, at the top of the wall to her left, men running along the battlements and crouching to shoot through the crenellations.

As the courtyard curved round to Ace's right it widened, and she saw that it opened on to a wide plaza. In normal times it would be a pleasant open space, she thought. She saw avenues lined with what appeared to be lamp-posts, topiary shrubs in huge containers, banners flying from flagpoles. Now it was full of carts and vehicles, with lines of soldiers carrying boxes to and fro, and officers shouting to be heard above the noise of the gunfire.

Ace retreated into the shadows and watched for a moment. This is where it's all happening, she said to herself. The King's men on this side and, on the other side of this wall to my left, the other lot trying to get into the palace. And although I've been lucky so far, I think I'd be rumbled if I tried to carry off my serving-wench impersonation in the middle of a firefight – so I can't get any closer to the action.

It was tempting to stay where she was and lob lighted sticks of explosive towards the carts and trucks. They'd burn well, and if they contained ammunition they might make some truly awesome explosions.

But the vehicles were surrounded by soldiers. She couldn't do it.

She retraced her steps into the narrow, curved space between the high walls. She looked up. Here the battlements were deserted, as the soldiers were concentrating their fire further along, opposite the plaza. And here, she realised as she felt along the wall, there was a doorway. And the door was unlocked.

She slipped inside, into a dark passage that ran along the base of the wall. When her eyes were accustomed to the gloom she began to look for places where explosive charges would do the most damage to the fabric of the structure.

The sounds of the battle hardly penetrated into the passageway, buried in the thickness of the wall. Ace worked patiently, knitting together the fuses. She hadn't been able to resist packing all ten of the cylinders together: if you're going to make a bang, she reasoned, make it a big one.

She struck a match, put it to the end of the fuse, and watched for a few seconds to make sure it burnt well.

She grinned in the darkness. Best not hang about, she told herself. Back to the throne room, I think. That'll be the best place to watch the action.

Lafed's troops were becoming a motley crew. Madok might have laughed had the situation been less serious. In addition to Madok and the five men from Harran, who were dressed as farmers, there were now clowns, acrobats, robed mystics and black-suited mourners fighting alongside the surviving uniformed men from Lafed's original force: three of the covert teams had emerged from the city, drawn by the sound of the battle.

'It makes no difference, Madok,' Lafed shouted. 'We're still stuck here. Pinned down.'

The wall behind which they were sheltering consisted now of only a few courses of bricks, and these were being shot away. Madok and Lafed were lying on their stomachs, and Madok knew that within minutes they would have to crawl back to a less exposed position.

'Great heavens!' Lafed exclaimed. 'What was that?'

The ground beneath them had moved. It had leapt up and struck Madok's chest, winding him. It was still shuddering.

He became aware of a rumbling that seemed to come from below the ground. It was so profound that he felt rather than heard it. The gunfire petered out. The rumbling, too, faded, but only to be replaced by another sound: a wrenching, cracking noise, as of a thick branch being slowly broken – but much, much louder.

'Ammunition dump gone up,' Madok choked out. 'Must be. Big explosion.'

'The wall, Madok,' Lafed said. He was pointing away to the right of the twin-towered gateway. 'Look at the wall.'

A section of the stone-block wall appeared to be quivering. Smoke billowed from cracks that widened and raced across the surface even as Madok watched. Cries of alarm could be heard from within the gates.

And then the blocks began to fall. The battlements toppled, and slid down the cracked face of the wall, smashing the cobbled streets where they fell. The structure began to lean outwards. The topmost blocks of stone curved gracefully away and seemed to hang unsupported in the air before plummeting to the street.

'Pull your men back now,' Madok urged Lafed, 'while the King's men are still wondering what's going on. And then form them up. The wall's breached, and we'll force our way in.'

It was dirty, frenzied, hand-to-hand scrapping. Madok and Lafed were at the front of the squad that ran in first, before the stones had stopped falling. Madok yelled at the top of his voice, because the smoke and dust, as thick as autumn fog, blinded everyone. He charged up the jagged hillock of fallen blocks and hoped his men were behind him. To his right he heard Lafed's voice. In front of him, flashes of light and sudden shocks penetrated through the dust: the two reserve squads were throwing grenades through the breach in the wall to deter the defenders.

Madok did not expect to be fired upon from within the palace. The guard commander would know that he had to keep out the attackers, and therefore he couldn't afford to have his men stand back from the wall and try to pick off the attackers as they came through the breach. Sure enough, Madok's charge was opposed by guards wielding swords. They appeared suddenly out of the mist, scrambling up the other side of the fallen wall, trying to take the peak before the attackers could reach it.

Madok had time to fire two shots, and then he drew his knife and it was steel against steel. He could barely see the man in front of him, but he could hear all around the clanging of swords, and cries and grunts.

He won the crest of the jumbled hillock of stone blocks. On both sides he heard his own men pressing forwards. He spat to clear the dust from his throat. Fortune was playing tricks with Kedin's cause, he reflected. To be held at bay at the palace gates, until failure seemed certain, and then for the wall to be blown down by some unknown agency – it was beyond belief.

Now they could succeed. Vethran would be overthrown, Tevana would be reunited with Kedin. Why, Madok himself might even find Ace, eventually.

He sheathed his knife, readied his gun, and strode forward into the palace.

Ace smiled as she ran. She was deep inside the palace again, but even here she felt the floor shudder beneath her feet. There was almost nothing she liked better than a good, big explosion, and it was particularly satisfying when she caused one herself.

Soldiers appeared in a doorway ahead of her. She slowed to a walk, and balanced the pitcher on her shoulder. Frankly she had the impression that she wouldn't get arrested now even if she started shouting and breaking the furniture: everyone she came across was running and looking very preoccupied. But there was no point in taking unnecessary risks.

She turned to her right at the next junction, in order to avoid meeting the soldiers, and found herself walking down a set of stairs. She was in a part of the palace she hadn't yet explored.

At the bottom of the stairs was a door. It was locked, and bore a sign which said PRIVATE. It was the first such sign Ace had seen in the palace.

'Well intriguing,' she said, and kicked open the door.

There was nothing of interest beyond the door: just a long, narrow, dark corridor. But Ace could hear the booted feet of the soldiers approaching the top of the stairs, so she took the key that was in the corridor side of the lock and set off at a jog along the passage.

As she ran she tried to estimate the length of the corridor. It seemed to go on for ever. It had taken her below ground level, far from the front wing of the palace, where she had gone down the steps. She reckoned that she was once again close to the dungeons.

At last she reached the end of the corridor. Another locked door. She opened it with the key. She entered a small chamber, lit by gas lamps on the walls. A narrow staircase wound upwards. In front of her was another door marked PRIVATE. It also said KEEP OUT.

Or in other words, Ace thought, INTERESTING STUFF IN HERE.

The door wasn't locked.

Truly, wickedly interesting stuff, Ace thought, as she surveyed the laboratory that she found she had walked into. Around the walls were cabinets full of glass jars containing powders and specimens of plants. Sprawling across two wide benches were labyrinths of tubes and flasks that reminded Ace of old horror movies. She recognised some of it as distillation equipment.

What's this lot for, then? she asked herself. What are the King's scientists cooking up down here?

She found the answer on a desk at one end of the room. She put down her pitcher and studied the row of exhibits, which were conveniently labelled as if in a museum.

At one end of the row was a nondescript plant which, according to its label, was called spore or spore-weed. Ace didn't recognise it, and she wondered whether it was a species indigenous to Mendeb Three.

Next came a little dish of the plant's seeds, and then a dish of the seeds ground to a powder, and then a flask containing spore-seed powder in a solution. Next to this was a smaller flask containing a clearer fluid: spore-seed distillate.

Finally there was a row of ten stoppered test tubes, each containing a fluid of a slightly different colour. The first was labelled SS1, and the last SS10.

'What are you doing in here?' a voice said, suddenly. 'Return to your duties at once.'

Ace turned. A man with a deeply-lined face, spectacles and a white coat was standing in the doorway. He approached Ace cautiously.

'You're his Majesty's new Two,' the scientist said. 'You shouldn't be here.'

Was there any chance at all, Ace wondered, that this bloke would be fooled by her dumb waitress act? No harm in trying, she supposed.

She kept her face blank and her voice expressionless. 'His Majesty sent me here,' she said. 'The guards who came with me were called away. His Majesty said I would be interested to see the work you are doing here.'

The scientist appeared sceptical. 'Do you have any knowledge of the science of chemistry?'

'Yes, sir,' Ace said. 'I almost got an O-level.'

'I see.' The scientist seemed impressed. 'So you understand the procedure for which this equipment has been designed?'

'Yes, sir. It's for distillation.'

'Quite right,' the scientist said. 'But there's more to it than that. The seeds of the spore-weed plant, in their natural state, work on humans as a mild narcotic. Our ancestors discovered that smoking the powdered seeds in a mixture of dried leaves produced feelings of relaxation and well-being.'

'Yes, sir,' Ace said. She wanted to keep him talking. She had a premonition that he was going to reveal something dark and terrible.

The scientist warmed to his theme. It seemed he rarely had a captive audience for his lectures. 'But we have found that the seeds of this plant are very adaptable. The distillation of the essence, the application of different levels of heat, the addition of various chemicals – by these means we have been able to produce a range of complex compounds, each with its own unique effect on the human physiology.'

Hurry it up, Ace thought. There's a big fight going on upstairs, and I want to be there at the finish.

'And here are samples of the ten compounds,' the scientist said, moving to stand in front of the desk. Ace stepped back as he waved his arms to indicate the row of test tubes. 'Our crowning achievement, of course, is SS10. That's the compound that you were given when you were processed, before being brought to this planet to serve us. Its effect, as you know, is to remove the subject's volition, without affecting intelligence or memory. It makes remarkably good servants, and its effects are permanent.'

That's what you think, Ace silently told him. 'And you invented this stuff, did you?' she said.

'Oh yes,' the scientist said proudly, reaching for the tube of SS10. His hand stopped: he had realised that Ace had spoken without being told to. 'Perhaps you'd like to try some more of it?'

'Born yesterday, was I?' Ace said, and clocked him on the back of his head with the butt of her gun.

He fell to the floor. Ace resisted the urge to give him a good kicking. No time for that: she wanted to get back to the fighting.

'Great heavens, what are those?' Lafed's hand pointed to the row of posts that lined the wide path that led across the plaza from the gatehouse.

Madok turned. 'Disgusting, isn't it? Vethran calls it Traitor's Way: the bodies of the poor wretches he executes are strung up in those cages. I imagine the display is intended as a deterrent.'

Lafed swore. 'It's reassuring to be reminded we've right on our side,' he said. 'Have your men cleared the buildings on the far side?'

Madok nodded. 'Vethran's guards have pulled back into the central wing of the palace,' he said. 'I doubt we'll meet much resistance until we reach the throne room. Is the gatehouse secure?'

Lafed looked up at the twin towers. 'There wasn't much structural damage,' he said. 'We've patched it up as well as we can.'

'In that case,' Madok said, 'I'll borrow your radio set, if I may. I'll tell all units to come through here. And I'll give Kedin the signal to come in now. You know, Lafed, for the first time I really believe we're going to do this. In an hour or less we'll have no king.'

'And then what?' Lafed said. 'There's much to be set right.'

'More hard work, eh, Lafed? It never stops.' Madok cast his gaze round the perimeter of the plaza, stopping when it reached the gaping breach in the outer wall. 'I wonder what caused that explosion,' he said. 'I suppose we'll never know.'

He turned, entered the gatehouse, and made his way up the spiral stairway. Lafed's radio set had been installed in the topmost garret. Madok had good news for Kedin Ashar.

The throne room was eerily quiet. Polygonal ribbons of light still hung against the night sky; lamps still burned along the walkways and on the tables. But the diners had gone, and had left their meals half-eaten and their wine glasses undrained. Chairs lay where they had been pushed over.

The servants and the Twos, who had a short time ago outnumbered the noble guests, and who had scurried back and forth across the concourse bearing plates of food, silver cutlery, pitchers of wine, napkins, were also all gone.

Except one. With a studied air of detachment, and still carrying her pitcher, Ace made her way up the steps of the Grand Terrace and towards the throne.

Outside the dome, and seemingly in another world, there were occasional sounds of battle: a gunshot, an exchange of fire, a shout. All around the perimeter of the dome, facing outwards, crouching behind the bases of statues and behind stone paling, there were guardsmen, silently waiting for the inevitable assault.

Still, Ace said to herself, old Vethran doesn't look that bothered.

The King was lounging in his throne, listening to the animated conversation of his Councillors. One of the dining tables had been dragged up to the terrace, and was now set in front of the throne, covered in charts and papers and surrounded by nervous aristocrats. Ace recognised among them the stocky figure of Balon Ferud.

'Your Majesty,' one of them was saying, 'I spoke only moments ago to the technician who operates the Citadel's radio set. He has received messages from the Duke of Jerrissar. And the Duke knows nothing of the attacks on the palace.'

Vethran laughed. 'He says he knows nothing.' He leant forward and struck the councillor on the head. 'You're an idiot, Chalon. He's close. He's here. I can almost smell him. Go and fetch Tevana Roslod. Bring her to me.'

The councillor hurried away. Vethran looked round and saw Ace.

'Ace. You've returned. Where have you been?'

'Been busy, your Majesty,' Ace said. 'Things to do.'

The King gazed at her, letting his eyes linger as they scanned her body. 'Come here,' he said. 'Stand beside me. You can be my lucky mascot in the coming struggle.'

'Yes, your Majesty,' Ace said. I'll lucky mascot you, she thought, you lecherous git.

She had to grit her teeth to prevent herself shuddering as he touched her. But he seemed lost in thought, and simply caressed the material of the sleeve of her jacket.

The Councillors continued to gabble to each other. As far as Ace could tell they were merely reiterating, over and over again, the positions and likely movements of the opposing forces. A soldier ran towards the terrace and up the steps to the throne. He knelt in front of the King, then stood and saluted to one of the Councillors.

'We've had a message from the last of the far riders, sir,' he reported. 'The Norbalt regiment has been alerted and is marching south with all speed. That means all but one of the riders got through, sir.'

The Councillor turned to the King. 'All but one of the far

riders have delivered your orders, your Majesty,' he said. 'The Norbalt regiment will be here by tomorrow night.'

'I know,' the King said. 'I heard this trooper say so. Do you think I'm deaf?'

'Of course not, your Majesty. I apologise. But the news is good. The Norbalt men alone could deal with these insurgents. And there are five other regiments, and three motorised units, all making their way here as fast as is possible.'

Vethran shook his head. 'And they will all be a day too late,' he said. 'This business will be settled within the hour. Ah! But look! My beloved approaches.'

Ace tried to look sideways without turning her head. The Councillor named Chalon was walking up one of the staircases, and behind him were two soldiers and a tall, slender woman with a mass of golden, curly hair. In principle Ace held the view that blondes look dumb, but she couldn't help feeling a pang of envy. The woman was a real looker, Ace decided: not merely beautiful, but poised and elegant with it.

This, then, was Tevana Roslod: the woman prisoner with whom Ace had held a whispered conversation through a locked door.

Ace had thought at the time that she sounded like a cool customer. As she glided along the terrace towards the throne she looked completely calm.

'Tevana and I are to be married,' the King said. There were stifled exclamations of surprise from the Councillors. 'Isn't that so, Tevana, my love?'

'Yes, Vethran,' Tevana said with a smile.

'Sit by me, my angel,' the King said, and Tevana took his proffered hand and arranged herself on the ornate seat next to the throne.

Another soldier ran up the steps. He knelt before the throne. 'Strategic report, your Majesty,' he gasped.

'Stop!' The King held up his hand. 'Let me guess. There are still incidents occurring across the city which require the presence of my guards, but the perpetrators of the incidents have yet to be apprehended. The gates of the inner city are still broken open. The west gate of the Citadel is still in the hands of the attackers, who are still moving through the palace and converging here. There is still no clear identification of the attackers, although a suspiciously large number of them have been recognised as coming from the estates of the Duke of Jerrissar. And where is the Duke himself? No one has any idea.'

The soldier bowed his head. 'Yes, your Majesty,' he said.

'I know where the Duke of Jerrissar is,' the King said.

The Councillors gasped, looked towards the King, and then followed his gaze, which was fixed on the apex of the dome. Ace, too, contrived to look up. The Duke of Jerrissar sounded like he was a tough operator, and Ace wanted to see him.

There was something above the dome: something large, darker than the night, hovering just outside the tracery of illuminated metal frames.

All the glass panes in the top of the dome shattered at once. The noise was deafening. Shards fell like rain on to the abandoned tables and chairs. A cold wind howled through the gaping holes in the dome. 'Protect me!' the King barked.

The Councillors gathered around the throne.

A voice, loud, harsh and distorted by electronic amplification, issued from above. 'Surrender, Vethran. You're surrounded.'

The voice sounded familiar to Ace, but she couldn't place it.

There was a moment of silence, and then from all around the dome there came the rattle of gunfire, followed by a long tinkling of falling glass. The guards at the perimeter threw themselves to the floor as the windows around the base of the dome blew inwards. Ace could see figures moving outside the dome: the attackers had entered the palace and had reached the throne room. She congratulated herself on a well-placed explosive charge.

'Stay close to me,' the King hissed to his Councillors. He pulled a long knife from the jewelled scabbard at his side. 'I'll skewer the first man who moves. And don't whine: you'll be safe. He won't shoot down unarmed men from his own class.'

'Well, Vethran?' the amplified voice said.

'No surrender,' the King shouted from the midst of his huddled courtiers. 'You'll have to fight your way in.'

The prone guards at the perimeter of the dome started to fire their guns through the shattered windows into the darkness outside. Ace heard, coming from below, the sound of many running feet.

The King, too, had heard the noise. 'At last,' he cried. 'Reinforcements. My guards are gathering. I can still crush this rebellion.'

Endless corridors, numberless rooms. Bep-Wor's mind felt as numb as his pounding feet. He had no idea how many were behind him as he raced through the maze: hundreds, certainly. Bep-Wor had never been inside a building as large as this palace. It seemed as wide as a town. Towers projected upwards; layers of cellars and dungeons lay below. It was a place without sides, without a top or a bottom. It went on for ever.

He was leading his army only in the sense that he was at its front. Chanting and baying, it pushed him onwards. It moved forwards in spasms, stopping in a courtyard or in a suite of rooms, wherever there were people to be freed or guns to be captured, and then rushing on again through the never-ending corridors, up and down the infinite stairs.

Having somehow returned to the subterranean levels, they were now running upwards again. There was light ahead, and Bep-Wor hoped, as he had hoped many times already, that light might reveal to them a way out of the palace.

An incredible noise, like the sound of a ship grounding on rocks followed by the shattering of a thousand plates, rebounded down the stairs and rolled over the heads of the army. Bep-Wor's people stopped chanting. They stopped advancing. Then, when there was no more sound, Bep-Wor led them forwards again, up the wide stairway.

He heard the sound of gunfire before he reached the topmost step, but there was no way to turn his people back: the stairs were crowded with men and women pressing forwards. The swollen army now consisted mainly of people who were under the influence of the dreadful potion, and those still in possession of their own minds were outnumbered. It was more a herd than an army.

Bep-Wor shouted for joy as he emerged into daylight, and outdoors. Then, as he began to understand what he was seeing, he realised that he was still in the palace and the light was artificial. He was in a room as big as the widest field, its roof a glittering, tattered web set impossibly high in the night sky. All around him his followers were emerging from the stairway and gazing up in awe at the distant, shining, broken dome above them.

But this was no place to stand and gawp. Bep-Wor tried to orient himself. There, covered in the shining fragments that had fallen from the damaged roof, was an area for taking meals; there, a garden, with trees and walkways; there, all around the edge of the entire space, were soldiers shooting their guns at unseen enemies outside the dome. And there, on a raised terrace, surrounded by a scrum of richly-dressed men, sat the King. In the chair beside his throne sat a tall, handsome woman, very pale of complexion and hair. And standing next to the throne, holding a jug, stood the young woman who had released him and his people from the dungeon.

The King and his fellows seemed as surprised to see Bep-Wor's ragged, filthy army as Bep-Wor was to find himself in the King's throne room.

Bep-Wor had no idea what was going on. He tried to make sense of it. This was the King's place: it contained his throne, and he was with richly-dressed men who had to be his advisers. Therefore the soldiers shooting out through the broken windows were defending the King from outside attackers. And Bep-Wor assumed that the attackers must be fighting the cause of Kedin Ashar, the languid, clever man whom he and the Doctor had met just before they were captured.

From there the logic was indisputable: the King wanted to enslave the inhabitants of Bep-Wor's world; Kedin Ashar was opposed to the King; therefore Bep-Wor would join with Kedin Ashar.

'There is your enemy,' he shouted, turning in a circle to indicate the soldiers around the edge of the dome. 'Take their weapons!'

The battle lasted only a few minutes. Caught between the incoming bullets of the attackers outside the dome, and the furious and unexpected onslaught of Bep-Wor's army from inside it, the King's guards could not even flee. They threw down their guns.

And then a loud, distorted voice bellowed from the skies.

'Well done, Bep-Wor. Magnificent. I can't possibly thank you enough. I'm forever in your debt.'

Bep-Wor looked up. There was something above the broken

roof of the dome. Presumably some sort of flying machine. The voice, in any case, was Kedin Ashar's.

When the prisoners from the dungeon came surging up the stairway Ace had to bite her lip to stop herself shouting with excitement. They had destroyed the King's hope of a last-minute reprieve, and had overwhelmed his final line of defence. The whole room was swarming with soldiers and prisoners, and buzzing with noise.

The prisoners were bellowing a victory chant: a name, shouted over and over again. And then Ace recognised the word, and had to suppress a laugh. They were shouting for the Doctor. She might have guessed he'd be involved. But she couldn't see him anywhere.

It was almost impossible to remain still and impassive, particularly as she wanted to look for the Doctor, but she forced herself to remain where she was: standing beside the throne, with her wine pitcher in her hand, pretending to be a mindless serving-girl. No one paid her any attention, and she had an excellent view of the whole of the throne room.

And still there were things to watch. The attackers were entering the throne room, clambering through the broken windows all round the edge of the dome. Ace saw that they had had to fight hard to reach their goal: every man's face was black with smoke, and many wore makeshift and bloodied bandages. The most remarkable thing about them, however, was their clothing: while some were in uniform, others were dressed in various civilian outfits, and a few were wearing outlandish costumes that were more appropriate for performing in pantomime than for warfare. They mingled with the defeated King's guards and the prisoners from the dungeon, filling the floor of the throne room with a milling, variegated crowd.

Ace saw someone she recognised.

It was the way he moved that she noticed first. Everyone else in the crowd was moving without purpose: the King's guards, their shoulders slumped, were huddled in groups; the prisoners were talking excitedly among themselves; the newly-arrived soldiers were relaxing, sitting on benches and chairs, but keeping wary eyes and ready guns on the guards and the prisoners.

One figure – burly, tall, erect – was pushing through the throng, making for the stairs that led up the gallery and the throne. It was Madok.

What was he doing here? The last time Ace had seen him had been on the space station. He'd been back-up man for that despicable creep Kedin. He must have taken part in the attack on the palace. Perhaps he wasn't all bad, then.

He looked up and caught her staring at him. She looked away quickly. I don't want anything to do with you, she thought; leave me alone. She fixed her gaze on the shattered roof.

Soldiers were dropping through the broken polygonal panes of the dome. Hanging on ropes, they came sliding from the roof towards the floor. Their uniforms were immaculate; their guns were pointing at the throne. More and more of them appeared: the sky was raining soldiers.

Through the hole at the apex of the dome descended a platform, hanging from four ropes. Standing nonchalantly on the platform was Kedin Ashar.

Ace's stomach clenched. She felt sick. There were quite a few people, in several planetary systems, that she hoped never to see again, but this particular long streak of aristocratic slime was right at the top of her hate list. He'd seduced her, lied to her, and pumped her full of a drug that had turned her into a slave. She stared straight ahead, and hoped that her face didn't betray her loathing and disgust.

'Kedin!' It was Madok's voice, calling up to his leader.

'Is that you, Madok?' The platform stopped in mid-air, so that Kedin was suspended above the centre of the throne room, on the same level as the throne. Ace tried to avoid his searching gaze. Kedin grabbed one of the supporting ropes and leant carelessly over the side of the platform. 'Madok, old friend, we've done it. There's just one final detail.'

Kedin straightened, and waved his arm to indicate the host of his soldiers filling the hemispherical space of the dome. 'Vethran!' he shouted. 'I've captured your palace, I've disarmed your guards, and there are a hundred rifles trained on you. You've been King long enough, Vethran. I think it's time for you to abdicate.'

'Out of my way,' the King yelled. Ace staggered as the King's Councillors scattered to right and left along the gallery. She felt suddenly very exposed: all eyes in the throne room, and most of the guns, were trained on Vethran, leaning forward in the throne. On one side of him sat Tevana Roslod, still looking unperturbed; on the other stood Ace.

'Think again, Kedin,' the King said. 'As you see, I have Tevana with me. And I have a knife.'

He lunged towards Tevana, and the blade of his knife was at her throat.

'Tell your men to lower their guns,' the King said.

Kedin shrugged. 'I have no intention of killing you, Vethran,' he said. 'I won't descend to your level.' He leant forward to look down to the floor. 'At ease, everybody,' he shouted. 'Put your firearms up, for the time being.'

The dome echoed to the sound of rifles being shouldered.

Ace remembered where and when she had heard Tevana's name before. Kedin had said it. Tevana, he had said, was his goddess. Ace felt her face redden. Perhaps she had been too hasty in judging Kedin. All right, he was still a lying toerag, but he had taken the trouble to overthrow Vethran, who was even more despicable then Kedin himself. Ace reminded herself that she had already discovered that it was Vethran, not Kedin, who had invented the stuff called SS10. And she realised that if Tevana had been in Vethran's clutches all along, as seemed likely, than Kedin had had to keep his opposition secret.

'I won't have you shot, Vethran,' Kedin shouted. 'Now let Tevana go.'

Vethran laughed. 'Look, Kedin,' he said, and thrust the point of his knife into Tevana's neck. A bead of blood grew and then trickled down her pale skin. 'If you and all your men surrender immediately, I'll let Tevana live.'

Ace could see that Kedin was finding it increasingly difficult to maintain his air of confident detachment. He had flinched when Vethran's knife had sunk into Tevana's neck.

'If you harm Tevana, Vethran, I can promise you that I will kill you. Release her, and I'll be merciful.'

'I am your King, Kedin Ashar, and you are a traitor. I do not need your mercy. Surrender now and I will spare Tevana.'

The two men stared at each other.

The throne room was silent.

The silence lengthened.

Kedin made a signal in the air, and the platform on which he was standing continued its descent to the floor of the throne room. 'I'll consult with my officers,' Kedin called to Vethran, 'while I'm waiting for you to come to your senses.'

'I can wait, too, Kedin,' Vethran replied. He flourished the knife. 'And I can make Tevana uncomfortable while I'm waiting. So don't make me impatient.' He laughed when he saw Kedin scowl in impotent rage. 'Balon!' he called out. 'Come here.'

Balon Ferud brushed past Ace as he hurried from the end of the gallery to the throne. Surreptitiously Ace slid closer, so that she could overhear the deliberations of the King and his Councillor.

'Balon,' the King whispered, 'we know that loyal regiments are on their way. We have to play for time. I want you to go and negotiate with Kedin Ashar. Let him think that I'm prepared to give up the throne. Involve him in lengthy discussions about what lands and titles I'm to retain, the guarantees each side will give – you know the kind of thing.'

'Yes, your Majesty,' Balon said. 'But surely Kedin will expect precisely this gambit? It will be difficult to inveigle him into negotiations.'

Vethran smiled mirthlessly. 'Quite right, Balon. But he won't be expecting this. Come closer. Let no one see.' Ace glimpsed the tiny glass phial that he produced from inside his jewelled cloak. 'This contains concentrate of SS10,' the King said. 'Drop it into his drink or on to his food, or simply throw it into his face if you have to. Do it at the first opportunity. If you succeed, the Duchy of Jerrissar is yours.'

Balon took the slim tube between trembling fingers. 'All the lands of Kedin Ashar?' he whispered.

The King nodded. 'Lands, titles, everything,' he said. 'But do it quickly. And be careful, Balon: the phial is delicate.'

It seemed to Ace that from that moment events moved in slow motion. A part of her mind was watching the portly body of Balon Ferud trotting down the steps of the gallery, towards Kedin. Another part was caught in an endless loop: Kedin Ashar isn't too bad really, and it's reasonable for him to want to save his lover and to get Vethran off the throne, but Vethran's going to poison him, so Kedin's going to lose after all.

And, seemingly quite independent of her mind, her limbs were moving. She leant forward; she let her arm brush against Vethran's as she righted the engraved glass that had fallen over on the table in front of him. She pulled the glass nearer.

Vethran looked at her in surprise. He had forgotten that she was standing beside him. He smiled to see her.

'Still here, Ace? It's good to see I've still one faithful servant.'

'Thank you, your Majesty,' Ace said, returning his smile. She lifted her pitcher, tipped it, and filled the glass.

Vethran picked it up.

Balon was making his way towards the huddle of officers around Kedin and Madok.

'Kedin!' Vethran shouted. 'Balon Ferud has my authority to parley with you.'

He held up the glass as a salute.

The officers around Kedin made space for Balon to approach.

Balon held his left hand behind his back.

Vethran brought the glass to his lips.

Balon was almost within reach of Kedin. His shoulders tensed.

Vethran drank.

Kedin extended his hand to greet Balon.

Vethran fell face forward on to the table.

'Kedin!' Ace yelled. 'Look out! Balon!'

Kedin ducked to one side, turning left and right to try to identify the source of the warning shout. Balon swung his left hand around his body, aiming to throw the phial into Kedin's face. His arm was stopped: Madok held it. Balon's fingers opened, and the phial fell to the floor, and shattered. Kedin, Madok and the officers stared in horrified silence at the dark, viscous liquid that stained the carpet at Balon's feet.

'Balon Ferud,' Madok announced, 'you are under arrest.' He summoned two soldiers. 'Lock him up,' he told them.

Kedin ran to the foot of the stairs that led up to the throne. 'Ace,' he said 'thank you. You had every reason to wish that Balon would succeed. And yet you saved me. I already owe you more apologies than I can pronounce in a lifetime, and now I find myself indebted to the same degree in gratitude.'

Ace grinned down at him. 'I sorted out the King for you, too,' she said. She turned to the slumped body beside her, and nudged its shoulder. 'Oi, wake up, mate,' she said.

Vethran sat up. His face was expressionless.

'Say hello to Kedin,' Ace told him.

'Hello, Kedin Ashar,' Vethran said. He remained motionless, with a faint smile playing on his lips.

Kedin bounded up the stairs. He gazed in awe at Vethran. 'What have you done?' he said to Ace.

'I've given him some of his own medicine,' she said, waving her pitcher in the air. 'I found his laboratory.'

Kedin continued to stare at the man who had once been the King. 'I suppose it's what he deserved,' he whispered. He turned to Ace. 'I'll see to it that every drop of that pernicious liquid is destroyed,' he said. 'Even the new, temporary formula that we administered to you. It will be another happy event in a day full of them. And,' he added, turning towards the figure sitting beside Vethran, 'the best event is still to come. I have my Tevana again. Why are you still seated, my love? Come to my arms, my dearest angel.'

Tevana stood. She seemed to Ace an eerie figure, so quiet and restrained in the midst of the evening's turmoil, so deathly pale, with a trail of bright blood down her neck. She turned towards Kedin. She didn't smile.

Oh, no, Ace thought. I can't bear it. It's too awful. Vethran had made sure of Tevana before he even brought her to the throne room. Ace remembered the guards arriving at the door of Tevana's cell: they had brought food and drink. That was probably when it had happened.

Kedin was backing away from Tevana as she advanced towards him. His mouth and eyes were wide with shock.

'Madok!' Ace almost screamed. 'Get up here! Kedin needs you!'

She looked from Tevana to Kedin.

I can't handle this, she thought. I'm off to find the Doctor.

Chapter Six

There had been nothing Madok could do for Kedin. In the end he had posted guards around the gallery in the throne room, and given orders that the Duke was not to be disturbed. He left Kedin sitting on the throne, cradling Tevana in his lap. Kedin had stopped weeping: he was simply rocking back and forth with his eyes closed. His grief was inconsolable.

Then Madok had done his best to help Ace. He couldn't blame her for the resentment he saw in her eyes whenever she looked at him. He deserved every pang of guilt she made him feel. He introduced her to Lafed, from whom they had learnt about the Doctor's meeting with Kedin on the eve of the attack on the city. He had sought out the leader of the escaped Twos, a simple but imposing man named Bep-Wor, who had recounted the story of the Doctor saving most of a consignment of Twos from enslavement, and then the tale of the Doctor's capture by Vethran.

As Bep-Wor's account led inexorably towards the Doctor's death, Madok felt a wave of hopelessness overwhelm him. He was utterly weary. It seemed like years since he had last rested; sleep was a state he had forgotten. He was drained of all energy, and yet he knew he would have to find from somewhere great reserves of compassion. As Ace realised that her friend the Doctor was gone for ever, she would need Madok's comfort and support.

It came as a surprise, therefore, and something of a disappointment, that Ace appeared unmoved by Bep-Wor's harrowing tale of the Doctor's poisoning.

Madok had expected her to turn to him with tears in her eyes. Perhaps, he had thought, she would collapse into his arms, and he would stroke her hair as he tried to summon words of sympathy and consolation.

In the event she had tutted and said, 'Silly old sod. Where's his body, then?'

He led Ace to the plaza inside the palace gates. Bep-Wor insisted on accompanying them, and Bep-Wor's followers could not be dissuaded from coming too. Many of Lafed's men, along with some of the King's guards, followed the crowd. The plaza became as crowded as the throne room had been, and the throne room became empty but for Kedin, Tevana and their guards.

Ace punched Madok's arm. 'Nice one, eh?' she said with a grin, pointing to the ruins of the palace wall.

Was it possible that Ace had engineered the breach in the wall that had allowed Lafed's troops to take the palace? Madok told himself that he should simply admit that where Ace was concerned anything was possible.

'You, my lady?' he said.

'You bet,' Ace said. 'A neat piece of demolition, I reckon.'

Madok managed to smile. 'Indeed, my lady. But look.' He sighed, and lifted his arm to indicate the row of gibbets lining the thoroughfare from the gates to the central block of the palace.

'Oh my god,' Ace said. 'That's grisly.'

Six of the cages were occupied. The bodies inside them were in varying stages of decomposition.

'Which is the Doctor?' Madok said gently.

'The one with the silly hat,' Ace said. She picked out the cage containing the freshest body: a small man, lolling within the iron bands that would have held a larger body upright. 'Well, get him down,' Ace said.

Madok gave the order. He looked searchingly at Ace's face. Had she misunderstood? Did she not realise that the bodies in the cages were dead? Or was she unable to accept the truth?

The Twos were maintaining a mournful chanting of the Doctor's name. It was beginning to irritate Madok. Was there no one who realised that this crumpled little man was just a shell: the lifeless husk of the man who had once lived?

The Doctor's body was laid on the cobblestones. Ace knelt beside it. She put her ear to his chest.

'One heart's out of action,' she reported. 'And if he's breathing it's very shallow.'

'He's dead, Ace,' Madok snapped. 'In heaven's name, come away.' He couldn't bear to see her deceive herself. But she ignored him, and began to shout into the Doctor's ears, and slap his face.

There was, of course, no response.

'Hello,' Ace said, 'what's this?' The encircling crowd of Twos gasped. Ace had found something in the Doctor's mouth. Under Madok's appalled gaze she began to prise apart the corpse's jaws.

The inside of the Doctor's mouth looked like an oily well. It was as black as tar. Madok grimaced as Ace inserted her fingers, making exclamations of disgust.

She pulled from the Doctor's mouth a slick serpent of black matter. It slithered between her fingers like jelly, issuing from the Doctor's mouth in ripples and falling on the cobbles in quivering coils. It seemed as though it would never stop.

'That's well disgusting,' Ace said. She shook drops of the substance from her fingers. The Doctor coughed, and a gobbet of black mucus exploded from his mouth. The Twos cried out.

The Doctor sat up. 'I quite agree, Ace,' he said. 'I haven't tasted anything as unpleasant as that since the last time you offered to make me a real English fry-up.' He looked around at the stunned faces of the crowd. 'I take it I've been unconscious for some time.' He stood, with Ace's support. 'It was touch and go, I can tell you. I've had to regenerate most of my internal organs. Have I missed anything important?'

'No,' Ace told him, 'unless you count armed rebellion and the dethroning of a King as important. Otherwise it's been very dull. You've obviously been making an impression, though.'

The Twos were beside themselves with joy. Their chant of 'Doctor! Doctor!' was so loud it made Madok's head ring. Bep-Wor was on his knees at the Doctor's feet, gazing up in an ecstasy of wonder.

The Doctor shook his head, as if he too found that the chanting made it difficult for him to think clearly. 'Ace,' he said. 'I left you on the space station. Did anything happen to you? Was there any trouble?'

Madok wondered how Ace would reply. She had, after all, been betrayed by Kedin and Madok, and had spent almost a week as a slave. Madok wasn't impressed by the Doctor's appearance, but he didn't want to be on the wrong side of anyone who had the power to cheat death. He exchanged a look with Ace.

'Nothing I couldn't handle,' Ace said, airily. 'These days I can look after myself, you know.'

Madok stepped forward. He extended his hand. The Doctor looked at it, and then appeared to remember the correct procedure. He took it and shook it. 'I am astonished, sir,' Madok said, 'but very pleased to see you so well. I am delighted to meet any friend of my lady Ace. I am Madok, sir, aide to Kedin Ashar.'

'Lady!' the Doctor snorted. 'Well, it's a pleasure to meet you, Madok. I hope you've been taking care of Ace. And how is Kedin, by the way?'

Madok and Ace exchanged another glance. 'Not good,' Ace said. 'You'd better come and see.'

* * *

Bep-Wor stood at the tall window and looked out across the courtyard. Beyond it there were more solid, stone-built extensions of the palace; beyond them the sea of roofs of the city houses; in the distance, the surrounding, forested mountains.

He longed to see the ocean.

It would have been unthinkable to refuse Kedin's hospitality. How could say that he didn't want this suite of high-ceilinged rooms, that he preferred his filthy rags to these heavy, itchy clothes, that the endless exquisite meals tasted bland and too rich?

He would have liked a simple meal of seared fish.

The convoluted carvings on the furniture made him uncomfortable, as did the extravagant patterns on the flouncy curtains. He wasn't used to walking on floor-coverings into which his feet sank.

On the open sea, or tilling the fields, on his home world, he had felt alive. Following the Doctor, freeing his people, flirting with danger as he led his growing army across the foreign landscape – then, too, he had felt alive.

Now he felt nothing. No – that wasn't true. He forced himself to look again at Kia-Ga. She hadn't moved: after all, he hadn't told her to. She was sitting, very upright, in one of the gilt-decorated chairs, her hands folded in her lap. In her borrowed clothes she seemed more distant from him then ever.

He turned away. What he felt, rising again from the pit of his stomach, swamping every other emotion, was hopelessness.

The Doctor had saved him from Kia-Ga's fate. The Doctor had proved he could revive the dead. Surely he could easily restore Kia-Ga, and all of Bep-Wor's people who had been poisoned and enslaved? Then why was there no word? What was taking so long?

Had the Doctor abandoned him?

There was a knock on the door. Bep-Wor leapt to his feet: perhaps this was a message from the Doctor. He ran to the door and opened it.

Madok stood in the corridor outside.

'Bep-Wor,' he said, 'the session of the Grand Council is ended. Kedin Ashar has asked specifically for you and Kia-Ga to attend the announcement of its deliberations.'

Bep-Wor nodded dumbly. What did the Grand Council matter to him? He didn't understand the complex structure of the society on this world. He had grasped that, thanks to Vethran's plans to proclaim himself even more absolutely the ruler of both his own world and Bep-Wor's, all of the most important people were already gathered in and around the palace. It had therefore been possible to summon a great meeting on the day after the overthrow of Vethran. The Grand Council had been in session for hours.

'Would you care to follow me?' Madok said. He looked expectantly from Bep-Wor to Kia-Ga.

Bep-Wor nodded again, and went to whisper instructions to Kia-Ga. He could feel Madok's eyes on him. He knew Madok was a good man, but he hated the way that, like everyone else here, he treated Kia-Ga as if she were in her right mind.

She's not like this, Bep-Wor wanted to shout. This isn't my Kia-Ga. This is a shell, a doll made to look like her. My Kia-Ga looks at me from the corner of her eye as she drinks cold beer at the beach; she dances as she walks; she tells lewd jokes and laughs before she finishes them; she clenches her warm thighs around my waist and makes me gasp. I want her back. I can't go on without her.

With Kia-Ga at his side he followed Madok along the crimson-carpeted corridor.

The proclamation was to be made in the throne room. Bep-

Wor saw that the broken glass and damaged furniture had been removed, but there were still bullet-holes in the plinths of statues. And small, winged animals, able to fly through the shattered roof of the dome, were circling above the heads of the assembly. Once again the enormous room was crammed with people.

To Bep-Wor's surprise Madok escorted him and Kia-Ga up the steps to the gallery. The throne was empty, but the row of chairs on either side of it was occupied. Bep-Wor recognised among those sitting along the gallery the Doctor, Ace, Lafed and Tevana. Madok offered Bep-Wor a seat, and Bep-Wor took his place in the row, with Kia-Ga beside him.

Feeling on display and self-conscious, Bep-Wor waited. The crowd below, many of them wearing ornate uniforms, or jewels and precious metals sewn into their colourful clothes, carried on so many animated conversations that the air in the dome seemed to vibrate with the noise.

Bep-Wor wondered whether he would offend against etiquette if he were to stand up, go to the Doctor and insist on hearing what the Doctor had done to find a cure for Kia-Ga, and all the other people from Bep-Wor's world who had been poisoned. He was gathering the courage to do so when the hubbub from below suddenly ceased.

A tall man with a lined face was climbing the stairs. At the top he turned, waited until the silence was complete, and addressed the assembly.

First of all the man made sure that the members of the new Council were present, and that also in the room were representatives of the guilds of the city and of the army.

Bep-Wor didn't understand all of the words and expressions that the man used in his speech, which was a report on the decisions reached by the Grand Council. He gathered that Vethran's claim to be a king was a crime, and that Vethran had therefore never been a king. All laws passed by Vethran were bad laws, and were no longer in force. For some reason the man spoke particularly about the property rights of women, which he said had been diminished by Vethran.

There seemed to be a never-ending list of decisions. Vethran's personal estates were to be administered by the Council; each nobleman – or noblewoman, the man stressed – would have legal authority in his or her own lands; but in cases of disputes, or in matters such as trade and dealings with other worlds, the Council would have the ultimate power.

Bep-Wor had almost stopped listening when the man started to make announcements about the people from Bep-Wor's world. All Twos were to be freed, without compensation being paid to their owners, and would be taken home to their own planet. People who had profited from the trade in Twos would be made to pay for the rebuilding of the houses destroyed by Vethran's army on Mendeb Two.

'And finally,' the man announced, 'it was the unanimous decision of the Councillors that the Council shall be led by Kedin Ashar, Duke of Jerrissar.'

Waves of thundering applause crashed against the gallery. Bep-Wor almost recoiled from its intensity. He formed the impression that Vethran had been unpopular, despite his military successes, and that Kedin was genuinely well liked.

Kedin, his head bowed, walked from the side of the gallery to its centre. He lifted his head, and the crowd cheered. He turned, and began to extend his hand towards Tevana. Bep-Wor saw his hand falter, and his head droop. Bep-Wor knew how he felt.

Kedin turned again to face the crowd, and lifted his arms for silence.

'My lords,' he began. 'My ladies. My friends. I have done nothing but restore the customary governance of our world. I

268

neither want, nor will I accept, any reward. There are others – and I intend to thank them soon – who did more than me. And no reward could recompense me for the loss I have endured.'

As Kedin turned again to look at Tevana, Bep-Wor saw the glint of tears in his eyes.

'I accept the leadership of the Council,' Kedin went on. 'Not because I believe I merit the position but because it will give me an opportunity to serve you all. What I will never accept,' he said, 'is this.' He turned, and with surprising strength he hauled the throne to the front of the gallery. 'Stand clear below,' he shouted, and with a twisted smile on his lips he pushed the throne over the edge. Bep-Wor heard it land with a splintering crash. The crowd roared its approval.

'And now,' Kedin continued, 'it is time to record the deeds of those who struggled to end the tyrant's reign. I will not list here the names of those from my own household who gave their loyalty, their energy, and in some cases their lives. Their duty was to follow me, and they did their duty. Others, however, had no obligation, but nonetheless fought bravely in the cause. Their names will be written in the account that will be published in every domain and posted in every town and village. Without them we would not be free now from tyranny, and I will not allow them to be forgotten. First, I present to you Bep-Wor.'

Bep-Wor stared at Kedin, who was scanning the row of seats. Kedin's searching gaze found Bep-Wor. Kedin gestured for him to stand.

As Bep-Wor rose stiffly from his seat, the crowd burst into applause.

'Bep-Wor and his comrades are the living proof that Twos are not naturally slaves. On his home planet, Mendeb Two, his people live as freely as we do. Vethran's armies conquered Bep-Wor's world; Vethran's technicians created the potion that enslaved Bep-Wor's captured people.' Kedin hung his head. 'I confess that I assisted Vethran in both crimes.'

Kedin extended his arm towards Bep-Wor. 'Bep-Wor avoided the potion. He found himself stranded on an alien world, where every hand was turned against him. Did he falter? No: he organised. He led a group of his people from the landing site to here, where Vethran's troops captured them. He escaped from the dungeons, and led his people up from the depths to emerge here, in Vethran's throne room, at precisely the right time to undermine Vethran's last defences. You were invaluable, Bep-Wor, and you are a credit to your people. When you go home we will remain in communication.'

Kedin rekindled the applause. Bep-Wor bowed, and continued to bow until the applause died. He sat down. He felt nothing.

'Next,' Kedin said, 'I would like to thank the man who helped Bep-Wor and his comrades to avoid taking the potion, and who kept Bep-Wor's Twos alive during their journey from Mendeb Two. He is known only as the Doctor.'

Bep-Wor leant forward to peer along the row of seats. The Doctor was reluctant to stand, and did so only when the strange young woman called Ace pushed him from his chair. Wringing his hands he uncomfortably acknowledged the applause of the crowd.

He looks small, Bep-Wor thought. Insignificant. But then, he reminded himself, that is the Doctor's way. He doesn't make a show of his power and strength.

'The Doctor,' Kedin continued, 'accompanied Bep-Wor on his march, and was captured along with all of Bep-Wor's free Twos. He knows as well as anyone the injustices of Vethran's rule: Vethran personally fed him fatal poison. As you can see, it takes more than that to dispose of the Doctor.'

The crowd cheered, and the Doctor gratefully returned to the safety of his chair.

'I have – we all have – one more reason to be thankful to the Doctor. He brought us Ace.'

Bep-Wor had thought the earlier applause excessive, but as Ace stood up the noise from below was deafening. Bep-Wor watched her as she waved cheerfully to the crowd. She seemed not at all abashed.

She was still wearing her outlandish black costume. Bep-Wor could not understand why the people here found her attire so shocking: her clothes were bizarre, and revealed her feminine shape, but she was decently covered. Whereas the wealthiest women here at the court wore dresses which were designed to show off the wearer's shoulders, or the curves of her bosom, or a length of her leg.

'The part that Ace played in yesterday's events is well known,' Kedin said. 'She released Bep-Wor and his people from the dungeon; she laid the explosive charge which breached the palace wall; she gave Vethran a dose of his own poison; and she saved me from assassination. I owe her a boundless debt of gratitude. We all do.'

It seemed as though the cheers would never cease. They continued while Kedin summoned Ace to his side, and embraced her. They continued even after she had resumed her seat.

Bep-Wor studied Kedin's face. The shadow of his loss lingered there, tingeing his smiles and his victory salutes.

But at least he's won his battle, Bep-Wor thought. He has Ace, and Madok, and the entire population of this grateful world.

What have I got?

He looked at Kia-Ga.

Nothing.

Less than nothing.

* * *

271

The Doctor was pretending not to listen. He was sitting at the desk in Vethran's underground laboratory, his head cradled in his hands as he pored over the notebooks that had been written by Vethran's scientists.

Ace prowled among the benches, watching him through the convoluted coils of glass tubing.

He hadn't once congratulated her on the things she'd done here on Mendeb Three. He'd asked her over and over again whether she was all right, and he'd told her how pleased he was that she had survived the ordeal of being robbed of her volition and her sense of herself. She didn't doubt that he really did care for her. But why couldn't he give her credit for a job well done?

She'd reached a turning point, a crossroads in her life. She had insisted on being put down, alone, on the space station, and she had proved that she could look after herself. And she could look after Kedin, too. Everything was different now. Couldn't he see that?

'Doctor,' she said, 'we have to talk. It's important.'

The Doctor sighed, and looked up from his studies. His face was drawn and his eyes were tired. 'Later, Ace. I have to try to help these people.'

Ace didn't understand. What was getting at him?

'We have helped,' she said. 'We've stopped the bad things happening. No more invasion of Mendeb Two; no more slavery; no more Vethran. We've stopped all that.'

The Doctor's expression was even more pained. 'But we haven't put things right, Ace. How many thousands of Bep-Wor's people have been left as –?' He stopped, searching for words.

'Zombies?' Ace suggested.

'That sums it up,' the Doctor said. 'I have to do something for them.'

Ace shrugged. It was obvious that the Doctor was blaming himself. And that was crazy. It had been Vethran who had invaded Mendeb Two, who had created the poison called SS10, and who had encouraged the trade in slaves.

'You've been working down here without a break since yesterday,' she began.

'And I would work better without interruptions,' the Doctor snapped. 'You know that Kedin intends to destroy this workroom and everything in it. I have limited time.'

'You'd better read on, then,' Ace said, pointing to the open notebook. 'You've been on the same page since yesterday evening.'

The Doctor put his head in his hands. His voice was low and empty of emotion. 'That's because it's hopeless,' he said.

The door swung open. Kedin, Madok, and Bep-Wor walked in, and the laboratory was suddenly crowded.

Ace noted that her heart skipped when she saw Kedin. He was just too tasty, that was the trouble. And there was something particularly appealing about the troubled frown he seemed to wear permanently these days. She caught his eye and flashed him a grin. His lips twitched into a brief smile, and Ace felt a warm glow.

She'd thought she would hate him for the rest of her life. She remembered the cliché about love and hate being the two sides of the same coin. Then she realised what she was thinking. Love? Was that what it was?

As Kedin went to stand in front of the desk, he rested his hand for a moment on her shoulder. She shivered.

Madok was staring at her. She smiled at him. She liked Madok: big, reliable, sturdy old Madok. 'How's it going?' she asked him. 'Managed to get any kip yet?'

'My lady,' Madok said. 'Thank you for your concern. I rested for a few hours last night.'

'That's good.' Ace turned to Bep-Wor. He didn't see her. He was staring at the Doctor. Ace saw that his whole body was quivering. He's losing it, she thought.

'Doctor,' Kedin said. 'I've come to see you in the hope of news. Have you been able to decipher the records left by Vethran's technicians?'

'Yes, yes, of course,' the Doctor said. 'And I've interviewed the people who worked here. They were anxious to co-operate. It's all quite clear.'

'I'm impressed,' Kedin said. 'Our chemists – my chemists, on the station, were I'm sure cleverer chaps than Vethran's. They never did succeed in analysing SS10. We wasted weeks on that, and on studying the effects of diluting the distillate.'

'You were attempting to create a new version of the drug,' the Doctor pointed out, 'not an antidote. You wanted something that produced the same symptoms, but not permanently. I'm not surprised you found it difficult. Dilution of the solution would be useless.'

'As we discovered, Doctor. Below a certain concentration the potion had no effect at all; above it the effect remained permanent. We were searching for a formula that would produce a temporary effect, so that Vethran wouldn't suspect that we were working against him. We didn't know how long we would have to wait before making our military moves.'

'So I got the temporary formula?' Ace said.

Kedin swung round and rewarded her with one of his dazzling smiles. 'Precisely, my dear Ace. We had only just created it, by altering the chemical composition of a sample of SS8. I'm so glad it worked.'

Ace basked in Kedin's attention and tried to apply her mind to the problem of spore-seed derivatives. 'But that's no good as an antidote,' she said. 'You'd need a completely different approach.'

'It can't be done,' the Doctor said abruptly.

Everyone turned to look at him. Ace saw that Kedin's face was suddenly pale.

'SS10 has a permanent effect on the physiology of the brain,' the Doctor said. 'It's fundamentally different from all of the other formulas derived from the plant. What it does is –' He paused, his face screwed up with disgust. 'It's diabolical. As far as I can tell – and you will recall that I have ingested this foul brew, although my brain is organised rather differently – it has several active ingredients that perform different functions. One is a powerful sedative; one reduces inhibitions; another increases suggestibility. These are common to most of the spore-seed distillates. In SS10, however, there is an ingredient that proceeds immediately to the hypothalamus, where it performs some drastic surgery and then transforms a clump of cells into a factory for producing a second agent which cauterises nerve endings as they are called into play by the victim's desires and wishes.

'All of the other effects wear off in time. This one causes permanent damage. It's irreversible.'

Kedin was standing completely still, with his eyes closed.

'My lord,' Madok said. Kedin brushed off Madok's comforting hand.

Ace couldn't bear to see Kedin crushed. 'There must be something you can do, Doctor,' she said. 'Can't you grow new nerves from stem cells? Or the TARDIS could create an organic substitute for the damaged tissue.'

The Doctor glared at her. 'Do you suppose I haven't considered every possibility?' he shouted. He calmed his voice. 'The problem is the capacity of the human cranium. The damaged cells are still there, in the brain, woven among the healthy cells. They die, but they are replaced by cells that become as useless as their predecessors as soon as the victim uses them.'

Kedin lifted his head. 'Is there no hope at all?' he asked.

The Doctor rubbed his forehead. 'There is always the possibility that the passing of time will bring about a partial cure – perhaps a complete cure. Eventually the body's defences may reject the altered cells occupying the hypothalamus. But I have no idea how long such a change might take, were it to happen at all. In the meantime Ace is right: I can give you the means to grow additional, healthy cells from each victim's stem cells. But any recovery will be only partial: it would be dangerous to replicate the full complement of damaged cells. I have the necessary equipment in the TARDIS. That's the best I can do. I'm sorry.' He jutted his jaw, and swept his gaze around the room. 'Where's Bep-Wor?' he said.

Bep-Wor had gone. Ace hadn't noticed him leaving. He must have slipped away quietly, she thought, when he heard the Doctor's news.

'Find him, Madok,' Kedin said. 'He will have taken this badly.'

'Yes, my lord,' Madok said, and marched from the room.

Ace looked from Kedin to the Doctor. The Time Lord was staring at his shoes, his shoulders hunched. Ace had never seen him looking so forlorn. Kedin was in no better shape: he was gazing into the distance, his eyes bright with tears. Ace tried to imagine what it must be like to love someone as deeply as Kedin loved Tevana, and what it must feel like for him to lose her. She felt her own eyes stinging with tears.

She went to him and slipped her hand into his. 'Come along,' she said gently. 'We can't have this. You're making me cry. Let's get out of here.'

She led him away. She resolved to have her talk with the Doctor later.

The barrel of the pistol was still hot; the smell of burnt

powder still hung in the air. Madok dropped the weapon and returned to the first body.

Kia-Ga was sitting upright in a chair next to the bed. It crossed Madok's mind that in death she looked scarcely less animated than when she had been alive. He cursed his ignoble thoughts.

Bep-Wor must have shot her as soon as he returned to the suite of rooms he and Kia-Ga had shared. Madok had raced up stairs and along corridors, heading directly to this room, but he had been too late even to hear the shots.

Bep-Wor had shot Kia-Ga in the centre of her forehead: the black, blood-rimmed hole was neat and small. The back of the chair, however, was soaked in blood and brains. Kia-Ga's eyes were open. It was as if, Madok thought, Bep-Wor had tried to obliterate the illness in her brain by shooting her there.

Bep-Wor's body was lying by the open window. What had gone through his mind, Madok wondered, as he had stood looking out across the city with the mouth of the gun touching the side of his head?

Madok walked slowly to the door. 'Stretcher bearers,' he said to the soldier he had left on guard outside. 'And two stretchers. Then take four men down to the dungeons and bring back half a dozen of Vethran's former Councillors. They can have the pleasure of cleaning up the blood.'

Once the lords were on their knees and scrubbing with sufficient vigour, Madok left them under the supervision of his lieutenant and went to report to Kedin.

As he dragged his feet along the corridors of the palace, Madok rehearsed how he would break the news of the deaths of Bep-Wor and Kia-Ga. Kedin's situation was too similar to Bep-Wor's for Madok's liking. On the other hand, he couldn't imagine Kedin taking Bep-Wor's route out of his misery. Kedin didn't clutch grief to himself: he was, Madok supposed, too sensitive to bear it for long. And so Kedin had not kept Tevana at his side, as Bep-Wor had kept Kia-Ga: Tevana was being cared for by her servants, who had been brought from Cathogh.

Madok was still deep in thought as he approached the entrance to Kedin's apartments. And he still hadn't decided on the wording of his report. The guards saluted as he passed between them. He knocked on the wide doors.

One of the doors was pulled open – by Ace. Madok was speechless with surprise. He knew that Ace paid no heed to convention, or even to everyday etiquette. But if she was alone with Kedin, and with Tevana in the palace, and in daylight, in front of the guards... Although by night would have been even worse...

'Hello, Madok,' Ace said. 'Come in. Kedin's having a lie-down. But don't worry, he'll be OK. I'll look after him.'

Madok followed Ace through the hall and into the reception room. She had removed her jacket, and the sight of her naked shoulders disturbed him. He saw her jacket, lying where she had discarded it, he supposed, across a chair. It was as if she was treating the Duke's rooms as her own.

'He's in the bedroom,' Ace said. 'You want me to give him a message?'

In the bedroom. Madok imagined Ace going to Kedin there. 'No, my lady,' he said. 'I must speak to Kedin Ashar myself.'

'OK,' Ace said. 'Come on, then.' She went towards the door that led to the private suite. Madok couldn't believe that she could behave so immodestly. 'Is it bad news?' Ace asked. Her eyes widened. 'It's Bep-Wor, isn't it?'

'I must report to my lord,' Madok insisted. 'I'm sure that he'll be able to withstand the shock. With your help, of course. My lady.' He didn't even regret the sarcasm in his voice: it was clear that Ace was oblivious to it.

* * *

Ace watched the Doctor as he paced back and forth in the tiny circular room he had chosen to stay in, at the top of one of the palace's tallest towers. She clutched the soft package in her hands. She wanted him to have it, but now that the moment had come she couldn't part with it. Not yet.

'So what do you think?' she said, turning in a circle. 'Is this smart or what?'

The Doctor looked at her. She was wearing the tunic of her new uniform, and she desperately wanted him to understand what it meant. She needed his approval.

He frowned, as if he hadn't noticed her new clothes, and then, to her relief, he smiled. 'Very military,' he said. 'But quite fetching. The colour suits you.'

'And I'm on the Council,' she said, trying not to rush her words. 'I've been co-opted, whatever that means. Special adviser to the Duke of Jerrissar. That's quite something for a girl from Perivale, you know.'

'Very impressive,' the Doctor said. He stared out of the narrow window. 'It's time to go, Ace,' he said. 'I've done everything I can here. The first ship's leaving today. Taking some of the people of Mendeb Two back home. We should be on it.'

He sounds defeated, she thought. It's unreasonable. We've done well. Baddies vanquished, evil overcome, all of that stuff. And he still doesn't understand.

'But there's so much still to do,' Ace said. She had to try to keep the excitement out of her voice. 'Here, and on Mendeb Two. I can help. I can explain the technology on the space station. Computers, quantum machines, even things like the food replicators. The whole of the north of Mendeb Two has to be reconstructed. Then there's the treatment programme for the ones affected by SS10. There's enough to keep me busy for years.'

The Doctor turned to face her. 'They'll work it out for themselves, Ace. It will be better that way.'

He still doesn't get it, she thought. He doesn't realise I'm staying.

He tugged at his sleeves, as if that way he could remove the creases. He picked up his hat and placed it on his head. 'Are you coming?' he said.

'I'll come to Mendeb Two,' Ace replied.

'That was Bep-Wor's house,' the Doctor said.

Madok's gaze followed the Doctor's pointing finger. The house, like most in the village, was a ruin. Vethran's troops had been systematic in their destruction. Fronds of vegetation had already climbed over the fallen walls.

There was nothing Madok could say. He and the Doctor continued to walk, away from the self-propelled vehicle that had brought them from the transport ship, and towards the centre of the square. The large blue box that the Doctor claimed was his spaceship was standing there. Kedin and Ace, walking hand in hand, followed them.

This was only the third time that Madok had been to this planet, and on his previous visits he had hardly strayed from beside the ships that had brought Vethran's soldiers and had taken away the captured natives. Even here, though, he was struck by the ethereal beauty of the place: the vast sky, the warm breeze, the long shadows, the strange shapes of the trees.

The Doctor's craft looked incongruous, but Madok suspected that it would look out of place anywhere. It seemed impossible that it could fly, let alone travel between stars. As he and the Doctor drew closer to it, he could see that its paintwork was scratched. It looked almost as derelict as the surrounding houses.

The Doctor produced a key from a pocket. 'I'll nip inside and fetch the cell culture kits,' he said. He glanced over his shoulder. 'It will give those two time to say their goodbyes.'

'But –' Madok began, and then realised that it was not his place to interfere. He had thought that Ace intended to stay with Kedin. Hadn't she told the Doctor yet?

Kedin and Ace wandered up to the blue box as the Doctor disappeared through its door.

'I've still got to give him this,' Ace said. She looked tense.

Kedin took the package from her hands. He tore it open. Ace stared at him as he unfolded the contents: her black jacket, covered with badges and signs. He placed it over her shoulders.

'What's this for?' she said.

Kedin put his hand under her chin and lifted her face. 'Ace, my dear, you must go with the Doctor.'

'You what? But we've talked about this. We've got plans.'

He placed his hands on her shoulders. 'You've told me many stories about your travels with the Doctor,' Kedin said, 'and jolly exciting they were too. But they set me thinking. I've done quite a bit of thinking about you, you know. And you're getting into that remarkable box thing with the Doctor, where you belong.'

Madok turned away. He felt he was intruding on a private conversation, but to step away would only draw attention to his presence. He couldn't bear the look of sorrow in Ace's eyes.

'He needs you, Ace,' Kedin said, his voice trembling with intensity. 'He can't function without you. And, from what you tell me, he has a great burden to carry and much to do.'

Madok glanced at Ace. Tears were running down her cheeks. 'You're only saying that to get rid of me,' she said. 'You don't want me at all.'

Kedin leant forward and kissed the tears from her face. 'Ace, Ace,' he said, almost moaning as he spoke. 'Nothing could be further than the truth. But listen to me, please. You know that if you don't go with the Doctor-now, you'll never get another chance. If that box flies away, or whatever it does, and you're not inside it, you will come to regret it. Perhaps not at once, but eventually, and more and more as each day passes. You know that's true.'

Ace stared up at him, her mouth moving soundlessly. 'But what about us?' she whispered at last.

Kedin smiled. 'Well, as the foremost member of the aristocracy I suppose I should know all there is to know about being noble. We have to make sacrifices, Ace.' He swept his hand in an arc across the sky. 'There are millions upon millions of worlds out there, my darling. Our broken hearts don't really matter. Not in the end.'

Ace wiped her eyes with the back of her hand. She seemed to Madok, suddenly, to look no older than a child. She gazed at the scene of destruction around her, as if searching for some hope or purpose. 'I wanted –' she began.

Kedin placed a finger on her lips. 'None of us has what we wanted, Ace.'

The Doctor emerged, carrying a large box made of translucent material. 'Here are the kits,' he said. 'Complete with instructions. Your scientists should be able to work out how to use them.' He looked from Madok to Kedin, and from Kedin to Ace. 'Ready, Ace?'

Ace lifted her hand to touch Kedin's face, and then turned away. 'Yes, I'm ready. Goodbye, Kedin Ashar.'

Madok and Kedin watched the blue box as it became transparent, and then disappeared.

A part of me has gone, too, Madok thought. I'll never see her again.

'Remarkable mode of transport,' Kedin observed. He stood for a moment, in silence, staring at the place where the Doctor's craft had stood. 'Ah, well,' he said, rousing himself. 'There's work to be done. The call of duty, and so forth. We must all do our duty, eh, Madok?'

'Yes, my lord,' Madok said.

About the Author

To my chagrin I'm old enough to remember seeing the broadcast of the first episode of *Doctor Who* in 1963.

A lot has happened since then, and most of it – what it was like to be educated at a traditional selective grammar school, the counter-culture scene of the early seventies and its merging into glam-rock and then punk, why I missed the Pertwee years, how I sold *Dungeons & Dragons* to teenagers throughout the land and came to publish *White Dwarf* magazine, my first company directorship, when I wrote my first *Fighting Fantasy* gamebook – you really don't want to know in any detail.

In 1989 I was trying to make a living from writing, and not succeeding. I applied for a part-time job: *Doctor Who* Editor at book publishers W H Allen. The books concerned were novelisations of the TV stories. W H Allen became Virgin Publishing, I became the Fiction Publisher, we acquired a licence from the BBC to publish original *Doctor Who* novels, and in 1992 there began a five-year stint of almost uninterrupted publishing fun. We did *Doctor Who – The New Adventures*, and then *Doctor Who – The Missing Adventures*. We published non-fiction books and illustrated books about *Doctor Who*. I wrote my first *Doctor Who* novel: *Deceit*. We published books about other television programmes: *Red Dwarf*, *Blake's 7*, *The Avengers*, *Babylon 5*, right up to *Buffy the Vampire Slayer* this year. We published the infamous Black Lace imprint: erotic fiction by women and for women.

I'm in Southampton now, writing this, and also writing other books and doing bits of freelance copy-editing and proof-reading. I miss my London friends, and the talented people I worked with. But there are compensations.

> 'True ease in writing comes from art, not chance,
> As those move easiest who have learned to dance.'

Alexander Pope
An Essay on Criticism, 1711.

Peter Darvill-Evans
June 2000

DOCTOR WHO

PRESENTING
AN ALL-NEW AUDIO DRAMA

Big Finish Productions is proud to present all-new *Doctor Who* adventures on audio!

Featuring original music and sound-effects, these full-cast plays are available on double cassette in high street stores, and on limited-edition double CD from all good specialist stores, or via mail order.

Available from September 2000
THE FIRES OF VULCAN
A four-part story by Steve Lyons.
Starring **Sylvester McCoy** as the Doctor
and **Bonnie Langford** as Mel.

Two thousand years ago, a cataclysmic volcanic eruption wiped the Roman city of Pompeii from the face of the Earth. It also buried the Doctor's TARDIS...

Arriving in Pompeii one day before the disaster, the Doctor and Mel find themselves separated from their ship and entangled in local politics. With time running out, they fight to escape from the shadow of Mount Vesuvius. But how can they succeed when history itself is working against them?

If you wish to order the CD version, please photocopy this form or provide all the details on paper. Delivery within 28 days of release.
Send to: PO Box 1127, Maidenhead, Berkshire. SL6 3LN.

Big Finish Hotline 01628 828283.
Other stories featuring the Seventh Doctor still available include:
THE GENOCIDE MACHINE   THE FEARMONGER

For more details visit our website at
http://www.doctorwho.co.uk